James George Semple

The Life of Major J. G. Semple Lisle

A Faithful Narrative of his Alternate Vicissitudes of Splendor and Misfortune

James George Semple

The Life of Major J. G. Semple Lisle
A Faithful Narrative of his Alternate Vicissitudes of Splendor and Misfortune

ISBN/EAN: 9783744728232

Printed in Europe, USA, Canada, Australia, Japan

Cover: Foto ©Raphael Reischuk / pixelio.de

More available books at **www.hansebooks.com**

MAJOR JAMES GEORGE SEMPLE LISLE

Pub.d September 1 1799. by W. Stewart 194 Piccadilly

THE

LIFE

OF

MAJOR J. G. SEMPLE LISLE;

CONTAINING

A FAITHFUL NARRATIVE

OF HIS

ALTERNATE VICISSITUDES OF SPLENDOR AND MISFORTUNE.

WRITTEN BY HIMSELF.

THE WHOLE INTERSPERSED WITH

INTERESTING ANECDOTES,

AND

AUTHENTIC ACCOUNTS OF IMPORTANT PUBLIC TRANSACTIONS.

————— *Aspera multa*
Pertulit, adverfis rerum immerfabilis undis.

HORACE.

LONDON:

PRINTED FOR W. STEWART, NO. 194, OPPOSITE YORK
HOUSE, PICCADILLY,

1799.

W. Blackader, Printer, 10, Tooke's Court, Chancery Lane.

P R E F A C E.

WHEN any one offers his own Memoirs to the world, it is very natural to afk what are his claims to the notice of the Public? To this the Author of the following fheets can juftly reply, that perhaps there exifts not another individual who has been fo much the play-thing of Fortune as himfelf; and he can boldly add, that few have been fo unjuftly calumniated. With fhame he acknowledges that there have been parts of his life he can neither juftify, nor means to defend; but this Work, the truth of which refts not upon his own teftimony only, but upon that of characters whom fufpicion itfelf would not dare to doubt, will prove that his life has been, by no means, a feries of difgraces.

a 3

Such

Such as it has really been, he lays it before the world, ready to receive from the impartial voice of the Public that praise or that cenſure to which he may be found entitled.

To the republic of letters he feels the neceſſity of apologizing for any inaccuracies which may be found in the compoſition. Born a ſoldier, though happy in an excellent education, the profeſſion of arms engaged his entire ſoul; ſomething muſt, therefore, be allowed for the production of one no way in the habit of writing beyond private correſpondence or military orders. Beſides, ever accuſtomed to execute his ideas with rapidity, he confeſſes his want of patience to touch, retouch, and ponder, words and ſyllables; but though his periods may want that harmonious chime which amuſes the ear, they ſhall never be deficient in truth and candour.

The many exalted characters whoſe names are introduced in this work, will, the Author truſts, excuſe the freedom he has uſed with them; he has, indeed, had the honour of ſtanding by their ſides in the field of battle and in the drawing-room; and he hopes, that

not

not one of them will be afhamed of appearing along with him on paper.

In fome parts he has, however, fuppreffed circumftances which, though highly honourable to himfelf, are neverthelefs improper for publication; but when his readers reflect, as he hopes they will have the goodnefs to do, that he has been entrufted with important ftate fecrets, by the moft potent Princes in the world, they would, he is fure, confider him as far loft to all honour, indeed, fhould he fuffer them to efcape him, merely to gratify his own vanity.

Finally, fhould any material fact be miftated, which may eafily happen to any one who writes from memory only, he will readily and thankfully rectify his miftake on being informed of it. Of thofe defpicable fcriblers, who, without knowledge of him or his hiftory, have dared to publifh their anonymous libels, he fhall, at prefent, take very little notice; though, perhaps, fome future day he may recompence them as they deferve.

C O N T E N T S.

CHAP. I.

CHAP. II.

CHAP. III.

rives

CONTENTS.

CHAP.

CHAP. VI.

CHAP. VII.

CHAP. VIII.

CHAP. IX.

CHAP.

CHAP. X.

CHAP. XI.

CHAP.

CHAP. XII.

CHAP. XIII.

CHAP. XIV.

CHAP. XV.

CHAP. XVI.

CHAP. XVII.

CHAP. XVIII.

CHAP. XIX.

CHAP. XXII.

CHAP. XXIII.

CHAP. XXIV.

in

CHAP. XXV.

CHAP. XXVI.

CHAP. XXVII.

E R R A T A.

Page 65, Line 5, *for* was, *read* were.

89, 3, *for* high juſtice, *read* the executioner of high juſtice.

90, 9 from bottom, *dele* to them.

—, —, *after* they, *read* all.

105, 2, It was not *Maſſena* who commanded, but another General whoſe name I cannot recollect.

112, 4, *for* Brunſwic, *read* Orange.

121, 5, *for* from, *read* for.

126, 5, *for* drawn, *read* driven.

273, 10, *dele* and.

311, 9 from bottom, *after* they, *read* therefore.

313, 4, *dele* and.

314, 4, *after* long, *read* ſtrait.

315, 2, *for* friends, *read* my friends.

CHAPTER I.

Among the throng of scribblers, who, without any personal knowledge of me, or my
family, have done me the honour to write my
history, there is a prodigious variety of asser-
tion concerning my parentage. Some have af-
serted that my father was a farmer, some a
tradesman, some a clergyman, and some, I believe, will hardly allow me any father at all.
Had my family no more reason to be ashamed

B

of

of me than I have of it, I might here produce a long roll of honourable and virtuous anceſtry: ſuffice it to ſay, that my deſcent is too well known to every family of diſtinction of my country to render it neceſſary to refute the calumnies of anonymous libellers.

My education was what *ſome* of my biographers have condeſcended to allow, of the genteeleſt ſort; and my friends gave me that encouragement which is naturally given to lads of parts, an encouragement that too often leads into unconquerable habits of expence and diſſipation; and a too liberal ſupply from my opulent connexions made me equally careleſs and extravagant. With the advantage of at leaſt a tolerable figure, great activity, and a perfect knowledge of all the polite manly exerciſes, I very early was initiated into the gay world. My ſkill in arms introduced me to the moſt celebrated profeſſors of that art; as a horſeman, I likewiſe received the higheſt praiſes; and naturally gay, fiery, and haughty, my vanity was proportionably inflated, till it laid the foundation of my ſubſequent misfortunes and diſgrace.

It would be mere impertinence to take up the time of my readers with details of juvenile amuſements and juvenile amours: and it would be downright cruelty to expoſe names yet un-
polluted

polluted by the peſtilent breath of ſlander; I ſhall therefore confine myſelf to obſerving, that my military *debût* was made in America, in the year 1775, at the age of ſixteen.

My adventures there were not much varied beyond thoſe of my brethen of the ſame rank. I was, however, taken priſoner in 1776; but was relieved early in 1777, by Lord Percy, whoſe retirement from the army his country may juſtly regret, and Sir Peter Parker, then commanding at Rhode Iſland. I was ſoon after wounded; and was in conſequence ſent home from New York, in the Bridget of Liverpool, Captain Gilbody.

I landed in Ireland, and came from thence to Wales and to Bath; where I met with the beautiful, but unfortunate, Mrs. Gooch. I was in the rooms; but as my wound rendered dancing impoſſible, a party at picquet was propoſed, which laid the foundation of a connection that induced me to retire to Liſle in Flanders. My amour with Mrs. Gooch having been related by the lady herſelf, in her Memoirs, though not *quite correctly*, I leave as it is: neverthelefs, my reader may perhaps ſmile with me at her boaſt of " then, and not till then, I fell," when they are informed that our joint ages did not amount to forty.

B 2

Had

Had she not mentioned uncandidly a transaction which I cannot think upon without regret,
I should have wished it to have been buried in
eternal silence; I mean where Mr. K. and
myself are reported by her to have used unfair
conduct to a young Irishman in a duel. The
young gentleman, who was about my own age,
undoubtedly fell; but nothing unfair took
place: the whole business passed in the presence
of Mr. D., a respectable inhabitant of London,
who is yet alive; and him I expect and entreat
to expose me as a villain if there was any foul
play on my side. Besides, if there needs a
stronger proof of my conduct, I myself carried
the unfortunate man to his lodgings, where, at
his own request, I remained with him several
hours, till prudence obliged me to provide for
my own safety from the effects of the law, by
leaving Lisle, and retiring to Tournay. The
process was carried on in Mr. K.'s absence and
mine; and we were, as Mrs. G. justly relates,
hung in effigy, the form of declaring outlawry
there; a ceremony which I was rash enough to
come into Lisle to see; a rashness which had
nearly cost me dear, for I was discovered, and had
much difficulty to effectuate my retreat to the
Imperial territory: and after remaining some
time at Tournay, I went to Brussels.

CHAP.

CHAP. II.

Goes to Bruffels.—Interview with Mr. Fitzherbert, now Lord St. Helens.—Leaves Bruffels, and accompanies the army of Frederic the Great, and the Emprefs Queen of Hungary to the field.— Returns through Holland to England.—Marries. —Goes to France; and from thence, at the inftance of the Duchefs of Kingfton, to Ruffia.—Adventure at Riga in Livonia.—His arreft there.— Goes to St. Peterfburg, and is introduced to Prince Potemkin and the Emprefs.—Curious particulars of the Duchefs of K.'s family.

A_T Bruffels, in the beginning of 1778, I met with General Lockhart and the Earl of F——r, by whom I was prefented to Mr. Fitzherbert, now Lord St. Helens, then Refident at that court. I remained in Brabant till Frederic the Great marched againft Maria Terefa, the Emprefs Queen: I followed thefe armies during that little war, which as the Germans themfelves call the " *Kartoffel Kreig*," or *Potatoe War*, I pafs over as of no importance to my readers. I held no confiderable fituation at that time; but I gained fome experience by obferving the manœuvres of the King of Pruffia and the celebrated Laudhon.

B 3

In

In 1779 I returned to England, by the way of Holland; and paffing immediately again to the continent, I met at Harwich with an amiable and accomplifhed young lady, of a highly refpectable family, then with her mother and fifter, going to the Hague: with her I formed a connection of the tendereft nature, which in a fhort time terminated in our marriage, and return to Britain. After fojourning fome months in London, I went with my wife to France; where I was prefented by her to the Duchefs of Kingfton. I remained in that country fome time; when being folicited by the Duchefs to go to Ruffia, I confented to follow her, as I was obliged, by affairs of my own, to take a circuitous route to Pruffia; from whence I went through Courland to Riga, the frontier town of the Ruffian territory, where I had letters of recommendation to all the principal merchants.

At Riga, according to my ufual bufy fate, I met with an adventure worth relating, as it, perhaps, ferved as the foundation of my future fortune in that country. A perfon of the name of *Sauvage*, a Hanoverian, and who had been employed by the Britifh government, during the adminiftration of Lord North, to recruit in Germany, was then in that city; where he paffed for a Major of the Britifh army, and

wore

wore the uniform of the Guards. Owing to some improprieties of his conduct, which I considered as incompatible with the character of a British foldier, I found myself obliged to call upon him for an explanation; which he was not only unable to give, but behaved with such insolence that I was reduced to appeal to the military judicature of the fword. His wife, who was in an inner apartment, (for this happened in a large anti-chamber at an inn,) hearing what was going forward, fprung out; and, with all the fury of a tygrefs, entangled me in a no very loving embrace. Swords being already drawn, there was no time to trifle; fo, fomewhat roughly difengaging myfelf from the lady's arms, I beckoned her hufband into the ftreet, and fairly locked her into the room. I was making the beft of my way to the ramparts, when he told me there was a fhorter cut; on which I followed him till he ftopped oppofite a guard, when, without further ceremony, he began to roar out for affiftance. I went home to my inn, where I had not long been when the Deputy-Governor, (who commanded in the abfence of the Governor-General of Livonia, Brown,) fent a guard for me, at the inftance of the Fort-Major, who was a countryman of Sauvage's. The officer of the guard acted with great politenefs; and took my word

that

that I would attend at the Governor's houfe: I
went accordingly, and found the Lieutenant-
Governor talking with fome officers in the yard.
His behaviour to me was rude, which did not
produce any excefs of politenefs on my fide;
he did not take off his hat to me, and I refufed
to do fo to him; in fine, without any examination had, I was put under an arreft.

My recommendations to the Britifh merchants had been of the ftrongeft kind; and they
no fooner heard of my adventure, than they
offered and became my fecurities until the Governor-General, who was daily expected, fhould
return. I then fent off an exprefs to the
Duchefs of Kingfton, at her feat near Narva in
Livonia; and Sauvage's wife fet off in perfon
for St. Peterfburgh.

The Lieutenant-Governor, finding me fo re-
pectably fupported, and that I was provided
with the neceffary paffports for entering the
country, made little objection to leaving me at
large in the town until the Governor-General
fhould return. Mrs. Sauvage, who in the
fcuffle had received fome flight hurt in her face,
having procured recommendations from the
Fort Major, (who himfelf began to be apprehenfive for his own fafety, from the fteps he had
taken againft me,) laid her complaint before
the Emprefs, through the Chancellor Count
Ofterman.

Ofterman. The Emprefs heard it with attention; and as Mrs. Sauvage had fuffered by the froft in her journey, by which fhe had nearly loft one of her ears, fhe had an apartment ordered for her at an hotel; and one of the Empreffes phyficians, Dr. Rogerfon, to attend her. In the mean time, General Brown, the Governor-General, arrived, examined into the bufinefs between Sauvage and myfelf, and fent a true ftatement of the facts to the court; the confequence of which was, that Sauvage and his family were conducted out of the country, and I received permiffion to proceed to St. Peterfburgh, which I immediately did; and the Duchefs of Kingfton's houfe laying in my way, I paid my refpects *en paffant* to her Grace.

On reaching the capital of Ruffia, I waited on Sir James Harris, then his Majefty's Envoy at that court, who had been made acquainted with my adventure at Riga; and who was fo pleafed with my conduct, that he, without a moment's delay, prefented me to Prince Potemkin. After fome converfation with that illuftrious general on my affair, and on general military fubjects, he afked me if I would ferve in the Ruffian army, which I confented to do; and was that fame evening appointed Captain. My appointment was extremely rapid, for the Prince having called for his Secretary, fpoke a

few

few words to him in Ruffian, which I did not then underftand; the latter retired, and in a few minutes returned with my commiffion ready made out, which he handed to the Prince, who immediately prefented it to me, acquainting me at the fame time, that he had done me the honour to place me in his fuite, and that he gave me two months leave of abfence to pre-pare myfelf for the enfuing campaign.

I remained a few days in town to be prefented to her Majefty the Emprefs, and then returned to the Duchefs of Kingfton to acquaint her with my good fortune. I took with me Thomas Mackenzie, Efq. Brigadier of Marines, and Cap-tain of the Ruffian navy, an officer who, both as a private gentleman and a foldier, has ever held the higheft place in the efteem of all that have the happinefs to know him; he had not before been introduced to her Grace.

I was a good deal furprifed, that the Duchefs did not receive the news of my fudden and honourable appointment with all the warmth I expected; but, as I afterwards found, that fhe wifhed to retain me about her perfon, the myftery was cleared up. The night of our arrival at the Duchefs's feat was fortunate to Mackenzie; for as we were enjoying our bottle, a meffenger brought him down a brevet of Rear-Admiral, and the intelligence that he was

appointed

appointed to command in the Black Sea: he therefore immediately repaired to St. Petersburgh, and soon afterwards to his station.

I continued with the Duchefs. In her company were a French lady Mad. de Porquet, sister to Monf. de Cocove, and a French Secretary, whose name I do not recollect. At my arrival, I found they had all quarrelled, and were not upon speaking terms. Mad. de Porquet was in fact so much chagrined, she kept her room. On which the Duchefs, in all the native violence of her disposition, *locked her in*, and actually detained her a prisoner in that state for some days, in spite of all my remonstrances.

The poor French Secretary was so much terrified at these tyrannical procedings, that he ran away the same night, without even venturing to take a great coat with him. In an almost desolate country, in the dead of winter, and without the smallest knowledge of the language, he had to travel twenty miles to the Baron Rosen's, who, in that dreary spot, is called a *neighbour*. He luckily overtook a peasant with a sledge by the way, to whom, by repeating the name of *Rosen*, he fortunately made known his wishes; and being placed in the vehicle, and covered with a sheep skin, he,

at

at length, reached the Baron's more dead than alive.

As foon as we arrived, the Baron fent a fervant to me with a letter, wherein he ftates that he could not refufe the poor Secretary the rights of hofpitality; adding, that he could wifh the Duchefs would abftain from fuch acts of violence; and concluded, by defiring me to endeavour to effect a reconciliation between them. I laid this letter before the Duchefs, who fent me to the Baron's; but the Frenchman would not liften to the propofals I was authorized to make, which were to pay him his wages, but perfifted in his intention of going to Peterfburgh to intereft the French Minifter in his caufe.

I returned next morning, and prevailed upon the Duchefs to permit Mad. de Porquet to go where fhe would. This lady, who, it feems, had preconcerted matters with her lover, the Secretary, went to St. Peterfburgh, and laid her complaint before the Marquis de Verac, the French Minifter there. The Marquis apprifed the Duchefs of the complaint, and I was fent to St. Peterfburgh to negotiate for her with them; the confequence of which was, that the Duchefs was to pay Madame de Porquet fix hundred ducats in fpecie, on condition

of

of immediately returning to France; and I was, at the expence of the Duchefs, to conduct her to Dantzic, whether I was going to meet my own family, to bring them to the houfe which the Duchefs had given me on her eftate, within a fhort league of that fhe inhabited.

The Duchefs had taken my receipt for the money with which fhe had entrufted me to pay Madame de Porquet on her arrival at Dantzic, charging me to take her receipt there; a feeming reconciliation then took place, and Madame de Porquet ftaid a few days at her Grace's feat to pack up her effects. In the mean time, the Duchefs ordered her fteward Mr. Wilkinfon to prepare one of thofe carriages, which are ufed in Ruffia in time of fnow, and which refembles the body of a coach, only much longer, to be got ready. Thefe carriages are furnifhed with beds; and when Mr. Wilkinfon informed her Grace that the machine was ready with two beds, fhe fmartly enough replied:—
" You have done well, Mr. Wilkinfon, but
" your precaution was unneceffary; I will an-
" fwer for it, one bed will ferve them before
" they reach Dantzic."—

Having obtained, with my commiffion, two months leave of abfence, and permiffion to leave the country, I fet forward without any further application to court.

CHAP.

CHAP. III.

The author performs his miſſion to Dantzic, and re-
turning is met by a meſſenger to haſten his journey.
—Arrives at St. Peterſburg, and is ordered to
wait the Empreſs's diſpatches.—The Ducheſs of
Kingſton's conduct.—Determines to remove his fa-
mily to Narva, on account of the Ducheſs's tyran-
nical diſpoſition.—Leaves the capital, with per-
miſſion to go to the Ducheſs's houſe.—Laws re-
ſpecting travellers in Ruſſia.—Quarrels with the
Ducheſs.—Removes his family to Narva, and
ſets out for Cherſon.

I PAID the money on my arrival at Dantzic to
Madame de Porquet, and took her receipt for
it, according to the Ducheſs's directions. My
family were waiting for me; I however found
it neceſſary to remain ſome days there; and I
was further ſo delayed by the badneſs of the
weather and roads, that my two months had
ſome time expired. In the mean time, Prince
Potemkin, finding himſelf obliged from circumſtances to ſet off immediately for the army,
had applied to Sir James Harris to know where
I was. In conſequence an expreſs was ſent off
for me, (whom I met in Livonia, about a hun-

dred

dred miles from the Duchefs's), to acquaint me with the Prince's orders, and to haften my journey.

The inftant I met the courier I left my family to come forward as their heavy carriages would permit them; and procceded with the utmoft rapidity to the Duchefs's houfe. She expreffed much fatisfaction at my arrival, and the great anxiety the length of my abfence had given her on account of the Prince's want of me. Without more lofs of time I fet off for St. Peterfburgh. I immediately went to Sir James Harris, who feemed hurt at my delay, and told me that there were inftructions for me at the War Office, but that Potemkin was gone: he preffed my departure to follow the Prince, adding, (for I will ufe his own words,) " You " may make your own terms with him; he " cannot do without you."

I went immediately to court, and received inftructions to wait her Majefty's difpatches, with which I was to follow the Prince to Cherfon, who had taken the circuitous road of Warfaw. Having received thefe directions, and not being able to leave St. Peterfburgh without the commands of the Emprefs, I wrote a letter to my wife, to endeavour to foothe the feelings which an amiable, virtuous, and affectionate woman muft naturally feel at the depar-

ture

ture of the hufband fhe loved, and who doated
upon her: nor was it an eafy tafk to frame a letter
capable of producing fuch an effect, in a country where fhe knew not a face except the Duchefs, nor could make her defires known in the
language of the place. I reprefented to her
that my ftay at the army would be but fhort;
that my being in the fuite of the Prince would
infure me from much danger, even fuppofing
there fhould be any war, which I did not imagine there would, for that certainly the Crimea
would be taken poffeffion of without a fhot
being fired: finally, I promifed to fee her previous to my departure, and bring her to Narva,
where I had already fent to take a houfe.

The fame courier carried a letter to the Duchefs, in a fomewhat more military ftyle: I
dwelt upon the valour of Potemkin, and his
turn for enterprize; I declared that, not contented with following where he would lead, I
would endeavour to be foremoft in the field of
glory; for that I was determined to fhew the
Ruffians that a Scot was neither their inferior in
fupporting fatigue, nor encountering danger.

The Duchefs betrayed the confidence I had
repofed in her; for when my wife fhewed her
the letter fhe had received from me, and even
which was hardly enough to enable her to fupport my departure, her *Grace,* with that hypo-

critical

critical cant she so well knew how to assume, inveighed against my false representations; and, by way of completing her cruelty, concluded by showing the letter she had received from me.

The effect of this frightful ecclaircissement, upon the sensibility of a delicate woman, may be easier conceived than expressed. She wrote a letter to Sir James Harris, and another to myself, in the most pathetic terms that affection could possibly suggest. She expressed the most anxious solicitude, lest the impetuosity of my temper should hurry me into unnecessary dangers; in fine, she wrote, to use Sir James's own words, " *as none but an Englishwoman could* " *write.*"

It will be readily believed that the Duchess's behaviour to Mad. Porquet had not contributed to raise in my mind any high veneration for her character; and the idea of leaving a wife and children, whom I loved with the tenderest affection, in the power of a woman, who already had sported in the most unfeeling manner with her sorrows, became unsupportable. I had in fact dreaded something of the kind, and had taken a house at Narva, distant between twenty and thirty miles from the Duchess's estate, to serve as a retreat to my family; and I now resolved, without loss of time, to remove

C

them

them thither.   I therefore wrote to my wife to console her as well as I was able, telling her, that Sir James Harris had acquainted me with some paſſages of her letter, and deſiring her to prepare for her departure without giving a hint of it to the Ducheſs, till I ſhould come down. In the courſe of a couple of days I was ſent for to court to receive the diſpatches of the Empreſs for Potemkin; it was then evening : my orders were to leave St. Peterſburgh that night. A ſum of money was paid me by the Secretary of War for the expences of ſo long a journey, and a Serjeant of the Guards (who bears the rank of Lieutenant in the army,) and who ſpoke the French and German languages, was ordered to attend me. My route to the army lying through Narva, and my diſpatches requiring no haſte (as it was expected I ſhould be at Cherſon before the Prince got there,) on taking leave of her Majeſty, I ſolicited permiſſion to go off my road to the Ducheſs's houſe for twenty-four hours; this favour was benevolently granted; and I went to take leave of Sir James Harris, and then to the hotel where my carriage and ſervants were, from whence I meant to have ſet off immediately. While my equipage was preparing, I was prevailed on by ſome officers to gamble ; at which we continued till it was announced to me that all was ready. Unfortu‑

nately

nately, however, I had not only loft all the Emprefs's money; but all my own; and had no
other refource but to fend immediately to Sir
James Harris to acquaint him with my embar-
raffment; who immediately, though he was then
in bed, difpatched his butler to me with five
hundred roubles. Thus reinforced, I inftantly
fet off.

When I reached Narva, I left there my military equipage, and went in a fmall carriage of
the country to the Duchefs's feat. I found my
wife and family already in the houfe her Grace
had given us. I then began to explain the motives of our intended removal; I told her Grace
that, confidering the hazardous fervice I was
going upon, and that no military man who was
going to the field of action could ever fay his
return was certain; I thought it neceffary my
wife fhould have fome eftablifhment to call a
home; that though fhe could as often and as
long as fhe chofe take up her abode with her
Grace, ftill, fhould any thing happen to me,
Narva would always, particularly in the event
of the Duchefs leaving Ruffia, prove a retreat
where fhe would find friends of her own nation; whereas, in her prefent fituation, fhe was
an entire ftranger to every one, nor had more
than one fervant who underftood the language
of the country. To this the Duchefs replied;

firft

firſt with a flood of tears, and a complaint that I was depriving her of her only companion ; and then (finding me unmoved) with a torrent of abuſe that would have done credit to Billings-gate, concluded with ſaying, we might both go to the d—l.

It is neceſſary to inform my readers that, by the laws of Ruſſia, no perſon can travel from the capital without a paſſport deſcribing his route, which he is not at liberty to alter ; in the country, travellers muſt have a paſs from the perſon whoſe eſtate they may have been upon, before they quit it, or no poſt-maſter dare fur-niſh them with horſes.   On my application at the poſt-houſe, which was not above half a mile from the Duchefs's, I was not only told that they durſt not ſupply me with horſes, but that they had her Grace's expreſs prohibition to that ef-fect.   I anſwered the poſt-maſter, that I ſhould remove that difficulty by taking his or her horſes by force.   I inſtantly removed my family to the poſt-houſe.   I juſt then recollected that I had given the receipt I had obtained from Madame de Porquet at Dantzic to the Duchefs, without her Grace having returned me that which ſhe required of me, when ſhe entruſted the money to my charge.   I begun to be apprehenſive of her making a bad uſe of it ; I therefore wrote a note to Mr. Wilkinſon her ſteward, requeſt-

ing

ing my receipt. The Duchess shuffled with ex-
cuses, that she could not come at it; that she
would give it to my wife, and such like eva-
sions; and instantly jumping into her carriage,
drove into the woods, to prevent further applications on my part. I sent one of her own servants after her Grace to tell her, that unless I
had my own receipt, or a discharge from her in
one hour from that time, that I would force my
way into her house, and carry off her *cassette*,
which I would lay at the Prince's feet, and intreat him to judge between us. In a few minutes, Mr. Wilkinson brought me the receipt
I demanded, and I set out for Narva, where I
rested scarcely one moment before I proceeded
for Cherson to join the Prince.

C 3

CHAP.

CHAP. IV.

*The author arrives at Cherson, and delivers his dif-
patches to Prince Potemkin.—An exprefs arrives
from the Duchefs of Kingfton complaining of him
to the Prince, which is received and anfwered in a
very mortifying manner.—Some acconnt of Cherson.
—The Corfes Expulfés, a corps of them given to
the author to organize.—Aftonifhing atchievement
of the Emprefs in building fhips.—Mode of launching and navigating them down the river Nieper.—
Admiral Mackenzie and Captain Taite.—Military arrangements.—Mutiny among the Corfes
Expulfés.*

In fpite of my delays, and the heavinefs of my
equipage, having with me all my baggage for
the field, I reached Cherfon in twelve days
from the time of my leaving St. Peterfburgh. I
there found the Prince, who had not arrived
many hours before me. I delivered to him the
packet I had received from the Minifter of War
Count Moufchkin Poufchkin, and the letter
from her Majefty, the contents of which was
not lefs pleafing to myfelf than the Prince, as
the Emprefs fpeaking of me, concluded by faying, " May you in battle always have a man
" like

" like him by your fide, and a friend like me
" wherever you go."

Next day an exprefs arrived from the Duchefs.
for the Prince, with heavy complaints of my
conduct to her, my delays upon the road, and a
long ftring of &c.'s. This furnifhed matter of
amufement to the Prince, who could not endure her; for fhe, partly through her ignorance
of the Emprefs's permiffion for me to go out of
my route, and partly through malice, had fo
caricatured the ftory, that it became the fubject
of laughter to all who heard it. To add to her
mortification, he made me not only read it to
him, but anfwer it forthwith; which I did in
French to the following effect, fometime in the
month of July 1783: " Madam, I had the ho-
" nour to receive your difpatch from his High-
" nefs; I had alfo the honour to read it to him;
" and am, by his Highnefs's commands,

" Madam, &c. &c. &c."

Cherfon is a town which the Emprefs built
on the river Nieper feveral leagues above its
mouth, with the view of forming a new colony
there; for this purpofe fhe iffued, by her Minifter at Leghorn, a proclamation to the exiled
Corficans, by the title of *Les Corfes Expulfés*;
under which name perfons of all nations affembled at her rendezvous, and were tranfported by
the way of the Dardenelles and Black Sea to

C 4

Cherfon.

Cherson. Of the real Corsicans, about 250, who were all military, she formed a corps, distinguished by the appellation of Royal Corsicans, which I was directed to organize. Here it was the Emprefs put in practice the exalted scheme of building ships of war for the expedition on the Black Sea. They were constructed upon a river scarcely navigable for a small sloop, the wood and iron for their construction brought from a distance of 700 miles up the country, some of it much farther, and every gun came not much less than 1000 miles by land. The mode of launching and navigating these vessels down to the sea was curious; the Nieper, as before observed, being extremely shallow, and not very broad, a fort of pool was first formed in the bed of the river opposite to the dock, then two large rafts, which were called *Camels*, were placed so as to receive the vessel as she slid from the stocks, from which she was eased down without much rapidity; being seated between the camels, as in a cradle, she was thus floated down the river past the Turkish fortress of Ofchacow, and into the Black Sea. Had not I been an eye-witness to this stupendous work, I should hardly have ventured to have related it; it was truly worthy the comprehensive mind of such a sovereign; it completely formed a maritime barrier against her troublesome neighbours the

Turks,

Turks, and opened a channel for trade from her territories to the Mediterranean.

Admiral Mackenzie, whofe name may truly be faid to have graced an early part of this narrative, had gone round to the harbour of Actiare, now called Sebaftapole; he had there, with the rapidity which diftinguifhed all his movements, begun to build a houfe for himfelf, marine barracks, hofpital, ftore-houfes, erect batteries, and put the harbour in a refpectable ftate of defence.

A vice-admiral remained at Cherfon with feveral captains, among whom was Captain, now Admiral Taite, who, at the time I am writing this, is lying with a Ruffian fleet, which he commands, at Yarmouth, a moft amiable man and intelligent officer; for whom, in common with all who knew him, I entertained the higheft efteem; an efteem which I exhibited in my ufual imprudent manner, by vifiting him at a time when we were directed not to go near his houfe, becaufe he was fick (fuppofed to be of the plague, which had broke out among us) a precaution ufed to prevent the fpreading of the infection: but, independent of his focial qualities, he had another ftrong claim on me, he is a Scot. For this vifit I was feverely reprimanded by the General of the day, Solticoff, and dared not to approach the Prince for feveral days.

The

The now well-known Field-Marſhall Suwarrow, and Ramſay Count of Balmain, were already in the Crimea, whither Potemkin followed, leaving me behind to organize the corps of Royal Corſicans, and then to join him. The Prince of Wirtemberg, whoſe ſiſter was married to the Grand Duke of Ruſſia, arrived at Cherſon about this time; he was then Lieutenant-General, and was left there by Potemkin to command the reſerve.

My Corſicans, though brave fine fellows, were, as is their character, quite undiſciplined; and, as they were the objects of cyrioſity to the whole army, our manœuvres were interrupted by the numbers thus drawn together; I therefore retired with them from the ground where the Ruſſians lay to a little ſpot on the other ſide of the town, between that and the Biſhop's palace, where I daily trained them.

To ſhew the turbulent diſpoſition of the Corſicans, I ſhall give the following inſtance: I had given them permiſſion to ſell ſome old ſtores and copper kettles which they had brought with them in the ſhips, and for which we had no uſe. About the produce of theſe articles they diſagreed. One evening, while I was at the Ruſſian camp, on a viſit to the Commanding General, a letter was delivered to me from the officer I had left on command, which I in-

inſtantly

ſtantly read. By this I was informed that my camp was in confuſion, and that the men were firing upon each other. Without ſaying one word to the general, I inſtantly roſe from table, and having previouſly requeſted a colonel of in-fantry, whoſe regiment lay neareſt me, to ſend a detachment of his men before day-light to ſurround my camp, I galloped home as faſt as I was able. The night was dark; and I had a vaſt open common to paſs: however, I reached my camp, being partly guided by the flaſhes and reports of the muſkets. On my arrival I inſtantly began to fire among them with my piſtols; and, as my voice was perfectly known, all was preſently quiet, and each in his tent. I gave orders to be called at day-break; when aſking the officer of the guard if he ſaw any thing near the camp, he told me there were ſome ſmall bodies of infantry on three ſides, the fourth being covered by the river; on which I ordered the drums to beat to arms. As ſoon as my men were on the parade, they were diſarmed, and the cauſe of the quarrel en-quired into; when the kettles, &c. appearing to be ALL they had fought about, the leaders were ſeverely and inſtantly puniſhed: thus tranquillity was reſtored.

CHAP.

CHAP. V.

*Improvements in the Russian army by the author.—
Remarks on military uniforms.—Russian peasants.
—Remarks on the proper use of the bayonet in
exercise.—A refutation of an anonymous libeller.
—The author having compleated the organization
of the Corsicans, sets off to the army in the Crimea.—His flattering reception.—Character of the
commanders, Potemkin and Suwarrow.—Russian
soldiers, their character and hardiness.*

DURING my first conversations with Potemkin
at Petersburgh, he had asked my opinion of the
Russian army; and I frankly told him that improvements might be made, in both their dress
and manœuvres.

The Russian uniform consisted of a green
coat, lined and faced with red, very tight, and
so long that it incommoded the wearer, by
beating on the calves of his legs; the breeches,
which were also tight, did but barely cover the
knee-joint; and as the Russian soldiers, both
cavalry and infantry wear boots, though of a
different form, a vacancy between the knee-
welt of the breeches and the boots became unavoidable; the hat was very small, and unfit for

a covering in a cold country; on which account the foldiers added a piece of flannel on each fide to cover the ears, and guard againſt the feverity of the weather. This cloathing being very inconvenient, to ſhew the Prince my ideas on the ſubject, I had dreſſes made for myſelf and a private, of the uniform which is ſtill retained, without any material alteration; and which was allowed to be at once elegant, convenient, and well adapted to the feverities of the climate. I muſt here remark, that elegance ſhould always, in ſome degree, be conſulted in the formation of a military uniform; for if we wiſh the foldier to keep up that nicety of appearance which is ſo becoming in military men, we muſt make him proud of his own figure. In Ruſſia this was more than any where neceſſary, for the peaſantry, (who ſupply the recruits for the army), are the moſt ſlovenly of mortals; their outſide dreſs being made of ſheep-ſkin, which they wear with the woolly ſide inwards, unleſs here and there, in the vicinity of noblemen's ſeats, ſome have them of coarſe cloth: yet ſuch is the effect of making men pleaſed with themſelves, that at preſent the Ruſſian army may vie with any in the world, for appearance and ſubordination. The Prince, thinking to improve upon me, put in orders, (without my knowledge) that the hair of the foldiers ſhould

be

be cropped, and that the bayonet should only be fixed when they were about to charge the enemy. As I was the acknowledged author of the alteration in the uniform, these novelties were likewise attributed to me, and I was heartily abused for all. The cropping of soldiers' hair, (unless occasionally for a partisan's corps) I always disapproved, as by giving an opening to negligence, it serves to introduce slovenliness; and whoever will reflect for a single moment on the different poise of a musket with and without the bayonet fixed, as well as on the absolute necessity of learning to load and fire with fixed bayonets, will, I trust, suppose me incapable of proceeding on so erroneous a principle; and will, with me, think that the musquet and bayonet should be inseparable. Accordingly, in a few days, the *crops* were supplied with false tails; but I had some difficulty to prevail upon the Prince to reinstate the bayonet in its proper place.

I did not, till this moment, know what the author of the Life of the Empress Catherine II. (published by Longman of Pater-noster Row, and Debrett of Piccadilly) has thought proper to say of me (vol. iii. p. 20. 2d edit.) respecting my situation with Prince Potemkin and the Duchess of Kingston:

" By *his* advice the Prince introduced several

" new

" new regulations into the army, both in regard
" to drefs and manœuvres ; and had it not been
" for fome manœuvres of another nature, fuch as
" writing to the Duchefs of Kingfton, that he
" would come by night with fome foldiers, and
" break into her houfe, unlefs fhe fent him a
" certain fum of money, &c. there is not a
" doubt but he would foon have been raifed to
" the rank of a general officer, or appointed
" conful at whatever place he chofe."—He
goes on to fay, that, " After his difmiffion from
" the confidence of Prince Potemkin, on his
" way to England, Major Semple laid the mer-
" chants of Peterfburgh, Narva, Riga, &c. un-
" der contribution by a variety of impoftures."

It is the eternal fate of falfhood to contradict
itfelf: and though I have given in the preceding pages an account of my affair with the Duchefs of Kingfton, which I challenge earth or
hell to contradict, ftill, as this worthlefs fcrib-
bler, who would tremble at my very fhadow,
may gain credit with fome, I will, in one moment, point out his abfurdities. Had I dared
to have threatened the Duchefs of Kingfton, as
he has afferted, a well-founded complaint (to
which my own letter muft have given an irrefiftible weight,) would have procured me a ba-
nifhment for life to Siberia ; befides, this quarrel happened before I joined the Prince at Cherfon ;

fon: and was it, I will afk, probable, that he would have received me into his favour, intrufted me with the organizing of a new corps, and after-wards treated me as will appear hereafter, had I been ftained with robbery? As to my frauds on the merchants, *while I was in favour*, they might have been poffible; but, *for a man difgra-ced*, they would have been an utter impoffibility. Befides, I did not pafs through, or near Riga; for I went from Petersburgh to Narva, where I embarked, and went down the Eaft Sea to Co-penhagen.

Such peftilent libellers are unfit to be fuffered in the world. Such have been my ruin; and the author of the above, who, I am informed, is a prieft, certainly affords a fhocking proof of that depravity which perhaps may, if ever I live to meet him, render his gown but an infecure protection. If he has any honour, let him contradict his unfounded affertions: but why fhould I afk him? Had he any honour, he would not have wrote it. One good, however, refults from his fcurrility: I am enabled by thefe anecdotes of myfelf, to judge of the authenticity of thofe parts of his hiftory which I have not yet had time to look at.

Having trained and difciplined my Corficans, I proceeded to the army, and joined the Prince on the heights above the town of Karafu-bafar,

in

in the Crimea; where my pride was not a little flattered by feeing the uniform of which I had given the model worn by an immenfe army, and my manœuvres adopted and applauded. I was then about twenty-five, and with my natural vanity, this diftinction almoft turned my brain, as it perhaps might have done to men much older and wifer then myfelf; and if I had no very great fhare of prudence in pecu- niary matters before, this made me quite re- gardlefs of them.

I was now at the Prince's right-hand day and night; he loaded me with honours, and I left nothing in the line of duty undone to deferve them. Potemkin was juftly placed among the firft characters of this or any other age; brave, open, rough, and impetuous, he was firft in every exploit of danger; fudden in his manœu- vres, his plans were conceived and executed with unparalleled rapidity; in the field he knew no character but a foldier, nor could age or rank plead with him any excufe for relaxation from the rules of duty.

Suwarrow was with us, already acting a diftinguifhed part. Bold and impetuous as his commander, he was indefatigable in duty, and feemed to afpire, by copying fo great a mafter, at that rivalfhip of glory to which he has now arrived.

D

The

The Ruſſian ſoldiers ſeem fitted by nature for war; their hardineſs is unparalleled, as eaſily may be imagined from the manner in which they live. Their magazines are not as with other armies, depoſited with even a finical care; their proviſion, which is rye meal, is piled up like pyramids in bags in the open air, where, by alternate expoſure to rain and ſcorching ſun, I have ſeen it ſo baked together that it was obliged to be hewed out with axes. The raw meal is ſerved out to the companies; and where they have no wood; (as was the caſe with us while in the environs of Cherſon where no wood grows, (and the chips of the dock-yard hardly ſupplied the hoſpital and General Officers,) they collect weeds and the dung of the cattle, with which they heat it as well as they are able, and eat it half raw. They are not leſs hardy in their tents than in their eating; ſtraw or blankets are never thought of by a Ruſſian ſoldier: his cloak ſerves him at once for bed and for covering; and wrapped up in this, he lies down contented on the bare cold ground. As an inſtance of their contempt for theſe *luxuries*, I had entruſted a ſoldier with the care of a conſiderable number of valuable articles, at a time when I was at a diſtance from the Prince. I had got a trench dug in the earth to ſerve as my cellar;

and

and over it a tent was erected, partly to ferve
as a ftorehoufe, and partly as an habitation
for the faithful veteran who was to guard my
ftores. Willing to make him in love with
his duty, I had got raifed for him a wooden
bench, with a mattrafs to fleep on, which indeed, though a moft vile one, coft me no fmall
trouble to procure; but bad as it was, I concluded that he would efteem it a luxury. I
was however miftaken; for about a week after,
going to look at my waggons, &c. I faw a
mattrafs laying like a piece of lumber. En-
quiring how it came there, I was informed,
that it belonged to the foldier I had placed on
my cellar, whom I inftantly fent for. Upon
afking him how he came to throw away his
mattrafs, he cooly faid, that it was not fit for
a foldier, and that he could not fleep upon it.
I then went to fee what he had fubftituted
for this defpifed couch, and found a hard
common ftraw mat of his own twifting.

Such is the real character of a Ruffian foldier, and to the portrait I can only add, that
their fidelity is equal to their other qualifi-
cations, for defertions are hardly known among
them: they are in fhort formed by nature and
education for the trade of war: for while they
acquire hardinefs by their ufual mode of living,
their minds are not eftranged from the paths

of

of obedience by thofe fmatterings of knowledge which only ferve to lead to infubordination and mutiny.

CHAP. VI.

Mr. Fitzherbert, now Lord St. Helens, arrives at St. Peterfburgh.—The author fent from Karazubazar to Afliare, where he again meets Admiral Mackenzie.—Vifits a curious old building there.—Mackenzie and he receive prefents from fome of the Tartar Chiefs.—Returns to head-quarters, and has a narrow efcape.—Potemkin retires to Krementchuck on account of his health.—The arrival of a Circaffian Prince there as hoftage.—Plain where the battle of Pultowa was fought.—Splendour of the Viceroy of Mofcow.—Anecdotes of Potemkin, the Emprefs Catharine, and other remarkable perfons.—The author prepares to leave Ruffia; quits the Ruffian fervice, and fails for Copenhagen.

As it is my intention hereafter to publifh a hiftory of my campaigns, I fhall hear fay very little on that fubjeft. Some time in Auguft 1783, we learnt at the army that Mr. Fitzherbert, (now Lord St. Helens,) had

arrived

arrived at St. Petersburgh to replace Sir James Harris. The Prince was most particularly curious to know his character, and I had many conversations with him on the subject; for Sir James had been among the most peculiar friends and intimates of Potemkin. No ceremony, no dress, no etiquette was observed, however much the Prince might be engaged. Sir James in his pelice and cap always found immediate access, even though other foreign ministers had been some time in the anti-chamber, and perhaps after all could not obtain an audience.

From Karazu-bazar, I was sent on military business to Actiare, where I met my old friend Admiral Mackenzie, with his little fleet. His fortifications and other works were in great forwardness, and every thing bore the aspect of improvement. We went to visit an antient building, called, I think, the antient Cherfonefe, which is near Actiare, and lays in a cove almost inacceffible. We in vain endeavoured to reach it by sea, the rocks were so perpendicular that they defied our attempts, and with much difficulty we scrambled over the top of them from the land side. The building, if it can be so called, is compleat, and is almost intirely cut out of the rock; but it is uninhabited, except by one man; and whether he lives there from motives of religion, or of concealment, I

cannot

cannot fay. The few remaining natives however fhewed him much refpect, and fupplied him with all neceffaries; and Admiral Mackenzie gave ftrict orders that he fhould not be molefted.

While I was at Actiare, Mackenzie and myfelf received the compliments of fome of the Tartar Chiefs of that country, together with a prefent of each a horfe. Mine was very richly caparifoned indeed, but his was almoft covered with filver. The faddle was of purple cloth, all ftudded over with filver nails, and from each fide depended a huge ftirrup of the fame metal, made, as is the fafhion of the country, the fize and fhape of the fole of the foot; nor were the crupper and bridle left without their due fhare of ornaments, which at every ftep made almoft as much noife as the fore-horfe of an Englifh waggoner's team. Mackenzie eyed the gawdy beaft with much pleafure, and in the prefence of the whole company jogged my elbow, and, poifing a ftirrup in his hand, faid, " Take you the horfe, I will have the " ftirrups, by G—d; each of them will make " a pair of candlefticks:" had he faid two pair, I do not think his calculation would have been extravagant.

I had been taken ill at Actiare with a fort of ague, which prevailed in the army, and on

my

my return to Karazu-bafar, my diforder was very much increafed; however, as I found the Prince juft changing his pofition, great part of the army, and moft of my own baggage already gone, I determined not to be left behind. Being too ill to mount my horfe, I got a bed put into one of thofe carriages which are commonly ufed there, and ordered horfes. I could get none but thofe of the irregular Coffacs, which were totally wild, and had hardly ever feen, much lefs drawn, a carriage before. My harnefs was of rope, fuch as I could pick up, and I was to be driven by a fellow equally unufed to his bufinefs. My curious equipage had nearly made me violate a general order, by which we were forbidden to enter any houfe or town on account of the plague; for being laid in my bed with my valet, (an honeft faithful Wirtemburgher, whom I had from the prince of that name, then along with us,) our cattle fet off at a moft furious rate. For fome time they galloped along the precipice that almoft overhangs the town of Karazu-bazar, till at length the carriage overturned, and we all tumbled down the fteep; and had we gone a little further, fhould have fairly tumbled into the town. Of three horfes which drew the carriage, two were killed on the fpot, and my poor valet de chambre broke his arm; I efcaped by being fairly turned out

D 4

with

with my bed into a bush; my Russian driver, who had received no hurt, comforted me, as he would have done, had we all broken our necks, with *Nebos! Nebos!* 'tis nothing! 'tis nothing! The Cossacs galloped on without taking the least notice, and supposing we must be all infallibly killed, cooly informed the officers at head-quarters, that the English Adjutant with his *Kebeetky* had fallen down the precipice. This news reached the Prince's ears, and an officer with one of his Highness' carriages was sent to my assistance. I met the officer upon the road; for, resolved to shew the Russians that I was as indifferent to accidents as themselves, I lay quietly in the bush till a new carriage could be procured, and then remounting with my unfortunate valet, I resumed my journey with all the *sang froid* I could muster.

In the end of the winter of 1783 the Prince, whose fatigues had much exhausted him, retired from the Crimea to Krementchuck, to recruit his strength. In the mean time, Prince Alex. Potemkin, who had been sent against the Circassians, forced them to conclude a peace. They had, together with other petty states, been waging a pilfering war against Russia; but were now compelled to send the young Prince, son to the reigning Prince, to Potemkin as a hostage. He was accordingly put under the care

of

of an officer of dragoons, and conducted.towards Krementchuck, near which place I was appointed to receive him. On meeting him, then a boy, seven or eight years old, I informed him, through the medium of the interpreter, that the Prince-General, though much indif-posed, and even confined to bed, meant to see him on his arrival; adding such other blandish-ments as were likely to soothe his mind. As we approached his Highness's quarters, which I pointed out to him, this young Circassian seemed quite diftressed at the noife of the bell, worn by the shaft-horse of his carriage; and which is the diftinguishing mark of an officer and the Imperial post. The amiable boy had no servant near him, and was too mild to ask such a thing of me; he therefore requested, by the interpreter, that I would allow him to alight and take off the bell, leaft it might dif-turb the Prince who was fick. Immediately on my arrival I related this puerile anecdote to the Commander, who inftantly received the young Tartar into his favour; and continued to shew him every mark of regard and attention.

We remained at Krementchuck fome time in cantonments; when the affairs of the Crimea being fettled, Potemkin returned to the capital. As I wished to vifit fome parts of the country,

he

he gave me leave to proceed, as I pleafed. In my progrefs I again paffed through Pultowa; and being more at leifure than when I came to the army, I vifited with increafed intereft and attention the plain where the famous battle was fought between the Czar Peter the Great and Charles of Sweden. The mound ftill remains that was built with the bodies of the flain. On being dug into, it exhibits an awful *melange* of fkeletons of men and horfes, with the iron heels of boots, rufty fpurs, and broken weapons.

Here it was that Charles XII. difmounted to charge a body of Ruffians, at the head of his own regiment of infantry. His orders were not to fire till he fhould command them; however, on approaching the enemy, they fired: but, though fuccefsful, the Swedifh hero was fo mortified at their difobedience, that he mounted his horfe, and rode away without fpeaking one word.

On my arrival at Mofcow, I paid my refpeĉts to Count Chernecheff, the Viceroy, who lived in a ftyle of incredible magnificence. I had the honour of dining with him the day after my arrival. About a hundred guefts fat down to table, behind each of whom ftood one of the Count's own fervants, in very fplendid liveries; he himfelf was furrounded by a hoft of upper

fervants,

fervants, dreffed in the moft fuperb manner: indeed, befide a, body guard, he kept no lefs, than three hundred domeftics.

At Mofcow I met feveral cart-loads of Eng-lifh midfhipmen; who being thrown out of employ by the conclufion of the American war, had entered into the Ruffian fervice. They were under the care of a ferjeant and two ma-rines, and were going to join Admiral Macken-zie on the Black Sea.

After having fpent a few days at Mofcow, I continued my route to St. Peterfburgh; and, having taken up my family at Narva, I reached the capital about the beginning, of the fum-mer 1784.

As it may probably intereft my readers to learn, a few authentic particulars of the great Potemkin, I fhall here prefent them with fome which are not known to the common herd of fcribbling travellers, but my fituation in his fuite enabled me to collect.

His levée commenced about eight in the morning; at which time a little fhabby anti-chamber, and a billiard room adjoining, were crowded with general-officers. Thefe apart-ments, with a bed-room, were all he ufually inhabited, though he had feveral magnificent ones in the fame houfe: the way to thofe he occupied led through a fuite of large rooms.

The

The firſt enquiry made by thoſe who appeared in the anti-chamber was, " In what humour is the Prince?" If it was known he was out of temper, it was not unuſual for many of the viſitors to depart immediately, well knowing that no good was to be done that day. Prince Serge Galitzin, who married one of the Prince's nieces, had the greateſt influence; for his great livelineſs, added to the high favour in which he ſtood, and which enabled him, like Sir James Harris, to make a viſit any hour without ceremony, ſeldom failed to cure the gloom of Potemkin.

Nor was the dreſs of this renowned commander on theſe occaſions leſs extraordinary than his apartments. It conſiſted of a looſe *robe de chambre*, which in winter he wore of velvet, and in ſummer of ſilk or chintz, flowing round him; his neck and breaſt were bare; and his ſilk ſtockings hung about his heels. No Highlander had a more cordial hatred to a pair of breeches; theſe he never wore but when he dreſſed. His hair flowed about his head in a moſt diſorderly ſtate; and in this naked ſlovenly trim he would ſit down to table with all the princes or general officers of Ruſſia.

His behaviour at table was as far removed from the common road of life as his dreſs; ſometimes he would ſit ſullenly without ſaying a word; and this was not without its due effect

on the countenance and appetites of his guests:
at others he was all gaiety, and kept the table
in a roar, so that nobody could eat for laugh-
ing; and I have seen him more than once, after
eating a few morsels, suddenly start up, as if
some important idea had struck him, and go
into his bed-room. This was the signal for
rising from table, for no one would sit when he
he was up; and the guests were expected to follow the Prince to take coffee: very often, indeed, when he retired with a louring aspect,
many of his visitors had not courage to follow,
but took coffee in the anti-chamber; his favourites, however, never failed to stick close to
him.

He was passionately fond of mimicry, and
was himself a tolerable mimic. He actually
raised a genius of this kind from Lieutenant to
Lieutenant-Colonel for no other merit. This
man was constantly kept attending in the anti-
chambers; and was occasionally called upon to
divert his patron by *taking off*, as the phrase is,
all his acquaintance. I alone escaped; for having plainly told the silly buffoon, that if he
presumed to take any liberties with me, I would
chastise him, he prudently abstained, even
though the Prince, (who had heard of my me-
naces, and wished to get him into a scrape,)
often desired him.

He had an extraordinary and whimſical manner of puniſhing his aides de camp, when they
exhibited any thing unmilitary in their dreſs
and behaviour. Inſtead of verbal reproof, he
uſed to ſend them long diſagreeable journeys;
and would take care they ſhould ſet off when
leaſt prepared. As an inſtance, a young gentleman who had lately been appointed, and who
had no other recommendation than his being
protected, appeared at dinner dreſſed in all the
frivolity of a coxcomb: Potemkin looked at
him with a louring obliquity of countenance,
and ordered his ſecretary to prepare ſome diſpatches. When theſe were ready, and before
dinner was ended, the young beau was called
for, and commanded inſtantly to ſtep into a
carriage that was waiting to carry them to the
Viceroy of Moſcow. There was no refuſing or
heſitating; and without even the neceſſary
cloathing for the ſeaſon, he had ſeven hundred
verſtes, (five hundred Engliſh miles) to travel in
the dead of winter.

After the Prince's return from the Crimea,
the firſt of the nobility gave him entertain-
ments, in which invitation, his ſuite was always
ſuppoſed to be included. The Ducheſs of
Kingſton, willing to immitate thoſe of the moſt
diſtinguiſhed rank, and wiſhing at the ſame time
to affront me, ſent an invitation to Potemkin;

but

but inftead of faying nothing about his fuite, fhe fent letters of invitation to every indivi-dual officer except myfelf.

The Prince, who hated her, was refolved to take the fame opportunity to mortify her that fhe had deftined to gratify her malice to me; fo contriving that I fhould be on his duty that day, he told me he would give me my revenge, for I fhould not only go with him, but I fhould fit next her at table.

Being on duty, I was obliged to attend him every where, and accordingly attended him to the Duchefs's, where I, with the reft, proceeded to pay our compliments to her Grace. My bro-ther officers fhe received with politenefs, but when I approached to make my bow, fhe turned afide from me. When we went to be feated at table, the Prince, under pretence of fpeaking to me on bufinefs, kept me near him, and fo arranged, that he feated me at the Duchefs's elbow. It would be difficult to depict the manner in which fhe fate fretting and fuming all the time of dinner; however I was feated, and fhe could not move; fhe had therefore nothing to do but conceal her anger, and that, to a woman of her violence, was no eafy tafk.

Though Potemkin had long ceafed to be the lover of the Imperial Catherine, he ftill con-tinued to govern; and though he was no longer an inhabitant of the palace, his houfe had *a* private communication with the Emprefs's a-partments. Potemkin had fucceeded Orloff in her affections; and Lanfköi, who had been a *Chevalier Garde*, with the intervention of a few fhort lived favourites, fucceeded Potemkin. It would however be an endlefs tafk to enume-rate all the lovers, who fucceffively occupied the favourite's apartments. Thefe confift of a fuite of rooms on the *entre fol*, very magni-ficent, in which the *Favourite* (for fo he is always called,) is little better than a ftate prifoner, as he cannot mix in fociety, and all his mo-tions are clofely watched.

Such was the afcendancy of Potemkin, that I have feen him tear an order figned by the Emprefs, and which only wanted his fignature, becaufe it had not been obtained by his means. The Emprefs frequently vifited him in his own apartments, at which time we, (the officers of his fuite) were ordered to attend in the anti-chambers; fome times fhe came unawares, and then all fled helter-fkelter, and, without waiting orders, repaired to our pofts.

Befides the houfe where he ufually lived, he had feveral rich palaces in the town, to which he occafionally went, and where he kept fer-vants; he had alfo fome fplendid apartments in the houfe I have juft defcribed, but thefe he

feldom

feldom ufed unlefs by chance in an evening, when he meant to receive vifits in fome fort of form, but ftill *fans cullottes.*

Notwithftanding he treated officers in general very roughly, I always experienced politenefs from him, nor was he even offended with me when I out-manœuvred him, which I once did as follows.

A Colonel who wifhed to have his regiment removed from the place where it was, to another province, applied to the Prince for an order, the Prince who had no favourable opinion of the Colonel, felt no wifh to oblige him; neverthelefs he told him to direct the fecretaries in the office to make out the order; this was accordingly done, and, in the routine of bufinefs, prefented with a mafs of other papers to the Prince for his fignature, which his Highnefs however evaded, and continued to do fo for feveral months together, till at length it begun to look fomewhat dirty and was eafily diftinguifhed.

When papers of this nature were brought before the Prince, it was cuftomary with the officers to arrange them in fuch manner as they thought fit; and as the Colonel had applied to me, I endeavoured to place it uppermoft; but the Prince continually difappointed me, by fhuffling the papers together like a pack of cards,

E   and

and whenever he came to this, he always threw it aside unsigned.

. Anxious to serve the gentleman who had so long waited for it, I procured it to be new drawn out and somewhat altered in form; when placing it near the top, I presented the whole together.. The Prince shuffled them as usual, but not expecting to see his old friend with a new face, and it happening to fall into his hands, he signed it without discovering what he had done; nor was he displeased when I told him (which I did some time after) how he had been tricked.

I was likewise treated with much distinction by the Emprefs, from whom I received many presents; one in particular I mention, not from its value, but because it does away every idea of my having left Ruffia in disgrace; she gave me, for some little services I had rendered, a present of 500 ducats of Holland in specie, a very few days before my departure. The court of the Emprefs was very splendid, but she was herself a wonder of regularity and exertion. Every morning at five her Secretary (Befborodko) attended her, at six the intendant general of police and others had their audience and received their orders. She dined precisely at twelve, and every evening at nine there was a supper for the party at court. The Emprefs amused herself with

walking

walking about, till she saw the guests seated, and then retired without saying a word or being observed by the company.

The great encouragement I had hitherto received, had naturally encouraged me to splendid living; few can bear the idea of retrenching; and I am unfortunately not one of that self-denying class. While I had the Duchess of Kingston's house, it saved me much money, but now, though I myself had a lodging and table at the Prince's, I was obliged to provide quarters for my family at an enormous expence, for houses are not easily to be hired at St. Petersburgh. Besides, the day of active service was over, and the Prince, though he treated me with much politeness, did not find me the indispensible officer I once was; I therefore obtained leave to retire to Narva, and soon after from the service.

I immediately sailed from Narva to Copenhagen, furnished with letters of recommendation for Prussia from several of the most distinguished characters at the Russian court; particularly from the Count de Goertz, minister from Berlin, to his brother, then Major-General of cavalry and Aid-du-Camp General to Frederic the Great.

CHAP. VII.

The author arrives at Copenhagen just after the revolution there.—Anecdotes of the King of Denmark.—Goes to Pruffia.—Ceremony of entering Potfdam.—Frederic the Great's mode of receiving reports.—Waits on Comte de Goertz.—Etiquette of prefentation to the King.—Meets feveral diftinguifhed charaEters.—The Hereditary Prince's apartments defcribed.—Receives permiffion from the King to attend his manœuvres.—Prefented to the Queen, at the palace of Shöen Haufen, near Berlin.—Accompanys the Prince on fome private expeditions.—Is ordered to leave Potfdam.—The order revoked next day.—Defcription of Potfdam. —Defcriptions and anecdotes of Frederic the Great. —Excellence of the Pruffian troops.

I ARRIVED at Copenhagen in September 1784, and was received in a very flattering manner by feveral perfons of diftinction; here I met that worthy and exalted character, Hugh Elliot, Efq. the Britifh Minifter at the court of Denmark. To this gentleman's friendfhip I have the higheft obligations; his praifes I need not write, they are in the mouths of all who knew him; but I fhould be even more loft to honour

and

and gratitude than calumny has dared to repre-
fent me, did I not here in the moft public manner return him my moft fincere thanks for the
almoft innumerable favours he has done me,
though I will not pain his generous mind by a
recapitulation of them.

The little revolution of Denmark, if indeed
it merits that name, had juft taken place, and
the Queen-Mother, to whofe tyranny the late
Queen owed her misfortunes, had been banifh-
ed to an eftate fome miles from Copenhagen.
Affairs had been placed in the hands of the celebrated Bernfdorff, and a law was paffed (on account of the King's weaknefs, which had induced him to give his fignature to any thing laid
before him) that no edict fhould be valid unlefs
counterfigned by the Prince Royal.

The King whofe derangement had rather reduced him to the ftate of boyhood than deprived
him of reafon, did not much relifh this arrangement, though he knew it would be in vain to
make complaints. He however contrived to
fhew his diffatisfaction; for one evening having a
number of papers to fign, he defired they might
be left till morning, when they fhould be ready.
In the morning the Minifter went to receive
them, but to his great furprize, he found the
King had fomewhat exceeded his promife; the
papers were indeed figned, but his Majefty had

E 3

made

made an addition to his name, and figned them
Chriftian and Company.   A thoufand droll anecdotes might be related of this monarch, but I
cannot confent to raife a laugh at the expenfe of
fallen worth and greatnefs.

Having paffed fome time at Copenhagen, and
the time of the King of Pruffia's evolutions being
at hand, I fet off for Berlin. I croffed the Belt,
and went through Pomerania to Potfdam, the
refidence of Frederic the Great.

Knowing the cuftomary mode of prefentation,
and the difcipline practifed here, I was not furprifed at the ftrictnefs with which I was ex-
amined at the gate of the garrifon. Every ftranger is afked his name, his age, to whom recommended, his bufinefs in the garrifon, and feveral
other queftions of the fame nature.   On being
afked " What are you ?"   I anfwered " A Scots
Highlander."   " Whence came you ?"   " From
the Black Sea."   " What is your rank ?"   " Major of the Ruffian Army and Aid-du-camp to
Potemkin."   " What is your bufinefs here ?"
" To compleat my education as a foldier under
the firft mafter in the world, your King." " Have
you any letters for the King ?"   " No; but I
have for feveral officers, particularly Count de
Goertz, his Majefty's Aid-du-Camp General."
" What inn do you go to ?"   Having anfwered
all thefe queftions, I was fuffered to proceed.

The

The accounts given by all ftrangers are laid before the King; and are, if there is any thing extraordinary in the report or perfon, noticed by his Majefty. The old warlike monarch ufed to receive reports in the moft perfect military ftyle; for however engaged in ftudy or bufinefs, his *paraphernalia* of fword, cane, hat, and gloves, always lay fo that he could reach them in a moment. A fingle page waited in the anti-chamber; and when any reports were brought, announced them to the King, who putting on his hat, cane, and gloves, and fticking his fword by his fide, made a military hobble, (for age at that time prevented him from raifing his boots,) into the anti-chamber. Here the great Frederic, with all martial form, ftood with his hat in his hand till the officer had made his re-port; and then facing about, he retreated in the fame manner he had before advanced

As foon as I had dreffed myfelf, which in compliment to the King, I did in the Pruffian ftyle, with boots half way up my thigh, and a *queue* down to my rump, I waited on thofe to whom I had letters, particularly the Count de Goertz, his Majefty's Aid-du-Camp. I afked him how I might accomplifh the object of the voyage to Potfdam. He informed me that perfons who came recommended it has the quette to write to the King, and afk

miſſion to be preſented to him, and to appear
at his parades and manœuvres.

I immediately went home, wrote a few lines
to the King, addreſſed, (as the Count de Goertz
had inſtructed me,) ſimply *au Roi*; and ſent my
letter by my own ſervant, in the uſual way.
Next morning, at ſix o'clock, I received an
anſwer, brought to me at my hotel by the King's
running footman. The letter was in amount
as follows:

   " MAJOR SEMPLE,

      " It is with pleaſure I permit you to
follow me to the manœuvres of my troops. As
to the preſentation, you muſt addreſs yourſelf
to Count de Goertz, my Aid-du-Camp General,
who is charged with ſuch affairs. Upon which,
(Major Semple) I pray God to have you in his
holy keeping.

               " FREDERIC."

This laconic epiſtle was ſomewhat curious in
s form, for it was begun ſo cloſe to the top of
paper that there was hardly room for the
rs. About an hour after it reached me, I
ved a viſit from Count de Goertz, to whom
ajeſty had wrote concerning me, ſignify-
intention of receiving me that ſame day,

at

at eleven o'clock; and at the parade I was prefented to the Prince.

When thefe prefentations were over, and the
parade ended, the King's running footman met
me in my way, giving me an invitation to dine
with the Prince. This was the etiquette at
Potfdam; for though you are entertained at the
Prince's, the invitation is really the King's.
The Marquis de Bouillé, Monfieur De Cuftine,
(fince guillotined at Paris,) and feveral other
officers were the fame day prefented, and received fimilar invitations.

Notwithftanding the King had feveral empty
palaces, the Prince was obliged to content himfelf with a lodging at a brewer's houfe. Here
we all met, in a fmall dining-room; where we
had an elegant entertainment, very handfomely
ferved.

This fuite of apartments might be called the
Prince's *oftenfible* lodgings; but he had extended
them far beyond the brewer's houfe, by occu-
pying parts of two or three adjacent houfes.
His Majefty was equally niggardly with refpect
to fervants, of which he allowed the Prince
very few; but feveral handfome young fellows,
who had no warlike inclinations, were glad to
purchafe the Prince's livery, and wear it without wages, as a protection from being forced
into the army. Though the enlargement of the

apartments

apartments might possibly be concealed, forty or fifty stout handsome domestics could not escape the penetrating eye of Frederic : he knew in fact every body in Potsdam; and when he met any of these volunteer lacqueys, never-failed to bestow reproachful epithets on them.

The King, whose curiosity was raised by the exploits of Potemkin in the Crimea, honoured me with some marks of attention; and thus I obtained a sort of indirect leave to reside at Potsdam, (a favour very rarely granted, particularly to military men); nor was I unnoticed by the Prince, at whose parties I frequently made one. Having seen the King, and having attended different manœuvres where that in-imitable soldier commanded in person, I was recommended by my friends to go to Berlin, in order to be introduced to the Queen.

I went accordingly; and Prince Dolgorouki, the Russian Envoy there, having introduced me to the rest of the foreign ministers, I was on the first public day presented to her Majesty, by her first Chamberlain, Pritwitz. It was on this visit to Berlin that I had the good fortune to become acquainted with the amiable Duke Frederic of Brunswick, and General Mollen-dorff, Governor of the capital.

After having remained a few days to enjoy the pleasures of Berlin, I returned to Potsdam,

not

not without feeling some reluctance at leaving certain connections I had formed. On my return to Potsdam I waited on the Prince, who now admitted me more frequently into his private parties. The Prince constantly attended the King's military manœuvres, and I always accompanied him: his Royal Highness had, however, certain *private manœuvres* of his own, at which I also attended, and with which the King was not acquainted. The great Frederic, as is perfectly known, had no high veneration for the fair sex in general; while the Prince Frederic William was, like myself, their devoted slave. Though it was no easy matter to elude the vigilance of the old warrior, the Prince, Baron Groothaufen, and myself, contrived now and then to steal to Berlin without his knowledge.

Though these sallies were some time concealed from the brave old King, it was impossible they should be hid for ever; in fact they were detected, and I had the honour of an intimation from the Governor of Potsdam, acquainting me that my presence was no longer necessary in that garrison. He would in fact have used his oldest general the same way or worse. This happened on the parade, in the presence of the Prince, of whom I immediately took leave; and repaired to my hotel, in order to prepare

for

for my journey. The Prince, well acquainted with my extreme extravagance, and fufpecting I might want money, though he feldom had fufficient for his own purpofes, fent a fervant to me with a handfome fupply. I then took horfe, and, attended by one fervant, left Potf-dam.

I ftopped at the houfe of a friend, with the intention of paffing the night, and waiting the arrival of my baggage and fervant. I wrote from hence, by a meffenger, to the Governor, acquainting him that I had obeyed his Majefty's orders with the alacrity and difpatch I owed to fo great a monarch; that I hoped he would facilitate the departure of my fervant, by furnifh-ing him the neceffary paffport: I added, that the keys of Spandau * had made a man tremble who would ftand undaunted before all the artillery of the Houfe of Brandenburgh.

The Governor granted my requeft, inti-mating at the fame time that I might, when I pleafed, return to Potfdam. After paffing fome time at Berlin, where I had now a numerous acquaintance, I accepted the invitation, and returned to that grand military academy, though not as a permanent refidence.

* Spandau is a garrifon not far diftant from Potfdam, where Frederic the Great frequently fent officers who gave him of-fence, and kept them as long as he thought proper.

Potfdam,

Potſdam, though certainly the firſt ſchool for war, was in fact no very pleaſant place to inhabit. The ſtrictneſs of the diſcipline rendered every man no better than a ſlave; nobody could paſs or repaſs the gates without being reported; and to the very garriſon it nearly was intolerable, as the ſoldiers had there no opportunity, as elſewhere, of earning any thing by their labour, as there was no trade or commerce whatever in that town, its inhabitants being, to a very few exceptions indeed, military.

The King endeavoured to amend their condition, by ordering numbers of houſes to be built every year: ſtill the ſoldiers were miſerable; but, though ſuicide was frequently the reſult of diſtreſs, the veteran monarch was abſolutely idolized by them.

Frederic the Great had in his younger days been a very active man; but when I ſaw him, he had upon him much of the infirmity of age. That ſharp, penetrating look, which would have marked him as an extraordinary man, even at a glance, ſtill remained; but he ſtooped much, and his legs were ſcarcely able to ſupport his weight, which, however, was not enormous.

He wiſhed, as far as poſſible, to conceal every appearance of decay; and would have felt himſelf hurt had any one obſerved him mounting his horſe. Unable to vault into his ſaddle as he ufed to do, he always got between his horfe and a wall. This was a fignal for all, except thofe employed in mounting him, to look another way. As foon as he had got his foot into the ftirrup, a powerful huzzar, in a twinkling, hoifted his Majefty into his faddle; once there, he galloped off immediately.

Perhaps, fince the time of Charles XII. of Sweden no prince ever paid lefs attention to drefs than Frederic the Great. His coat was always military, and feldom, I believe, had its nap difturbed by the officious intrufion of a brufh: this he wore buttoned tight round him; and his legs were cafed in a pair of large ftrong boots. Thefe laft, the date of whofe antiquity I am not chronologift enough to fix, had been held facred from brufh and blacking; but when overloaded, with mud, having been wafhed with a fponge, had gradually deferted the fable, and affumed a mahogany hue.

His hat was no way calculated to put the reft of his drefs out of countenance; it feemed their coeval fellow-foldier, and was fharp before. As he never fpoke, even to a private foldier, without uncovering and holding it in his hand, the right corner, by which he always held it, fhewed evident marks of hard duty.

His fnuff-box, the only gaudy thing about him, was of gold, of an enormous fize, and to

this

this he was almoſt perpetually reſorting, not for pinches, but, I had almoſt ſaid, handfulls.

Such was the exterior of Frederic! In ſuch a homely caſket was contained a ſoul capable of conquering and governing the univerſe! This was the truly great man who, amidſt all the hurry of war, cultivated arts at home! The companion of a Voltaire, the avowed enemy of kings; he eſteemed this philoſophical republican, and was beloved in his turn by philoſophers of all deſcriptions. This was he who in the midſt of diſaſters, roſe in proportion to his ſufferings, and not only reſcued his kingdom from ruin, but raiſed it to a pitch of greatneſs unparalleled in Europe! Invincible in war, indefatigable in exertions, and inflexible in juſtice, he never had a ſuperior, hardly an equal.

At Potſdam this incomparable Prince occupied but three ſmall apartments, and thoſe in a corner of the vaſt palace there. They conſiſted of a *Salle à Manger*, which ſerved likewiſe as an anti-chamber, a bed-chamber and a library; theſe, like all the other apartments he uſed, were hung with blue ſatin. It muſt be confeſſed that the hangings were ſomewhat worſe for wear, the moths having made free with ſuch parts as beſt ſuited their palates; the very curtains of the King's own bed were ſo full of holes, that he might have pretty tolerably reconnoitred the

approach

approach of a vifitor, without the trouble of withdrawing them.

He lived however but little in this palace, as his principal refidence was at *Sans Souci*, a fhort diftance from the gates of Potfdam. Here was his favourite retirement; here he unburthened himfelf from the cares of ftate; here he was the philofopher, the polifhed fcholar, and he may be properly ftyled the father of the Pruffian *belles lettres.* His company at *Sans Souci* was extremely felect; it confifted of the firft literary characters and a few diftinguifhed generals; with thefe he paffed his time in converfation and mufic, in which his excellence, both as a compofer and performer, is admitted by all the world.

While I was in Pruffia, his Majefty had a violent illnefs, a little before the time appointed for the Silefian manœuvres; his attendance was thought to be impoffible, a circumftance the more remarkable, as, during his long and glorious reign, he had never been difappointed of any military operation for which he had fixed the time, either by ficknefs or bad weather.

However, juft as the feafon approached, and as if fuch was decreed to be the unchangeable fortune of the Great Frederic, he recovered, contrary to all expectation, and was perfectly able to review his gallant troops as ufual.

During

During his illnefs he was fo reduced, that a lufty ftrong huzar was obliged to lift him from his bed to his chair, and back again. One day, when this faithful domeftic was lifting his royal mafter from his bed, the iron heel of his boot flipped on the wax-rubbed boards, fo that he found he muft unavoidably fall; he had however the prefence of mind to tofs his Majefty on the bed, while he himfelf meafured his length on the floor. Frighted to death, the huzar did not venture to raife his head, and the King who was hardly able to fpeak from debility, was rendered perfectly fpeechlefs with laughter at the droll accident. As foon as he recovered his fpeech, he encouraged the honeft foldier to rife, and conceived fuch a liking to him for his fudden refource of thought, that he never would part with him from about his perfon.

From *Sans Souci*, the King ufed to gallop al-moft full fpeed to Potfdam to the parades, which he feldom miffed; he was attended only by two pages, who not being fo well mounted, had frequently much difficulty to keep up with him. When he arrived there, he rode brifkly along the line, fometimes without fpeaking a word, and, fometimes he would converfe with the Governor, the other general officers, and fuch ftrangers as had been prefented.

F

It

It is impoffible, without having feen the Pruffian troops, to form an idea of their appearance
and difcipline; no miftakes ever happen, no
awkwardnefs is to be feen; they feem rather different branches of the fame grand machine than
diftinct beings. Every thing is perfect, every
thing is in a ftate of readinefs; fo that were it
neceffary to fend the whole army to the frontiers,
or further, in an inftant they would begin their
march.

The Great Frederic ufed to pay vifits on horfeback, with little ceremony; of which an inftance
happened, in the beginning of the winter 1784,
when the then reigning Duke of Courland came
to Potfdam, to pay his refpects to his Pruffian
Majefty. The Duke had taken up his refidence
at an hotel clofe to the parade, but by no means
the beft in the place. Here in a little, fhabby
parlour, was his Serene Highnefs, dreffed in the
moft fplendid ftyle, blazing with diamonds, and
covered with the richeft embroideries. In this
place, immediately on his arrival, he had the
honour of a vifit from the King, who in his old
uniform coat and other ufual accoutrements,
rode up to the door of the hotel, alighted in a
moment, and without further ceremony went
into the parlour; he ftopped a few minutes in
converfation, when he took leave, remounted his

horfe,

horfe, and rode away with as little ceremony as he had approached.

The Prince and Princefs was kept under fuch reftraint by the King, that it was next to impof-fible for them to enjoy any pleafure. But when his Majefty was gone to any diftance, which pre-cluded the poffibility of his return for a day or two, the Princefs never failed to give a ball, at the palace of Charlöttenburgh, in the park of Berlin. To thefe affemblies, which were very gay, the officers of the *Gens d' Armes*, and variety of the moft fafhionable and noble perfonages were admitted ; but the Princefs was obliged to be at home before the King's return to Potf-dam.

CHAP. VIII.

The author leaves Pruffia and returns to Denmark.— Sets out for England, where he arrives in December 1784.—Frequently vifits the Continent in the courfe of the two following years.—Befpeaks a travelling poft-chaife of Mr. Lycet.—Mr. Lycet, not being able to arreft him for the DEBT, *twelve months after the delivery of the carriage, proceeds* CRIMINALLY *againft him.—The unhappy confe-quences.—Sends a model of a faddle and accoutre-*

ment

*ment to the King of Pruffia.—Obtains his pardon,
and goes to France.—Forms an intimacy with some
of the moft diftinguifhed characters there.—Proceedings of the Convention, and anecdotes of the perfons principally concerned in the maffacre of the
King, with the proceffion to his trial.*

In November 1784, I left Pruffia, and by the
way of Lubeck, went again to Copenhagen;
here I ftaid a few days. I then fet out for England, charged with letters for government from
Mr. Elliot, and arrived on the 23d of December. I delivered the packet, with which I was
intrufted, according to inftructions, and having
fpent fome little time in London, I returned to
the Continent, partly to gratify my turn for
military operations, and partly on confidential
bufinefs. I continued to go backward and forward as bufinefs or inclination led me, till an
event took place, which firft fitted my name for
the mouth of calumny, and which has humbled
me in my own eyes, more than in thofe of the
public. Though this has been told and retailed
a thoufand times, and though I am far from ac-
cufing either a judge or a jury, of willing injuf-
tice, ftill will I boldly affirm, that it is not only
poffible for both to be miftaken, but that it is
often impoffible for any but the man himfelf to
judge of his own *intentions.* The cafe ftood thus
with

with me: I had befpoke a travelling poft-chaife of a coach-maker, Mr. Lycet. -It was ordered to be finifhed on a particular day, and on that day he fent it home. My then fituation render-ed fuch a carriage neceffary for me, and I was at that time able to pay for it; but my fatal turn for extravagance foon put that out of my power. After remaining fome time in town, I went again to the Continent, and during twelve months, paffed and repaffed very frequently; on which occafions feveral attempts were made to *arreft me for the debt,* nor was there any idea of calling it *a fraud, till a year after the carriage was delivered to me at my lodgings at Knights-Bridge.* I am far from vindicating the non-payment of a juft debt, but I folemnly declare that I had not the fmalleft idea of defrauding the coach-maker. I had occafion for a carriage; I was in a good fituation, though very carelefs and extravagant. But were every fafhionable young man, who buys a poft-chaife, without confidering how it is to be paid for, as ftrictly dealt by as I was, the Newgate Calendar would, I fear, become an al-moft indifpenfible fupplement to the Red Book.

It is true, Mr. Lycet fwore that I had hired the carriage *only for a week*; but had he not fworn it, would it have appeared credible, that he would fit up a new carriage for a week's hire? The attempt to arreft me was admitted; befides,

in

in his books there appeared an *erafure*, where the word *hired* was. Had it been originally fo, what need to alter it? If it was not, fome other word muft have occupied that place. What that word was, or when erafed, Mr. Lycet beft knows.

It is further remarkable, that he produced no perfon in court to whom he had complained of the robbery ; he had applied to no magiftrate, nor had he even entertained an idea of commencing a criminal profecution, till, as himfelf confeffed, he had been *advifed* to it. Contrary however to the expectation of every *Lawyer* in court, the judge who tried me, was of opinion that the jury fhould find me guilty of *a felonious intention*.

After fuch a charge delivered by the Judge, it cannot excite much furprife, that I was found guilty, and that I was fentenced to feven years tranfportation.

Notwithftanding this had been the opinion of the *Judge*, and the determination of the *Jury*, it weighed very little with thofe who knew me, and who exerted themfelves to extricate me from my difficulties.

I was of courfe committed to the charge of the keeper of Newgate, by whom I was lodged in the ftate apartments of that prifon. Here I had a room to myfelf; and having much fpare time,

time, I invented a faddle and accoutrement for cavalry, which faddle I find recently adopted in the British army, with little alteration.

My model I fent to his Majefty Frederic William of Pruffia, who had then juft fucceeded the immortal Frederic the Great, accompanied by a letter, of which a tranflation is here annexed, and which, at that time, appeared in moft of the periodical prints, in French and Englifh.

(TRANSLATION.)

(The original being wrote in French.)

"To the KING.   POTSDAM.

"*SIRE*,

"WHEN I had the honour of being prefented to your Majefty, on my return from the invafion of the Crimea, the gracious reception which I met with, and the ftrong proof which your Majefty deigned to give me, (in a* moment of difgrace,) of your uncommon generofity and condefcenfion, rivetted thofe chains, by which, as a man devoted to the profeffion of war, I was already attached to your perfon.

* See Page 60.

F 4   " Such

" Such, Sire, is my paſſion for martial affairs, and ſuch my veneration for the Pruſſian arms, that even in diſgrace and bondage, while afflictions are dealt to me with more than common liberality, ſtill my whole ſoul is occupied by the glorious ſcenes I have ſeen, and ſtill my diſtracted imagination holds to my view your Majeſty's godlike troops.

" Your cavalry, the fineſt in the world, I have often gazed on with rapture, and the particular attention which I payed to their accoutrements, occaſioned me to make ſome remarks, which I now beg leave, with the moſt reſpectful ſubmiſſion, to lay before your Majeſty, along with an accoutrement for light-horſe, an invention of my own, and which I had prepared to lay in perſon at your Majeſty's feet, when I was prevented by the diſgrace and deſtruction, into which I was plunged, by unbounded extravagance, and ungoverned paſſions. Unable to adorn my tale, I will without further apology, proceed in the plain language of a ſoldier, to point out the diſadvantages which your Majeſty's, and indeed all the cavalry on the Continent of Europe, labour under by the preſent mode of ſaddling.

" It is an eſtabliſhed cuſtom in your Majeſty's cavalry to place the ſaddle on the ſhoulder

der of the horfe, by which means he is confined in his movement, travels with great inconvenience to himfelf, is foon fatigued, is fubject to have fiftulas from the continual motion of his fhoulders under the faddle; and, when be becomes fatigued, having the weight of his rider fo much forwards, is fubject to ftumble. Was the faddle placed in fuch manner as to expofe entirely to view the fhoulder, it would add grace to the appearance, give eafe to the horfe, render him more active, lefs fubject to an ulcerated back, lefs apt to ftumble, and when he did ftumble, would be eafily recovered by his rider, who, being feated about the middle of his horfe's back, would fit firm, and have great command.

" My prefent fituation renders it impracticable for me to convey my accoutrement for light-horfe to your Majefty by any other means than that of your Majefty's Minifter at London. To enter into a defcription of this accoutrement would exceed the bounds of a letter. My earneft prayer is, that your Majefty would fuffer it to be laid before you, when I hope its appearance will fay more in its favour than I could fay in a volume. I will, however, fo far obferve, that it is well calculated for parade, for eafe, for fervice, and to encourage the men to clofe to the enemy, the only means by which

cavalry

cavalry can be redoubtable or fuccefsful. Should it meet with your Majefty's approbation, and fhould it be found to poffefs the qualities which I have attempted to defcribe, I fhall efteem myfelf the moft fortunate man on earth.

" The hour in which I muft be liberated, though, alas! 'tis too diftant, neverthelefs advances; and as it approaches, I tremble for the difficulties which I fhall have to encounter: that averfion which mankind in general have for the unfortunate, will throw unfurmountable difficulties in my way, unlefs your Majefty, as confpicuous for compaffion as for military talent, will fuffer me to ftand as a volunteer in the ranks with your grenadiers; there I may find an opportunity of perifhing as I ought; further I do not expect. I have forfeited all claim to confidence, of courfe, to command; and only feek fuch a grave, as (in fpite of my prefent difgrace) the hard fervice which I have feen, and the dangers which I have braved, give me fome title to demand.

" If it is a fact, Sire, that men of courage are ever poffeffed of the moft tender feelings, I can no where look for compaffion, for pity, or pardon, with fuch hopes of fuccefs, as to your Majefty, and your gallant army! Have mercy on me, Sire, and command your brave General de Mollendorff to announce to me, that you will fuffer me to carry arms with your Majefty's
grenadiers,

grenadiers, I fhall be happy! will wait the hour of my enlargement with refignation, and, when it comes, fly to your ftandard.

" With anxious impatience I attend the fen-tence which your Majefty will pronounce. On it depends my fate!

" I have the honour to be, Sire, with all that enthufiafm which fo great a Captain as your Ma-jefty can infpire in the foul of a foldier,

" Your Majesty's

" Moft humble,

Sept. 1790.

" Faithful and devoted fervant."

I remained a prifoner in the ftate apartments of Newgate a confiderable while. I was then fent to Woolwich, where, after fome time, I received his Majefty's pardon, on condition of going abroad.

The encouragement I had formerly received on the Continent, and the protection that I had fome reafon to expect from the King of Pruffia, inclined me to go to Germany; but my friends advifed me rather to go to France, then at peace with, and receiving fupplies of every thing from England. They very properly fupported their arguments by truths which I could not deny;

that

that the bare pay was too fmall for my turn of mind, and that France then deprived of her beft officers wanted men of tried fkill and experience, and therefore held out a fairer profpect to me. I yielded to thefe reafons and went to France, where I remained fome time an inactive fpectator, till want of fubfiftence forced me to apply to the Committee of War for employment. But already difgufted by their villainous proceedings, I declined accepting any fituation, though my advice was frequently taken refpecting the new corps they were forming. Curious however to fee the event of the King's trial, I determined to remain on the fpot until that was over, and was accordingly obliged to conceal my fentiments.

I had now formed a ftrict intimacy with General Beruyer, Commandant of the interior, a fituation often miftaken for that of Commandant of Paris, whereas in truth they are very different: the General has the command of all the troops in the interior, but the Commandant of Paris has only the command of the national guard in that city; the former, Beruyer, was an old and excellent foldier; the latter, Santerre, was a brewer. With Beruyer I went upon all his little excurfions. I was likewife very intimate with Pache, the minifter of war, Pethion,

Roland

Roland, and several others of the then leaders of France, moft of whom have fince been guillotined.

During my abode in Paris, I was an eye-witnefs of many fhocking maffacres, and I cannot help wondering at my own efcapes; for at a time when liveries were forbidden to all but the foreign minifters, and brilliant equipages wholly out of ufe, I had both of the moft fplendid kind, and was generally called an *ariftocrate*, a reproach I did not take much pains to contradict.

The time fixed for the trial of the unfortunate Louis now drew near, and vaft preparations were made for that purpofe. During this time the violence of the Jacobin party daily increafed, though it.had not then reached its height of wanton and indifcriminate murder.

When the day arrived for the King to appear before the Convention, I, with Mr. Maxwell, went in the fuite of Beruyer, to fetch him; the whole way was lined with troops, and the concourfe of people was immenfe. The unhappy monarch was found dreffed in a morning coat of grey Bath coating, a waiftcoat, and, I think, breeches of the fame; his hair rolled up, and his beard long, not expecting, as we imagined, a vifit of that kind.*

A fingular

---

* Clery fays that the King *had* received private intelligence, and defcribes the means by which fuch intelligence was obtained.

A singular delay happened, and for a time retarded the proceffion. The * decree of the Convention, ordering the King to be brought before them, had been forgotten; a meffenger was therefore difpatched for it, and on his return it was read to his Majefty, who bowed and complied. Though there had elapfed fufficient time from the hour of Chambon's arrival at the Temple for him to have changed his cloaths, he went dreffed as I have juft defcribed.

From the King's wavering conduct, in his attempt to efcape from the country, and on other occafions, I had formed the idea of his being a very weak and irrefolute character; but I was far miftaken, for his examination convinced me, that he wanted neither courage nor talents, and indeed from that day. I became devoted to him.

With the utmoft coolnefs and intrepidity, he anfwered interrogatories, which he could not poffibly forefee, and while his whole conduct

tained. But at that time this circumftance was unknown to any except thofe immediately concerned.

* Clery mentions, that though Chambon, *Maire* of Paris, was announced before eleven o'clock, as being with the council below, and coming up immediately to fpeak with the King, he did not appear before one; as the caufe of this delay was only whifpered among the general ftaff, it could not well come to Mr. Clery's knowledge.

evinced

evinced firmnefs of mind, his anfwers fhewed that he poffeffed a clear underftanding, far above the ftandard of mediocrity.

When the King arrived at the hall of the Convention, he alighted from his carriage, and the general-officers quitted their horfes. Santerre and the municipal officers led the van; the King walked next, clofe followed by Beruyer. They paffed along the Corridor till they came oppofite a fmall chamber, into which Santerre informed the King he muft go, while his arrival was announced to the Convention.

The King then addreffing himfelf to Beruyer, who always treated him politely, defired to have fome refrefhment; on which the General told him he might have bread and wine, and he immediately fent for a bottle of the beft claret, " *vin de-la fete.*"

His Majefty had drank a goblet of wine, eaten a morfel of bread, and was filling his glafs again, when Santerre entered the room, faying, " *Louis Capet! la Convention Nationale vous demande a fa barre.*" To this rude addrefs the King replied with a bow, and inftantly obeyed.

The firm conduct of this unfortunate monarch I have already remarked: it was fuch as difarmed many of his enemies; and every friend to humanity entertained hopes of the moft favourable kind. The examination ended, the
King

King returned with the fame guards. The whole was, however, thrown into confufion, by fome battalions refufing to let Santerre, (who had been delayed at the hall of the Convention,) pafs them, in order to get into his proper place, next to the King's carriage. Santerre rode very badly; and the guards, who were without difcipline, were afraid of his horfe, they therefore, after great diforder, obliged him to difmount, and, with much ado, permitted him to force his way through the mob, leading his charger.

The confufion ftill continuing, he no fooner got near the carriage of the King, than, with a fquadron of the regiment of the *Dragons de la Republique*, and a battalion of artillery, he rode off with his royal prifoner, leaving the guards to follow as they could. This procured him a public reprimand, as it was alledged that he might, for want of ftrength, have had his charge taken from him by fuperior force.

The King was left fome time before he was brought up to make his defence, of which he had regular notice: counfellors were alfo allowed accefs to him, and he chofe *Malfherbes* and *Tronchet* to defend him; *De Sèze* was afterwards added. *Target* had been applied to, but infamoufly refufed.

On the 26th of December the King was

again

again brought to the Convention, with the same ceremony as before; but as he was apprifed of it, he appeared dreffed, though very plainly. About ten in the morning he left his prifon. I had, however, feparated from General Beruyer, in order to introduce the Princefs Alexandre Luboumerfky and Mr. Ellis, an Englifh gen-. tleman, into the hall of the Convention, which was at that time a matter of no fmall difficulty. When I had placed them, I took, together with Mr. Maxwell and two fervants, the fhorteft cut acrofs the city to join the line of march; but coming to a ftreet that opened into the Boule-vards, we were ftopped by a cannon and a fe-male cannonier, who guarded the pafs. As I knew it was to little purpofe to argue with a *poiffarde*, I turned my horfe, and paffed through another ftreet. Having gained the rear of thofe who lined the road, I made up to the Com-mander, and defired leave to pafs his line when the head of the march fhould reach him: he in-ftantly confented; but in the mean time, and to cool our horfes, we walked them about in the rear. Here I was accofted by a patrol, who afked me who I was? I told him, an Englifhman, waiting to join the General Staff, with whom I had permiffion to ride, but had been left behind. He anfwered, " You are not, you are a *Ci-devant*;" and pointing a muf-

G

ket

ket at me, we were inftantly furrounded by a crowd of pikes, and a general outcry of " *Ce font des ci-devants.*"

All we could fay availed nothing; we were carried before the Commiffaries of the fection of the Temple; but not being able to fatisfy them, I was obliged to write to Beruyer in their pre-fence, who no fooner received my note than he came, with his whole General Staff, and deli-vered us.

A very pacific perfon, not yet mentioned, who was impelled by curiofity alone, was involved in this adventure, which, as Beruyer obferved, made him haften to my affiftance, leaft, by the fmalleft delay, he might have met my head on a pike. This was no other than *Mr. Newcomb, the Boot-maker, mounted on my beft charger*, which, at his own requeft, I had lent him, that he might follow me to fee the proceffion of the unhappy monarch to that tribunal which even-tually deprived him of life.

In his way to his former attendance the King had received fome, though not much infult, yet enough to difgrace, before all mankind, the un-feeling wretches who could be bafe enough to ufe it; but now a gang of fervants belonging to that UNIVERSALLY DETESTED ARCH TRAITOR, ORLEANS, together with a hireling crew devo-ted to him, uttered fuch fhocking abufe, fuch
inhuman

inhuman taunts, as could not fail of exciting horror in any bofom, not callous to every fenfe of mercy and decency.

So much has been faid on the fubject of the King's trial and defence, that I fhall be filent upon it, farther than that I was individually prefent. I fhall therefore proceed to the time of his execution, wifhing only to lay before my readers particulars that are not generally known.

CHAP. IX.

The Convention orders that the decree pronuncing the King's death fhould be made known to him within twenty-four hours.—His counfellors refufed admiffion to him.—His fentence announced to him.— Proceedings the evening previous to his execution: —The author attends at the Temple with General Beruyer.—Santerre's brutal behaviour at the Temple the morning of the King's death.—The Queen and Royal Family refufed to fee the King, by the Commiffaries, with an explanation of the reafon.— Santerre's fpeech to his Majefty when he came to fetch him, not related by Clery.—More brutality of Santerre.—A man murdered for pitying the

King.

King.—Preparations at the place of execution.— The King's behaviour, and the involuntary respect paid to him.—New insults of Santerre.—The King's death and burial.

It had been decreed by the Convention, on Saturday January 19th, 1793, that the executive body should, within twenty four hours, announce the King's fate to him. This, however, was not done till the latest hour of the time limited, though the Municipality did not neglect to take an account of the few trifles then remaining in the possession of a once great sovereign, even before the decree was passed.

For many days the sufferings of the unfortunate Louis had been wantonly aggravated by a series of unnecessary and unprovoked cruelties; the Queen, his children, and sister had been inhumanly torn from him; but now even his counsellor, the venerable Malesherbes, was refused admission.

On Sunday the 20th of January the decree of the Convention was brought to the King, with equal formality and rudeness: it was bluntly announced by *Garat*, Minister of Justice, and read by *Grouvelle*, Secretary to the Council, who, I have been assured by those present, seemed more terrified at its contents than the royal sufferer.

The

. The King had prepared a paper, which he delivered to Garat, defiring three days delay in the execution of the fentence, that he might prepare himfelf for the awful fcene he was to undergo; he alfo requefted to have a catholic clergyman, of his own chufing; to be freed from inceffant infpection, and to fee his family without witneffes. He added an earneft entreaty for permiffion to his family to go where.ever they would; and that the nation would confider the cafes of fome diftreffed perfons, chiefly old people, widows, and children, formerly fupported by his bounty.

The fame evening, about fix, the Convention returned an anfwer to this requeft of the King, purporting that he fhould fend for any clergyman he pleafed; that he fhould fee his family freely, and without witnefs; that they fhould be taken into confideration; that the creditors of his houfehold fhould be indemnified; but the delay of three days was poffitively refufed.

Before the clofe of the evening drums went through the feveral diftricts, with the Sectional Commiffaries, who publicly read a proclamation ordering all windows to be fhut next day; that no women or children fhould be feen in the ftreets; and that the men fhould repair to their refpective fections: they alfo vifited hotels where ftrangers took up their refidence, order-

ing

ing them either to march with the section, or
to remain at home; questioning them at the
same time concerning their situation, employment, and business in town. Among others
they came to me, when I told them, that I had
obtained General Beruyer's leave for myself and
Mr. *Maxwell* to march with his Staff; and that
I was to hold myself in readiness at his quarters
at four next morning.

I attended as was appointed, and rode with
the General to the Temple. During our march
he several times observed to me, that he was
surprised at my curiosity; that, for his own part,
were he not apprehensive that his declining to
attend, (though no part of his duty,) would en-
danger his own head, he could not have been
induced to be witness of so awful a scene. I
repeat this in respect to the memory of the
amiable Beruyer, who since paid his life as the
price of his unshaken loyalty; and who, though
forced to disguise his thoughts, was ever in his
heart the devoted advocate of the King. When
I add that he had a wife and six children, and
no fortune, his disguise will be thought very
excuseable.

Though I had hitherto avoided going into
the prison of the Temple, I now went with
Beruyer and his Staff into the apartment where
the Committee of the *Commune* was sitting. In
a little

a little time the Municipal Officer then on duty with the King entered, with a requeſt from
his Majeſty that he might have a pair of ſciſſars
allowed him to cut his hair, as he expected
every moment to be led forth. No oppoſition
was made by any of the Council, only one member aſked the officer who brought the meſſage, if
he thought the King might ſafely be truſted
with them? On his anſwering in the affirma-
tive, and that it was impoſſible for any man to
be more calm or collected, the voice of every
member concurred without heſitation in granting this requeſt.

Santerre, however, who, with his Staff, was
preſent, but had no ſort of concern or authority in the affairs of the council, as ſoon as he
heard the permiſſion granted, brutally exclaimed, " I oppoſe that! he wants to cut his hair
" to give it to his confeſſor, to be handed about:
" I will not have a relic of the tyrant left."
The Committee, over-awed by the opinion of
the General, adopted his deciſion; and the
Commiſſary, laying down the ſciſſars, returned
to his duty.

Some time after a Commiſſary came down to
the Council with a meſſage from the Queen,
purporting, (to uſe his own words) *that the
women wanted to ſee Louis Capet.* The decree of
the Convention, allowing the King to ſee his

G 4

family

family *when he pleafed*, was then read; but being found not to enjoin that they might fee him *when they pleafed*, the Council paffed to the order of the day. The Prefident, as foon as this was fettled, probably willing in compaffion to evade the decree, afked if the king had expreffed any defire to fee them; the officer faid *he had not*, (a circumftance confirmed by Clery,) and there the bufinefs ended.

About half-paft eight Santerre went up ftairs to bring his Majefty down; he was attended by feveral municipal officers and foldiers, fome of whom entered the King's apartment, while others took their pofts upon the ftairs. I followed them, and went fo far that I could, through the legs of thofe that were at the door, fee all that paffed between Santerre and the royal prifoner.

His Majefty appeared as if coming out of an inner apartment, with two perfons behind him, whom I was told were his confeffor and Clery. Santerre immediately addreffed him to this effect: *" Louis Capet, I am come by order of " the National Convention to take you to the " *Place de la Revolution*, formerly *Place de Louis*

---

* Clery fays nothing of this addrefs; but the anguifh and confufion of that faithful and affectionate fervant might well prevent him from attending to the difcourfe of thofe from whom he had nothing but barbarity.

" *Quinze,*

" *Quinze*, there to deliver you into the hands of
" high juſtice." I did not hear his Majeſty
ſay a word.

Before Santerre went up to bring down the
King, he had propoſed to the Council of the
Commune, to *tie him ;* but this was rejected, and
one of them exclaimed, " Why ſhould we tie
" him, are we not all his enemies." Santerre
vexed at having his cruelty thus diſappointed,
told them, that ſince they had refuſed to tie him,
inſtead of two Commiſſaries, he ſhould put two
gens d' armes, in the coach with him.

Before his Majeſty reached the carriage, he
had to paſs through the garden of the Temple,
and along a narrow paſſage, at the end of which
Chambon's ſhabby old coach was waiting for
him. On reaching this he looked round, as for
ſome one to give him a hand to help him in;
but no one came near, and the inſulted, fallen
monarch, was forced to get in without aſſiſtance.

Santerre performed his *promiſe;* for he put
two *gens d' armes* into the coach, while the Commiſſaries, whoſe duty it was to guard the King,
were obliged to follow on foot as well as they
could; this was however only the prelude to
thoſe ſcenes of anarchy when no ſafety was to be
found, and when nothing was more uſual than

for

for the tyrant of yefterday, to become the victim of to-day.

The proceffion went on very flowly, with
little infult; yet there were not wanting, fome
whom this awful fcene could not foften into
decency, a decency due to the feelings of even
the worft of criminals. In the principal ftreets,
through which the fad proceffion was to pafs,
not a window was open, and fome perfons who
imprudently looked out at windows in the bye
ftreets, were inftantly fired at.

After we had proceeded fome diftance, a
fhocking affair took place, which muft have filled with horror any heart, not loft to humanity.
A man as the King paffed, exclaimed " *Quel
trifte changément !*" " what a fad change !" He
had no fooner uttered the words, than he was
literally torn to pieces, and parts of his mang-
led body held upon pikes before the carriage,
to fhew the unhappy Louis, the end of what
they arrogantly called the *laft of his friends.*

The * proceffion met with no more interruption, till we arrived at the place, de la Revolution,

* The ftreets were compleatly lined with foldiers, cannon
were placed at every avenue, leading into the line of march,
field pieces and heavy artillery were likewife drawn in the
proceffion, both before and behind the carriage, and the guards,
who led and clofed the whole, were immenfely numerous.

the

the deſtined theatre of regicide. Here the fatal machine was erected in ſuch a manner, that the illuſtrious ſufferer, could, from the ſcaffold ſee at one view, the once pleaſing palace of the Tuilleries, and the pedeſtal and fragments of his predeceſſor's ſtatue.

The guillotine was ſurrounded by troops, of which the *Marſeillois* held the moſt conſpicuous ſituation, as it was between them and the ſcaffold that the King muſt paſs. A place on the right was kept open for the General Staff, and the cannon filed round into the front of the machine, where they were kept primed, with matches lighted, and *one* in particular was pointed at the place of death, with orders on the ſmalleſt cry for mercy from the people, to fire and put at once an end to all hopes,

When the carriage drew up oppoſite the ladder of the ſcaffold, M. de Frimont the King's confeſſor alighted, and his Majeſty was likewiſe preparing to do ſo, but was ſtopped as ſoon as he put his head out of the door by Santerre, who imperiouſly bade him go back; this order was inſtantly obeyed, and the King being heavy, ſhook the coach when he ſate down; hence aroſe the report that he had fainted on ſeeing the machine, than which nothing could be more falſe.

Santerre

Santerre then called to some of the *gens
d' armes*, and ordered six of them to draw up,
three on each side of the way, from the coach
door to the ladder, which was not more than
two yards distant.   In this place, the King who
had been made to alight as soon as these *gens
d' armes* were posted, undressed himself; first
throwing off his hat, which was instantly cut to
pieces and distributed among those present; he
then threw off his coat, which was treated in
the same manner, nor did he receive any assistance, except that some person folded his shirt
under the collar of his waistcoat, which seemed
to me to be of white cotton flannel.

He then prepared to ascend the scaffold, but
was told that his hands must be tied; to this he
quietly submitted, only saying *it was not neceffary*.   Mr. *Frimont* was going along with him to
administer the last offices of religion, but he was
torn away, and another priest, a meer raggamuf-
fian in appearance, was put in his place, as a
parting insult to the dying monarch.

Whether he had thus far attempted to speak,
I cannot say; for the drums and trumpets,
which by the express order of Santerre, were
placed in immense number in the front of the
guillotine, to use his language, " *to prevent Louis
" Capet from being heard should he attempt to speak,*"
made

made fuch a noife as rendered it impoffible to
hear a word. As foon as the King came upon
the fcaffold, he looked at the fatal machine, and
then walked towards the front, bowing to the
people as if he meant to fpeak. Notwithftanding the drums and trumpets had been placed
for the purpofe of drowning his voice, no fooner
did his Majefty appear to be preparing to addrefs the fpectators, than the noife ceafed in an
inftant, and the moft profound and folemn filence prevailed. He attempted to fpeak, but
inftantly Santerre called to the executioner to
do his duty, who going behind his Majefty, attempted to pull him away by the arms; but
not being able, his affiftant got before him, and
pufhing againft his breaft, they together forced
him near to the centre of the fcaffold, in a line
with the guillotine, he likewife called immediately to the drums and trumpets, who again
began to make a noife.

The prieft now approached; but the King
faid fomething to them, on which they retired
a ftep, and he continued uttering, probably a
prayer, for a few feconds. He then laid himfelf voluntarily on the board of the guillotine,
which was inftantly put in its place; the executioner immediately proceeded to tie him, and
his affiftant to fix the collar that was to fecure
his neck. While he was doing this with one
hand

hand, and before his master had done his part, he with the other hand held the string that was to discharge the machine, and ere the collar was fastened, pulled it, and put a period to the sufferings of the once great sovereign of France, who so lately, and so justly was idolized by all the people of that nation.

No sooner had the guillotine performed its dreadful office, than the executioner made a pretext to press the knife down, as if it had not gone quite through the neck, and that the head was taken off by *his hands*; but this was unnecessary, as the fall of the machine did its duty compleatly.

The assistant caught up the bleeding head, as soon as it was severed from the body, and holding it by the hair, exposed it to view on every side of the scaffold, crying out, " *Vive la repub-* " *lique, le tiran n'est plus;*" he then threw it down at his feet, and went to assist his master to put the body into a long basket, which was already bloody with the gore of numerous victims. The ruffian then again held up the head as before, and after exposing it some little time, standing a few paces from the basket, tossed it in with an air of disdain.

Many now pressed round to dip their handkerchiefs in the King's blood, and the city resounded with shouts of " *vive la republique:*" nay,

so

fo eager were *fome* for blood, that (I blufh to relate it,) the fon of an eminently rich Yorkfhire clothier gave to a *Marfeillois* fifty crowns, to ftain his handkerchief in that of the murdered King.

The body of the unfortunate Louis was then taken to the church-yard of St. Magdalen, where it was put into a hole fifteen feet deep, amidft a large quantity of quick-lime; a guard was fet over it for feveral days, that (to ufe their own expreffion,) *not a relique of royalty might be left.*

CHAP. X.

Santerre fends a letter to the Convention, announcing the King's death, which the Prefident declined reading aloud.—The city overwhelmed with for-row.—The author fends an account of the King's death to London.—Refolves to leave France, and receives a paffport for that purpofe.—In danger of being arrefted as a fpy.—Makes his efcape from Paris.—Paffes feveral garrifon towns by ftra-tagem, and reaches Bruffels.—Difficulty of paffing the Cordon, and the method he took to avoid Ant-werp, where Dumourier then was.—Arrives at Hoogftraten.—Stops for refrefhment at Baal-Her-tog.

*tog.—Reaches Bois le Duc.—Propofes an enter-
prize which is approved, and occafions him to go
to the Hague.—Returns with power to carry his
plan into execution.*

SANTERRE difpatched one of his Aides-du-
Camp to announce to the Convention the death
of the King, as foon as his head was ftruck off;
he himfelf ftaid to fee the body interred, and
then rode to the hall of the Convention.

The letter he had fent by his Aid-du-Camp
contained fo many boafts of his own fhocking
brutalities, that the Prefident refufed to read it
aloud, and contented himfelf by announcing the
event to the Convention. The whole city feemed quite melancholy: for fome days hardly any
one was to be feen in the ftreets, and the few
that ftirred out, wore evident marks of grief
and difmay in their countenances. On the night
of the King's death I went into feveral of the
theatres: they were empty; and I am well convinced that nine-tenths, not only of the people
of Paris, but of all France, at that time were
ftill devoted to their fovereign, but they wanted
a leader and confidence in each other, to enable
them to prevent, or to avenge his fall.

Mr. Newcomb, before-mentioned, who had
only waited in Paris to fee whether the Convention would dare to put their threat in exe-

cution,

cution, remained with me that night till I wrote an account of the shocking business, with which he and his son immediately set off for London.

The following evening, the theatres still continuing empty, the traiterous Orleans hired a mob to fill them, and to give to the place the air of chearfulness; but all was in vain; an evident gloom overspread the once gay metropolis, nor was it till several days had elapsed that joy re-appeared.

Disgusted to the highest degree with the excesses I daily witnessed in a country to which I had gone merely by the advice of my friends, and expecting war to be declared by my own sovereign, I determined to join the allies. I therefore addressed the Convention, telling them that my circumstances had induced me to offer them my services when they were at peace with, and receiving succours from my country; but that as firmly devoted to Britain as Frenchmen were to France, and perceiving war * at the eve

* I was so far right in my prediction, that before I had time to leave Paris, the Convention declared war, (to use their own words,) " *Non contre le peuple Anglais et Hollandois, mais* " *contre les tirans George et le Statbouder.*" Nevertheless, they commenced by waging war against the people. for they immediately laid an embargo on all British vessels, seized all British property in France, and in every way harrassed and imprisoned such of his Majesty's subjects as had not left the country.

H

of

of breaking out, I begged they would grant me a paſſport, that I might haſte to my poſt.

This requeſt they complied with, and even ſeemed pleaſed with my boldneſs. I was, notwithſtanding, under ſome apprehenſion of being arreſted as ſoon as I ſhould begin my journey, and therefore reſolved to depart unawares. In the mean time I paid viſits to all my friends, telling them that I ſhould leave France in ten or twelve days.

The precautions I took were not without reaſon; for the ſame day, while dining at the houſe of a lady where it was known I paſt all my leiſure moments, a perſon belonging to the Convention, whoſe ſole ſtudy has invariably been to do good, and to whoſe kind offices many ſubjects of all nations owe their exiſtence, came in diſguiſe, and acquainted me that I was denounced to the Committee of Public Safety as a ſpy, and as going to join the enemy, by Maxwell *, Le Brun, and my landlord; and that the

order

---

* This gentleman, I afterwards learned, was the Dr. Maxwell who had fled from Portland Road, on account of ſome improper meetings held at his houſe. I firſt met him at Pache's office. He attended there for months, offering ſome rifle barrels, which he brought from England, and ſoliciting the command of a company of rifle-men. He had been protected by Servan, the former Miniſter of War; but Servan having reſumed the poſt of General, Maxwell's intereſt was at an end; and

the

order for my arreftation had juft been iffued. I talked of furrendering myfelf, but he ftrongly diffuaded me, as faction, not juftice, then prevailed. As I had for fome days been preparing to fet off from that lady's houfe, I had removed nearly all my baggage thither piecemeal; and had ordered my valet, who remained at home, and on whofe fidelity I could depend, to leave fome of my cloaths, maps, arms, &c. in confufion, as if I had, as ufual, gone out; and to fay to any one that might enquire for me, that he could not tell when I fhould come in, but that I might certainly be found, as was my common practice, at eleven the next morning. It was, however, my intention to have fet out that night, and to have taken him with me.

A groom whom, from not fufficiently knowing, I had fufpected to be capable of betraying me, I kept conftantly near me; I would not fuffer him to go out of the lady's houfe; and when her fervant had prepared her *cabriole*, with which I meant to efcape, I made him get into it, and then followed myfelf. I drove to St. Dennis; where I told the Poft-Mafter that I was going upon military duty, defiring him to furnifh me

the firft Secretary having introduced him to me as my countrymen, I recommended him, and his fervices were accepted.

 with

with horfes, and to take care of mine until I came back; with which requeft he complied. I then judged it proper to explain myfelf to my fervant, who declared himfelf determined to fee me fafe over the frontiers, or to die by my fide.

By ftratagem I paffed Cambrai and Valenciennes. Arriving at the gates, I called loudly for the officer of the guard, and telling him that I came from Paris on urgent bufinefs, I demanded, in great feeming hafte, that he would give me one of his guard to conduct me to the Commandant's houfe; and leaping out of my chaife, directed my fervant to drive to the poft, and get frefh horfes put to the carriage immediately. By this means I prevented interrogation at the gates; and when we came to the Commandants, who were then men without military knowledge or experience, I pretended to have been ordered to join the army of the North by the Convention, and to inform him that fome troops of the line were on march to join Dumourier, whom he might expect in his garrifon in a few days.

A plaufible ftory was all that was neceffary; and, inftead of demanding my pafs, I was only afked queftions about the death of the King while the horfes were preparing.

Thus I reached Bruffells, where I confidered myfelf as fafe, having fo many acquaintances;

but

but the greateſt difficulty lay in paſſing the *cor-don* formed by the army: I therefore applied to Prince Louis d'Aremberg, who accompanied me to the quarters of General Moreton, then commanding at Bruſſells.

From Moreton I ſolicited a paſſport, which he readily gave me, but informed me at the ſame time that his paſs was but of little uſe, for that an Engliſh General, to whom he had given one ſome little time before, had, neverthelefs, been detained at Oſtend. Upon confulting with D'Aremberg it was refolved, that I ſhould pur-chafe a couple of horfes, and endeavour to go round Antwerp, as Dumourier, with a large body of his army, was then there; and I was well known to that General and moſt of his officers.

I immediately purchafed the horfes, and ſet out in a few hours from my arrival, contriving to reach Antwerp a little after the gates were ſhut. This precaution was neceffary, to furniſh me a pretext for ſtopping in the village; for had I arrived there before the gates were lock-ed, I muſt either have gone in, or have made myfelf the objeſt of fufpicion, by remaining at a paltry *cabaret* when I might have been elegantly accommodated in the town. To have reached the gates any confiderable time after their being ſhut would have excited as much fufpicion as

to

to have stopped in the village while the town was open: I was therefore obliged to calculate very nicely, and to assume the appearance of having rode furiously to reach the town in time. I managed this manœuvre so successfully that the inhabitants of the suburbs, concluding that I was in as great haste as I appeared to be, officiously called to me as I passed, that I might moderate my speed, for that I was too late to pass the gates. I however galloped on, with seeming anxiety, to the barrier, which I found shut. This was what I wanted; so, with apparent disappointment, I returned to the suburbs, and went into the first public-house I saw.

Here I ordered refreshment for my horses and myself, pretending that I must be ready to go into the town as soon as I could obtain admission; but having during the evening met with a person who had formerly served me, and in whom I could place confidence, I opened my mind to him, and he consented to be my guide round the town. In the dead of night therefore, when all was quiet, I again mounted my horse, and set out, accompanied by my guide, who conducted me so well, that before day-light he left me within sight of my direct road.

As the day approached, I consulted with my servant, when we determined, that if we fell in

with

with a centinel of the troops of the line, we should endeavour to approach and shoot him; but if he were a *Garde Nationale*, (whom we knew at that time to be wholly unacquainted with the bufinefs of fervice, and whom we could at once diftinguifh from the ftriking difference of the uniform,) that I fhould endeavour to get the counterfign from him; fortunately the firft we encountered was a *Garde Nationale*. He challenged me; I anfwered that I was of the General Staff, fent to vifit the pofts, and to examine the centinels, fome of whom had fuffered Auftrian fpies to pafs, and were fuppofed to have forgot the counterfign. He replied that it was not him, and after fome altercation gave it to me. I thereupon pretended great fatisfaction, and expreffing the uneafinefs it would have given me, to have been obliged to have ordered fo fine a young man to have been fhot, I rode on. Having obtained this, I had no difficulty to pafs another centinel, whom I foon afterwards met, and early in the forenoon, found myfelf in the Dutch village of *Hoogftraaten*, which lies about half-way between Antwerp and *Bois le Duc*; hither I learnt the enemies parties frequently came, even before the declaration of war.

My ftay in this village was confequently very fhort; and from thence I went to Baerle-Hertog,

but

but even here I was told I was by no means
fafe.   However both my horfes and myfelf being
much fatigued, I went to fleep in a part where
I thought I fhould not be readily found: my
horfes were likewife difpofed of fo as not to be
eafily come at, and I had directed my fervant,
in cafe of alarm, to turn them adrift.   After a
few hours reft, but before day-light, I again
fet forward, and without any interruption, arrived at *Bois le Duc* the fame forenoon.

The whole appearance of this place indicated
nothing but the profoundeft peace; the Governor, the reigning Prince of Heffe Phillipfthal,
and the Commandant, Major General Douglas,
feemed unconfcious of the prefence of war. The
French army, which under Dumourier had inva-
ded the empire, had juft been defeated near Aix
la Chapelle, by Saxe Coburgh, and the Duke
Frederic of Brunfwick, the former of whom
purfued the flying army into the country, between *Maeftricht* and *Leige*, while the latter with
his ufual promptnefs, marched immediately
from Aix into Holland by the way of the Rure,
and was then advancing towards Bois le Duc, to
prevent it from falling into the hands of the
enemy, an event which the garrifon did not
feem to apprehend, though they were not prepared to refift, and though a large army of the
                                French

French under General Maffena, lay at Antwerp, and were already preparing to attack
Williamftadt and Breda.

This was not a time for a man of any activity
to be idle. I had not paffed the French lines
without making fome obfervations on their pofitions. I therefore immediately propofed an
enterprize, which was highly approved by the
Governor and Commandant of *Bois le Duc*. I
was indeed received and attended to by them
with the utmoft refpect, as the Hereditary
Prince of *Heffe Phillipfthal*, fon to the Governor,
had ferved in Ruffia, and had conceived a high
regard for me, and a favourable opinion of my
talent as a foldier.

This enterprife which was deemed practicable by all the military men of experience, was
to furprife one of the enemy's Generals, and
carry him off from his quarters, a bufinefs
which only wanted a fmall fhare of refolution
and fome ingenuity; for that General, at that
period, expofed himfelf to fuch an accident, by
placing his quarters in a fituation totally detatched from his army, and having no other
guard than a few orderly commiffioned, and
non-commiffioned officers.

The Governor and Commandant not having
the power to carry my propofal into effect,
neverthelefs judged it proper to lay it before the
Stadtholder.

Stadtholder. This delay though probably short was too much for my impatience, and I was on the eve of setting out to join the Duke Frederic of Brunfwick, when I received a letter directing me to proceed immediately to the Hague.

I accordingly set off without delay, and had an interview with the Stadtholder, and some of his Generals, who finding my plan practicable, gave me an order to the Prince of Heffe Phillipfthal, inftructing him to give me from the Cavalry, in the garrifon of *Bois le Duc*, such a detatchment as I might judge neceffary.

CHAP. XI.

Change in the operations of the French, which defeats the author's plan.—He goes to cut off some forage belonging to the French, in the vicinity of Alphen. —Perfectly fucceeds.—Employs a bold ftratagem to reconnoitre Breda.—Finds the Duke Frederic of Brunfwick juft leaving Bois le Duc, and follows him to the village of Oofterwyk.—Without time to reft or take refrefhment, difpatched to Saxe Cobourgh.—Is prefent at the memorable battle of St. Tronde, which lafted three days.—The defperate taking of Ooftmaal.—Account of the battle, with an anecdote of the Arch Duke.—Returns to the Duke

of

of Brunſwick, after a moſt extraordinary journey of fatigue and danger.—Without ſtopping proceeds to the Hague, and gives a deſcription of the battle to the Stadtholder.

DURING my abſence from that city, the French had inveſted *Williamſtadt*. *Breda* had ſurrendered to them without a blow, and the Duke Frederic of Brunſwick, at the head of a ſmall Pruſſian army, had already reached Bois le Duc. The approach of this Prince, induced the French to be ſomewhat more circumſpect, and to make a retrograde movement; by this change of affairs, my plan neceſſarily fell to the ground. Neverthelefs, I had no ſooner ex-plained myſelf, with the illuſtrious Pruſſian General, whom I found in the houſe of the Prince of Heſſe Phillipſthall, than he diſpatched me at the head of a detatchment of huzzars, to pene-trate as far into the country as I could, and to prevent, if poſſible, the tranſport of ſome forage, which the French had collected near Alphen, into Breda.

I left Bois le Duc, with my detatchment, on the night of the 13th of March 1793, directing myſelf upon Tilbourgh, a Dutch village, where, though only three leagues from the gar-riſon I had left, I found the tri-coloured cockade diſplayed. I collected the magiſtrates,

and

and ordered them to publish immediately through the town, that wherever I found the cockade of the French, in one hour from that moment, I would treat it as an enemy.

I here learnt that the French General, commanding in Breda, had sent out detatchments into the country, towards *Hoogftraaten*, to force the farmers to send all their waggons during that night to Baerle-Hertog, for the purpose of tranfporting, on the following day, the forage they had been able to collect into the garrison. This appeared a meafure of too great importance to be overlooked: notwithstanding therefore there was much to rifque, by penetrating fo far into the country, ftill the object was worthy an attempt, even though I was forced to pafs the garrifon of *Breda*, and confequently expofe myfelf to the danger of being cut off. After having detatched an officer, with fome huzars to Kaam to deftroy fome forage I could not carry off, I marched by *Reil* to *Alphen*, a league from Baerle-Hertog. Here I lay upon my arms, till about two o'clock in the morning, watching the village, leaft intelligence of my approach fliould go to the enemy; leaving an officer and fome huzars to occupy *Alphen*. I then proceeded to *Baerle-Hertog*, where I knew the Commiffaries had directed the waggons and carts to affemble the preceeding night. I reached that village

early

early in the morning, which I entered full fpeed in almoft every direction.

The effects of this well concerted furprize were fuch as I expected; the Commiffaries and their guard fled with the greateft precipitation towards *Breda*, infomuch that I was only able to take two prifoners of the huzars *de la liberté*. I however prevented the waggons from putting in execution the bufinefs for which the French had collected them; and after cutting down the · *Bonnet Rouge* planted by the regicides, I began my retreat in the forenoon of the 15th of March towards Bois le·Duc. When I left *Tirlebourgh* on the 14th, I had difpatched a meffenger to the Duc Frederic, acquainting him that I found it neceffary to go on to *Alphen* that day, and might perhaps be obliged to go on ftill further; I therefore folicited his Serene Highnefs to fend out a detatchment of infantry to fecure my retreat, otherwife my return would become problematic. I delayed no time in regaining the village of *Alphen*, where I found the detatchment I left there forming *en battaille*, in confequence of fome of the enemy's fcouts having appeared at a diftance.

After having reconnoitred the country and given fome refrefhment to my huzars, I continued my march under fome anxiety, ufing every precaution to prevent furprife by the enemy,

enemy, who I was confident muſt have learnt the nature of my expedition, and the ſmallneſs of my force, and would probably attempt to cut off my retreat. I had not however proceeded far on my route, when I was met by a meſſenger, whom the Duke Frederic had ſent to recall me, and to inform me that that very morning, the firſt column of his army had left *Bois le Duc*, and part of it would that evening reach *Tilbourgh*, whether I was directed to repair, and where my detatchment was to return under the command of its proper officers, after which I was myſelf to join his Serene Highneſs.

This cheering intelligence removed all apprehenſions of danger, and in the evening I reached *Tilbourgh* without having met with any oppoſition, there I found the officer who I had detatched to *Kaam*, and who had executed the purpoſe of his miſſion. Here, in conſequence of the Duke's order, I gave up my charge; but inſtead of going immediately to *Bois le Duc*, I conceived the idea of reconnoitring the poſts occupied by the French in the environs of *Breda*. To effect this purpoſe, when midnight had ſcarcely yielded to the morning of the 16th of March 1793, taking with me a non-commiſſioned officer and a trumpet, *on my own authority*, I ſet out to ſummons *Breda*, about four or five leagues diſtant. I well knew that garriſon could

be

be no ftrangers to the advance of the Pruffian army, a circumftance which would give an air of truth to the *Rufe de Guerre* I meant to play upon them.

At day-light I approached the garrifon, and fummoned it to furrender to the Duke Frederic of Brunfwick, for the King of Pruffia with the ufual formalities. My fummons of courfe was but little attended to, but I had obtained all I wanted, a knowledge of the out-pofts held by the enemy. It was now about feven o'clock in the morning, and I returned to *Bois le Duc* fo much fatigued, that it was with difficulty I could fit my horfe. I there found the Duke preparing to follow his fecond column to the village of *Oofterwyk* about a league diftant, which he had appointed for his head-quarters. I reported to his Serene Highnefs the fuccefs of my expedition; he was but juft fetting off, and defired that I would dine with him at his new quarters.

This invitation was a command which I could not evade. I therefore haftened to my apartments to change my drefs, which I had not been able to do for three days before; but my horfes were no longer able to carry me, and my fervants were fo much fatigued, that I found they could not follow: I therefore borrowed a groom belonging to the *Chevalier d'Antras*, formerly a page to the prefent King of France; for him I alfo borrowed a horfe; and I myfelf mounted one which the Prince Frederic of Brunfwick had lent me fome time before, and then followed the Duke Frederic to *Oofterwyk*. I found his Serene Highnefs about to fit down to table; he placed me by him, and then informed me that, during my abfence, he had received different letters from Prince Saxe Cobourgh, who, with the Auftrian army, lay then between *Maeftrich* and *St. Tronde*, and which rendered it indifpenfibly neceffary for him to fend to that Prince. His S. H. further obferved, that, as I had been for fome time in that country, and knew better than any of his officers could do the exact fituation of the enemy, the Britifh, the Dutch, and his own army, that he had a defire to fend me, though he had felt much regret at impofing a tafk on me which could not but be irkfome to one who had been on horfeback fince the night of the 12th. I told his S. H. that on the day of fervice neither fatigue or danger were confiderations with a Briton, and that he would always find me ready to execute whatever he could command. To thofe who knew the gallant and amiable Duke, it is unneceffary to defcribe the effect which my anfwer had upon him; and to thofe who have not the happinefs to know him it is a matter of little import. I will therefore only fay, that

before

before his S. H. rofe from table, I was difpatched, attended by a huzar and the groom of
d' Antras.   I took peafants horfes and a guide,
from village to village, making a ftraight line
upon *St. Tronde*.   Arriving at *Heftell* on the
night of the 17th of March, I learnt that Saxe
Coburg was near *St. Tronde*, and that *Dumourier*
in three numerous columns commanded by himfelf, Valence and Miranda were preparing to
attack him, the fituation of the Auftrians was
defcribed to me as extremely critical; their
numbers far inferior to that of the enemy, much
fatigued by harraffing marches and almoft without cannon; in fhort, it was the general opinion
that they would be defeated.

As foon as the Mayor of *Heftell* could procure
me horfes and a guide, I continued my march
on the poft road to *St. Tronde*. As I approached
that town, (very early on the 18th of March,)
I heard very diftinctly a heavy cannonade, and
I met part of the Auftrian baggage coming away
in fome diforder. I found the town in the utmoft confufion, full of carriages, fome driving
off as faft as they could, and others waiting for
horfes; I then found that the two armies were
ferioufly engaged, and the defeat of the Auftrians from the great difparity of numbers was
deemed unavoidable.   With the affiftance of the
magiftrates, I procured frefh horfes and a pof-

I   tillion

tillion for a guide, and then went forth to look for Saxe Coburg in the field of action.

Being wholly unacquainted with the position of the armies, I left it to my guide to conduct me, which he did, until, to my surprise, I found myself in the rear of a French column. In such a position, there was little time for reflection, and I determined instantly to pass between this and another column, which I perceived at some distance on the right; the enterprize seemed fraught with danger, but it was authorised by necessity, as I could not tell whether there was not another French column to the left: in short it seemed to me, that the most certain and evidently the shortest road to the Austrian army, was through the French columns; this plan I adopted; I therefore directed my guide to look to his own safety: and telling the servant of *d'Autras,* that it was not his business to die, I advised him to accompany the guide, (my huzar I had already dispatched the night before, towards *Dieſt,)* but this intrepid boy refused to leave me. We then rode on at an easy pace, until we were on a line with the head of the columns most advanced. I could then perceive some part of the Austrians at a distance on my right front, and nearer and almost directly before me a body of cavalry; to those then I fled with all the speed the wretched horse on

which

which I was mounted was capable of. In the
buftle of action, I was not perceived by the
French, but as I approached the front of the
Auftrians, an officer rode up to examine me,
and a very few paces behind him, I perceived
on foot, coming towards me, the gallant young
Prince of *Wirtemberg*, who commanded that
body of troops. I acquainted his S. H. that I
was charged with a letter for Saxe Coburg,
from the D. of B. and begged he would inform,
me, in what part of the battle I fhould find him;
he affured me it was impoffible to determine
where he might be found, but to render it more
eafy for me, and to prevent me from falling into
any of the pofitions occupied by the French, he
fent an orderly officer with me. Between ten
and eleven o'clock in the forenoon of the 18th,
I found Saxe Coburg at the head of one of his
columns; after being announced in the brief
manner of the field, I prefented to him my letter, which he immediately read; and after afking me a few queftions, begged I would attend
the event of the day, that at night he hoped to
have more time to fpeak to me. I of courfe
joined the croud of officers, by whom he was
furrounded, and from them I learnt that Colonel (then Captain) Crawfurd, Aid-du-Camp to
his R. H. the Duke of York, had arrived before
me, and was ftill there; indeed I perceived him

at a little diftance.   Having a letter of recommendation from the Duke Frederic, for General
(then Colonel) Mack, I neceffarily enquired for
him; and on being told that indifpofition had
forced him to go to a fhort diftance in the rear,
where he was laying upon fome ftraw, I intimated a defire to go to him; and an officer of the
Prince's fuite offered his fervices to conduct
me. I found this eminently diftinguifhed officer
extremely ill, neverthelefs he quitted his ftraw,
and remounting his horfe, accompanied me back
to Saxe Coburg.   After a fhort converfation
with his Highnefs, partly on the fubject of the
letter, which I had juft delivered to Colonel
Mack, the Colonel had the goodnefs to propofe
to defcribe to me the order of battle. We rode
towards a height occupied by Imperial troops,
from whence I could diftinctly fee the heads of
the enemies columns, and the various pofts they
held. I vifited different parts of the pofition of
the Auftrians, and was filled with admiration,
at the determined countenance which that hand-
ful of men, though almoft exhaufted by exceffive fatigue, and labouring under every inconvenience to which a foldier can be expofed,
fhewed to an enemy, each of whofe columns
was nearly equal to their whole force, and whofe
front feemed covered with well ferved artillery.

The battle about this time, (the noon of the

18th

18th of March,) became very active in some parts; we rejoined the Commander in Chief, who was then at the head of a column, that bore at leaft its fhare in the fervice of that memorable day. As I had not then been prefented to the Archduke, whom juft then Colonel Mack perceived to have quitted his horfe, and to be walking at a little diftance from us, apparently to warm himfelf, he propofed to me to alight and he would prefent me. I difmounted immediately, and we walked towards his R. H. to whom the Colonel prefented me, as a man recommended by the Duke F. of Brunfwick. Some cannon fhot at that moment ftriking the ground very near us, this gallant Prince addreffing himfelf to me, faid, " This is a rude drawing-room, " Major."

A fort of paufe in this part of the battle prefently took place, which induced Saxe Coburg himfelf to difmount and join us for a few moments. One of the Archduke's fervants then produced a fmall quantity of bread and cold meat, with a fingle bottle of wine, which he laid upon a napkin fpread on the ground; having haftily partaken of this military repaft, we remounted our horfes. I then learnt that Captain Crawfurd had left the field, immediately after my arrival, in the forenoon, and was gone back to his R. H. the Duke of York, then with the

I 3

Hereditary

Hereditary Prince of Orange, at *Dortrecht*, where the Britiſh and Dutch guards lay.

The battle ſtill continued doubtful, alternately raging and ſlackening in the different poſitions. The village of *Orſmael* had for ſome time been occupied by the enemy. Saxe Coburg now determined to force it, and a body of troops was ſelected for that purpoſe; I was ſtill mounted on the miſerable poſt-horſe, which had brought me to the field, neverthelefs anxious to ſhare in the daring enterprize about to be put in execution, I ſolicited leave to accompany the dragoons, and that a horſe might be furniſhed me; but no horſe was at hand, and there was no time for delay, I therefore rode on mounted as I was.

The affair though very ſhort was inconceivably deſperate. Our way to the village, was the high road from St. Tronde, to Tirlemont, (encloſed by trees and a deep ditch on each ſide.) The enemy had planted ſeveral pieces of cannon to defend the entrance, and kept up a very heavy fire along the avenue; we however advanced undiſmayed, though nearly every horſe of the firſt ſquadron was either killed or diſabled by an unuaſually furious diſcharge of artillery. There was no ſtopping, and thoſe who were diſmounted, were forced to move forward on foot, to avoid being rode over; for ſuch was the confu-

fion,

fion, owing to the inceffant firing and fmcke, which the clofenefs of the trees and drizly weather would not fuffer to afcend, that it was impoffible to diftinguifh any object. For my own part, my poor poft-horfe having literally been blown from under me, I rufhed forward with the croud, unable to know where I was, until I actually run againft a cannon, which had been overfet, and which the thicknefs of the fmoke hindered me from perceiving, till I touched it.

The French being drove from this village, and fome other pofitions they occupied, and being overthrown in another quarter, by General Clairfait, declined engaging further, and retired to the pofition they had left.

Thus the bufinefs of that day clofed, juft before fun-fet, in a manner highly honourable to the Imperial troops. The approach of night and the fuperior numbers of the enemy, preventing Saxe Coburg from attempting to purfue. His army remained on the field of battle under arms, himfelf and the General Staff retiring to their quarters, at the villages of *Landen* and *Neerwinden*.

No fooner had the dawn of day appeared on the 19th, than the French columns were perceived in order of battle; the action confequently recommenced, and continued during that whole day with much obftinacy and various fuc-

ccfs.

cefs. The cool and determined bravery of the Auftrians however prevailed over the rude numbers and impetuofity of the French; about four or five o'clock in the afternoon they gave way, and were purfued to Tirlemont, but night coming on, prevented them from being further annoyed. By this compleat victory, fo truly glorious to Auftria, Holland, was for that year, (1793) refcued from the deftructive fraternal hug of the Conventionalifts.

I cannot avoid relating an anecdote of the brave Archduke, which will fhew more than any defcription I can give, the neceffity in which the Auftrian army were for bread. Riding over the field of battle, his Royal Highnefs obferved a fine dreffed Frenchman laying dead; the unufual fmartnefs of the dead man's appearance, firft attracted his notice; but perceiving a *black loaf* in his *havre fac*, he inftantly alighted, and feizing the valuable prize, he exclaimed, " That " gentleman did not fuppofe he was carrying " this loaf for me."

The defeat of the enemy being perfectly afcertained, about nine o'clock in the evening, Saxe Coburg ordered a *feu de joye* the whole extent of his front. The army as the night before remained on the field of battle, and Saxe Coburg, the Archduke, and the Staff, retired again to the villages of Neerwinden and Landen;

to

to the latter I accompanied Saxe Coburg, we reached his quarters about ten o'clock in the evening, and while some refreshment was pre- paring I received my letters from the Duke Frederic of Brunswic, and his Serene High- ness the Stadtholder; I then supped with the Field Marshal, and at midnight on the 19th, almost unable to carry my own weight, set off on my return to the village of *Oosterwyk*, where I had left the Prussian head-quarters.

I had now passed eight days almost continu- ally on horse-back, and without once having had time to undress: the state I was in can be conceived much better than related; but my zeal for the good of the service, and my anx- iety to carry the first intelligence of this so essential victory to the Duke Frederic, and to the Hague, enabled me to sustain the fatigue of the journey. I took the same road back, by which I had come to the Austrian army; and after much trouble to obtain horses, I reached *Oosterwyk* about ten o'clock, on the night of the 20th. I found Duke Frederic in his bed-room, standing and conversing with Captain, now Colonel Crawfurd, who had but a few moments before me arrived there, and who had acquainted his S. H. with the dan- gerous situation in which he left the Imperial army on the 18th.

I de-

I detailed the circumstances of the victory to his S. H. and then obtained his permission to continue my journey to the Stadtholder at the *Hague*. I was by this time almost unable to move, I could no longer stand straight, and it had become necessary for me to be lifted off and on my horse; while we were taking some refreshment in the Duke Frederic's anti-chamber, horses were preparing for me, but Colonel Crawfurd, who was going to the Duke of York at Dortrecht, consequently a considerable part of my road, and who had a *cart and straw*, very politely offered me a place in his equipage; I accepted it, for even such a conveyance was an indulgence to me, and we instantly departed.

We went through *Bois le Duc*, the gates of that town having been opened to let us in, I suppose about one o'clock in the morning, and we drove immediately to a house where a carriage had been previously ordered for Colonel Crawfurd; and though in this town I had appartments, my servants, and my horses, I did not go near them, but contented myself, while the chaise was preparing, to write a line, which I delivered to the stable-keeper for General Douglas the Commandant, announcing to him the victory gained by the Austrians. The instant the chaise was ready we continued our rout; when near the passage to the island of

Dortrecht,

Dortrecht, I parted with Colonel Crawfurd, and continued my journey to the *Hague*, where I arrived about two o'clock on the morning of the 22d. I went immediately to Major General Bentinck, Aide-de-camp to his S. H. the Stadtholder, and with him to the palace. The Prince was informed of our arrival, and immediately rofe to receive us. After giving his S. H. an accurate description of the battle, I was permitted to retire to a hotel, and to reft.

CHAP. XII.

The author fent for to court next morning, and forced to go dirty as he came from his journey.—Returns to Duke F. of Brunfwic—Capitulation of Breda.—Saxe Coburg's great actions.—Thofe excite fufpicions in the Convention, who fent to recall. Dumourier.—Dumourier fends the Commiffaries, and his intended fucceffor, Bournonvile, prifoners to Saxe Coburg.—The author arrives at Saxe Coburg's head-quarters.—Dumourier deferts with feveral others.—The author returns to Duke F. of Brunfwic at Bois le Duc.—Finds the Duke indifpofed.—Receives a moft extraordinary and honourable commiffion in the Dutch fervice at the Hague.—Returns to Bois le Duc and prepares to take the field.—Is fent on political

bufinefs

bufinefs to Bruffells.—Is induced to leave that army, and go to the army of the Upper Rhine.—Situation of the army, and Characters of the Generals.—The King of Pruffia leaves the field.—The reigning Duke of Brunfwic fucceeds him.—The author's diftreffed fitutation.—Retires to a fmall town in the interior.

BEFORE I went to bed I had purified myfelf as well as I was able from the inconveniences natural to my almoft incredible exertions; I had in fact neither enjoyed the comfort of a bed, a change of linen, nor a razor, for a week, during which I was hardly an hour out of my faddle. Once laid down I had refolved to recruit my ftrength with fleep, and had given orders that I fhould not be difturbed; about eleven, however, a meffage came from the Court, commanding my attendance there, and inviting me to dinner; though fcarcely able to crawl, I obeyed this honourable fummons, and proceeded to drefs myfelf, but perhaps in fuch a fafhion as never before appeared at that Court; I had only an old blue jacket and pantaloons, which, fullied with the dirt I had collected in nine days, were proof againft every effort of a brufh, and I was forced to borrow a fhirt of the perfon who kept the hotel; thus equipped, however, to Court I went, but fatigue made a moft awkward courtier of me.

The

The Stadtholder moſt kindly did every thing to render me comfortable after this immenſe exertion; for though he himſelf ſet out to viſit ſome forts the ſame afternoon, he recommended me to remain at the Hague to recover my ſtrength, offering to anſwer to the Duke of Brunſwic for my abſence for three days.

I remained only two days, when I returned to the Duke, by whom I was employed on different miſſions, chiefly to reconnoitre the enemies poſitions. The Duke of York had left *Dortrecht*, and was at that time approaching Antwerp by water, and the Prince of Orange with a ſmall Dutch army was marching upon Breda, ſtill in the poſſeſſion of the French.

About the end of March, or 1ſt of April, he ſummoned it to ſurrender, and the garriſon entered into a capitulation for that purpoſe; at this time the Duke Frederic ſent me to Saxe Coburg, to know how affairs were going on in that quarter he commanded: me to paſs by the way of the Dutch army lying before *Breda*, to receive the orders of the Hereditary Prince of Orange, who requeſted me to go to *Bergen-op-Zoom*, to the Duke of York who was then at that harbour on his way to Antwerp; and to inform his Royal Highneſs that *Breda* had capitulated: I obeyed his directions, and then took

the

the road for Bruffells, in which neighbourhood I expected to find Saxe Coburg.

In the fhort fpace of hardly a month had that gallant Prince drawn the immenfe army of the Convention through all Brabant; he had already purfued them beyond *Mons*, and was preparing to inveft *Velenciennes*. Thefe victories occafioned the fall of Dumourier, and indeed feemed fo extraodinary, that the Convention fent four commiffioners to direct him to appear before them; and appointed Bournonville, who accompanied them, to command provifionally in his abfence.

Dumourier, who forefaw what would be the event of his journey to Paris, and was un-willing to have his conduct made the fubject of enquiry by thofe that were ignorant of military operations, without delay feized on the com-miffioners, together with his deftined fucceffor, Bournonville, and fent them to Saxe Coburg: I met them at Bruffells, on the evening of the 4th April, under the charge of an Auftrian officer, who was conducting them to *Maeftricht*.

From this officer, I learnt that the head-quarters were at *Mons*, whither I immediately re-paired; and on my arrival, about four o'clock in the morning of the 5th of April, feeing a centinel ftanding at the gate of the inn where I alighted, I enquired who lodged there. To my

great

great furprife I was told the French General
Valence. I afked whether he was a prifoner, but
was anfwered that he had *deferted*, and had arrived there a few days before, and that he received all the honours of an Auftrian General.
I then went to Saxe Coburg's head-quarters;
he was in bed, but I was immediately introduced to him; while I was yet by his bed-fide,
one of his Aid-du-Camps came into the room,
to announce that *Dumourier, Egalité*, (alias
Duc de Chartres,) *Sullivan, Baptifte*, and another, (*Montjoy*, I think) were then in the anti-
chamber, fent in by General Clairfait, to whom
they had deferted; they were immediately ufh-
ered into the Field-Marfhal's prefence, and I
withdrew. Their interview lafted fome time,
and the event was, that in a few hours, a fort of
proclamation appeared, which, as it is fo well
known, I will pafs over. ·

At the Field-Marfhal's table, I that day met
thefe extraordinary deferters, each wearing the
three-coloured cockade.   After dinner the
Prince called me afide, and telling me that in
half an hour he would give me a letter for the
Duke F. of Brunfwic, and that he wifhed me
to haften back to inform his Serene Highnefs,
and the other Commanders, that Dumourier
had come over, and that he meant to bring him

to

to Antwerp, where a meeting of the Commanding Generals, and fome minifters of the allies,
was to be held on the 7th of April.

In confequence of my orders, I fet out immediately to carry my intelligence to the Duke
Frederic of Brunfwic, at Bois le Duc, who being
prevented by indifpofition from attending the
meeting at Antwerp, had deputed General Kno-
belfdorff in his place.   Breda laying very little
out of my road, I went that way to announce
Dumourier's *change of pofition*, to the Hereditary
Prince of Orange. By the road, as I expected, I
met the Stadtholder on his way to the conference, to whom I communicated the welcome
intelligence in his carriage, and then proceeded
to the place of my deftination.

I found the Duke ftill indifpofed, and feem-
ingly difatisfied; he talked of retiring, and I
fancied he was rather chagrined than fick. I
remained with him, going on fuch expeditions
as he chofe to command, until perfifting in his
refignation, he prepared to depart. I then applied to his Serene Hignefs the Stadtholder, to
place me in the Staff of his army. I was immediately appointed, and received the commiffion of
Major, in the fervice of the United States, on
the 6th of May 1793; but on account of my exertions on the expedition at *Baerle-Hertog*, my
commiffion

commiſſion bears in its body the date of March 15th, from which day my rank in the Dutch army takes place.

I remained at the Hague for a few days, and then returned to Bois le Duc, to prepare my equipage for taking the field. The Dutch army was collecting, and advancing towards the more active theatre of war. After being employed on different ſervices, I was, at length, while the Dutch lay at *Menin*, and its environs, fixed for a time at Bruſſels, for a political purpoſe. On my return from thence to head-quarters, an e-vent happened, which induced me to leave that army immediately, even without permiſſion, though not without announcing my departure, nor did I conceal the place of my retreat; it was to the army on the Upper Rhine:

The King of Pruſſia was there at the head of his own army. *Mayence* had fallen, after an obſtinate reſiſtance, and was taken poſſeſſion of in his own name; he afterwards prepared to inveſt *Landau* in *Alſace*, and was before it at·the time I arrived.

I acquainted his Majeſty candidly, with my reaſons for having left the army of the Low Coun-tries. I did not at the ſame time conceal the very haſty mode of my departure; to all which my relation, this illuſtrious Prince attentively and gracioully liſtened. Full of the higheſt con-

fidence

fidence in his juftice, generofity, and difcernment, I ventured to implore his royal protection, and permiffion to ftay with his army. This
I the more boldly did, as I well knew him to
be a foldier, and perfectly incapable of any thing
but great and benevolent actions. He was indeed
endued with a foul which was worthy the exalted ftation he held.

I likewife made my fituation known to the
gallant veteran General Wurmfer, who commanded the Auftrian army, and who, though far
advanced in years, feemed to lofe all fenfe of his
age in the hour of exertion; he then indeed
fhewed all the fire of youth; and if he fell
fhort in activity, his knowledge, his fkill, and
the maturity of his judgment, more than com-
penfated for the deficiency.

The reigning Duke of Brunfwick was with the
Pruffian army, and was left to command, when
his Pruffian Majefty took the refolution to retire
to his own territories. The brave Condé was
there with his little army of heroes, but never
was General better qualified to command the
moft numerous. When he, from power, from
extreme wealth and fplendor, was with the
whole of the nobility of France, fwept away
from his habitation, by the revolutionary torrent, he did not difpair. Deprived of his riches,
he abridged his expences; from a truly princely
                                        board

board reduced his dinner to a few dishes, and invited always a certain number of his followers in rotation. In the field with his little army he did every thing that could be performed; and so compleatly master is he of every part of the science of war, that he commanded the good wishes of all who knew how to appreciate his merits. His private life was in the highest degree amiable; a sincere friend, a polished and cheerful companion; the evenness of his disposition, and the benignity of his heart, attached to him all who approached him.

Soon after the affair of *Pirmasens* and *Weissembourg*, the King of Prussia withdrew from the field, and returned to his own dominions, leaving (as I before observed,) the gallant reigning Duke of Brunswick to command the Prussian army. This distinguished General's astonishing talents I will not attempt to describe, as they far transcend my abilities; but to him, and to every other General, I have endeavoured to do ample justice in a publication I now do myself the honour to announce, and of which I have already given some intimation. This will contain a complete account, illustrated with the most accurate maps and plans of every remarkable movement made by the allied armies during the three first campaigns of the war. As accurate plans are not easily forced to de-

ceive,

ceive, military men, who were not there, will then have an opportunity of judging whether the Generals I have named, did or did not deserve my praise.

When the King of Pruffia retired, all my hopes vanifhed into air; ruined in my fortunes, without home, without expectation of employ whichever way I turned my eyes, the profpect was equally dreary ; and, as if the hand of fate was lifted to my deftruction, I juft then received a defperate wound, under the pain of which I long languifhed.

Worn out with fatigue, fainting with the lofs of blood, and ftill more tortured with the anguifh arifing from the contemplation of the immenfity of my undeferved misfortunes, a retreat was neceffary; but, alas! where was I to find it? or who would open a hofpitable door to a poor wounded foldier, though I hope, at leaft, in that capacity not degraded? Thefe melancholy reflections had reduced me to a fhadow, and I looked forward to death as the moft defirable of events. Thus circumftanced I was induced to take up my refidence in a little town of the interior, till my health fhould again enable me to draw my fword.

CHAP.

CHAP. XIII.

The author's affair with Mrs. S.—Character of Col. S.—The author sets out for Augsburg in Suabia, accompanied by Mrs. S.—Becomes acquainted with Baron D'Ompteda.—Reaches Augsburg.—Suddenly arrested there, on the requisition of the the Baron D'Ompteda.—The Baron arrives at Augsburg, and makes some vague general charges.—Demands all the author's papers in the name of his Britannic Majesty.—The author writes to Mr. Dundas.—Was extremely well treated during his confinement.—Receives a letter from Mr. Walpole with an official denial on the part of the British government, of any knowledge of the transaction.—Decree of the Senate of Augsburg.—Remarks on the decree of the Senate.—Kind behaviour of Mr. Walpole.

It has been hitherto my study to conceal female frailties; for though I by no means pretend to the character of a stoic, there is a basenefs in publishing any thing which can hurt the feelings of those whom heaven meant us to protect, which my soul abhors. Yet I am now obliged to bring forward to the public an amiable woman, who owes her misfortunes to her husbands

K 3

brutaliy;

brutality; a woman who, adorned by very polite accomplifhment, and calculated by nature
to charm, would be an everlafting fund of happinefs to the man who had fenfe to efteem her
worth.

Colonel S. was the hufband of this lady;
and he of all men leaft knew, and leaft deferved
female merit in a companion; infenfible alike
to love and honour, he regarded a wife only
for what fhe brought him; if her purfe was but
to his mind, he cared not for her perfon. This
extraordinary Colonel having publifhed a moft
fcurrilous pamphlet concerning me, I fhall give
the public fome opportunity of judging between
us: not that I fhould notice any of his libels
fo far as I am alone concerned; but as his wife,
and even her relations, or thofe whom he thought
proper to call fo, came in for fo large a fhare
of mifreprefentation and abufe, that the fale of
his work was ftopped for fear of a profecution;
I feel myfelf called upon to refute his calumnies. However, we are not the only objects of
his fcurrility, as fome time before, without
knowing how to write, he publifhed a pamphlet in which he abufes almoft every man
whofe name he knows, and has even the impudence to level, particularly the low flander of
his malignant pen, at that illuftrious character

the

the Earl of Elgin ; fortunately for the author, the blackguard ſtupidity of the performance took away its ſting.

His origin is not worth tracing, but he firſt *ranked* as a Colonel in 1786, among the revolters in Brabant ; whence after their defeat he fled to Paris. He there became acquainted with his wife, who uſed to viſit a family of reſpectability, with whom he was in ſome degree of intimacy. The lady was not then quite ſeventeen, and through his perfuaſions, was induced to conſent to a private marriage. This ſtep, as might be expected, much offended her father, who refuſed to give any fortune to the Colonel, but, conſented to allow her a yearly income for her own uſe ; which the Colonel however turning to his purpoſes, ſhe became obliged to ſend her little bills for millinary and ſuch like to the old gentleman. Finding how the money he allowed was employed, he withdrew that fund, but continued to pay her bills.

This *gallant Colonel* next applied himſelf to the Princes of France, who were juſt then gone to Coblentz, ſoliciting leave to raiſe a regiment for them. As he knew the effects of beauty on men of profeſſed gallantry, he conſtantly made his wife the bearer of his meſſages ; thus at once expoſing her to every temptation, and plainly

K 4 proving

proving to the world that he did not think her virtue a price by any means, too high for his own promotion. Still however her fame remained unfpotted; nor was it till fhe was moft cruelly treated by him, till blows were added to infults of every other kind, and till fhe was left unprotected in a garrifon town, amidft feveral hundred officers, each of whom was ftriving to fhew himfelf as far as poffible the contraft of her hufband, that fhe fell.

That fhe fell into my hands, was more owing to the gentlenefs of her own heart than my defert. True it is that I left nothing undone that I could devife; but though fhe feemed to view my fituation with pity, for I was then fick and diftreffed, and fhe had feen me in highly honourable circumftances, and the favourite of the great, it was long before a tender paffion took place.

After fome time I went to Augfburg in Suabia, and in my road thither, paffed through Ratifbon. Here, among others, I became acquainted with the Baron D'Ompteda, Hanoverian Envoy to the diet; I likewife had the pleafure of finding the Count de Goertz, who had, as I before mentioned, given me a letter of recommendation, while Pruffian minifter in Ruffia, to his brother at Potfdam, who was Aid-de-

camp

camp to Frederic the Great, when I vifited that celebrated garrifon in the end of the year 17&4.

The feverity of my indifpofition had delayed me many weeks upon the road, and my expences had already far exceeded my calculation; the trifling fum too, which was yet due to me fiom the army, was by my own appointment to be remitted to me, at the place of my deftination: I therefore at leaving *Ratifbon*, borrowed 32 louis of the Baron D'Ompteda, for which I gave him my bill.

I continued my journey, and reached *Augfburg* without any material occurrence; but I had not been many days there, before I met with an adventure difagreeable enough for the time. As foon as I was fixed at my hotel, I communicated to the Right Honourable H. Dundas a plan which I had formed, and which though a very bold one had been honoured with the approbation of feveral diftinguifhed military characters. For its execution I had found near three hundred volunteers; the majority of them had been officers under Louis XVI. and all afked no other reward than the fanction of the Britifh government, and to proceed to the attack under my direction. I was now fo far recovered, that I felt myfelf ready to bleed again; and I once more ventured to cherifh hopes, that I might be fuffered to profit by my exertions without further

ther

ther moleftation, or perfecution; promptnefs, courage, and my fword were my only fortune, nor could I fo thriftily employ it as in the har-veft of danger.

I flattered myfelf with vain expectations, for at that moment, a new perfecution was levelled at me, from a quarter whence I leaft expected fo bafe an attack.

It was I believe on the firft of December 1793, I was fitting on a fopha, in the room I occupied, in my hotel, in the very act of fealing a fecond letter to Mr. Dundas, renewing my folicitations to be employed in the enterprife I had already defcribed to him. Mrs. S. was fitting by me, little fufpecting that any evil awaited us—when in a moment, two different folding doors, which opened into my room, at oppofite angles, were violently burft open, and I was inftantaneoufly encircled, by a detachment of infantry, to the number of thirty-fix. They were commanded by a Lieutenant, who told me I was his prifoner; I afked him on what account, but this he refufed to tell me, or by what authority he came to arreft me; I therefore refufed to obey, and affumed a pofition of refiftance, till I fhould be fatisfied by what right he prefumed to act in fuch a manner. The acting Burgomafter was at hand, and immediately entering the room, affured me that the magiftrates

were

were themselves ignorant of the *cause*, but that my arrest was in consequence of a request, made by Baron D'Ompteda, the *Hanoverian Envoy*, at *Ratisbon*, in the *name of his Britannic Majesty*.

His letter having been read to me, I surrendered immediately, as I knew that the city of Augsburg, at the request of any Sovereign Prince of the Empire, is bound by law to arrest any person and detain him for a reasonable time, to see if any charge is brought forward against him. Nevertheless I could by no means comprehend for what cause his Britannic Majesty had desired my arrest, and I was equally at a loss to know how the Hanoverian Envoy, could act in the name of the Court of Great Britain, when there was a British Envoy then actually resident at Ratisbon. Besides, my conscience told me that I had never by any act whatever done, or meant to do, the smallest harm to the person or interests of my Sovereign, towards whom I had ever borne the most unshaken affection and loyalty.

With these reflections I consoled myself; at the same time that I endeavoured to assuage the alarm of the unfortunate lady, who had accompanied me; I assured her that there *must* be some mistake in the business, that a few days *must* clear the whole up, and then I should be set at liberty.

That

That night I remained at the hotel, under a guard of thirty-six men; but as such a croud occasioned much confusion and trouble in the house, and I was unwilling to put the master to such inconvenience, I was next morning, at my own request, removed to the town-house. Two very comfortable apartments were prepared for me; an officer attended me, and there were constantly four soldiers in the anti-chamber; I was likewise refused the use of pen and ink, and my papers were all seized; but Mrs. S. was permitted to come to me every morning, and remain till evening, but always in the presence of the officer.

The moment of my arrest, an express had been sent off to Ratisbon, to Baron D'Ompteda, and we waited with some impatience the charges he was to exhibit against me. In a few days the Baron arrived, and came to the very hotel where I had lodged, and where Mrs. S. still continued to reside; he found fault in a very high tone, at the permission she had to visit me, mysteriously pretending that my crimes were of great magnitude, but still without condefcending to particularize *even one*.

Augfburg being a free imperial city, governed by its own fenate, in whom the fovereignty refides, he was obliged to give fome fort of account of the authority under which he demanded me

to

to be arrested and detained in *close-custody.* He now dared, in the name of his Britannic Majesty, to require that all my papers should be delivered to him and his advocate, whom, (the more to shew that he acted in an official capacity,) he styled his *charge d'affairs,* for their inspection.

The consequence of his making this demand in such a high official style, and in the name of the King, was my arrestation, a translation of the decree, for which purpose, I here annex, the original in German being deposited with the publisher.

TRANSLATION.

EXTRACT.

PROTOCOLLI CONSULARIS.

(Done at Augsburgh 11th December 1793.)

" His Excellency Baron D'Ompteda, *minister of the king of Great Britain and Elector of Brunswick Luneburg,* at the diet of Ratisbone, after having examined the papers of Mr. Lisle, declares, in the quality of requirer, in the name of *his British Majesty,* for the imprisonment of Mr. Lisle, calling himself a Dutch Major, as a Scotch sub- ject; and being under the necessity of going

from

from hence, in the courfe of to-morrow, he appoints Mr. Kephalides, I. U. D. prefent at the perufing of the aforefaid papers, for his *chargé d'affaire* in the whole caufe."

My confinement was therefore continued in a ftill clofer manner. Mrs. S. was denied the liberty of feeing me, and even my two fervants were from the firft, as clofely confined as myfelf. A croud of circumftances now preffed upon my mind, and a kind of elucidation of my myfterious imprifonment, feemed to glimmer before me. I recollected that Baron D' Ompteda, had always attempted to be *particular* with Mrs. S. and he might probably think that my confinement, and his threats would ftarve and intimidate her into compliance. In my own conduct I could find nothing of which his Britannic Majefty had any reafon to complain. I therefore applied to the magiftrates for leave to write to the Britifh Government, which being granted, I fent the following letter to Mr. Dundas, to whom I had indeed before found means of privately writing a few lines.

" *To the Right Honourable* HENRY DUNDAS.

" SIR,
" AUGSBURG, Jan. 7, 1794.
" I HAVE already had the honor to acquaint you, with the very fingular manner in
which

which I have been arrested and confined *au fecret* by the Baron D'Ompteda, in the name of the King, without, however the Baron having shewn any order for such conduct; that arreft ftill continues, to-morrow it is five weeks since it commenced.

" As a Britifh fubject, Sir, permit me to request that you will be pleafed to fay, whether the Britifh Government has any demands on my perfon? And whether the Baron D'Ompteda has been charged to arreft me in the name of his Majesty? And if fuch an order has been given, at what time it was forwarded to the Baron? This is a juftice which a Britifh Minifter will not deny, and which will enable me to expofe and punifh a man, who I am convinced fearches my deftruction, in hopes by that means to re- move a barrier, which lays between him and the poffeffion of a woman, by whofe charms he is captivated.

" The unrelenting fury with which he perfe- cutes me, and the act of oppreffion with which he difgraces himfelf, and the diplomatique body, by committing, prove that he is actuated by fome motive which touches him nearly, and that mo- tive muft be what I fufpect.

" You well know, Sir, that in fpite of the dif- advantages which I labour under, no man has been more indefatigable than I have been to re-

cover

cover myfelf; I have continually folicited the moft defperate expeditions from yourfelf. And the general officers under whom I have ferved will vouch that while at the army, I was ever clofe to the points of the enemy's bayonets. As a proof of my good conduct, Sir, at a moment when I was without protection, and furrounded by malignant enemies, the firft Captains under heaven gave me their confidence, and the Prince of Orange, as a reward for my alacrity gave me a Majority in the army of the ftate.

" I rely on your juftice as a minifter, your humanity. I have already experienced: and have the honor to be, with all that refpect, to which your perfonal merit, and high fituation intitle you,

" Sir,

" Your moft humble

" And very devoted fervant,

(Signed)   " I. G. Lisle,

Major."

" Pleafe, Sir, to obferve that I complain not of the magiftrates of this place, far from it; they are perfectly difpofed to humanity and juftice, they only comply with the requeft made in the name of the King: was fuch a requeft made with authority, I myfelf would bow with fubmiffion."

I was

I was extremely well treated during my confinement, an excellent table being kept for me ; and my servants were boarded at a considerable expence in the town house. A table was likewise kept for Mrs. S. at our hotel in the same style as we had lived there, of which I need hardly say, that it was not inelegant. In the mean time she had addressed a letter to Mr. Walpole, his Britannic Majesty's minister at Munich, in which she had stated the case so far as came to her knowledge.

I had remained in prison about six weeks from the time I had wrote to Mr. Dundas, anxiously expecting some determination from the court of Great Britain, when Mr. Walpole wrote to me, and transmitted the following extract of a letter from Lord Grenville : " The " British government has not demanded the " arrestation of Major Lisle, nor has his Bri- " tish Majesty any cause of complaint against " him."

Baron D'Ompteda had given orders that all letters addressed to me should be stopped at the post-office ; but this being directed to me at the town-house, went to the magistrates, who opened and sent it to me in that state. I at first refused to receive it, and asked them if they did not know that it came officially from a British minister. They replied, that they did; but that D'Ompteda, in the character of his Majesty's Envoy, had taken all consequences upon himself; and thus was I forced for the time, to submit to the insults of a man, who, intrenched deep in his diplomatic situation, evaded the effects of law, which justly awaited the audacious imposition he had practiced on the Senate of *Augsburg*, by profaning the name of his royal master.

The consequence of Lord Grenville's declaration was, that I was immediately discharged from prison, and the Senate pronounced the following decree:

(TRANSLATION.)

(Decree of the Senate of Augsburg.)

TUESDAY, the 11th of *March*, 1794.

" HIS Excellency Baron D'Ompteda, Minister Plenipotentiary of the *Elector of Brunswick Lune-burg*, at the diet of Ratisbon, having requested the arresting of Major Lisle, pretending he was an impostor, and having taken on himself every consequence of this imprisonment, and making himself answerable for it, his request was granted. But as his Excellency has not justified this imprisonment, either by the

charges

charges of which he accufed the Major, and which were partly of no confequence, partly not verified, or having fhewn any authority from the Britifh Court, (which, as he declared, was interefted in thefe charges) for making the requeft of arrefting him in its name, or having juftified it on account of the reclamation of 32 Louis, lent to the Major, this imprifonment of which the expences fall on his Excellency is finifhed, and the Major enlarged on conditions of engaging himfelf on *parole d'honneur*, not to leave this town or its territory without having paid the 32 Louis. With regard to further fatisfaction, the Major, according to his own declaration, muft addrefs himfelf to the King, his mafter.

" Alfo, that the paper exhibited the 20th of January, *cum adjunctis*, fhall be communicated *in copia* to Dr. Kaphalides, his Excellency's *Attorney*."

I muft here intreat the reader to obferve the different ftyle in which the Baron is defcribed in this, and in the decree of arreftation, in which he is called, " *Minifter of the King of Great Bri-* " *tain and Elector of Brunfwic Luneburg*," as he

had

had announced himself: But now the veil of imposition was removed, and they ftyle him what he
really was, " *Minifter Plenipotentiary of the Eleftor*
" *of Brunfwick Luneburg;*" and to the perfon
whom he appointed *charge d'affairs*, they give
the title only of *Attorney*. The charges he brought
againft me are feverely, but juftly characterized,
and his pretended authority declared not to
exift.   But the difgrace of the tranfaction did
not perhaps wound the Baron fo deep as the
expences; for as he had taken every confequence
upon himfelf, he was ordered to pay all that had
been incurred by my arreft, amounting to a
fum far exceeding my ideas, and far too heavy
for his purfe to bear without much inconvenience.   I pofitively refufed to fubmit to that
part of the decree, which required me to give
my word not to leave the territories of Augfburg, till I had paid the Baron his 32 Louis-
d'ors; for as I could obtain no fatisfaction for
my imprifonment without the tedious, and perhaps fruitlefs mode of applying to court, I was
refolved to detain the only trifling indemnity I
could hope for.

I was much indebted on this difagreeable occafion to Mr. Walpole, who fhewed me many
effential marks of friendfhip.   I cannot attribute thefe to any perfonal attachment, as I had
only feen him in my way to Augfburg, as I
paffed

paſſed Munich; but the groſs inſult offered to him in his official capacity, by a man who dared to his face uſurp his privileges for the worſt of purpoſes, to ſerve which he likewiſe audacioufly proſtituted the name of his Sovereign, might induce him to enquire into the affair; an enquiry would convince him of the injury I was ſuſtaining by ſuch cloſe and unwarrantable confinement, and this probably made him conſider me as entitled to his protection.

CHAP. XIV.

More accounts of the nature of the author's confinement.—Finds means to convey a letter to the Duke Frederick of Brunſwick.—Receives a letter from that great General in the moſt flattering terms.—Receives indulgences from the magiſtrates.—Writes a letter to Baron D'Ompteda.—Copy of it.—The Baron rather chuſes to ſit down diſgraced, than to give the ſatisfaction required.—Goes to Manheim. —A droll manœuvre there.—Receives a bayonet wound.—Proceeds to Cologne and Aix-la-Chapelle, where he finds Colonel S. has been bullying in his abſence.—Goes to Holland, hears the ſame acaccounts, but cannot find the Colonel.—Arrives in

England,

*England, where the Colonel has been more loud,
seeks him by every stratagem and in every place,
but in vain.*

I MUST now return again to what passed during my confinement; I had one servant assigned me by the Senate to attend on me, and to him I was obliged to speak in the language which the officer who was with me understood. My diet and lodging was perfectly good, and even elegant. Notwithstanding all this strictness, I however found the means of conveying a letter to the Duke Frederic of Brunswick, praying of that justly renowned General to give me a certificate of service. This letter was forwarded through the means of a Prussian officer who was there recruiting for the Duke's own regiment.

The brave Duke Frederic, with that soldier-like promptness which distinguishes every action of his life, immediately sent me a most flattering certificate, which I likewise contrived to receive privately. As soon as I had read it, I sent it to the Senate, who were astonished how I could manage such a business; but though they were very desirous of knowing *how* it was done, I gave them no satisfaction on that subject.

About a week before the arrival of Lord Grenville's letter, the burgomasters plainly perceiv-

ing

ing that D'Ompteda could not bring forward even the shadow of a charge against me, and suspecting from various circumstances that he acted in the name of his Britannic Majesty without authority, gave me the liberty of walking about the town with a single guard, more by way of form than security. The first use I made of this privilege, was to write to the Baron in a manner to try whether he could shelter his want of courage, as well as his want of honour behind his diplomatic character.

That letter having had no effect, I sent him another in French which I made public, and of which the following is an exact translation*.

" *To his Excellency* BARON D'OMPTEDA.

" *Hanoverian Envoy,*

" *Ratisbon.*

" Give me leave, Sir, to demand an explanation of your conduct towards me.

" 1st. By what title or by what right have you had the temerity to order me to be arrested? was it as Minister to his Britannic Majesty? But were you, Sir, invested with that character? You who are only received at the Diet of *Ratisbon* as

* For the original, see the Appendix.

L 4 Minister

Minifter of the Elector of Brunfwick Luneburg, and in whom the Senate of Augfburg has only acknowledged that title in its decree of the 11th of March 1794, which is here fubjoined.

" You have then done wrong to affume the quality of Minifter of his Britannic Majefty, as in the act done at Augfburg the 11th of December 1793, of which I fend you a faithful extract. It is not then by this title that you can have any authority over me.

" Was it as being authorized by his Britannic Majefty? But how could you have the impudence to make the affertion? When you know that the real Minifter of the Court of Great Britain, at Ratifbon, has declared that his Court has not demanded my arreftation, and that the King has no fubject of complaint againft me.

" 2dly. Suppofing you to have been invefted with all the titles which you have had the prefumption to arrogate to yourfelf, did my conduct merit fuch hard treatment on your part? The flattering teftimonials and honourable employment which have been beftowed on me by the Princes, under whofe ftandards I have ferved, fufficiently vindicate my actions.

" I will not here fpeak of my campaigns in the fervice of Ruffia, nor of thofe I made in America, in the army of his Britannic Majefty, my Sovereign; but I fpeak of the manner in which I

difplayed

difplayed myfelf in 1793, when fighting under the commands of his Serene Highnefs the Duke of Brunfwick Oels, and afterwards thofe of his Serene Highnefs the Prince of Orange. The honourable rank which this Auguft Prince granted me in the armies of their High Mighti-neffes, proves the confidence he repofed in me; and if I have been deficient in my duty, it is for him, not for you to complain of it.

" After having made me undergo the moft unjuft vexations, by condemning me for three months to the horrors of a prifon, where I, as well as my fervants were detained in the clofeft cuftody; and after I have ftaid another month in this city in order to give you time to prove the accufations you brought againft me, of which you were unable to verify even one ; there remains for you now, Sir, only to give me an explanation of thefe iniquitous proceedings ; you know the kind of reparation I demand; you wifhed to difgrace me before the face of Europe, and it is before the face of Europe that I de-mand the fatisfaction due to me.

" I wait your anfwer,

" And am, &c. &c. &c.

(Signed)   " J. G. LISLE,

March 1794.   " *Major*."

Previous to thefe tranfactions I had prevailed on Mrs. S. to leave Augfburg; for as there feemed to me no end to the Baron's fh ffling and chicane, I who was no way verfed in fuch practices, was determined to give him an invitation, to finifh the affair a little more in my own way: I was therefore anxious to remove her from a probable fcene of diftrefs. The letters I fent him certainly contained hints plain enough to be taken; as he, however, feemed very dull of apprehenfion, I determined to fpeak ftill plainer; but as I found him equally infenfible to the calls of honour, or the ftings of infult, and that he fhrunk behind his *diplomacy*, I left him, fully fatisfied, that his courage, his honefty, his veracity and his modefty were all upon a par.

As it was evidently in vain to feek any fatisfaction from fuch a character, beyond what I had already received, through the decree of the Senate of Augfburg, I determined to give up the purfuit ; I therefore fet out for the Low Countries, leaving the Baron, fufficiently incumbered by the expences his folly had incurred, an object of fcorn and ridicule to all who knew the ftory.

At *Manheim*, I found it neceffary to ftop a few days; during which, as I was not travelling with my ufual fplendor, I remained *incog.* On my arrival in that town, I was very much furprifed

prifed to find a guard placed upon me ; I naturally enquired what was the reafon of fuch treatment, and was told that it was in confequence of
the conduct of the Dutch and Britifh recruiting
officers. Thefe gentlemen ufed, it feems, to
hold out fuch encouragement to recruits, as the
Bavarian troops could not withftand, but ufed
frequently to defert to enlift with them ; a general order had therefore been given to place a
guard on every officer of either country that
might arrive there.

I immediately fent a meffage to the Fort
Major, to inform him, that if he had looked at
the report I made at the gate of the town on
my entering, he would have feen that I could
be by no means looked upon as a recruiter ; I
concluded with faying, that fuch being the cafe,
I expected my guard to be inftantly removed.
As he did not think proper to fend me any immediate anfwer, I determined at once to be re-
venged on him, and to remove this obnoxious
attendant; entering therefore into converfation
with my centinel, I prevailed upon him to defert, to which indeed he made very little objection, except the difficulty of getting away. This
was eafily obviated, by putting him into my
own chaife, in which I fent him to the adjacent
town of *Worms*, where an officer of my acquaintance lay, recruiting for the regiment of Salm

then

then in the pay of Britain. This was a dangerous bufinefs, but the pleafure of outwitting the
wife heads of the place was irrefiftible; nor indeed did any confiderations of danger ever prevent a plan I had formed.

In the evening, a non-commiffioned officer
arrived, with an apology for not attending
earlier to my meffage, which was owing to the
abfence of the Commandant of the place. He
next enquired for the centinel, who was not to
be found, and as I could give no account of
him, it was immediately concluded that he had
deferted through my perfuafions and affiftance;
but as the fecret lay between him and me, it was
in vain to make enquiries.

I left *Manheim* and paffed through *Worms*,
where I faw my deferter who had already put on
the Britifh uniform; but my chief reafon for
going that way was to folicit the protection of
that highly diftinguifhed General Field Marfhal
Mollendorff, who was in that neighbourhood.
Juft then fome affairs of pofts took place, not
far from where I was; curiofity induced me to
become a near fpectator, in confequence of
which I received a wound with a bayonet in my
breaft, which detained me fome time at the
houfe of a friend near *Bingen*.

When I was fo far recovered as to be able
again to travel, I proceeded to *Cologne*, and
thence to *Aix-la-Chapélle*.

At

At *Aix-la-Chapélle*, I learnt that Colonel S. the hufband of the lady who was with me at Augfburg, had been vowing the direft vengeance againft me; as foon as I knew this, I begun a very ftrict fearch after this furious antagonift, but to no purpofe; the Colonel had *prudence* in his anger, and very ftudioufly avoided my prefence.

I then paffed into Holland, where I again heard of this redoubtable champion, who had been loud in his threats of revenge; but here as at *Aix-la-Chapélle*, I could only find the *echo*, for the man was invifible. I had not been many days in England before I heard of the fame threats of vengeance; thus aggravated by repeated provocations, I determined to find him if poffible, and with this view fought him in every place where he was likely to be found; I even went to Meffrs. Learmonth's and Beazley's, in Parliament-ftreet, where he almoft took up his refidence, and after much converfation with thefe gentlemen, left an open letter for him, but this was infufficient to bring him forward.

The world will hereafter hear of this extraordinary Colonel no more from me; and if he chufes to attack me again with his pen, I fhall refer them *for his veracity* to *Monfieur de Calonne*, and the records of the Court of King's Bench.

CHAP.

CHAP. XV.

The author's reasons for returning to England.—He waits on the Ministers with some proposals which are rejected.—Becomes involved in another misfortune.—Is about to proceed to the Continent, and put back by a storm.—Apprehended and taken to Bow-street.—Repeated examinations there.—Ridiculous charges made against him.—Would have been discharged but for Mr. Flood.—Is tried and convicted, but retains many valuable friends. —Mr. Burke's friendly interference; copies of letters from him.—Mr. Boswell, with one of his letters.—Remarks of the author's friends.

THE ill usage I had received on the lower Rhine, by the repetition of things, which my conduct, during the time I had been with the army, ought to have cancelled, had driven me away; in fact, had I been contented to act simply in the routine of duty, I might have remained unnoticed; but as I had nothing to depend on but my sword, and the friends it might gain me, I had only to do bold and daring things, or to remain in want and obscurity. I had therefore on every occasion courted danger

and

and exertion; and I had gained the good opinion of the moſt diſtinguiſhed Generals, by
whoſe friendſhip (which I had determined that
my conduct if poſſible ſhould cement,) I ſeemed rapidly mounting to honour and independance.   Then it was that men whom indolence,
or ſomething worſe, prevented from following
my example, begun to envy my ſuccefs, and
they determined by the baſeſt arts to ruin the
man they could not imitate.

As the Pruſſians had retired from the field,
my hopes from that quarter were at an end; but
as I had received a liberal offer from a Sovereign Prince of Germany, to raiſe men on very
moderate terms for the Britiſh ſervice, I found
it neceſſary to repair to England to endeavour
to conclude the buſineſs. I laid my propoſals
before the proper officer, but they were not accepted, notwithſtanding I had full * powers
(which are ſtill in my poſſeſſion,) to contract
for raiſing a regiment of 1800 men, and my
zeal in a buſineſs, which offered me ſo many advantages, could hardly be doubted.

I now come to that part of my hiſtory,
which has been ſufficiently made the ſubject of
public diſcuſſion, and for which I now am ſuf-
fering, how meritoriouſly let others ſay.   I

* Thoſe papers are in the hands of the publiſher.

had

had bought of a linen-draper, near Welbeck-street, a quantity of cambric and other articles for which I paid him ready money; on the goods being fent home, there appeared to be not quite enough for the purpofe they were intended for, and I fome time after went to the fhop to compleat the deficiency. I had before mentioned to the fhop-keeper, that I was about to return to the army, and fhould want fome linen. I again mentioned this circumftance to him, and he fhewed me a fhirt, which he thought would anfwer my purpofe, but of which fort he had but a very few made. I propofed calling another day, when I fhould return to town with a perfon who was a better judge than myfelf of the value of fuch articles; but like all other tradefmen, anxious to fell, he requefted that I fhould take it with me, and abfolutely put it into my fervant's hand to carry home. If it did not meet with approbation I was to return it the firft opportunity, but if it was liked I was to order the quantity for which I fhould have occafion.

I was taken ill very fhortly after this event, and not being able, on account of various difappointments, to pay the money for a couple dozen fuch fhirts, I did not return; but continually in the hope that I fhould receive cafh, which I had reafon to expect, I delayed from

day

day to day; but my difficulties encreafed, and amidft a multitude of troubles, the fhirt was totally forgotten, and I was again going to join the army on the Upper Rhine, once more to try my fortune. I had embarked on board the Rheinhaufen, of Hamburgh, in December 1794; but the fhip in a tempeft having been drove on fhore at Sheernefs, and having received much damage, I came to town till fhe was repaired.

On my return to London, the fon of an old acquaintance, who lent me fome money, thought proper to have me apprehended; his charge againft me was however laughed at; but no fooner was the matter known, than perfons who had never feen me, came to fwear to frauds committed upon them by me. Among the number, a hatter and hofier, in Oxford-Street, fwore pofitively to my having cheated him of a bundle of filk ftockings and two hats. I was thunder-ftruck to hear fuch an accufation, as I had never feen the man before, and ftill more when he fwore to the 14th of June. On Mr. Bond afking him whether any other perfon could fwear to me, he produced his fhopman and an apprentice boy, both of whom fwore pofitively that I was the perfon who had defrauded their mafter. When I heard the time affigned for the tranfaction, I was perfectly eafy as to the event, being confident that I could readily

prove

prove my having been upon the Rhine at that time, and for some months after. Mr. Bond, who I believe was well acquainted with this circumstance, neverthelefs ordered the people of the houfe where it was faid I had lodged, and where the goods had been fent, to attend; they did fo, together with a hair-dreffer; and all of them declared that I did not in any refpect re-femble the *gentleman* who had done the bufinefs. The hatter retired with difgrace. As I was pretty warm with him, a fellow who had come for the purpofe of exhibiting a charge againft me, very boldly exclaimed, " Don't be fo impudent, Sir, " you know you robbed me the fame day!" but no fooner did it appear, that it was impoffible I could have robbed either of them, than he alfo, hiding his head, fneaked off.

Such tranfactions ought to make magiftrates very cautious how they receive informations from perfons pretending to be injured; the pof-fibility of miftakes is very great, and too many from an obftinate and foolifh pride, will fooner deprive their fellow-creature of life than acknow-ledge an error. I fay nothing of the vindictive, and cruel, nor of thofe whofe trade is blood, and who for a little money, are but too ready to fwear what (though it may be very true,) they do not know to be fo; I fpeak of the good, and them I wifh to remember, that a momentary view can

give

give but a very imperfect idea of a face, hardly indeed so much but that a change of drefs will efface it. In my own cafe, I am convinced that nothing lefs than my being able to prove myfelf on the Continent, faved me from being convicted by the hatter; for fuch was the power of prejudice againft me, and fo pofitively, and fo repeatedly did he fwear, that a jury muft have been compofed of no ordinary men to have refifted.

. A thoufand ridiculous charges of fwindling tranfactions were now brought forward; among the moft laughable were the following:

Mr. *Strongitharm*, of *Pall-mall*, feal engraver, being very fhort, had got himfelf perched over the heads of the reft of the affembly, like a creft over a coat of arms, and complained that I had defrauded him. Mr. Bond requefted to know in what manner; he faid I had ordered him to engrave a feal, after a drawing which I had given him, but had never called for it, adding that it was not quite finifhed; Mr. Bond advifed him to go home and finifh it, for that the Major would probably call for it.' A 'Mr. Warburton, a woolen-draper, in the Strand, likewife brought a charge againft me; this *heavy* accufation however appeared to be, by his own account, that I had afked him to give me credit, which he had refufed; but even that was more than

M 2

truth,

truth, for I folemnly fwear I never before faw the man, nor ever was in his houfe.

But the fummit of ridicule was climbed by Mr. Clay, of Birmingham, who bawled out aloud that I had cheated him. Mr. Bond immediately afked how I had done it. Mr. Clay faid he held a note of hand of mine, for, I think, ten pounds. Mr. Bond enquired where it was? At Birmingham was the reply. " What is its date?" " About ten years." A loud laugh immediately fhook the whole audience, and Mr. Clay was told that that office was not the place to recover debts; befides that the ftatute of limitations ftood as an infuperable barrier in his way. This was the more malicious on the part of Clay, owing to another laughable circumftance. About the time he fpoke to, I did really borrow the money of him, for which I gave him a note payable at the houfe of a very refpectable gentlemen, but whofe fingularity of name, gave rife to fufpicions in Mr. Clay's fapient brain. That night, or the night following, there appeared in the newfpapers, one of thofe paragraphs that are calculated to fet the world a ftaring, ftating that a fraud on the Bank to a very large amount had been committed, and giving a defcription of a perfon, which nearly agreed with my own. Clay read this, and forthwith went to confult with a juftice of

the

the peace in the neighbourhood, by whofe advice and affiftance I was taken into cuftody at
Shrewfbury, where they detained me till they
fent an exprefs to town. Sir Sampfon Wright,
who was then alive, on receipt of the letter of
thefe *wife men*, returned for anfwer, that "NO
"SUCH CRIME HAD BEEN COMMITTED, and that
"the beft thing they could do was to make the
"matter up with me." On account of the civilities I had received from every refpectable inhabitant of Shrewfbury, I was induced to drop
all ideas of profecuting Clay and the Juftice, and
contented myfelf with making them pay all expences there and my horfes back to town. I
further told Clay he might burn my bill, for I
fhould never pay it; nor did I hear of it from
that day, until he made as related his foolifh
harangue in Bow-ftreet.

Nothing of courfe could be made of fuch fri-
volous complaints, and the linen-draper, who it
feems belongs to that *moft creditable fociety*, infti-
tuted for the profecution of *fwindlers*, (a term
unknown in the law of England,) had applied
to the attorney of that body, who, on the feventh
or eighth time that I went up to the police
office, fent his clerk with a letter to the magiftrate. This letter was read and ftated, that
after the matureft deliberation, he could not
make any thing but a debt of the tranfaction,

M 3

and

and therefore he fhould not proceed further, nor would the linen-draper appear again at the office.

I now thought myfelf on the eve of liberty, when that *active magiftrate*, Mr. Flood, who had no concern at all in the bufinefs, being merely a fpectator, infifted that I fhould be fully committed; he maintained that if my former conviction was juft, (a point on which even yet lawyers are by no means unanimous,) then the prefent cafe muft be felony ; he further directed that the linen-draper fhould draw up his cafe, and lay it before Mr. Sylvefter, for his opinion ; in the mean while I was remanded for another hearing. The next day Mr. Bond fat at the office ; I was brought up, and Mr. Sylvefter's opinion upon the new ftatement, which the linen-draper had made out to lay before him, was, that the tranfaction was felonious, of courfe I was fully committed for trial.

My trial is yet recent in the memory of all the world ; how my obtaining the fhirt as rela-ted, and as it appeared in evidence, could be a theft, I leave to that world to judge ; but fo it was called, and the jury by their *fecond* verdict found me GUILTY.

As every one who knew my cafe, thought it (to fay no worfe of it) extremely hard, I with the more confidence applied to my friends, who

in

in their turn left nothing undone to ferve me. Among other diftinguifhed characters, the late celebrated Mr. Burke took amazing pains. to do away or mitigate my fentence. At firft indeed, before he knew my real conduct, he was not totally free from that univerfal prejudice which had taken place in the minds of almoft all the world; but his fentiments will be much better known from his own words, than from any defcription of mine. In fhort, Mr. Burke writing coolly and difpaffionately on any fubject, muft be read with pleafure by all mankind, and I therefore cannot conceal this letter, though not favourable to myfelf, from my readers.

(COPY.)

From the Right Honourable EDM. BURKE,
To I. E. DEVEREUX, Efq.
35, St. James's-Place, LONDON.

"OCTOBER the 19th, 1795.

" DEAR SIR,

" I do full juftice to the principles of humanity, which induce you to take
" an intereft in the fate of Mr. Semple. There are
" circumftances of compaffion in his hiftory, that
" would induce one to wifh that the feverity
" of the law was not to take place, with regard

M 4

" .to

" to that unfortunate gentleman. Had the judg-
" ment been capital, I should take a warm part
" for its mitigation.   But I have very different
" sentiments with regard to transportation.   A
" person without fortune or profession, and who
" has the misfortune, by the sentence of a court
" of justice, to lose his reputation, cannot pos-
" sibly live but by a repetition of the same, or
" similar practices to those, which have first
" brought him into his difficulties. I venture to
" say that it is nothing at all short of a moral im-
" possibility he should. Now, I submit it to your
" very good sense, whether, in such a case, the
" very worst sort of punishment, and that which
" admits no hope on this side of the grave, does
" not become an event very much to be appre-
" hended; and whether you or I would like
" hereafter, to consider ourselves by an ill under-
" stood lenity, to be the means of his losing his
" life with aggravated disgrace to himself and
" to his family? For my own part I look upon
" transportation, to be, without question, an
" unpleasant remedy; but still a remedy in a des-
" perate disease. He goes to a place where he is
" not oppressed by the judgment he has suffered;
" and where none but honest ways of life are
" open to him. The climate is good, the soil is
" not unfavourable. There is even some choice
" in the society. God knows that they who have

" suffered,

" fuffered, and even defervedly fuftered, by the
" fentence of the law, are very far from the
" worft or moft difagreeable men in the world.
" I affure you that if I were to fall into a mis-
" fortune of this fort, and to have youth and
" vigour of body and mind; I fhould think
" this change of place to be a thing to be de-
" fired, not fhunned. If I were a friend of Mr.
" Semple, I would of courfe advife him, after
" humbling himfelf before God, to look refo-
" lutely on all, in this kind, that man can do to
" him. He is a military man. Let him encoun-
" ter his ill-fortune bravely, and refolve to ob-
" tain by his fortitude and future integrity, the
" efteem of all thinking and worthy minds. He
" has no lofs at all in lofing a country where
" he has loft his place in fociety; and as to
" tranfportation to any other country in Europe
" or America, the Englifh newfpapers, among
" the infinite evils they produce, fpread fuch
" things as thofe that relate to him into every
" quarter, and never fuffer a man to recover
" his reputation. If I cannot give my affift-
" ance to this poor gentleman's releafe, it is
" upon motives of good will to him to the beft
" of my weak judgment; but if his powerful
" relations, or others who are his friends, and
" difpofed to compaffion towards him, will con-
" tribute to the alleviation of his circumftan-

" ces,

" ces, you fhall command my mite in the con-
" tribution ; and I fhall ufe my beft intereft with
" Mr. King, that Mr. Semple may be recom-
" mended to the Governor of the Colony, for
" every fort of attention to his perfon and his
" eftablifhment. I wait your commands.

" And am, &c."

After the receipt of this, I laid my creden-
tials of fervice before this great and good man,
and thefe foon infpired him with far other fentiments. . He now no longer confidered me as
the defperate depredator, but as (if I know myfelf, I really am) a man mifguided by violent
paffions, who had done wrong, but who never
laid any premeditated fchemes to deceive.

Impreffed with thefe fentiments, he wrote a
very warm letter to John King, Efq. one of his
Majefty's Under Secretaries of State ; which he
had the politenefs to fend to me under a flying
feal to perufe, and to forward. I now lay it
before my readers ; and if the former exhibits
all the placed benevolence, this latter glows
with all the fire of Burke.

(COPY.)

(COPY.)

From the Right Honourable EDMUND BURKE,
To JOHN KING, *Esq. Under Secretary of State.*

" MY DEAR KING,

" I SEND you a letter I received juſt
" now, which is written to a very much reſpect-
" ed friend of mine, by the unfortunate Major
" Semple ; it is attended with ſeveral documents
" tending to ſhew, what I believe is extremely
" true, that this unhappy gentleman ſo conduct-
" ed himſelf abroad as to obtain no ſmall degree
" of conſideration. You will be ſo good as to
" preſent thoſe papers with my moſt reſpectful
" and affectionate compliments to the Duke of
" Portland ; and you will, I am ſure, yourſelf
" warmly recommend them to his Grace's moſt
" ſerious conſideration, ſo as to obtain a reſpite
" of the ſentence 'till the next embarkation, and
" until the full extent and true nature of the of-
" fences are aſcertained, and compared with the
" rigour of the ſentence. If one great object
" of criminal juſtice, that is, the removal of the
" offender from the ſphere of his offences, his
" habits, and his temptations, is obtained, every
" rational as well as every humane perſon would
" wiſh him every means of becoming of uſe in
" ſome quarter of the globe, where, far from

" being

" being noxious, he might be ufefully and ho-
" nourably employed:

　" You are yourfelf a lawyer; you well remem-
" ber your friend, my late brother; you know
" that no man had a clearer head, or a more
" upright heart. He had, as Recorder of Briftol,
" a good deal of experience in the criminal law ;
" and I verily believe a better criminal judge
" never did exift.　I have often heard him ex-
" patiate with no fmall indignation againft the
" confufion which began to prevail in the cri-
" minal jurifprudence, by which the diftinctive
" lines of offences were effaced, or at leaft ren-
" dered mifchievoufly uncertain.　The confufion
" of fraud with felony (a new practice) he held
" to be highly pernicious ; and for one I look
" upon it with horror.　By this means men are
" entrapped by the law itfelf.　The law ought
" as religioufly to prevent one crime being pu-
" nifhed as another, as it ought to fave inno-
" cence from being punifhed at all.　The law
" itfelf getting into this crookednefs becomes
" the fwindler, and gets the blood of men under
" falfe pretences, much worfe is it than under
" falfe pretences obtaining their money.

　" On this head, I will fay no more juft now
" than this, that when the law (if it be law or
" can be law) is fo very vicious ; the mitigating
" power of the Crown, cannot be fo well em-
" ployed as in preventing its having its worft
" effects.

　　　　　　　　　　" I once

" I once more moft humbly and earneftly re-
" queft that this matter may be left open to the
" matureft confideration. I fhall be much obli-
" ged to you for your good offices on the oc-
" cafion; and am always, with moft fincere re-
" fpect and affection,

"My dear KING,

" Your moft faithful,

" And obedient humble Servant,

BEACONSFIELD,
October 26th 1795.　　　　" EDMUND BURKE."

" *You will be pleafed to return his papers to the un-*
" *fortunate Mr. Semple after you have made ufe*
" *of them ; there are eight pieces.*"

Among the number of thofe refpectable perfons, who applied in my behalf to thofe in
power, I cannot but mention James Bofwell, Efq.
the intimate friend of the great Dr. Johnfton.
He prefented a petition from me, and not receiving any anfwer, he called at the Secretary
of State's Office, where he left a letter, of which
he inclofed me a copy, in thefe words :

" *To* JOHN KING, *Efq. Under Secretary of State.*

" SIR,

" I LEFT at your houfe on Sun-
" day night a Petition from Major Semple
" Lifle,

" Lifle, to the Duke of Portland, which you
" had been fo good as to fay you would deliver;
" and I wrote on Monday to his Grace refpect-
" ing a fhort audience, as from my having feen
" the unhappy man's papers while he was laft
" upon the Continent.   I could enforce his ap-
" plication for the royal mercy, which he folicits,
" on condition of his tranfporting himfelf for
" ever, inftead of being. tranfported for feven
" years; by which commutation the public
" would be a gainer.

    " Having as yet heard nothing on the fubject
" from his Grace or yourfelf, Sir, may I beg to
" be favoured with a line, to inform me whether
" hopes of fuccefs may be entertained; and that
" you will be pleafed to contribute your humane
" influence.

" I am, Sir,

" Your moft obedient

" Humble fervant."

Secretary of State's Office,
FRIDAY, *April 10th* 1795.

    Thefe letters I have inferted, not becaufe
Mr. Burke and Mr. Bofwell were the only gentlemen of diftinction, who interefted themfelves
for me; but becaufe they are characters of fuch
celebrity and genius, that had my crimes been
                                        fuch

fuch as the world has been taught to believe, they muſt have feen them and defpifed me. Their friendſhip is my greateſt honour, next to that of the diſtinguiſhed Generals, under whom I ſerved on the Continent; and I am happy to ſay, that I have not yet found one enemy among thofe whofe friendſhip was worth the acceptance.

CHAP. XVI.

The author remains two years a prifoner in Newgate. —Begins to entertain hopes that he will not be fent away.—The ſheriff's attempt to fend him away in an abrupt manner.—His defpair and its confequences.—Reflections on this action, and the conduct of the ſheriffs.—Sent down to Portſmouth.— Receives the kindeſt treatment from Mr. Dyne, contractor for tranſports.—Embarks on board the Lady Shore.—Finds the ſhip in a ſtate of mutiny. —Different inſtances of the mutinous behaviour of the ſoldiers of the New S. Wales corps.—Puſillanimity of their officers.

I HAD remained a prifoner, in Newgate, on what is called the ſtate ſide, where I enjoyed an

apartment

apartment to myſelf, upwards of two years; during which time, many of the moſt diſtinguiſhed characters had, as I have already ſtated, done every thing they could to ſoften the rigour of my ſentence. Though I had received many aſſurances, that there was no intention of ſending me from that jail, ſtill, whenever I heard of the ſheriffs having obtained an order for the removal of priſoners to the hulks, I naturally felt myſelf uneaſy, and renewed my applications; the anſwers I received were of the ſame tenor, till my fears gradually ſubſided, and I concluded, that ſhould his Majeſty's miniſters in the end determine to ſend me abroad, they would at leaſt ſuffer me to remain where I was, until the ſhip in which it was meant I ſhould embark, ſhould be ready for ſea; and that after having been ſo long detained, ſome ſhort notice of my departure would be given me. . How much reaſon I had for my opinion, may be ſeen by the following extract of a note from Mr. Kirby, keeper of Newgate, a gentleman to whoſe humanity I have the higheſt obligations :

". MAJOR SEMPLE LISLE,"

" * * * * * * * Can you ſuppoſe
" any event hoſtile to your feelings ſhould take
" place, after what I have ſaid to you, and I not
" inform you? no, be aſſured you are ſecure—I
" need

" need say no more, you will rest satisfied till I
" see you.

J. K."

Early in the month of December, the sheriffs
had obtained an order, such as is ordinarily
given twice or thrice a year, for the removal of
convicts, in which it would appear, they were
determined to include me, though they kept
their intentions a secret. One evening as I was
sitting in my room, one of the turn-keys came
and told me that a gentleman who did not wish
to come in, desired to speak to me in the lodge.
As this had more than once been the case, I
went without delay, in my slippers, and without
a hat; but immediately found myself surrounded
by the officers of the place, who, shewing me a
coach then at the door, told me I was going
immediately into the *country*. I however found
the way back to my room; Mr. Kirby, junior,
and two of the turn-keys, who had ever behaved
to me with the greatest kindness, followed me.
I was now driven to distraction, but though enraged to the highest pitch of madness, I could
not raise my hand against those from whom I
had experienced nothing but friendship. I was
besides unarmed; but in my frenzy, I snatched
up a round pointed breakfast knife, with which
I made a blow at my breast; I struck too high,

N

and

and the knife would not enter; but I repeated the ſtroke lower down, and plunged it to the handle in my body. Thoſe about me were ſhocked and aſtoniſhed, and ſeemed incapable of thought or action, till Mr. Kirby drew the knife from my breaſt, and I deſired them to help me off with my coat, which being done, I calmly laid down.

I by no means intend to juſtify the violent act I committed, but I was driven to deſpair, by the unaccountable conduct of the ſheriffs. It ſeems they have the privilege of *ſelecting* the perſons, who are to compoſe the number ordered by the Secretary of State to be ſent off; and for reaſons which are yet unknown to me, they had reſolved not only to ſend me away, but to take me unwares in the ſingular manner I have already deſcribed. To take me unawares, was the only method in their power to diſtreſs me; and of this they determined to profit, well knowing that from my extenſive correſpondence with the moſt diſtinguiſhed perſons at home, and on the Continent, I muſt, if taken by ſurpriſe, leave many papers which I highly eſteemed at their mercy. I muſt beſides be unprovided with ſo much as a change of linen, till their *great humanity* might be pleaſed to order me ſome of my own little ſtock. But above all, they well knew that I muſt leave thoſe who are

dearer

dearer to me than life; and that to be thus torn from them, without even an Adieu! was the fevereft blow they could inflict.

The pretext, and it is a *mere pretext*, for thefe fudden removals, is, that the convicts are riotous and diforderly when about to be fent off; this is true in the crouded part of the prifon, where the poor wretches are, *without a moment's warning, awaked out of their fleep in the dead of night, and hurried off.* They then are apt to break the few trifling utenfils they have got, and to make much noife; but when they have had previous notice, I have feen them go away peaceably and quietly, without making any difturbance. But this did not even furnifh a reafon in my cafe, as I was neither in a crouded part of the prifon, nor had any communication whatever with thofe under fuch fentences as myfelf. Befides, the fheriffs ought to have confidered, that though I was all fubmiffion to the fentence of the law, I was not to be intimidated, and that it was poffible to drive even men of the mildeft temper to acts of madnefs by unneceffary feverity. Of this they would have been fatisfied, had they been prefent when their mandate was announced to me.

I fhould by no means have felt the leaft refentment againft the fheriffs, for having in my turn fent me away, but that turn had paffed for

twelve

twelve months and more; and it may be feen from Mr. Kirby's note, that I had no reafon to think that I fhould be hurried off without timely notice. I had even much higher authority, which I am not at liberty to give up, for believing that it was not the intent of government that I fhould go at all; indeed his Majefty's Minifters feemed inclined to take into confideration the blood I had fpilt for my country, and make fome allowance on that account. This their liberal conduct towards me, determined mine in the hour of danger, when the mutineers feized the fhip, and when my refiftance was firm, but rendered ineffectual by the *inaction* of the officers of the troops. Whether however circumftances might afterwards have induced them to fend me away, I cannot with abfolute certainty determine; but I am confident they would have fent me immediately to the fhip, and they would have given me fufficient notice, to make the neceffary preparations for fo long a voyage, and this was all I had defired! But the *benevolent fheriffs*, ————————————— ——————————— would have fuppofed themfelves degraded by a generous or humane act; and, I dare fay, would have thought it *rare fun* to fend a gentleman to the hulks.

I remained without any further interruption, till, I think, about the end of February, when,

after

after a notice given me of some days, I was re-moved to Portfmouth, after having received marks of the moft humane attention from fome of the firft perfons in the kingdom. On my arrival, I experienced the utmoft exertions of humanity from that moft worthy character, Mr. Dyne, the contractor for tranfports, to whofe care I was configned; that gentleman, far from wifhing to add to my fufferings, did every thing he could to alleviate them. Inftead of being fent on board a hulk, I was put on board, what is called, the hofpital fhip, where I had a cabin to myfelf, and every accommoda-tion I could wifh; and here I remained till the Lady Shore came round from the river.

When I went on board the Lady Shore, I found fome perfons, whom by their drefs, I fhould have fuppofed to be foldiers; but their diforderly and mutinous behaviour foon con-vinced me, that whatever they might be called, they were in fact moft daring mutineers. I had not indeed been many hours on board, when a fcene prefented itfelf, which ought to have warned any officer of his danger. Though the Britifh fleet laying clofe to us, was then in a ftate of open rebellion, the whole of the officers of the New South Wales corps went on fhore, and left the charge of the detachment, I think, 74 in number, to a Serjeant of the name of

 Hughes;

Hughes; in their abfence, Hughes thought proper to go on fhore too, and when the officers returned, was not come on board. When they came, which they did all together, the Commander enquired for him, and before an anfwer was well given, he appeared along fide in a boat. The commanding officer in perfon, ordered him on board, to which he replied, *he would not come till he had feen his goods out of the boat.* The officer repeated his commands, and Hughes replied in a language which I will not repeat; ftrange to tell, the officer calmly walked into his cabin, without taking the leaft notice of the infult.

The fame day, if I recollect well, Sir Jerome Fitzpatrick came on board, and to him 'I related the ftory, as I was even then convinced that the fhip muft fall a victim to mutiny; it was not however in Sir Jerome's province, who having introduced and recommended me to the officers, took leave.

The mutiny then raging on board his Majefty's fhips, by which we were furrounded, was, I fuppofe, the reafon why we were ordered to fail in an unufual hurry, and with the *Weft,* inftead of the *Eaft India* convoy. Of the mutinous ftate of the fhip, let the concurrence of Mr. Black, our purfer, bear teftimony with me; that gentleman, in a letter to his father,

dated

dated May 1ft, 1797, and which has fince been
publifhed, fays,

" I fincerely wifh (as do all the fhip's com-
" pany,) that we were now laying at Port-
" Jackfon, delivering our *precious cargo*, inftead
" of Torbay; for the foldiers are the moft dif-
" agreeable, mutinous fet of villains that ever
" entered into a fhip.—Two of the ferjeants
" behaved fo ill, that Captain Willcocks was
" obliged to infift upon their commanding offi-
" cer confining them in irons; for they have
" their own officers on board, and the Captain
" and officers of the fhip have no power over
" them. Major Semple is a quiet kind of a man,
" and I have no doubt will behave like a gen-
" tleman and give us no trouble.—He was fome
" days fince applied to by two of the villains,
" to know if he would head them in an attempt
" to feize the fhip after they fhould get well out
" to fea, and had left the convoy; one of them
" at the fame time telling him, this was the
" eighth time he had embarked for Botany Bay
" without reaching it; and he was determined he
" would not this time; and that he was fent on
" board by force from a Police Office. This
" was immediately reported to the officers of
" the fhip by Semple; in confequence of which
" the foldiers vow vengeance againft him,

N 4

" threatening

" threatening to throw him over board the' firſt
" opportunity."

In conſequence of theſe riotous proceedings, an order was given that none of the ſoldiers, but thoſe on duty, ſhould come on the quarter-deck. The day following, Hughes, the Serjeant, attempted to violate this order, which the ſentry would not permit, and told him the reaſon why he could not ; with which indeed the Serjeant muſt neceſſarily have been acquainted. He then requeſted to paſs the deck, to go down to the commanding officer's cabin, to have the order repealed; not being able to obtain this repeal, he came up again, threatening and ſhaking his hand in the firſt mate's face, who then, in the abſence of the Captain, commanded the ſhip. Continuing his inſolence, the mate went into his cabin and put on a dirk; when Hughes ſaw this, he went below, ſaying, that he had a longer ſword, and was coming again upon deck with it drawn, and had I not guarded the hatchway, he certainly meant to have attacked and murdered the Chief Mate. This as well as the former acts of mutiny paſſed unnoticed by the officers of the detachment.

CHAP.

CHAP. XVII.

Mutinous proceedings at Portfmouth.—The Chief Mate makes a complaint to General Pitt.—Sail for Torbay.—The mutineers difturb the Captain in muftering his men.—Captain Wilcocks complains to General Fox, who tranfmits his letter to the Duke of Portland.—Lieutenant Colonel Grofe, the Commander of the New South Wales corps, fent to infpeft them.—The fhips receive damage from a ftorm, and are obliged to go into harbour.—The Lady Shore fails after the Captain had addreffed the Minifter on the fituation of the troops, to which the author alfo added his teftimony.—The troops increafe in mutiny and difobedience.

THE fhort time we remained at Portfmouth was fufficient to demonftrate, that the officers entrufted with the charge of the New South Wales Corps, were inadequate to their duty. I intimated as much before we weighed anchor to feveral perfons of refpectability; and the Chief Mate of the fhip (who commanded in the place of Captain Wilcocks, then abfent,) complained to General Pitt, in confequence of the attack by Serjeant Hughes, which I mentioned

in

in the laft chapter. This complaint was rendered ineffectual, by our being ordered to fail in about 12 hours after it was lodged ; fo that the General had not time to punifh the mutineer, or enquire into the merits of the cafe.

We had not many hours left Portfmouth, till our convoy made a fignal for the fleet to difperfe, and to rendezvous at Torbay, according to our orders.   While we were fteering for that port, Captain Wilcocks fufpecting that the reafon of the fignal being made might be the approach of fome enemies fhips, and his men not having been appointed to their quarters, he ordered them to be muftered. He was in the act of telling them off, when a number of foldiers furrounded him, and drowned his voice by their noife ; he defired them to go forward, and not difturb him in the execution of his duty on the quarter-deck ; but they replied *that they would ftay where they were.* He then made application to Enfign Minchin, who prevailed upon the foldiers to defift, and fuffer the Captain to continue his bufinefs for the moment in peace ; no other punifhment however was inflicted, though we were foon in harbour, than laying one man under arreft for the evening.

How far fuch conduct was likely to ftifle mutiny I fhall not fay ; but when I remark that the foldiers on board were a mixture of fo-

reigners

reigners and criminals, enlifted from jails, and induced to enter for fear of worfe confequences, the due recompenfe of their crimes, I think my readers will agree with me, that the reins of difcipline ought to have been held with a ftrong hand.

A continuation of mutinous behaviour, every day more daring and aggravated, obliged Captain Wilcocks to addrefs Major General **Fox,** who had fent the detachment on board.

As the orders which the General had fent on board, were excellently well calculated for the fafety of the fhip, and the regulation of the troops; thefe flagrant acts of mutiny induced him to acquaint the Duke of Portland with Captain Wilcocks's letter; a written declaration, alluded to in Mr. Black's letter already quoted, which I had made, was alfo tranfmitted to his Grace; and which affords an honourable teftimonial, that however my character might otherwife have fuffered, as a foldier it ftill remained unfpotted.

The Duke immediately ordered Lieutenant Colonel Grofe, the Commander of the New South Wales Corps, to Torbay, to examine into the nature and accuracy of the complaint.

It is not perhaps improper for the information of fuch of my readers as are unacquainted with military affairs, to obferve, that it is a ftanding order on board tranfports, that no lights are to be fuffered, no tobacco to be

fmoaked,

fmoaked, nor cartridges to be allowed to remain between decks ; all which were grofsly violated by the foldiers, who, as muft already be evident, had no refpect for their officers, nor knew any controul of difcipline.

When the Lieut. Col. came on board he afked a few queftions of the officers of the fhip, but ex-amined more fully fome of the foldiers who were accufed of the diforders complained of, and feemed to give credit to their affertions.

The Captain expecting that the fignal for failing would be made foon, and apprehending that he might not have time to procure redrefs from another quarter, requefted that the Lieu-tenant-Colonel would take from the foldiers, the ball cartridges which Mr. Minchin had left in their poffeffion, as he entertained apprehenfions for the fafety of the fhip ; not only from the difpofition of the foldiers, but from fire that might be occafioned by their negligence and dif-order. This moft reafonable requeft was refufed by the Lieutenant-Colonel. . The judicious and foldier-like orders of that moft excellent officer, Major General Fox, which he had fent on board with the detachment, were then called to his recollection ; his anfwer was nearly to this pur-pofe, that the men were then under his (Lieu-tenant-Colonel Grofe's) command, that General Fox had no orders to give them. He then re-turned to his boat, and as he croffed the deck,

told

told the Captain that he would return next morning; but we faw him no more. The following afternoon, Captain Wilcocks was informed by the keeper of the inn, at Brixham, " that as foon as the Lieutenant-Colonel landed " from his vifit to the fhip, he took fome refrefh- " ment and fet off for London."

Juft at this time a very fevere gale commenced, which did much harm to the fleet in general, difmafted the frigate, under whofe convoy we failed, and did us fome, though not material damage; feveral fhips belonging to Admiral Sir R. Curtis's fquadron, then laying near us, likewife loft their mafts, and received other injuries. The tempeft having fomewhat abated, after raging two days, if I recollect right, the frigate was obliged to put into Plymouth to refit, and we with others of the convoy went round to Falmouth, efcorted by his Majefty's fhip Scourge, to repair our damages.

The fituation of Captain Wilcocks became now truly diftreffing, as he was on every fide furrounded by embarraffments, and uncertain how many days, or even hours he might have to remain in England. In hopes that the foldiers would at length behave with more decency and order, he wifhed to avoid further complaints; and as the Lieutenant-Colonel feemed to have forgotten him and his fhip, he likewife forgot the Lieutenant-Colonel. But their mutinous

difpofition,

difpofition, which could not reſt even for a day, plunged us again into confufion.

The foldiers, emboldened by impunity, infulted equally their own officers, and thofe of the fhip, till one day, a Corporal daring to ftrike the Chief Mate, in the execution of his duty, the Captain found himfelf impelled to addrefs the Minifter, and to furnifh him with a detail of the conduct of the troops, and his apprehenfions for the fafety of the fhip. About the fame time, my own affairs rendering it neceffary for me to addrefs the Duke of Portland ; I took advantage of the opportunity, to give my opinion of our fituation. A few days however put an end to our hopes, the fignal for failing was fuddenly made, and we went to fea, before any anfwer could be received to the Capt in's complaints.

During our paffage, the fame diforder which we had fo fenfibly felt in the harbour, prevailed and even encreafed; the fame Corporal, who ftruck the Chief Mate with impunity, ftruck and kicked his officer (Enfign Prater,) at fea; who, inftead of punifhing him with inftant death, tamely fubmitted to the infult.

It is with heart-felt pride, I write the hatred entertained towards me, both by the foldiers and their officers. The former, thought to have found in me a defperate advocate for mutiny, ready as themfelves to any act of villany or mur-

der;

der; whereas they found a determined enemy to every thing that tended to the want of difcipline, and fubordination; while the latter were fecretly enraged, that I fhould have dared to write as I had done on their fubject to his Majefty's Mi-nifter, and to their Lieutenant-Colonel, who furnifhed them with copies of what I had wrote; and one of which letters, wherein I defcribe the intention of the foldiers, and named thofe whom I fufpected to be the ringleaders, Enfign Min-chin read to the men on the quarter-deck, while we were at fea. The foldiers, however, though they ftruck their own officers and thofe of the fhip, only *threatened* me, nor did they ever venture to approach me, with the intention of put-ting their threats in execution.

The Captain's friendfhip for me merited the moft grateful return; whenever there was any difturbance I ranged myfelf by his fide, a con-duct which gave no fmall offence to the muti-neers; nor at laft, had not thofe whofe duty fhould have induced them to act far otherwife, hid themfelves in holes and corners, inftead of offering a manly refiftance, the mutiny would have ended in the death of the infurgents.

During the time we were at fea and under con-voy, though rebellion appeared every day and every hour, no attempt was made at feizing the fhip; the mutineers well knew that a fignal would

would bring the escort to act against them; and they equally knew that they had arms and ammunition adequate to their purpose, whenever they should think proper to make the attack; resistance they could expect but little of, since they had so many proofs of the tameness of their officers; they therefore suffered us to proceed without interruption on our course. Nevertheless, every day was marked by outrages, that loudly demanded the interference of authority, not only to quiet, but to disarm the New South Wales banditti, and inflict a signal and exemplary punishment on their infamous ringleaders.

In this state of continual apprehension, amidst the terrors of a mutiny we daily expected to break out, and which we were only too conscious, (from the causes already given,) we should not be able to resist, we proceeded on our voyage, proposing to touch at *Rio de Janiero*; and the convoy having left us in the proper latitude to proceed to their destination in the West India islands, we were left to our fate.

C H A P. XVIII.

The Lady Shore proceeds in safety almost to Rio de Janeiro.—The mutiny commences. Ensign Minchin

*chin refuses to act.—The Captain mortally wound-
ed.—The author endeavours to persuade the officers
of the troops to rally, but in vain.—He offers a
variety of practicable plans, but without effect.—
At the instance of the Captain and Minchin, the
author enters into a treaty with the mutineers.—
Minchin makes his submission, and the ship is given
up.—The officers who hid themselves, brought to
light.—The Captain's death.—The author wishes
to leave the mess, but at the solicitation of the officers, continues with them.—The officers endeavour
to procure a boat from the mutineers to carry them
to Rio Grande.—The author's stratagem to procure
leave for himself and the Purser to go in the
boat.*

W E proceeded on our voyage without any
event worth remarking, till we were very near
Rio de Janeiro, in the Brazils. On the 1ſt of
Auguſt 1797, about four o'clock in the morning, I was awaked by the report of fire-arms
and the ſcreams of women. I immediately
haſted from my bed toward the hatchway, which
I found ſtrongly guarded, and near it I met
John Curran, a ſailor, who had juſt eſcaped
from the ſcene of bloodſhed, then paſſing upon
deck; he told me that the ſoldiers had taken the
ſhip, and that if I went near the hatchway, I
ſhould be murdered by the mutineers.

O

Captain

Captain Wilcocks occupied the round-houfe, the Chief Mate, Second Mate, and Purfer, were in three fmall cabins in the fore-part of it; in cabins between decks abaft, and in the fteerage were the officers of the troops, Lieutenant Drummond, of the Bombay Marines, (doing duty as mate,) the petty officers of the fhip, the feamen, a paffenger with his family, and my-felf.

It was the Chief Mate's watch upon deck; him I had already heard calling aloud that he was murdered, and fall groaning at the feet of the affaffins; the Captain, whom the noife had alarmed, and who had run upon deck, was im-mediately mortally wounded, and in that ftate threw himfelf down the hatchway, but retained ftrength enough to drag himfelf into Enfign Minchin's cabin, and into his bed, which as he afterwards told me he found empty, the Enfign with his lady having already crept underneath it.

At the moment, when the Captain fell down the hatchway, in front of the ladder, I was be-hind it, at the cabin of Lieutenant Drummond, the Surgeon and the Steward, endeavouring to excite them to action, that we might not only defend ourfelves, but raife force enough to re-tain poffeffion of the fhip. I found the Steward's cabin empty, he having abandoned it; I then

went

went to Lieutenant Drummond's door, which communicated with the Surgeon's cabin, and which was fhut. After knocking and calling repeatedly on both thefe gentlemen, without obtaining any anfwer, the door was at length opened. The Steward, who had gone there to conceal himfelf, was the firft man I faw; Lieutenant Drummond was, I blufh to fay it, *under the bed of the Surgeon*, and pofitively refufed taking any active part; the Surgeon, a very good and very young man, faid but little, but I am confident, that had thofe whofe duty it was, made preparations for refiftance, he would not have been backward.

Juft then I heard the Captain calling me to come to his affiftance; I went round to him immediately, and found him laying in Minchin's bed, into which he had thrown himfelf. The bed ftood uncommonly high, being more than three feet from the deck, and under it I difcovered, by the day-light which begun to appear, ENSIGN MINCHIN, the COMMANDING OFFICER, with his wife. In fome fuch fituation, indeed, the knowledge I had of the man, and the clamorous outcry of " GIVE THEM THE SHIP! GIVE THEM THE SHIP!" which he had repeatedly vociferated at the very beginning of the conflict, taught me to look for him.

The Captain defired me to place him in an

eafy

eafy pofture, and then afked my opinion of our fituation. I frankly told him, that although the prefervation of the fhip was no way difficult, yet I had no hope of it, as I found no difpofition in thofe who had the power, to make any attempt; neverthelefs, if any active meafures fhould be determined upon, I was ready to lead the way to the deck. The Captain, the agony of whofe wounds was encreafed by feeing that he had nothing to hope for, feeling the approach of death, was difpofed rather to expire in peace, than fingly, and unable to ftand, to oppofe the fury of the mutineers; Mr. Minchin likewife, who had now fallied from his retreat, joined the Captain in conjuring me to go to the hatchway, to affure the mutineers that no refiftance would be made, and to entreat that, as they had no oppofition to expect, no more mifchief might be done. To the Captain I anfwered, that whatever might, in his own opinion, tend to his advantage or convenience, I fhould moft readily do, but to Enfign Minchin, I felt myfelf, as a foldier, obliged to fpeak in another tone. Him I told, that HE, and HE ONLY, was the proper perfon to fpeak to the mutineers; that they were committed to HIS charge, and that it was his duty TO SUBDUE THEM OR DIE! I called to his recollection, that he had more than force fufficient to infure.fuccefs; that all the ammunition of every

kind,

kind, except a few mufket-cartridges, were in our poffeffion, and that nothing was wanting, but for him to draw his fword and exert himfelf; but that if he thought attacking them on deck would be attended with more danger than he deemed *prudent* to encounter, we had ftill another and a fafer refource; that, as well as the ammunition, we were mafters of the provifions; that we had only to defend the hatchways, and keep the mutineers where they were; and that, having neither bread nor water in their reach, want of refrefhment and reft would foon reduce them to fue for mercy on their knees : I even propofed to him to choak the rudder, and cut away the mafts between decks, in which cafe the wreck would have fallen on their heads, and they had not one implement of any kind to clear it with; but fuch meafures he did not chufe to adopt, and repeated his defire of giving up the fhip; the Captain likewife again folicited me to communicate his and Enfign Minchin's propofitions to the mutineers, as the probable means of preventing more murders.

I went therefore to the hatchway, where the centinels prefented their pieces to my head; but three Frenchmen, a German, and feveral Irifh at that moment appearing, I communicated my bufinefs. They remained upon deck, and myfelf below; and while we were in that

fituation,

fituation, they affured me that they wifhed not to hurt any one; but that they wanted their liberty, and would have it or die: they added, that if the Captain and Mr. Minchin would come to the hatchway, and give their word of honour that no refiftance fhould at any time be made, all fhould be at peace, and we fhould be well treated. I reprefented to them the Captain's perilous fituation, and that it was impoffible for him to be brought to the hatchway, without encreafing the pain and danger in which he already was: they then replied that they would be fatisfied with receiving the declaration of fubmiffion from Minchin, and that they would make me anfwerable for the Captain's future conduct.

Minchin went to the hatchway, made the promifes demanded, and delivered up his arms. This point being fettled, thofe who had hitherto concealed themfelves began to appear. Anxious to know the fate of the gentlemen who lodged in the round-houfe, and of the failors of the watch on deck, I enquired of the mutineers whether many had fallen? They anfwered me, " But few." I then requefted to know if Mr. Murchifon, the Second Mate, Mr. Black, the Purfer, (whofe piftols I faw in the hands of a mutineer,) and Enfign Prater, were alive? They told me that Murchifon was in the cabin,

fhut

shut up under a guard, and that he should remain unhurt, provided he was quiet; that they sup-posed Mr. Black to have been killed and thrown over-board, as he was no where to be seen; that his pistols were found loaded at the head of his bed, and that there was much blood in his cabin; but as to Prater they knew nothing about him. The Chief Mate we already knew to be dead; so, that in addition to this, and the almost hopeless state of the Captain, we apprehended we had to lament the death of the other two gentlemen. However, about nine in the morning, *five hours after the affray was over*, Ensign Prater was found concealed among the women convicts, and about an hour after, much to our surprise and satisfaction, Mr. Black, the Purser, was handed down to us.

It now appeared that when the Chief Mate received his first wound, he fled into the cabin of Mr. Black, and threw himself upon that gentleman in his bed, the mutineers following, and firing upon him till he received, I think, eight wounds. Mr. Black, who is a very young man, at that time not above nineteen, and, as might be expected, totally unused to scenes of blood and horror, found himself awoke from his sleep by the noise of fire-arms, and the yells of the assassins, by whom he was surrounded; from the nearness of the discharge, his cabin

must

muſt have ſeemed filled with fire, and the weight
of his dying friend muſt have effectually prevented him from uſing his arms. Thus embar-
raſſed, ſurpriſed, and on all ſides ſurrounded by
armed ruffians, none could have ſuſtained ſuch an
aſſault but the man who, long accuſtomed to the
ſhock of war, has learnt to deſpiſe death, and who,
on all occaſions, even when the thunder of God
burſts round his head, claps his hand to his
ſword, and ſtands undaunted. Who then can be
aſtoniſhed that a youth, who neither wearing a
ſword, nor bearing a commiſſion, conſequently
had contracted no obligation to fight or die,
ſhould conceal himſelf? For him, therefore, no
apology is neceſſary; for the officers of the
New South Wales Corps and Lieutenant Drummond it may be, perhaps, difficult to find one.
Out of the reach of the mutineers, furniſhed
with every neceſſary, incapable of being attacked, except by the hatchways, which we
could eaſily have blocked, and ſufficiently numerous to have acted upon the offenſive, it is
their province, not mine, to account for their
extraordinary conduct.

Mr. Murchiſon had already obtained leave to
join us; and in fact, he and myſelf were the only two on board whom the mutineers treated
with conſideration; him they knew to poſſeſs
courage; that he was powerful, and would defend

fend himfelf with vigour ; and my uniform conduct towards them, from the hour I firft embarked, told them what they had to expect from me.

The former differences which had fubfifted between the military officers and me feemed now buried in oblivion, being as it were abforbed in our common misfortune; my time, however, was taken up in attending the Captain, who was very defirous I fhould not leave him; and who, after languifhing about forty-eight hours, expired in my arms. As foon as his body was committed to the deep, not wifhing to affociate with Minchin, for reafons that may be collected from the foregoing narrative, I left that cabin and returned to my own; but the fame day, at the hour of dinner, I was fent for, and folicited by all, but particularly by Enfigns Minchin and Prater, not to leave them ; I complied with their requeft, and we were no more feparated.

Some hours before our unfortunate Captain was buried, the mutineers did the fame to one of their comrades, named Delahay, who was killed in the conflict, not, as was firft suppofed, by Mr. Lambert, the Chief Mate, but by an accidental fhot from one of their own party ; on this man's body they affixed the following infcription, " *Il eft mort pour la liberté.*"

Previous

Previous to the Captain's death he defired me to cut off fome of his hair, to fend to his wife; a tafk which I carefully performed.

The direction of the fhip was now in the hands of a few foreigners, and the knowledge I had of their different languages often obliged them to have recourfe to me as their interpreter: thefe fervices enabled me to obtain from them fome indulgence for my friends and myfelf, by way of recompenfe. From the moment we were taken we never ceafed to folicit the mutineers to give us a boat, that we might land at *Rio de Janiero*; but this they refufed, from an apprehenfion that fome Portuguefe fhips of war might by laying there. As they had declared their intention of making for the *Rio de Plata*, and landing at fome of the Spanifh fettlements in that river, they thought, that if we reached our port foon, we might procure a Portuguefe fhip of war to be fent after them, which might reach the mouth of the *Rio de Plata* before the Lady Shore, and thus intercept them. On this account they pofitively refufed us a boat, till we fhould be fo far to the fouthward as to enable them to reach the *Rio de Plata* before we fhould be able, in all probability, to reach the *Rio Grande*, the fouthernmoft fettlement of the Brazils.

Every individual who formed our table folicited

licited leave to embark in the boat, and all obtained a promise, except Mr. Fyfe, the Surgeon, and myself; and though the most active in the mutiny were against my leaving the ship, as being useful to them, the majority of voices were in my favour: they also entertained an idea of detaining the Purser, to furnish them with an account of the quality and value of the cargo.

Notwithstanding these unfavourable appearances, I still flattered myself with expectations of vanquishing the opposition that obstructed my desires. An opportunity soon offered, which I seized, and found the means of turning to the advantage of the Purser and myself; and this we owed to a report which had reached the ears of the mutineers, that a chest of money or plate, and a box of watches were somewhere in the ship.

The three Frenchmen, who then governed the Lady Shore, were desirous that these should be made their own exclusive property; they spoke to me on the subject, making me very large promises if I would obtain them such information as might enable them to come at it without the knowledge of their companions. I communicated this business to the Purser, telling him, that if he knew of any such thing in the ship, and would give them directions where to

find

find it, he would procure his own liberty and mine; for if we were once in a fecret of that nature and importance, they would, for their own fecurity, fend us away, in preference to any other perfons. The Purfer affured me that there was neither money nor plate in the fhip, but that in one of the lockers of the cabin there was a fmall cafe of watches, his property; and this information we agreed to give them the fame eyening. Some days p..vious to that time they had been in the cuftom of fending for the Purfer and myfelf every evening, to affift them in examining the fhip's papers; the ufual hour arrived, and we were called for. We found the three chiefs alone in the cabin: I communicated to them what Mr. Black had told me, and he pointed out where the watches were. The cafe contained fifty-two, of different forts; they prefented him with fix, and me with two, of the beft; the reft they divided equally among themfelves.

This done, I knew no more objections could be made to our departure, and, indeed, from that moment they became very indulgent towards us. The ringleaders, being naturally afraid that if we were offended we might expofe their infidelity to their comrades, were extremely anxious to furnifh us with an opportunity of leaving them: in fact we were now become dangerous

gerous perfons, and their fafe poffeffion of their booty rendered our departure highly defireable to them; nay, even their lives were held by a precarious tenor while we remained on board.

After the fhip was given up the mutineers never treated us with cruelty; though fenfible of their fituation, they were very cautious: they kept fentries at the cabin door, and they would only permit one or two of us at a time to walk the quarter-deck.

One day Enfign Prater, having got drunk, entered into converfation with one of the failors publicly on deck, on the facility of retaking the fhip: he was over-heard, and the ring-leaders, telling him he fhould be hung in the morning, hand-cuffed him, and put him to bed, obferving, that though *he*, (Prater,) was no way formidable, yet, by fpeaking to the failor, he had incurred the penalty pointed out in the orders they had publifhed, which forbid any officer to fpeak to a failor or foldier. This harangue effectually fobered Prater, and put an end to his military prowefs; he lay howling in fuch a manner as was heard to the remoteft parts of the fhip; and, as the Purfer has obferved in his narrative, utterly prevented all who lay near him from fleep.

On Sunday, Auguft the 14th, 1797, the mutineers told us that they intended to give us the

boat

boat the next day; and on Monday morning, as a preparative to our departure, they brought us some papers, which we were compelled to sign. One was a certificate, purporting that we engaged not to carry arms against France for a year and a day; and there were other certificates for the petty officers and seamen, setting forth that they were detained, against their confent, to carry the ship into the *Rio de Plata*. Some of our *non-refifting* officers pretended to have obferved an unufual alacrity in the failors in obeying the orders of the mutineers, and muttered that they did not deferve fuch certificates; but I folemnly declare, that, in my opinion, thefe fufpicions were unfounded; and as to the remonftrances faid to have been made by the officers of the troops, their conduct, as already defcribed, will hardly give room to fuppofe them too loud. Befides, we were all in bondage, and no one durft refufe any thing required of us: could we then wonder at the conduct of ignorant failors?

In return, the mutineers gave us a certificate that their infurrection was not owing to any ill treatment from the Captain or any officer belonging to the fhip; but becaufe they had been trepanned into the Britifh fervice, without any means of redrefs, and had otherwife been ill treated by their Commander. This certificate, which was committed to my care, does fo much

honour

honour to the memory of Captain Wilcocks, and compleatly vindicates him from any charge of misconduct to the troops, that I thought it my duty to give it to his widow.

CHAP. XIX.

The officers and some others are allowed the boat.— The author procures leave for a boy committed to the Captain's care to go with them.—Obtains a knowledge of the ship's place by a stratagem.— They embark, after being searched for money.— Ensign Minchin's conduct and good luck.—The boat sets sail, and meets with a terrible gale.— She is nearly lost in the breakers as she approaches the coast.—Those on board forced to throw their trunks overboard; when, in the utmost distress, they see a boat coming towards them.—They make the harbour, and are hospitably received.—Minchin refuses the Purser and Mr. Murchison any assistance.—They send a report of their situation to the Governor-General.—Are sent for to Port St. Pedro, where they are hospitably received.— Their splendid entertainment by the Governor-General.—A second report made, in which, as well as the first, the author did not join.—Hospitality

of

of the Commandant.—The author is prefented with a fword by the Governor-General.

On the morning of Monday Auguſt the 15th, 1797, the intimation we had received the day before that we ſhould leave the ſhip was con-firmed to us, being then nearly in the latitude of 34 S. about 60 leagues from the ſhore, and from 80 to 100 from the mouth of *Rio Grande*; the boat was hoiſted out, and every other neceſſary preparation made. Juſt then Michael Richards, a fine boy, about fourteen years of age, and of very reſpectable connections, who was entruſted to the care of Captain Wilcocks before we left Falmouth, and who ſince that gentleman's death had been abandoned by every body, ſolicited me to procure him permiſſion to accompany us. His helpleſs ſituation determined me to exert myſelf to procure him the melancholy privilege he ſo much wiſhed, and which ſeemed entirely neceſſary for him: I applied to the mutineers, and was ſucceſsful. I took him under my protection, which he did not leave till he was reſtored to his family.

In the morning a liſt of names, twenty-nine in number, was made out of the perſons whom it was determined ſhould go in the boat; this was delivered to us, and we were informed that thoſe who had any property might take each

one

One trunk. · During the afternoon our baggage was fearched, when I found means to conceal in fome foap a confiderable fum in gold : when they had taken from us every thing they fan‑cied, they gave us fome provifions, and we were fuffered to embark.

Previous to our embarkation I had obtained a tolerable opportunity of afcertaining where we were, by the following ftratagem : The mu‑tineers, not fufpecting that a foldier knew any thing of navigation, had permitted me to fee them work their * day's works for determining the fhip's place ; but though I knew fomething of the fcience, I wifhed to have the opinion of a better judge than myfelf. Mr. Black, being an incomparable navigator, was the perfon I wifhed to confult ; but there arofe a confidera‑ble difficulty in accomplifhing my defign, as the mutineers were not very willing that he fhould fee the fhip's log‑book, or the chart of the coaft, on which they had traced her route.

One of the chief mutineers, named Thomeo, who was the beft navigator among them, fhew‑ed me the chart as ufual, and pointed out to me the fituation of the fhip, in which I pre‑tended to differ from him, jocularly offering to

* A term ufed for the calculations every day made to deter‑mine the fhip's place.

P

back

back my opinion with the wager of a guinea: he laughed at my feeming ignorance; but he was my dupe, and accepted my bet, propofing to refer it to any perfon who had competent ability to decide.   This was all I wanted, and, apparently with the greateft indifference, I pro- pofed Mr. Black; he was accordingly called for, and allowed to infpect the charts and books: I payed the lofs of my wager; and we thus were enabled to determine our diftance from *Rio Grande*, and the courfe we had to fteer, of which the mutineers feemed inclined to keep us ignorant.   We were compelled to get into the boat one by one, after being previoufly fearch- ed for money, contrary to the promife of the mutineers; none, however, was found; but they had previoufly feized about a *hundred dollars* which Minchin had to pay the foldiers, and which was the property of government; for this they gave him a receipt for a *hundred pounds*, with a view of enabling him to recover that amount from the State.   He had fo little bag- gage that he not only faved it all, but fucceeded in getting fafely to fhore *eighteen whole pieces of printed cotton, and fome packages of flockings and women's fhoes*, which Mr. Black had thrown down in the cabin the day we were preparing to embark.

About half-paft fix in the evening we left the
fhip,

ship, and, anxious to make land as foon as poffible, fteered but little to the northward of weft. At our departure the weather was tolerably moderate; before midnight we were affailed by a moft violent ftorm, attended by the heavieft rains I ever witneffed. The tempeft fomewhat fubfided toward morning, but as we approached the land, blew with redoubled fury; fortunately we had fixed up fome ftanchions on the boat's gunwale; and nailed a breadth of canvas, brought with us for that purpofe, fore and aft, which we found of great ufe in keeping off the fpray; and to this we owed much of our prefervation.

Mr. Black, Mr. Murchifon, the Second Mate, and Mr. Drummund undertook the management of the boat; Enfign Prater, who, in his earlier days, had been fome voyages to the Eaft Indies and other parts, being fuppofed fomething of a failor, was added to their number; myfelf and the others were conftantly employed in bailing; for, independent of the boat being very leaky, the fea run fo high, and the rain fell fo heavy, that fhe was continually filling with water. The quick and violent motion made even the beft feamen fick; poor Black was rendered incapable of action, and Prater, after all his profeffions, was in due form pronounced *neither failor nor foldier*; he was turned

from

from the helm, and I took his place. To describe our situation is no easy task; expecting every inftant to perish, lumbered with baggage, with sick useless soldiers, women, and children, loaded almost to the water's edge, and the crowd so great that in going back and forward to work the boat we were obliged to tread on the carcases of those whom sickness or fear had forced to lie down.

On the morning of the second day we had soundings, and early in the fore-noon saw land, which we knew to be the flat sandy coast which runs from the southward of *Rio Grande* to *Cape St. Mary's* on the *Rio de Plata*. The extreme lowness of the coast causes the breakers to run very high and very far into the sea, in so much, that had the coast promised food and shelter, we could not have reached it alive, as the boat must have swamped in the breakers; we therefore determined to steer more to the northward, still keeping the coast in sight. That day we had an imperfect observation, according to which we were then above 20 leagues to the southward of *Rio Grande*; and, though the boat seemed almost to fly through the water, we did not expect to make the wished-for river that day. A strong current that set from the south having, however, carried us beyond our reckoning, we were surprised, about 3 P. M., to see something re-

sembling

fembling the maft of a fhip; we ftood towards it, and found it to be a wreck; ftill no land was to be feen, but we perceived, more in fhore, feveral mafts which we concluded were of veffels laying at anchor, and though on ftanding yet farther in, nothing was to be feen as far as the eye could reach but fand, we were convinced it muft be the mouth of *Rio Grande*, fince we knew that the coaft from thence to the *Rio de Plata* does not afford a fingle harbour.

The banks, which run far into the fea, made our fituation horrible, as we feemed to be embayed by breakers. There did not appear any retreat for us, nor any poffibility of fafety, except ftanding to fea, and that, with the gale ftill blowing in all its violence, and night advancing, offered only a forlorn hope. Befet with dangers and threatened on all fides with fudden diffolution, one bold and laft effort remained; we determined to ftand through the breakers and to fteer a direct courfe for the fhips we faw riding at anchor!

On approaching the fhore I had yielded the helm to an able pilot, Lieutenant Drummond; confident in his fkill, forwards we went, while all who dared look up, fixed their eyes on the tremendous breakers we were about to encounter, and waited in filence that fate which feemed inevitable. In an inftant the fea burft over us

in

in every direction, our quarter-cloaths were torn away, and the boat was filling with water. Mr. Drummond, ſuppoſing that nothing could ſave us but lightening her, called out to throw the trunks overboard, and deſired me to drive thoſe forward who were abaft. Mr. Murchiſon (the Mate) with that manly promptneſs and liberality which he never fails to diſplay, ſet the example with his own trunk ; the baggage was thrown overboard without diſtinction till we ſufficiently lightened our veſſel, and thus to his and Mr. Drummond's ſkill and activity we are indebted for our exiſtence. Having paſſed the firſt range of breakers, and finding ourſelves in much ſmoother water, but ſtill with breakers between us and the ſhore, we came to an anchor, and hoiſted an Engliſh jack at the maſt head ; but this the violence of the wind compelled us to lower the moment it was hoiſted. We were, however, perceived by the ſignal-houſe at the mouth of the river, which anſwered us with a Portugueſe flag, and by the help of a glaſs we could ſee a boat coming towards us ; but finding we were faſt driving to ſome breakers which lay between us and a point of land that runs out into the ſea, we again got under ſail and ſtood for the river.

Providence directed us to the right channel, and we met the boat very near the ſhore. The

Maſter

Mafter Pilot, and a Captain of militia were in her, who received us with the utmoft kindnefs, and conducted us to the houfe of the former, where nothing that could give us comfort was omitted by that good man and his family. Mr. Black, Mr. Murchifon, and feveral others landed with all their poffeffions on their back, their trunks having been thrown overboard. The former of thefe gentlemen naturally applied to Enfign Minchin, who had, as before obferved, faved *more than his own baggage*, but to little purpofe, and he abfolutely was forced to afk me for a change of linen. This was the more vexatious, as Mr. Black had a compleat claim on him on account of the goods which Mrs. Minchin had faved, and which were the property of Mr. Black ; however, as my baggage had efcaped, I had the pleafure of fupplying both him and Mr. Murchifon.

When we had refted about an hour the Pilot requefted that we would inform him who we were, the better to enable him to make his report to the Governor-General of the province, Lieutenant-General Sebaftian Xavier da Vega Cabral e Cemara, who then, on account of the probability of war with Spain, refided at Fort St. Pedro, above four leagues up the river ; he added, that we muft remain where we were until an anfwer came from his Excellency.

It

It was natural for me to wish that the disadvantages under which I laboured should not be unnecessarily published; I well knew that neither Mr. Black nor Mr. Murchison, the Mate, were capable of an unkind action, nor did I entertain any doubts of Mr. Drummond. I had done every thing for the general good, and I was sure, that from them at least, I should meet with a proper return; but my opinion of the Ensigns Minchin and Prater was very different. I therefore called those two into another room, and requested them to tell me what was their intention in regard to me. They both answered, by all means to conceal every thing disagreeable, for that it was not their business to publish my misfortunes. I told them, that though I was sensible of their kindness I was indifferent to what they might have determined; but that it was necessary before I saw the General, that I should know what their determination was. I cautioned them at the same time not to deceive me, but if they thought it their duty, or felt disposed to relate my circumstances to the General, to say so, and I would do the same, when his Excellency would act as he thought proper. If, however, they first concealed and afterwards exposed me, they would only expose themselves, and might be assured, that I would not peaceably submit to any thing so mortifying. They

then

then repeated, that it could never be their intention in any report they might be required to make, to fay more on my fubject than my name and military rank. On this I left them, and *they* propofed to Mr. Murchifon, Mr. Black, &c. to do the fame, to which they readily confented, and the report of the fhip's name, the place of our deftination, with the names and rank of every individual was given to the pilot, in which I was ftyled Major Semple Lifle (a Dutch officer) *a paffenger.*

The Pilot conveyed this report to the Governor-General, and the next morning his Excellency fent a Non-commiffioned Officer with his inftructions. The Pilot was by thefe directed to fend all who were Officers immediately up the river to him, for that he would not dine until they arrived, and the foldiers and women were ordered to follow in our own boat; Enfign Minchin, with his Lady, Prater, the Purfer, and myfelf, accordingly embarked in the Pilot's boat, while Mr. Drummond and Mr. Murchifon remained to take charge of the launch and fuch bagage as we had not been compelled to throw overboard.

We had not proceeded more than a league up the river, before we met the General's barge, with an officer, who informed us, that he was fent by his Excellency to congratulate us on our efcape, and to conduct us to the town; we

thereupon

thereupon went into the General's barge, and foon reached Fort *St. Pedro.*

We found the Governor-General in a large audience-chamber at the head of the Officers of the garrifon.all in full uniform. The benevolence apparent in his countenance, his manly form and the elegance of his manners filled me with admiration and refpect, and infpired me with ideas of the moft favourable kind, which a further knowledge amply confirmed. That inimitable General, having fpent the laft thirty years of his life entirely in the Brazils, would not that day venture to fpeak to us in French, as the few opportunities he had enjoyed of converfing in that language, might, he apprehended, have rendered him unable to exprefs himfelf in the manner he could wifh; but a Lieutenant-Colonel of Engineers, converfant in that language, was commanded by the General to enquire into our adventures, and to affure us that his Excellency would give us every affiftance in his power.

The Lieutenant-Colonel immediately addreffed himfelf to me; but anxious as I was to avoid, as far as might be, implicating myfelf in any concerns of the officers or foldiers, I told him that I had not, as he might perceive by the report fent from the mouth of the river, any authority or connection either with the fhip or

the

the troops; that for information in whatever regarded them, his beft way would be to addrefs himfelf to the proper officers who were no doubt able to account for the mutiny, and to explain their own conduct, fubjects upon which I did not wifh to talk ; I then pointed out to him Enfign Prater, who I informed him could fpeak French, and that the Steward, who was likewife prefent, could fpeak both French and Italian.

The bufinefs having been by them explained to his Excellency, he informed the officers of the troops that we fhould experience the liberality due to the fubjects of an antient ally of the Queen his Sovereign, and that they and the foldiers fhould be treated as his Britannic Majefty's troops were on his own eftablifhment. The General then did me the honour to addrefs a few words to me, and we took leave till the hour of dinner.

To amufe us till the table was prepared, a number of officers conducted us to the houfe of the Commandant Colonel *Manuel Marquez de Lima de Souza.* There we found a large company, who were affembled for the purpofe of offering their fervices, and congratulating us on our happy arrival in their country. Various refrefhments were prefented to us, and among the reft, fome extremely fine bottled porter, which, as that part of Brazil has no traffic what-

ever

ever with any other quarter of the world, is esteemed more than Imperial Tokai is in Great Britain. Every individual of this truly respectable assemblage loaded us with caresses, and seemed to vie with each other in acts of kindness towards us.

We returned to the General's about four, when dinner was announced, and we were most sumptuously entertained; we sat down, about forty in number, to a splendid dinner of three courses, and an elegant desert; but such is the style in which his Excellency lives.

In the evening we were conducted to the quarters which had been provided for us. His Excellency had already distinguished me, and said, as we took leave, that as he was unable to accommodate me in his own house, he had directed half of his Adjutant-General's to be prepared for me; Lieutenant Drummond expressed a desire to be lodged with me; when, finding there was sufficient room, I requested that a bed might be prepared for him which was accordingly done. Next morning the Lieutenant-Colonel of engineers, who had acted as interpreter the day before, came to my quarters to require that I would accompany him to the General's. In compliance with this request I immediately went, when, after some conversation on various subjects, his Excellency told me, that it would

be

be neceſſary for me, together with the officers of the ſhip and troops, to make a report of every particular regarding our voyage, to be tranſmitted to the Viceroy. I told his Excellency, that, ſituated as I was, I could make no report, as I had not the honour to ſerve Britain ; I had even left it under unpleaſant circumſtances, and had no concern whatever with the ſhip or troops, being only a paſſenger, as his Excellency would perceive by the report made by his Majeſty's officers and thoſe of the ſhip, on our arrival in his government. The General's requeſt was therefore communicated to Enſign Minchin, and the other gentlemen, who, in conſequence, drew up a report every way ſimilar to the former one, but more ample ; it was ſigned by all, myſelf accepted, and certified regularly to be a TRUE REPORT. In this document Mr. Minchin ſtyled himſelf *Lieutenant and Adjutant*, a title which he had indeed aſſumed from the day we left Falmouth, ſaying, that he had that day received his promotion.

The invitation to dine with the General was continued during our ſtay, and it was further intimated to me, that his Excellency wiſhed to ſee me every morning at eight o'clock. On the third day, waiting upon him according to his deſire, he moſt politely addreſſed me, telling me, he was confident no man deſerved better to wear

a

a fword than myfelf, and concluded by prefent-
ing me with a moft elegant one.

Flattering as it was to be thus diftinguifhed
by this excellent and accomplifhed General,
ftill my pleafure was not totally unmixed with
pain. I knew the effect this diftinction would
have on the minds of our *military gentlemen*, and
apprehended fome unpleafing event in confequence of their envy; I however continued my
exertions to acquire and to deferve the friendfhip and protection of his Excellency, and the
efteem of the garrifon.

CHAP. XX.

News comes of the Lady Shore being brought into
Monte Video on the Rio da Plata.—Enfign Min-
chin and the Purfer fend each a report to the
Spanifh Governor.—Enfign Prater's behaviour to
the author, and the confequences of it.—Prater,
who was in difgrace, again admitted to the Ge-
neral's table at the author's interceffion.—De-
fcription of the province of Rio Grande, the man-
ners of the inhabitants, and their uncommon hofpi-
tality.—Scandalous behaviour of the Englifh fol-
diers.—A child of one of the Englifh foldiers
chriftened

christened at Port St. Pedro.—The Governor and a Lady of distinction stand sponsors.—The Author and his companions prepare to leave Rio Grande. —Detained by contrary winds.—The mode of catching wild cattle in that country.—The author resolves to go over land to Rio Janiero, and obtains the Governor's leave for that purpose.—The same favour refused to Mr. Minchin.

ABOUT the middle of September, the General received a letter from the Governor of *Monte Video*, a Spanish settlement on the north side of the Rio de Plata, acquainting him that an English ship had been brought in there by mutineers; that the ship's name was the Lady Shore, bound for Botany Bay, with British soldiers and female convicts; that the Frenchmen who then commanded her, declared that they had revolted in consequence of having been FORCED INTO THE SERVICE AS SOLDIERS; that they had made themselves masters of the ship near the *Rio Grande;* in doing which the Captain, Chief Mate, and a soldier were killed, and that they had given the ship's launch, with all things necessary, to a Major, two officers of the troops, two of the ship, and several others, at some distance from *Rio Grande*. The Governor of *Monte Video* expressed the greatest concern to know whether we got safely on shore, fhore, and folicited his Excellency, in cafe we were with him, to engage us to fend him a report of the tranfaction: he added, that he was the more anxious for this, as he could rely upon our report, though not upon that of the mutineers.

His Excellency communicated the purport of this letter to me, and urged me to make a report, to be tranfmitted to the Governor of *Monte Video*; but I returned the fame anfwer that I had done before, and excufed myfelf to him as having no command in the fhip, and having left home in difgrace.

Two reports were then made, one by Enfign Minchin, and one by Mr. Black, the Purfer; the latter was done with candour, good fenfe, and propriety; but the former was of a very different defcription. Minchin, whether he really thought what he wrote, or whether he had private reafons for mifreprefentation, repeated the ridiculous charge which has been already hinted, of the prompt obedience of the failors to the mutineers; this he reprefented in a criminal light, though it was evident to every perfon on board that they only obeyed from neceffity, and becaufe a refufal would, in all probability, have been punifhed with death.

The Surgeon of the fhip, a fpirited, amiable, and intelligent young man, had, as I before ob-

ferved,

ferved, been forcibly detained by the mutineers; for him I entertained the high regard he
fo well deferved; and, by the advice of his Excellency General da Veiga, wrote a letter to the
Governor; in which I accounted for not making
a report; intreating him to diftinguifh that me-
ritorious young gentleman; and as an act of
juftice and humanity, to enable him to return
to London as foon as poffible. I addreffed, at
the fame time, another to the Surgeon, both of
which the General indulgently inclofed in his
own letter to the Governor of *Monte Video*, and
which he difpatched by a courier.

The effect which the partiality the General
did me the honour to beftow upon me, began
now to manifeft itfelf in the conduct of fome of
my companions. Enfign Prater, in contempt
and contradiction of the various reports he had
figned; in violation of every focial tie which
arofe from thofe habits of intimacy in which we
lived from the day of our arrival at *Rio Grande*,
gave a loofe to that malice he could no longer
contain. He not only divulged what, by the
common confent of all parties, was judged proper to be concealed, but uttered a number of
malicious flanders againft me. Thefe his *brother
Enfign* reported to me, with many fevere ftric-
tures on fuch unwarrantable conduct; and added,
that, as he had put us all in an aukward fitua-

Q

tion,

tion, if I was difpofed to let him pafs unpu-
nifhed, *he would not.*

In the courfe of a few minutes, and while I
was yet glowing with feelings much eafier to be
imagined than defcribed, I faw Prater walking
with Mr. Murchifon, the Mate, in the ftreet.
Smitten with confcious guilt, he fled, and attempted to hide himfelf in the houfe of a
burgher; I followed, and, having reached him,
faid, that, though I felt more afhamed than
proud of drawing my fword againft him, ftill
the wanton flanders he had uttered had placed
me in fuch a fituation, in a ftrange country, as
reduced me to the neceffity of vindicating myfelf with the arms of a foldier; he had therefore no remedy, no hope, but in a manly defence. He ftood hefitating, and I was tempted
to haften him by a hearty kick, but in vain; I
told him, that, after having abufed me in the
manner he had done, he could not hope to
fcreen himfelf behind his want of courage; ftill
he refufed to draw. My fword was already in
my hand, and my point directed to his bofom,
when Mr. Murchifon, the Mate, (who, together
with the Steward, into whofe quarters he had
fled, and was prefent at the whole affair,) feized
my arm; and, perhaps, prevented me from doing that, in a paroxyfm of paffion, which might
have embittered every cool moment of my future

tufe life. I, however, made him leave me his
fword, and then permitted him to fly; but unfortunately, Mr. Murchifon, whofe goodnefs of
heart induced him to interfere, received a fevere
wound acrofs his hand, when he threw himfelf
before me to fave Prater.

That night I was put in arreft by the Commandant, who, early in the morning, carried
me to the Governor; by that excellent General
I was treated with great and even unufual kindnefs; and had the proud fatisfaction to hear
from himfelf the warmeft encomium on my
conduct, which he faid had given me a frefh
claim to his friendfhip. Mr. Minchin likewife
waited on his Excellency, to exprefs his difapprobation of his brother officer's conduct; and
faid, that though I had fuffered fome difficulties in my own country, which it was not his
bufinefs to explain, ftill Prater, as well as himfelf, knew me to be a gentleman and an old
officer. I then wifhed to relate to the General
all the circumftances of my difgrace; but that
truly great man impofed filence upon me, faying, " I will not fuffer you to call to your me-
" mory any painful event."

Prater, as well as myfelf, had been put under
arreft, and was not yet enlarged; I folicited
his Excellency to difcharge him, promifing
upon my honour, that I would no more lift my

 hand

againſt him while in the government of *Rio Grande*; his Excellency replied, that after ſuch a promiſe from me, itwas no longer neceſſary to keep Prater in confinement, for he was confident that *there was no danger of that gentleman's attacking me.* He therefore ordered an Aid-du-Camp to announce to him that he was at liberty; but that his appearance at the General's table would be diſpenſed with for the future.

The next morning Prater ſent to me to propoſe to make any apology I might require; I anſwered him, that *I* could receive no apology from him, but I thought he would do well to apologize to the Governor for the impropriety of his conduct. He accordingly ſent to the Colonel of engineers, the General's Aid-du-Camp, and myſelf, and addreſſing himſelf to them, he begged of them to aſſure his Excellency that he lamented his miſconduct; and ſolemnly declared that what he had done proceeded from the effects of ENVY and WINE. This meſſage was immediately delivered to the General, who ſmiled and ſaid, " Tell the poor " gentleman to come and dine at my table when " he pleaſes;" and Prater, to the utter aſtoniſhment of every one who knew the tranſaction, never failed to appear at dinner as if nothing had happened.

The province of Rio Grande lies about the

6th degree of fouth latitude, and 34th of weft longitude; the foil is extremely fertile, producing all things in the greateft abundance, with which the inhabitants are well fupplied; in fact, the luxury of the firft clafs of the people is exceffive, and fnch as one would fcarcely expect in a place almoft fhut out from the reft of the world. The town of *Port St. Pedro* is fituated about four leagues from the mouth of the river, from which the province takes its name; it is moftly of wood, ill-built, and ftraggling, with very few good houfes; nor did I fee above two or three that confifted of more than one floor. The Governor's houfe is fmall, but convenient and laid out entirely on a military plan. It confifts of a fuite of apartments, all on the ground floor. There is a handfome cathedral, with very fuitable eftablifhments about it; and I fhould fuppofe that here, as well as every where, the clergy are well taken care of.

The people, unlike thofe of the mother country, are remarkably clean, and drefs in a fplendid manner; their linen, which feems with them a favourite article of drefs, is exceedingly fine, and is always fo clean that it really prepoffeffes a ftranger in their favour; notwithftanding I have ever carried cleanlinefs to a finical nicety, I made but a fecond-rate figure at *Port St. Pedro*; for fuch is the effect of the fun, and the

Q 3

pure

pure water, that their linen is white beyond all imagination.

The hospitality of the *Rio-grandians* far exceeds all I ever saw in any other part of the world; they are not contented with the cool civility which is dignified with the name of hospitality in other countries; they court the society of strangers, merely for the sake of heaping benefits upon them, and they are ever upon the watch for opportunities to do service to all that approach their dwellings. I have already said a few words on the manner in which the officers were treated, but Brazilian hospitality stopt not here; the inhabitants followed the very soldiers in the streets, giving them invitations to their houses, and pressing favours upon them. How the soldiers returned these acts of kindness will be seen hereafter.

Besides the regular forces, the whole males are enrolled in the militia, and form, if not perhaps the best disciplined, by far the best dressed corps in the world; their waistcoats and breeches are generally silk, as are the linings of their coats; these, with the excessive whiteness and cleanness of their linen, render their appearance truly elegant.

The orderly and civilized manners of this elegant corps formed a striking contrast to the behaviour of our British soldiers (two Serjeants,

two Corporals, and two privates) who were
there. These *heroes* were perpetually quarrel-
ling, not only among themselves, and with their
own officers, but with their benefactors in the
town, on whom they never failed to beftow
every abusive epithet their knowledge of the
Portuguefe language afforded them, by way of
return for the civilities they received. This irregular and brutal conduct occafioned the General, though the mildeft and moft humane man
living, to imprifon them in the guard-houfe;
nay, fuch was their behaviour, that during the
feven weeks we were there, they were never *all*
at liberty. So much was his Excellency difpleafed with them, that I have heard him repeatedly fay, he would rather fend them home
at his own expence, than fuffer them to remain
in the country he governed; and all the officers
of the garrifon declared with one voice, that for
the laft ten years fo many punifhments had not
been known in that country. Sorry am I to
add, that fo frequent vifitors thefe foldiers were
to the prifon, that the inhabitants gave it the
name of the *Englifh barracks*.

I might fill a volume with particular inftances
of the kindnefs we experienced, but the following will certainly fhew that the foldiers ought
to have at leaft comported themfelves with
decency. One of their wives who came with

us had been brought to bed a few days before
we left the ship; the infant as well as the mother arrived safe, and were by a Brigadier-Ge-
neral's widow, received into her house. She
cloathed the mother, and finding the child
had not yet been christened, resolved to have
that ceremony performed according to the rites
of the church of Rome. A christening is a very
important concern in this country, and managed with much splendor; accordingly the
soldier's wife was dressed very handsomely, or-
namented with diamonds which the lady lent
her. The Brigadier's widow and the General
stood sponsors; the ceremony was conducted in
a most magnificent style, and when it was over,
the General presented the father with a small
sum, which would probably afterwards have
been augmented, had not his misconduct pre-
cluded his Excellency's bounty.

We had been six weeks in *Rio Grande,* every
day experiencing fresh marks of kindness from
the General and the inhabitants ; it may indeed
be truly said, that his Excellency makes humanity his employment, and that those under him
strive to imitate him. To myself he was continually shewing new proofs of friendship, and
when I was about to go, earnestly intreated me
to remain with him; an invitation too honourable and too flattering to have been declined,

clined, had I not, for many reasons, thought my presence in Britain absolutely neceffary.

About the 20th of September we prepared to go on board some coasting vessels for *Rio de Janeiro*; Ensign Minchin, his Lady, the Purser, and myself, embarked in one vessel, and Ensign Prater, Mr. Drummond, the soldiers' wives, and the rest of our company on board four others. The General made me several valuable presents at my departure, and besides filled our ship with abundance of all kinds of provisions for the passage.

The wind proving unfavourable we remained three weeks at the mouth of the harbour, where we amused ourselves with shooting. We found vast numbers of a kind of plover, called by the Portuguese *Quero-Quero*, from their cry; partridges are by no means plentiful, but there are abundance of snipes, storks, sea parrots, &c. The great number of vultures that abound here are a real blessing to the inhabitants, who kill every year vast quantities of wild cattle for the sake of the skins; the carcases which they leave in the woods would, by their putrefaction, occasion pestilence, did not they find a ready sepulchre in the rapacious maws of these voracious birds.

They take these cattle in a very singular manner. One of their methods is by means of a thong of plaited leather, from thirty to forty feet in length ; a ring of iron at one end ferves to pafs the other end through, and thus form a running noofe. The Indian who ufes this, gets within reach of a horfe or bullock, and taking a large coil of the thong in his right hand, and feveral others ready to veer away in his left ; he dexteroufly throws it over the animal's head, while he is flying from him full fpeed, and by a fudden check brings him to the ground. Their other method is by three balls connected by a thong, two of which are about three inches in diameter, and the third, which is to be held in the hand about two inches. The hunter, when he wifhes to ufe this, takes the fmall ball in his right-hand, and fwings the other two round his head till he has got the proper aim and velocity; he then throws it at the legs of the animal he is purfuing, with fuch dexterity, as either to break or entangle them as he thinks fit. With thefe inftruments, it is computed that from three to four hundred thoufand head of cattle are annually flaughtered.

We were feveral days detained by contrary winds, and it being the general opinion of all who knew the coaft, that the wind would not fhift till the moon changed, my anxiety to return to Europe increafed, and my natural impatience of temper rendered me quite unhappy.

I

I therefore resolved to solicit the Governor ot permit me to go over land, in spite of the danger and difficulty attending such an expedition ; but before I applied to his Excellency I prevailed on Mr. Black the Purser, to promise to accompany me.

In consequence of this resolution I dispatched a messenger to his Excellency the General, who, with his usual kindness and politeness, returned me an immediate answer, allowing me to go when I pleased, and to take with me whom I might chuse.

Next morning, at day-break, we disembarked to return to town. When we left the ship the wind was contrary, but just as we reached the shore it chopped about ; the pilot made the signal for the vessels, ten in all, to weigh ; we stood on the brink of the river, and, with some regret, saw them stand to sea, and every ship, except that which we had just left, pass the bar in safety. She struck upon a bank, and a violent gale springing up at that moment, the pilot went to her assistance, but thinking her lost, his own boat and the ship's launch took out all the persons on board. Mr. and Mrs. Minchin saved all their property, but Mr. Black's trunk and mine were left on board, and the ship presently after going to pieces, the unfortunate Purser was again stripped of almost every thing.

Mr.

Mr. Minchin landed on the north fide of the river, which is very broad, and we were on the fouth, where no boat was to be had; they therefore went to the pilot's, and we mounted our horfes to proceed to the town. The General had already learnt from the fignals, that one of the fhips had been loft on the bank; from us he learnt all the particulars, and next morning fent his barge to bring Mr. and Mrs. Minchin to town.

' Mr. Minchin requefted the General to permit him to proceed over land, but his Excellency thought proper to refufe, telling him, that he would provide him a paffage in one of the next fhips, which would fail in the courfe of a few days. The General added, that fuch an indulgence was very unufual, and that his granting it to me was purely the effect of private friendfhip, as he muft anfwer himfelf for any confequences that might enfue.

CHAP. XXI.

The author prepares for his journey, accompanied by Mr. Black, Richards a boy, a Brazilian fervant, two dragoons, and two Indians.—Set out, and lay the firft night at Tropa Velha, where the country begins to grow fertile.—Elegant entertainment there.

there.—Dine at the hut of a poor Farmer.—Sleep at the house of an officer of auxiliary dragoons, where the entertainment is magnificent.—Remarkable situation of Moiſtardio.—Manner of marking horses on the royal farms.—Dexterity of the Indians in the use of two very ſingular weapons.—A merry prank played on a Farmer.—Torres, a fort on the frontiers of the province of Rio Grande, deſcription of it ; vaſt number of ſeals there.—Brazilian cavalry.—Charaĉter of the inhabitants of Rio Grande.—Farinha, a root uſed as a ſubſtitute for bread.—Difficulty in croſſing a large river.—A curious old Frenchman.—Extraordinary mode of fiſhing.—Mountains near Laguna.—Part with their former guides.—From Laguna the road towards St. Catharine's very bad.—Stop at a whale fiſhery, and next day arrive at St. Catharine's.

WE now prepared for our journey, with the fatigues of which we were made fully acquainted, both by the General and others, who knew and had experienced them. They repreſented to me in very urgent terms, that none but a ſtrong man inured to fatigue, could ſupport ſuch an expedition, through a country in many places deſolate, and in all but thinly inhabited; for my ſafety they expreſſed no apprehenſion, as my habits had ever been of the laborious and enterpriſing kind; but they with a well-meant

earneſtneſs

earneſtneſs of intreaty, deſired me by no means to think of taking Mr. Black or the boy Richards with me.

Though Mr. Black was not an expert horſe-man, and the boy had never been in the ſaddle; the former treated the fatigue and danger with contempt, and I was moreover, beſides the wiſh I had for ſuch a companion, bound to him by a promiſe; as for the boy, his artleſs intreaties were irreſiſtible; and he had ſo long been uſed to look up to me as his only protector, that he would not be diſſuaded; I was therefore obliged to permit him to join in the expedition.

The mode of travelling in that country is truly ſingular. There are no inns or any place where freſh horſes may be regularly procured, the traveller therefore takes with him from *fifty to a hundred horſes*, by far the greater part of which have never been mounted; theſe are driven be-fore him quite looſe, by one or two Indians, and when the horſe on which he rides is fatigued, the Indian catches him another. This would to an European be no eaſy taſk, but here it is far otherwiſe; for you have only to point out the horſe you wiſh, and the Indian makes directly at him, throws his *thong* or *lace*, before de-ſcribed, over the animal's head, and, in ſpite of all his efforts, leads him to you.

His Excellency had given me an old dragoon,
who

who knew the country, for a guide, and a militia dragoon, to add to our force; we had also two Indians to drive our horses. We were furnished with leathern baskets for our baggage, which are laid on the backs of the horses, somewhat like panniers; we had, however, not much to carry, the whole consisting of a few changes of linen, and a spare coat, our heavy articles having been left in the ship and lost by her being wrecked.

We took leave of our most worthy friend and benefactor the Governor, who, together with most of the officers of the garrison accompanied us to the river side. Our conductor, who was already in the north town, having prepared every thing for our departure, we crossed that evening, a distance considerably above a league. On the fourth of October, about seven in the morning, Black, myself, little Richards, and a servant I had engaged at *Rio Grande*, began our march. About eleven we reached the village of *Estreito*, where we dined with the curate, who gave us a very friendly reception. After dinner we resumed our route on fresh horses, and in the evening, about six, we arrived at the house of a captain of auxiliary cavalry, about eleven leagues' distant from the place whence we set out.

We were elegantly entertained, but sat down to supper by ourselves, the whole family being
nder

under the deepeft afflietion for the lofs of a near
relation, who died a few days before.   This relation had come to a tragical end while we were
preparing for our journey, having been found
murdered upon the fhore near St. Pedro.   It
was generally fuppofed that he had been detected in an intrigue, as he had been feveral times
obferved by his fervants to go out late in the
evening, difguifed and armed ; from the mark
about his neck it was evident that he had been
fuddenly caught by a * *lace*, no very unufual
mode of affaffination in that country, and having
been thus ftrangled was thrown into the water.

A little before we reached this place, where
we took up our firft night's quarters, the country begun to look more fertile, and cultivation
to appear.   This captain's houfe is one of thofe
appointed for the reception of the Governor, in
his journeys between *Port Allegro*, a town fituated about 60 leagues up the *Rio Grande*, where
he ufually refides, and Port *St. Pedro*, which he
only occafionally vifits. Our fupper was, as I have
before mentioned, very fumptuous, and might,
at leaft, have handfomely entertained forty perfons ; a vaft quantity of provifion went away
untafted, and after a fine defert, and plenty of
excellent wines, we retired to reft ; our beds

---

* The natives give the name of *lace* to the plaited leather thong with which they catch animals.

were

were fuitable to our fupper; I flept in that ap‐
propriated to the General, and Mr. Black in
that of his Adjutant. The whole of this feat
is extremely pleafant, and the gardens are laid
out with tafte; it belongs to Captain *Luiz da
Souza*, who, from his being the oldeft captain,
called it *Tropa Velba*, or the old troop.

After a hearty breakfaft we took leave of our
hofpitable entertainer, and proceeded on our
journey through a fine romantic country.
About eleven we reached a hut, where we could
have nothing to eat till they killed a fheep, upon
part of which we dined. In this hut the crew
of a fouth-feaman, wrecked upon the coaft fome
years ago, lived a confiderable time, and one of
them who embraced the Roman Catholic faith,
ftill remains a few leagues off. The General,
whofe humanity every ftranger is fure to expe‐
rience, not only ftood fponfor to him at the time
of his fecond baptifm, but fhewed him many
marks of favour, which, fo far as I could learn,
he very little deferved.

After a fhort repofe during the heat of the
day, when, in fact, travelling is almoft impof‐
fible, we again proceeded on our journey, and
that night were entertained at the houfe of a
Captain of dragoons, named *Joze Carneiro Ge‐
yaldes*. This gentleman's houfe is likewife one
of thofe where the General repofes in his pro‐

R   greffes,

greffes, and here again we were feafted in a
fumptuous manner. Our beds were extremely
magnificent, and here, as the night before,
and I may add, fo long as we flept at his
Excellency's houfes of reft, I was compli-
mented with the General's own bed, and
Mr. Black with that of his Adjutant. Next
morning we were furnifhed with provifions and
other neceffaries, and after breakfaft fet forward.

About our ufual hour we reached the village
of *Moiftardio*, where we dined with the vicar, a
man of good education and polite manners, who
gave us a very kind reception. This village is
remarkable for its fituation, being in the middle
of a fand, though furrounded by a very fine and
fertile country; it confifts of one large ftreet of
tolerably well-built houfes. After dinner we
continued our route to *Naftantia de Pavoz*, a royal
farm. Here, to the number of horfes we had
already collected, and were driving before us, we
added about a dozen; they are the property of
the crown, and are diftinguifhed by having one
ear cut.

The adjacent country, as far as can be feen, is
covered with infinite numbers of wild horfes,
fome few of which may indeed have been once
or twice mounted, and then again loft or turned
loofe, but by far the greateft part are in a ftate

of

of nature. The inhabitants keep a few, and but a few domeſtic ones, and when they want any for the King's ſervice, for which demands are frequently made, they catch the wild ones, and among the number thus collected, the traveller muſt ſelect thoſe he means to ride. As neither of my Britiſh companions nor my ſervant were expert horſemen, I always deſired that they ſhould have the tameſt horſes. Little Richards, on account of his youth, I mounted on the moſt tractable, Mr. Black claimed the next preference, and then my Brazilian ſervant ; as to myſelf, the dragoons, and the Indians, we took any that offered, if they only appeared to be able to perform their work.

Next day we reached the houſe of an auxiliary Captain, where we dined, and were entertained in a plain hoſpitable manner; after dinner we again proceeded, and I was eye-witneſs to a piece of Indian dexterity and addreſs, which I cannot forbear relating at full length, as it will more forcibly than any deſcription exemplify the manner in which they uſe their plaited thong, called in that country *lace*, and their *balls*.

Towards evening one of the horſes which we were driving before us, contrary to the common practice of thoſe animals, ſeemed determined to eſcape from his companions. After ſeveral

fruitleſs

fruitlefs attempts, he at length fucceeded in detaching himfelf, and gallopped away at a moft furious rate; one of the Indians purfued him, I accompanied him in the chace. After follow-ing him for at leaft an hour, over every obftacle, during which time the Indian made feveral vain attempts to noofe him in his *lace*, no refource was left, ·fince night was coming on and we were drawing near a wood, but the *balls*. Thefe. are never unneceffarily ufed, as the danger of laming the animal is confiderable; but the profpect of lofing the horfe in the thicket, and perhaps a little pique at the trouble occafioned by the unruly beaft, induced the Indian to apply to this laft expedient. He therefore took his balls, as before defcribed; holding the fmall one in his right hand, he followed the object of our purfuit, whirling them round his head till he faw his opportunity; when (at about forty yards diftance) he threw them with great force at the animal. The balls flew whirl-ing through the air, and completely entangled the hind legs of the horfe, fo that they were de-prived of all motion unlefs together. Thus hampered, the furious beaft dragged himfelf near a mile, until fatigue compelled him to ftop, when the Indian, with great dexterity, threw the lace over his head, and hawled it tight round his neck. Curious to know how he would un-

fix

fix the balls, which were twifted in a very extraordinary manner round the horfe's hind legs,
I offered no affiftance, but fuffered him to manage the bufinefs entirely by himfelf.

He begun by difmounting, and ftill keeping his *lace* tight, tied a knot with the end
of it round the fore legs of the horfe, by the
means of which he in a moment threw him
upon his fide; he then fet his foot on the
horfe's neck, but without flackening that part
of the lace which was round it, and crawled
down over his body, till he could reach the
hind legs, from which he difentangled the *balls*;
after this he flipped the knot which tied the
fore legs, and allowing him to rife, led him
away. We then rejoined our companions, and
reached the houfe of a farmer, who was alfo an
auxiliary Lieutenant, fituated in a moft romantic fpot; on one fide, the view is bounded by
mountains, and on the other, it opens to an ex-
tenfive profpect, where woods, lakes, and rivers
afford a moft charming relief to each other. The
country is very fertile, and the uncultivated
parts abound in game, and immenfe numbers of
wild horfes and cattle; oftriches are alfo very
plentiful here.

We were hofpitably received, and provided
with good accommodations of every fort, and
in the morning purfued our journey. About

R 3   noon

noon we arrived at a very poor farm, where we could procure no refreshment, except a little milk : we therefore had recourse to the provisions we had brought with us, and in the evening found ourselves at a farm not much better than that we had lately left ; here we passed the night.

Next morning, about ten, we came to a river, which we forded, and about noon came to some fishermen's huts on the banks of the river, near its mouth ; we were again compelled to dine on our own provisions, and then forded the river a second time. About five we arrived at a cluster of ruined huts, occupied by a few negroes, and a new unfinished house at a small distance. Here we found nothing but some beef, milk, and eggs, and the negroes huts were so ruinous and filthy, that it was impossible to enter them without disguft; the new house was shut up, the windows were barred on the inside, one door was bolted within, the other locked, and the owner, who was gone to another estate he occupied at a confiderable distance, had the key with him. Notwithstanding I had often lain in the fields, I did not feel myself at all disposed to do so when a good house presented itself, but the difficulty was how to get in. We could not force the windows without doing injury, on account of the strength of the bars ; but an open-

ing

ing of confiderable fize over each door, though too fmall to creep through, gave us a view of the interior of the houfe. By looking through the hole over the door which was locked, I could perceive where the bolt on the infide of the other was; one perfon was therefore held up by the reft of us, who, putting his arm and a long ftick through the aperture over the bolted door, with much difficulty, after a number of ineffectual efforts, withdrew the bolt.

We found the houfe totally unfurnifhed, but there was a fide of bacon and a cheefe, with which we made free to augment our fupper; we then made our beds of our horfe cloths and went to reft. In the morning, when ready to depart, we refolved to play a fly joke upon our landlord, and accordingly firft bolted the locked door, fo as to render his key ufelefs. We then all went out, except the boy Richards, who, having bolted the other door, built himfelf a little ftage, by the help of which he reached the hole over it. Through this we with difficulty dragged him, and then having pufhed down the ftage with a ftick, and bribed the negroes to fecrecy, we departed, leaving the owner to exercife his ingenuity in contriving how he might enter his own houfe.

The evening was almoft dark when we arrived here; but the beautiful view which opened upon us in the morning, made me quit this place with regret. The country round was astonishingly fertile, and abounded in all sorts of game; the house itself stood about half a mile from a noble and extensive lake, bordered by a margin of luxuriant grass; beyond this arose a grove of stately trees, which never lose their verdure, while the range of mountains, which runs along the coast, bounded the prospect, and harmonized in a most picturesque manner, with the pure azure of the sky. Having quitted this beautiful scenery, we proceeded on our march, and having refreshed ourselves at a farm, went on to *Torres*, a fort situated on an eminence by the sea on the frontiers of the province of *Rio Grande*.

About a league before we came to *Torres*, the road led us down to the sea coast, where we travelled along the sands, close to the water, for a considerable distance. Here we had a full view of the mountain on which the fort is built, and of another abreast of it, each of which presents a perpendicular front of rocks, of amazing height, to the sea; these with some small craggy islands very near the shore exhibit a majestic view, and form a striking contrast to the scenes of fertility we had just left. The fort, though it might be rendered impregnable, in its present state, hardly merits the name. Some batteries

are

are indeed begun, but none are finifhed; nor did I fee more than two guns mounted.

The dragoon, who had been our conductor on our march, was now fo fatigued that reft was indifpenfibly neceffary for him. His exertions had really been furprifing; for he had the charge of every thing, and had rode at leaft three miles where we had rode one; my fervant like-wife was totally worn out; I therefore confented to ftop twenty-four hours. To this I was the more readily induced as the fociety we met with was highly amiable; for the Lieutenant who commanded, had two charming daughters who fung delightfully, and played with much tafte on the harp and other inftruments.

The morning after our arrival I explored the mountain on which the fort ftands, as well as the adjacent one, each of which, efpecially the latter, is perpendicular towards the fea. The rock forms a cove, at the bottom of which is an inacceffible cave; into this, even in the moft moderate weather, the fea rolls with a moft tremendous noife, that may be heard many leagues, and fometimes, in ftrong eafterly gales, even rifes above its roof. From hence, as well as from the fort of *Torres*, we could dinftinctly fee thofe fmall rocky iflands, which I have before mentioned; from this place, they feemed alive on account of the great number of feals with

which

which they were covered. The Lieutenant shewed me several skins of such as he had killed, many of which were fully as large and coarse as a bull's hide.

This is the northernmost frontiers of the province of *Rio Grande*, and though but thinly inhabited, the Lieutenant assured me he could, whenever it might be required, collect five hundred men in twenty-four hours, all of them trained to arms. I must here remark that this gentleman was more than commonly intelligent, and very capable of shining in a much higher sphere than that in which he then moved.

The only commodities of this fertile and beautiful country are corn and hides; with the former, they supply the rest of *Brazil*, and the latter are exported to *Rio Janeiro*, and thence to Europe. The Brazilian cavalry might be made the best in the world, especially for that country; the horses are excellent, and will live where an European horse could not exist. The men are robust and hardy, and being accustomed from their infancy to the saddle, support fatigues on horseback in an astonishing manner. Every dragoon, besides the horse on which he rides, has from two to five spare ones, which accompany the regiment; he carries, besides the usual arms of a horseman, his *lace* and *balls*, and when he finds his horse tired, he turns him loose, and

catches

catches another, which he immediately mounts. Their elegance is very great; even the privates having their large fpurs and their fword hilts of maffive filver.

The inhabitants of the province of *Rio Grande* differ confiderably from thofe of the reft of Brazil, as well as from thofe of Portugal; they are active and induftrious; remarkably hofpitable to ftrangers, and exhibit ftrong marks of cheerfulnefs and good temper in every look.

We refted at Torres one day as had been agreed upon, and our guide finding himfelf capable of travelling we refumed our march. We fet out at day-light, and immediately on quitting Torres entered the *Captaniha* of *Santa Catherinha*. Our route lay along the fea fhore, and about noon we came to an hut where we could procure no provifions except milk and a little rum, fo that we were compelled to dine upon this and a little *farinha* which we carried with us.

As I may have occafion to mention the *farinha* again, it will not be, perhaps, wandering too far from my line to give fome account of this fingular production. The Portuguefe call it *farinha de pao*, or *flour of wood*, and prepare it from the root of a fhrubby plant, every where to be found in Brazil; the root is fucculent, and about an inch in diameter at largeft. When roafted it taftes very like a potatoe; but to pre-

pare

pare it as a fubftitute for bread, they employ a fort of mill, which carries a large circular grater; this machine reduces the *farinha* rather to little lumps than to the ftate of flour, and it is thus eaten by the country people, either alone, or mixed up with cold water into a fort of pafte. When the Portuguefe fhips of war are on the Brazil ftation, it is ferved out to the people under the name of *farinha de guerra*; they feem to like it much, and fometimes eat it baked with fugar or treacle, when it forms a fort of fweetmeat, far from difagreeable. *Farinha* and *bananas*, which are equally plentiful, form almoft the fole food of the negroes; and all the inhabitants, without diftinction, are fo accuftomed to it, that very little bread is made ufe of.

Having waited to refrefh ourfelves during the heat of the day, we proceeded on our route, and in the evening reached a river which it was necef-fary we fhould crofs, in order that we might procure quarters at a guard-houfe that has been built on the oppofite fide. It was fo dark that we could not be feen by the guard on the other fide, who are placed there to ferry paffengers acrofs in canoes, and the river was fo broad that we could not make ourfelves heard. Notwith-ftanding the rapidity of the ftream my fervant ftripped and fwam over; he found the foldiers,

who

who inftantly came for us.   Our horfes, to the number of about fifty, we fwam acrofs, and turned them to feed, during the night in a meadow near the banks; we ourfelves were compelled to fleep in a forry guard-houfe, occupied by about a dozen militia foldiers.   We could meet with no fort of provifions, except fome badly dried fifh, not even fo much as *farinha*; fortunately, however, in the bottom of a bag, in which we had carried fome provifions, we found a few handfuls, on which, and a little rum, we had brought from the hut where we had ftopped at noon, we made our fupper.   Our faddle cloaths were our beds for the night, during which a vaft quantity of rain fell ; the roof was totally inadequate to keeping us dry, and we were almoft as completely drenched as if we had remained in the open air.

Early in the morning we were vifited by a little old Frenchman who lived farther up the river; he had come into that country as a foldier, and had lived there twenty-fix years, during which time he had never heard his own language fpoken.   Through want of practice he had almoft forgotten it, nor yet could he explain himfelf in Portuguefe; in fhort, none but his own family could comprehend him.   Not being able to make himfelf underftood by words, he attempted to do it by figns and geftures;

tures; in thefe, by long habit, he had acquired a moft grotefque facility, and abfolutely fometimes, might have been miftaken for a great baboon.

At feven next morning our horfes were collected, and we prepared to continue our journey. We found ourfelves obliged to pafs another branch of the fame river, not lefs rapid than the former; the horfes were fent over by the dragoons and Indians; and we followed in a canoe.

Here we faw an extraordinary mode of fifhing, almoft incredible indeed, and what I fhould not perhaps have ventured to mention, had not Mr. Black, in his narrative, already publifhed it. The fifh, at the river's mouth, are fo very plentiful, that the fhoals feem to cover the furface of the water, and nothing more is done than to beat the waves with the paddles of the canoes. The fifh, thus alarmed, having no room to fave themfelves by fwimming, leap out of the water in fuch numbers, that thofe which accidentally fall into the canoe, are fufficient to load it in a few minutes.

When we had croffed this river, one of our horfes took in his head to leave his companions, and fet off as faft as he could; he was followed by many others, and we were in danger of lofing feveral more. The fame Indian, who

had

had fo nimbly purfued the former fugitive, whofe adventure I have already related, immediately gallopped after them, and I thinking he might be unable to manage them all, joined the chace. We followed them a long time over the hot burning fands, in many places almoft up to our horfes bellies; but at length we fucceeded in bringing them all back, and about noon refted at fome huts, where we procured a little rum, and dined upon fome fifh we had bought from the men we faw catching them at the mouth of the river.

After dinner, we refumed our journey, depending upon the information of our guides, that we might reach the town of *Laguna* that night, which they faid was only about five leagues off. We were, however, difappointed, and in the evening found that we were fome leagues from that town; we therefore went to the houfe of a prieft, who was not at home, but having got fome fowls from the flaves, who alfo killed a fheep to accommodate us, we ftaid there that night, and in the morning fet off for Laguna.

Here we met with the only mountains except thofe at Torres, which we wereo bliged to crofs. We paffed feveral hills of fand, of great magnitude, and at laft reached the top of a rocky precipice, where we found that our guides
had

had miffed the way.   We were unwilling to return the road we came, and therefore endeavoured to find fome place, where the defcent might
be practicable ; we found one, which we
thought tolerably fafe, and having difmounted,
drove our horfes down the defcent, following
them on foot.

As we approached Laguna, the country had
a very romantic, hilly, and wild appearance.
We had much difficulty in finding our way, we,
however, at length, after croffing an immenfe
meadow, reached the river, at the mouth of
which, on the north fide, the town of Laguna
lays.   The horfes we had been thus far fupplied with were to ftop here; we therefore dreffed ourfelves under a tree, while the canoe was
getting ready to carry us to the town.   Before
we reached the river which leads to the bar we
had a lake to pafs which is very broad, very ftill,
and very fhallow.   The river, on the contrary,
is very deep, and the current, in fome places,
extremely ftrong.   After a paffage of about an
hour and a half, we arrived in the harbour,
which we found full of fmall veffels, remarkably
well built, and much appearance of commerce
on every hand.   We were conducted immediately to the Commandant, by whom we were extremely well lodged, and entertained in a very
handfome manner.

Laguna

Laguna is a small town, but well built, the people dress well, and seem to live in great plenty; the country round it is uncommonly beautiful, and every-thing seems to conspire to render the place rich and flourishing.

At *Laguna* we dismissed our dragoons and Indians, by whom I wrote a letter of thanks to the Governor of *Rio Grande*, acknowledging all the favours we had received from him and his garrison. At the same time I assured him that our journey had, instead of abounding in hard-ships, been exceedingly pleasant and entertain-ing. Had I been able to foresee the inconve-niences we were to meet with the next day, I might not perhaps have wrote so gaily..

From *Laguna* we took fresh guides, who, as well as the former, were dragoons ; we also had fresh horses, and on the morning of Sunday, October 16th, we resumed our journey. About noon we arrived at *Villa Nova*, a village most beautifully situated on the side of a hill, where we rested during the heat of the day, and then again changing horses and guides, we rushed into scenes new to us. Our road lay through immense forests, where the path was so narrow as to preclude the possibility of two going abreast ;. in many places it was indeed almost too narrow for one; and Mr. Black was once li-terally jammed between two trees, so that it re-

quired

quired our united efforts to difengage him. In many parts the road was fo fteep that I, though vanity flatters me with being a fkilful horfeman, could with difficulty keep my feat; nor is this all, for the trees over-hang the way in fuch a manner, that during many hours we were forced to crouch down upon our horfes necks, and in that painful pofture we had to afcend and defcend precipices.

We marched to a fpecies of mufic every way adapted to the rugged fcenes around us ; the roaring of different favage beafts, and the hiffing of ferpents were heard every moment; but though we often judged from the horrid founds that they were very near us, we faw none. After a moft troublefome and fatiguing march we reached a whale fifhery, about eleven or twelve leagues from St. Catharine's, a little after funfet.

Here we were kindly received by the fuperintendant, apparently an intelligent man ; he inhabited an excellent houfe, the beft I had till then feen in the country, and fhewed us all the works and buildings belonging to the place. From the complaints he made againft the Britifh whale-fifhers, it fhould feem that in this place they fenfibly, and to their lofs, feel the effects of the induftry and activity of my countrymen.

By

By his advice we agreed to proceed from
hence to St. Catharine's in one of his whale-
boats, being quite difcouraged by his defcription of the road, which he reprefented as even
worfe than that we had paffed. We left the
fifhery early in the morning, and about two
o'clock reached the place of our deftination.

This paffage for beauty exceeds any thing I
have ever feen or heard of, laying between a
range of moft fertile mountains, diftant from
each other, in the narroweft places, about a
league. The whole coaft, on both fides, feems
an *orangerie;* on our paffage we were induced
to ftop at a farm-houfe, in a moft delightful
fituation, to refrefh ourfelves, and there the
people almoft loaded our boat with excellent
oranges.

CHAP. XXII.

*Arrival at St. Catharine's, honourably received
there.—The Portuguefe fleet from Rio de Janeiro
laying in the road of St. Catharine's, the author's
arrival is announced to the Admiral.—Superb ceremony at the Admiral's landing.—Character of
the troops there.—The curious manner in which*

the

the Indians ride.—The author meets with an old acquaintance.—Is most kindly treated by the Admiral.—He and Mr. Black go to dine with the Admiral, and visit the other Captains.—They pass their time in every pleasure.—They sail for Rio de Janeiro.—The author is treated with much distinction by the Admiral.—He presents his letters to the Adjutant-General and the Viceroy.—The perfidy of Ensign Minchin, who gets into disgrace for it.—Minchin and Prater make application to the Viceroy to be paid as in England, which is refused.—The author refuses to receive any money.—They prepare to depart, and the author is sent on board the Ulysses.—Mr. Murchison and Mr. Black embark on board two South-sea whalers. All, except the author, ordered on board.—Ensign Minchin's humorous embarkation.

ON our arrival at St. Catharine's we were conducted to the Governor, to whom I presented the letter of recommendation which the Governor-General of Rio Grande had given me: We were received with much politeness, and apartments in the palace assigned to us. I acquainted the Governor with my desire to continue my journey to *Rio de Janeiro* immediately by land, if it were possible, if not, to be allowed to embark in the first ship; he told me, that we were very fortunate, for that Admiral *Antonio Januario*

Januario de Valle, had arrived from *Rio de Ja-neiro*, only two days before, with a fquadron of four fhips of the line, three frigates and a brig. He added, that the Admiral with his fleet lay in the road, about four miles below the town, and that he had not yet been on fhore, but was expected the next day, and that, moft probably, he would furnifh us with a paffage to the port we wifhed to reach. The Governor the fame night fent his Aid-de-Camp on board the Admiral's fhip to acquaint him with our adventure and arrival at St. Catharine's.

The fecond day after our arrival the Admiral came on fhore with great ceremony. Not only the garrifon of the town and all the militia of the ifland, but a battalion of infantry then in that place, on its march for *Rio Grande*, were af-fembled, and formed in two lines from the pa-rade before the palace to the landing-pace, to re-ceive his Excellency.

The troops made a very fine figure, were well dreffed, and the cavalry particularly verified the opinion I had formed of them in Rio Grande. The militia uniform of that ifland, both for cavalry and infantry is light blue ; they are ftout, well made men, and the horfes are better than in *Rio Grande*. This is owing to their eating corn, which thofe of *Rio Grande*, ex-cept fuch as are tamed and accuftomed to it,

S 3

will

will not touch ; but the great number of them, which are every where to be found, renders a single horse of very little importance. The Indians, who are very dextrous in catching them, ride in a very singular manner; their saddle is coarse, and the girths are of hide ; their bridles exactly resemble those of the Moors, Turks, and Tartars, a circumstance which the more astonishes me that there is no connection between the countries, but their stirrups are widely different, and truly singular in their con-struction ; they consist of a piece of wood which forms a sort of semicircle, about an inch diame-ter, and there is a hole through each end of this to receive the stirrup leather. The Indian fixes his *great toe* in this curved piece of wood, which is just large enough to receive it, nor does he touch the stirrup with any other part of his foot; in fact, they ride (contrary to the practice of the Moors, &c.) with such long stirrups, that it requires the utmost extent of the leg, to reach them even with the toe.

The Admiral's departure from his ship was announced by the usual salute, and a signal gun was fired from every fort on the coast between the road where the ships lay and the town ; these forts, as he passed them, likewise fired a royal salute. This great ceremony was performed because his Excellency had come from Lisbon,

invested

invefted by the royal commiffion with extraordinary powers to infpect into the affairs of Brazil. He came on fhore in a very elegant barge,
accompanied by all the Captains and other fuperior officers of his fquadron, whofe boats followed his in order, according to their rank and
feniority.

As he approached the landing-place, Mr.
Black and myfelf accompanied the Governor
and Staff to receive him ; we were there prefented merely as matter of form, but no converfation took place at that time. From the landing-place the Admiral went in ftate to the
church, and having heard mafs, he entered into
converfation ; for it is the etiquette of Portugal
never to enter upon any bufinefs-till the cere-
monies of religion have been complied with.

Among the officers who attended his Excellency, was a French nobleman, who had known
me on the Continent with the army of the
Rhine, at a time when I was honoured with the
friendfhip and confidence of the diftinguifhed
perfonages whom I have already mentioned.
The Admiral having feen the letter of recommendation which I brought, and being himfelf
a man of amiable manners, fpoke to me in the
moft polite terms, begging that he might have
the pleafure of fupplying the lofs I had fuftained
by my feparation from fuch a friend as General

 da

da Veiga. He returned on board very late that evening, and on leaving us, invited us on board his ship the following day. One of the commanders of a line-of-battle ship also gave us an invitation to spend a day with him, and told the Admiral that he would send his barge for us; this gentleman was our countryman Captain Thompson, an officer whose praises need not my feeble pen to enumerate them.

Next day Captain Thompson's boat came for us, and we went immediately to the Admiral's ship; he received us with the greatest politeness, and having paid our respects to him, we made visits, in the course of the forenoon, to all the other Captains. We returned to dine with his Excellency, and when we took leave in the evening, he told us to look upon his ship as our home. While we remained there, he added, that for the voyage he would accommodate me, the boy, and my servant, on board his own ship, and that he would provide a passage for Mr. Black in another of his squadron. Captain Thompson, on learning this from us, solicited that Mr. Black might go with him, to which the Admiral gave his assent.

On board the Admiral's ship we had the pleasure to meet with a countryman, Phillip Hancorne, Esq. equally distinguished by the elegance of his manners, his talents, and his ap-

pearance;

pearance; he then held the honourable rank of Captain of the Fleet, or what they call *Major General da Esquadra*; and of this gentleman, to whom I stand infinitely indebted, I shall have to say much hereafter.

We returned to the palace of St. Catharine's, and during our stay there, which was about three weeks, we were treated with the most polite attention by the Governor and principal inhabitants of the island. Our amusements were various; the Governor, who was very fond of music and dancing, gave frequent balls, at which many of the officers of the Fleet attended; and the more to encourage the Admiral, who would not sleep out of his ship to come on shore, he left the town of St. Catharine's, and removed to a house at St. Antonio. This is a most pleasant situation, and much nearer to where the fleet lay at anchor than the town of St. Catharine's, where we continued to reside, paying frequent occasional visits to St. Antonio, and passing our time in a most pleasant manner. I here contracted an intimacy with Major Joaquim Correa da Serra, Chief of Engineers, a man of universal knowledge, whose professional talents intitle him to the most brilliant situation; such, indeed, are his various accomplishments, that I never think of him, without lamenting that he is not more usefully employed.

The

The ifland of St. Catharine's is remarkably fertile, and might, with a little pains, be made a moft productive fpot; but fo great is the lazinefs of the inhabitants, that little or nothing is done by them, even the cattle for the market being brought from Rio Grande.

On the 31ft of October 1797, while we were enjoying all the amufements of the place, our approaching departure was announced to me by Phillip Hancorne, Efq. in the following polite note:

"The Major-General of the Efquadra prefents "his compliments to Major Lifle, has the ho- "nour to inform him, that the * General would "wifh him to embark to-morrow, and that a "boat fhall be at the town of St. Antonio, "agreeable to the wifh of Major Lifle. Cap- "tain Thompfon begged of the General to fuf- "fer Mr. Black to embark in his fhip, which "he fuppofes Major Lifle to be acquainted "with.

"31ft October, 1797."

Addreffed "*Major Lifle, &c. &c.*"

On the 4th of November the fleet failed for *Rio de Janeiro*, where we arrived on the 18th. During our voyage I had a very neat and commodious cabin affigned to me, and lived at the

---

* In Portugal, the Commander, either by land or fea, is ftyled General.

Admiral's

Admiral's table; nor did I ever meet with a better seaman, a better commander, or a more accomplished gentleman. To him, in the course of conversation, I communicated my real situation, and found, to my great satisfaction, that he was disposed to judge for himself, as he was free from those narrow prejudices which haunt little minds; nor had the discovery I made to him any other effect than of making him, if possible, redouble his kindness to me.

Immediately after we had come to anchor, Brigadier General *Gaspar Joze*, Adjutant-General to the Viceroy, came on board from his Excellency, to compliment the Admiral on his arrival; having letters of recommendation to him, I likewise committed to his charge those I had to the Viceroy. The night we arrived some South-sea whalers came into the harbour, and Mr. Black, by the desire of Captain Thompson, went aboard one of them, to purchase some porter for him; on board this ship he met with some of our officers, all of whom had arrived before us, and who had gone to enquire after English news; by whom he was told, that, *somehow*, my real situation had come to the ears of the Viceroy. This he immediately communicated, with a very friendly solicitude, and seemed alarmed at it; when I told him not to fear, but to hold himself in readiness to go on shore at eight next morning.

morning. Not chufing, however, to involve himfelf in any difagreeable affair that might happen
to me, he avoided going under pretence of
ficknefs, and thus miffed the honour of being
prefented.

Next day I went, accompanied by an officer
of the fleet, to the palace, where the Viceroy
received me with much politenefs. I requefted
his permiffion to refide on fhore, with which he
readily complied, and informed me, that next
day he would give directions for a houfe to be
prepared for my accommodation. Having likewife a recommendation to the Bifhop, I paid
my refpects to him, and was received by that
excellent Prelate with every mark of kindnefs;
I then went with the officer, who came with me
from the fhip, to the houfe of the Interpreter,
where Minchin and his wife lodged. He
feemed almoft petrified with furprize at feeing
me, and told me, it was generally fuppofed,
from the length of time we had been on the
road, we had found fome fhip bound for Europe
at St. Catharine's, and had embarked in her.
He complained in the moft bitter terms of the
Viceroy, who had, he faid, refufed to fee him,
and had only allowed him and his wife each
12 vintins (about 17*d.*) a day, to fubfift upon;
that the fame fum was given to the foldiers,
women, and children; and that he had *heard*

that

that some one, Drummond and Murchifon, as he
fuppofed, had acquainted the *Viceroy* with every
thing relating to me. I at once faw fhame and
confufion in his face, and concluded very naturally that he had done what he attributed to
them; an action which he had fo much repro-
bated in his brother officer at *Rio Grande,* and
for which he dreaded the fame vengeance I had
there inflicted on the other delinquent. I however faid nothing, but immediately took my
leave, and a few fteps, from the door, met the
two gentlemen he had fo flandered. I at once
put the plain queftion to them, when both folemnly declared, that nothing concerning me
had been afked of them, nor had they uttered
one fyllable; but they had heard from the perfon who tranflated Minchin's letter, that *he* had
wrote to the Viceroy every thing that I could
fuppofe moft unpleafing.

Having obtained this information I repaired
immediately to the caftle, but the Viceroy having retired, I could not have an interview with
him; I therefore inquired for the Count Don
Luiz his fon, who was his Aid-de-Camp. To him
I acknowledged what my circumftances really
were; I likewife told him that the gentlemen
who accompanied me had, of *their own accord,* as
appeared from the reports previoufly figned by
them, concealed the difagreeable part of my
hiftory,

hiftory, and I could not therefore, at that time, fuffer them to circulate one word that fhould give me pain; I added, that from him, as a man of rank and an officer, I could not but expect liberality, and I therefore conjured him to tell me, with the franknefs of a foldier, if any thing had been faid, and by whom. With open candour, he at once acknowledged, that *the officer in the fcarlet uniform who came laft*, had fent a letter on the fubject to his father, but that it would do me no injury with him, as he had that very day faid, that the recommendations given me by General da Veiga and the Admiral, as well as my own appearance, gave me a claim to his protection, and that he would diftinguifh me from the reft. I affured the Count Don Luiz of my gratitude for the kindnefs of the Viceroy; then taking leave, and it being already late, I ftepped into the Admiral's barge, which was waiting for me, and went on board.

Next day I returned, and having found a retreat, I wrote to the Admiral, *Major-General de Efquadra*, and the Viceroy, acknowledging every thing, but telling them, that I trufted to their liberality, and expected they would treat me as a gentleman, whofe conduct, *when there was nothing but that to fpeak for him or againft him*, had acquired their friendfhip and efteem. The Viceroy affured me, that I fhould always be

well

well received by him, and fent me the key of a neat houfe, which I immediately occupied ; a few days after which I received the key of a *loge* in the theatre, from the fame generous fource of benevolence.

The Admiral, knowing how neceffary money was to a man in my fituation, and fufpecting I could not have much left, fent me a handfome fum by the *Major-General da Efquadra*, who, adding as much to it, delivered the whole to me. The Bifhop was in nothing behind the others; his houfe was open to me at all hours, and as it was fome diftance, he furnifhed me with a'carriage during my ftay at *Rio Janeiro*, that I might, to ufe his own words, with the greater facility come to him, when my engagements would permit.

Thofe diftinctions could not but be as peafingly flattering to me as they were mortifying to the two Enfigns, who were by this time fecluded from every fociety. Determined to give Minchin the chaftifement he fo well merited for his duplicity, I placed a centinel on his door to inform me if he fhould go out ; but the affair I had with his *brother officer*, Prater, at *Rio Grande,* effectually locked his door, and he did not, during his abode in that town, think proper to ftir from home. To avoid a fimilar difgrace, he complained to the Viceroy, demanding protection ;

tion ;

tion; to this demand, according to some accounts, he received no answer; but, according
to others, the Viceroy sent him a brace of good,
substantial, holster pistols,—a hint, one would
think, sufficient for a soldier. In the mean time,
the Admiral became acquainted with the transaction; and Captain Thompson, one morning,
came to me, desiring me to promise, that I
would not attack Minchin in that country. As
my situation was such, that it would neither have
been pleasing nor prudent to quarrel with the
exalted characters who had so nobly and gene-
rously protected me, I readily gave my word,
which satisfied *them;* but *Minchin* was not so
easily persuaded of his safety; he therefore kept
close to the house, equally despised by the officers of the fleet, of the army, and the inhabitants
of the town.

During our abode at *Rio de Janeiro,* Ensigns
Minchin and Prater made various applications
to the Viceroy, soliciting his Excellency to pay
them, for themselves and the soldiers, their full
pay, according to the British establishment, from
the day of their arrival in that country. The
Viceroy declined complying with this request,
alledging that he had no authority to grant it;
that the trifle he had ordered to be paid to
every individual, without distinction of age, sex,
or rank, was an act of hospitality, which he had

taken

taken on himfelf in confequence of the harmony which for fo long a time had fubfifted between our countries, and which never would be charged to the Britifh Government; but if thefe gentlemen thought they had a claim to further affiftance, they muft each of them addrefs a petition to the Sovereign, ftating their demand, and lodge it at the office of the Tribunal, which reprefents Majefty in that country, and of which his Excellency the Viceroy is Prefident, and they would determine whether the requeft fhould be refufed or granted; their petitions were accordingly prefented, Minchin figning himfelf Lieutenant and Adjutant, and demanding to be paid as fuch. Some days before the meeting of the Tribunal I received a vifit from the Secretary, who enquired why I had not already given in my petition; I told him, that having no claim of any kind on the Britifh government, I could not, like the others, petition; that his Excellency the Viceroy knew every thing concerning me, and that if he or the Tribunal, in the name of the Sovereign, thought it proper to prefent me with fuch a fum of money as would pay my paffage to Europe, I would accept it; but that the eighteen pence per day, which the officers of the New South Wales Corps, men, women, and children, had received, I neither yet had, or ever would touch; that the Viceroy having given me a good houfe, and the

T

generous

generous Admiral furnishing me, from time to time, with the means of supporting that house handsomely, I could dispense with further assistance, and the more so, that I was confident he (the Admiral) would also provide me with a passage in some ship of his fleet to Lisbon. The Secretary desired me to put that answer in writing; I did so, and in a few days it was intimated to all of us, that for the time we had been in the country, the Tribunal would allow nothing more than what the Viceroy had before ordered to be paid, and which I ever refused to take, lest it should be charged to the British Government. Mr. Black likewise declined receiving any allowance of this kind. It was further intimated, that the masters of the merchant ships of the convoy, in which we should be sent to Europe, would be paid for each officer, in advance for five months, at the rate of one cruzade, about half-a-crown per day; and for the soldiers, women, and children, half that sum. The hour of our departure drawing near, the Admiral was pleased to order a passage for me, the boy Richards before-mentioned, whom I had taken under my charge, and my servant, on board her most Faithful Majesty's frigate, the Ulysses, commanded by Captain *Joao da Costa de Cabedo*, one of the most active officers in Europe, and who already did me the honour to count me amongst the number of his friends.

This

This gallant officer refused positively to receive the money allowed by the Tribunal; but as it was a present made in the name of the Queen, and could not be returned, he ordered it to be paid to me.

During our abode at *Rio de Janeiro*, several British ships bound to the South Seas came into that port, when leave having been given to any one of us to embark in any ship in which we could obtain a passage, Mr. Murchison, the Mate, suspecting that the convoy would be delayed long in Brazil, and have a long passage when it did sail, went on board one of them; and about a month afterwards, when we were on the point of going to sea, the Purser entered on board another vessel, also bound to the South Seas. As I had with some trouble prevailed on the mutineers to give that gentleman the ship's charter, and every other paper which he thought could be useful to the widow of the unfortunate Captain, I endeavoured to persuade him to remain with us, because I thought his presence in England would be necessary; and to me it seemed impossible, that a ship bound to the South Seas could reach Europe before a convoy going immediately thither. A young man (James Macleod) who left Britain as a soldier in the New South Wales Corps, but with his discharge in his pocket, a problem which I cannot explain, and one of the *ladies* bound to New South Wales,

T 2

went

went on the fame expedition, fo that his Excellency, the Viceroy, had four lefs to provide for.

About the 24th of January laft, the fleet being
ready to fail, all thofe belonging to the Lady
Shore, myfelf excepted, were ordered to embark; boats belonging to the Cuftom-houfe were
provided for them, and an officer charged to conduct them to their refpective fhips.   The boats
were drawn up at the landing-place near the
Palace, and every one embarked, except Enfign
Minchin, who delayed it till the lateft moment.
I happened to be walking on the wharf at the
time, which he perceiving from the window of
the room where he had remained fhut up fo long,
and confcious that he merited chaftifement from
my hand, folicited from the Adjutant-General,
and obtained an efcort to conduct him to the
boat.   Accompanied by two fuzileers and a
non-commiffioned officer, he croffed the parade
amidft the burfts of laughter of all who beheld
this extraordinary proceffion.

CHAP. XXIII.

*Defcription of the town of Rio de Janeiro.—Mili-
tary eftablifhment there.—Uncommonly fine mulatto
regiment of militia.—Produce of the country.—Defcription*

ſcription of the port.—The author ſails from thence for Bahia de Todos os Santos.—Meets with an honourable reception from the Governor.—Writes to Enſign Minchin.—The effect of his letter.—Minchin requeſts to be left behind.—Reſcues Drummond from an attack made upon him by Prater and ſome of his companions.—Laughable adventure with a taylor.—Has a fracas with a Portugueſe gentleman.—Is attacked by aſſaſſins at night time.—Character of the inhabitants of Bahia de Todos os Santos.—Deſcription of the place.—The author prevails with the Admiral to allow Minchin to remain behind.—Singular theft on board one of the ſhips of war.—The fleet ſails for Europe, and arrives at Liſbon.

Before I take leave of *Rio de Janiero*, it is incumbent on me to ſay a few words concerning the place, and alſo of the Portugueſe fleet. The town is well built, buſy, conſiderably large, and ſurrounded by gentlemen's ſeats and gardens. The palace is large, commodious, and magnificently furniſhed; the ſtreets are remarkably well paved, but never lighted; the houſes are generally good, but have, for the moſt part, lattice windows; and there are a prodigious number of rich churches. The vaſt influx of trade renders ſome of the inhabitants

T 3

extremely

extremely opulent; and an air of plenty appears throughout the whole. The amusements are chiefly confined to the opera, for which they have a small theatre; but private societies are very engaging. The people are not, however, so hospitable as in some other places, particularly *Rio Grande*; but they are not morose, and treat their negroes remarkably well, many of whom at an early age are enabled to purchase their freedom.

The women here are by no means patterns of chastity; and those of the class of courtezans are remarkably extravagant in the prices they demand for their favours, twenty and even a hundred half joes being no uncommon present. Among the singularities of the place we may enumerate the frequent, or rather inceffant use of baths of tepid water. Whether this gives rife to any peculiar disease I leave to phyficians to determine, but two pretty extraordinary ones almost univerfally prevail here. Thefe are swellings of the legs, which fometimes arrive at vaft magnitude, and *hydroceles* of aftonifhing bulk; both are at times, but not conftantly, attended with violent pain, and the latter not unfrequently defcends below the knee.

The military eftablifhment of the town of *Rio de Janeiro* confifts of two fquadrons of very fine dragoons, which ferve as a guard to the

Viceroy,

Viceroy, two regiments of regulars, and a battalion of artillery, who, though far better in appearance than thofe in Portugal, are not to be compared to the militia. Thefe confift, befides whites, of a black and a mulatto regiment; and the laft, in appearance, exceeds any thing I have feen. At prefent, however, they are holiday foldiers, and almoft without difcipline; but a hard campaign or two would, in all probability, make them good troops. It muft be remarked, that the mulatto militia are all men of fome property, and drefs at their own expence; they wear light blue, with red facings, and gay fpangle filver lace; which gives them a remarkable fhowy look.

The reafon why the regiments of colour are fo much more fplendid than the whites is owing to this circumftance; the whites are a promifcuous affemblage of *all* the males, poor and rich, whereas the others confift only of fuch as are rich enough to have been able to purchafe their own freedom; befides, when once free, they, through fuperior induftry, acquire independance much quicker than the others.

The principal produce of the country is cotton, coffee, dyeing woods, fugar, hides, gold, and tobacco. With thefe they load a hundred and fifty, or two hundred fhips, which ufed to rendezvous yearly at *Bahia de Todos os Santos*,

T 4

and

and from thence continue their voyage to Portugal; but now they are divided into feparate fquadrons, one of which fails every three months. Befides thefe articles of commerce, there are a few diamonds; but not fo good as the oriental ones, from which chemifts affert they differ, in not being inflammable; chryftal is alfo produced here, of very great bulk and beauty; and furnifhes the optician with the very beft lenfes for fpectacles. There is likewife a fpecies of cotton, which, from its filky appearance, is called *filk cotton*; but its fcarcity excludes it from commerce; and, though it might certainly be raifed in any quantity, the lazinefs of the inhabitants proves an infuperable bar to its cultivation. Fruit is remarkably plentiful here, though not at *Rio Grande*; but, in return, horfes are fcarce whereas, as has already been feen, there they abound.

The port lies a confiderable diftance inland; the channel is ftrongly defended by iflands which are well fortified, and is in many places fo narrow that a cannon-fhot will reach acrofs; in fhort, if well defended, I deem it impoffible for an enemy to enter it.

The harbour is large enough to hold all the fhips in Europe; and in it, oppofite to the town, is a large ifland, called *Ilha de los Cobras*, which ferves for a ftate prifon; the fortifications upon it are

of

of confiderable ftrength, and might be made impregnable ; the paffage from hence to the town is allowed to one ferry-boat only, and it is befides guarded by foldiers.   No accefs is allowed to ftrangers, though fome of our enterprifing Englifhmen, with their ufual ingenuity, contrived to vifit it *according to law*.

I did not embark for fome days atfer the reft. As I had now loft my friend Black, our company was reduced to myfelf, the boy Richards, and my fervant. I the more lamented his departure fince, on account of his fkill in navagation, he was highly efteemed by all the Portuguefe Officers, particularly by Captain Thompfon and the *Chevalier de Drocourt*, Captain in that navy, a Commander of the order of Malta, and late Aid-de-Camp to the celebrated Count d'Eftaing. From what thefe gentlemen faid, I am convinced that he might have obtained very rapid promotion in the Portuguefe fervice, if his inclination had led him to ftay there.

I embarked on board her Majefty's fhip the Ulyffes, on the firft of February, and failed the fame day, with a fquardron of fhips of war, commanded by Rear Admiral *Francifco de Paula Leite*, and the convoy, though we did not arrive at *Bahia de Todos os Santos*, till the third of April.   Notwithftanding our tedious paffage, we reached our port eleven days be-

fore,

fore the convoy; this quicker difpatch was owing to our having met with the miffortune of running down one of the merchant fhips at fea, which we were obliged to efcort to the place of her deftination without delay.

From the day of my arrival the Govenor had given me a houfe, and a general invitation to his table; acts of politenefs which I had uniformly received during my journey. With the reft of the convoy, Enfign Minchin arrived, and as I now confidered myfelf abfolved from the promife I had made of not attacking him in *Rio de Janeiro*, I did every thing in my power to induce him to give me a meeting. Unwilling that he fhould difgrace the name of a Britifh officer, I imagined that the readieft way to induce him to think of his fituation was to paint its horrors out to him. I accordingly wrote him the following letter:

" Sir,

         " Flattering myfelf with a hope
" that the time you have had for reflection,
" and that the forlorn ftate into which the black
" ingratitude of your conduct to me has plun-
" ged you, will have convinced you of your
" error, I again folicit you to do away, in as
" much as you can, the injury which you at-
" tempted to do me at the very moment in
                                " which

" which I protected you from infult, and ren-
" dered you various fervices. Wearing, as you
" do, the uniform of a crown to which I am
" and ever fhall be devoted, I could wifh at
" leaft that you would fupport the reputation
" of a man.

" You cannot have forgot, while you lived
" with me in the habits of intimacy, while you
" courted my fociety and my advice, and while
" you entrenched yourfelf behind me from dan-
" ger, you dared fecretly to aim at my deftruc-
" tion, and to contradict papers which you had
" before figned. The gallant officer, (Philip
" Hancorne, Efq. Major-General of the Ef-
" quadra,) to whom you addreffed yourfelf, as
" well as the Commanding Admiral, to whom
" he reported the tale you baiely told, FOR
" THAT ACT held you in deteftation, and
" neither of them would fee you more; even
" the Viceroy of Brazil, equally unacquainted
" with yourfelf or me, fo perfectly defpifed the
" treafon you committed, that he loaded me
" with acts of kindnefs and diftinction, while
" he left you and Mrs. Minchin to lodge with
" the interpreter, and to eat at the fame table
" with a woman common to the whole race of
" man.

" Let me call to your recollection, Sir, that
" you are of a nation, (Ireland,) whofe fons

" are

" are diftinguifhed for courage; draw not on
" them a difgrace to which they will be very
" fenfible, and which will make them execrate
" all who bear your name: be gallant then for
" once, and give me the meeting to which I
" have fo juft a claim.   The more to induce
" you to comply with my requeft, I promife,
" by every thing facred, that if you give me
" a rendezvous, from that moment, on my
" part, all animofity fhall ceafe; but if you
" continue to refufe to fee me, and to fcreen
" yourfelf from my juft vengeance, by fhutting
" yourfelf up as you did at Rio de Janeiro, I
" will expofe you by every poffible means on
" your return to Europe.   If it is the fear of
" offending the laws of the country, or any
" other etiquette, that prevents you from ac-
" cepting the arrangement, ftill the bufinefs
" may be done, and the guilt, (if there is any,)
" attach to me alone; you have only to ap-
" pear publicly; I will attack wherever I fee
" you, were it even at the right hand of God!
" Surely you may defend yourfelf.

            " I am, Sir,

                " Your obedient humble fervant,

                        " J. G. S. Lisle."

" St. Salvador Lodiera de Mifericorde,
        9th April, 1798.

    " Enfign Minchin, on board the Invincible."

                                        The

The receipt of this epiftle, far from roufing him to vindicate his honour, only induced him to confine himfelf as clofely to his fhip, as he had done to his lodgings at *Rio de Janeiro*; nor did I ever fee him till we were on the point of failing. He then fent the Mafter of the veffel, in which he was, to our Rear-Admiral *Francifco de Paula Leite*, to folicit his leave to remain behind; his pretence being that he was fo afflicted with the fcurvy that his life would be endangered by purfuing his voyage.

During our ftay at *Bahia* I principally fpent my time with the military, or at the houfe of an eminent merchant named Lifboa, a gentleman whofe doors are open to every ftranger of decent appearance; and where there is at all times a large and good fociety. I likewife frequently faw the Count Barbafini, Governor of the province of *Minas*, fo called from the mines there, who, with his lady and family, had come in the Admiral's fhip from *Rio de Janeiro*. To this nobleman the Governor gave frequent *fetes*, to all which I had the honour of being invited; in fhort, the utmoft harmony fubfifted between them, for both were accomplifhed literary characters. With them I too affifted at a very grand ceremony performed annually here, upon a holiday whofe name I have forgotten. On that day the Governor, attended by all the

principal

principal nobility, vifits all the churches; when fuch was the profufion of riches I faw, that even in a country where gold and diamonds are the natural produce of the foil, I fhould hardly have thought fuch quantities could have been col- lected in one place, and for one purpofe, that of adorning the images in the churches.

Every where as I walked through the ftreets the ftrong and lufty appearance of the negroes forcibly ftruck me. I learnt that they came from a part of Africa different from thofe ufual- ly imported; and that their treatment far ex- ceeded even what they received at *Rio de Ja- neiro*.

Mr. Drummond had taken his paffage in one of the merchant veffels of the convoy; and on his arrival I found that he was very indifferently fi- tuated both in point of accommodations and pro- vifions. I therefore, having obtained the Gover- nor's permiffion for him to remain on fhore, invited him to my houfe, and he refided with me during my ftay. Having a fpare apartment, I gave it to a foldier, whofe conduct had been more to my fatisfaction than any of his comrades, and whofe wife, a decent woman, and whofe infant child feemed almoft worn out with remaining fo long on board.

While we were here, Prater prevailed on fome perfon to advance him about twenty pounds.

Drummond

Drummond, hearing this, thought it the beſt time to recover a trifling debt the other owed him; he accordingly went to a billiard-room, where he was, with ſome maſters of merchant-men, to demand the money, and a ſquabble enſued. It was about ſunſet, and I was taking my evening's walk, when paſſing the door of the houſe, I heard a noiſe, and could eaſily diſtinguiſh the voices of Drummond and Prater. I looked in, and ſaw Prater, with a rabble of his companions, all beating Drummond with *queues* and other weapons, and endeavouring to drive him down ſtairs; while the maſter of the houſe, a little dwarfiſh fellow, attacked him with a ſword. I immediately aſſailed this burleſque imitation of man, and giving him a hearty kick in the belly, diſarmed him; I then attacked the other combatants, and without loſs of time, or diſtinction of perſons, cleared the place of them, and reſcued Mr. Drummond. The guard having been called upon by the inhabitants of the houſe, I told them to return, and to inform their Captain that I ſhould myſelf call upon him, and explain the buſineſs; I went in a little time, and was thanked for my pains.

Another laughable adventure befel me here; a taylor whom I had employed to do ſome work for me, had delayed ſo long, that I was apprehenſive leſt we might be called upon to embark

before

before he had done. I in vain fpoke to him; till at length I fent the boy Richards to bring the cloth, finifhed or not, which he did, without delay, to the great difpleafure of the taylor. Next morning early, before I was out of bed, the taylor came to defire I would let him finifh the things; and, as I fpoke to him rather fharply about his neglect, he took upon himfelf to give me a great deal of abufe. Enraged at being difturbed by fuch language from fuch a vifitant, I jumped out of bed, feized a cane, and made after the offender, who fled with great nimblenefs into the ftreet, whither, with nothing on but a pair of flippers, I purfued him. The chace was long ; for though he was never quite out of my reach, I was not able to get a blow at him ; at length he found fhelter, and I, for the firft time during the purfuit, recollected that I was naked. I need hardly add that my retreat was as fpeedy as I could make it.

These trifling adventures I fhould not have thought worth relating, were it not, as will hereafter be feen, that they led to ferious confequences, though I may chiefly attribute many unpleafant things to an affair which I yet know not how I could have avoided. It was as follows:

At a route given at a gentleman's houfe, where were prefent all the officers and inhabitants

tants of diſtinction, a converſation was introduced about the invaſion of England then
threatened by the French. A Colonel of infantry enquired of the *Chevalier de Drocourt* what
was his opinion of the probable ſuccefs of ſuch
a plan, ſuppoſing the attempt to be made; the
Chevalier replied, that the ſuperiority of the
Britiſh fleet would baffle any attempt of that
nature; beſides, ſhould any accident enable
them to land, they would find a very warm reception, for that, independent of the troops of
the line, there was an immenſe body of militia,
fencibles, and volunteers, which altogether
formed one of the fineſt armies in the world.
A gentleman who ſtood near us, and whom I
had never ſeen before, immediately ſaid, in Portuguefe, " The Engliſh troops are worth no-
" thing! nothing!!!"

Such a declaration in the preſence of a man
whom he knew to be a Briton, was, to ſay no
worſe of it, indecent, and ſuch as I could not
paſs without notice; but there being not only a
great number of ladies in the room, but the
Admiral under whom I ſailed, beſides ſome
other General Officers, I was obliged to ſuſpend
my vengeance for a few moments. Had I taken
the advice of ſome of my friends I had let the
affront paſs with impunity, as the gentleman
was the *protegè* of one of the Miniſters at Liſbon.

U

I very

I very foon, however, found an opportunity to give him all the mortification fuch infolence deferved; but, though my conduct on this occafion was generally applauded, fome of thofe higheft in rank felt themfelves difpleafed. They were hurt that I fhould dare to reduce a Portugueze gentleman to fuch a ftate of humility; and though the Rear-Admiral never noticed the bufinefs to me, I learnt that he was highly difpleafed. He even took the advantage of his privileged fituation, and behaved on another occafion with a rudenefs that fhould not long have gone without the chaftifement it merited, had not prudence prevented me. I however hinted to him that on our arrival in the Tagus, where we fhould once more be upon an equal footing, I would fpeak to him in a plain and effectual language.

The firft ferious inconvenience my imprudence brought upon me, was an attack with an intention to murder. The plan was not fo privately laid but that it came to the knowledge of Mr. Drummond and my fervant; by him it was communicated to me. At firft I treated it as a trifle; but one night Drummond having been followed by miftake for me, I looked upon it in another light. In this country the negroes are the affaffins, and in the execution of their hellifh bufinefs they ftrip themfelves naked,

they

they then furround their victim, and from fome of them he feldom fails to receive a mortal wound. The villains are fure to efcape, for fuch is their activity and the lubricity of their fkins from the oil with which they befmear themfelves, that it is next to impoffible to lay hold of them.

It happened one evening after the intimation had been given me of their defign, that I was going to vifit a lady, and that I might at leaft have one affiftant at hand, Mr. Drummond accompanied me. When I arrived at her door he left me, and I went in. In a moment the lady, with the utmoft earneftnefs, intreated me to be going, as her houfe was befet by affaffins, whom fhe fufpected were looking for me. I run to the balcony, hoping that Drummond might not be gone very far; I called to him, but in vain; I therefore immediately departed with my fword under my left arm, but not drawn. I walked for fafety in the middle of the ftreet, and was within a few yards of home when juft as I was entering the ftreet where I lived, called *The Ladeira de Mefericorde,* on a fudden I beheld fome negroes gathering round me. I put myfelf in a pofture of defence, and endeavoured to gain a wall, but before I could effect my purpofe, a negroe came behind and gave me a flight wound. Mr. Drummond,

who

who had not yet got home, hearing the noife, came to my affiftance, but I had already difperfed the affaffins. Fortunately my wound was fo flight as not even to confine me to my houfe, nor had my enemies the pleafure of knowing that I was hurt.

Here among other advantages I met with the Governor General of *Angola*, a man beloved wherever he is known; he was on his return from Africa to Lifbon, and had come to *Bahia de Todos os Santos*, that he might be under the protection of the convoy. This amiable General had in his fuite Dr. *Azeredo*, a native of *Rio de Janeiro*, who, with his brother, had fome few years before ftudied phyfic at Edinburgh; the firft two Brazilians who have ever been educated at a college in Scotland.

The inhabitants of *Bahia* are exceedingly hofpitable, remarkably gay, and paffionately addicted to gambling; they drefs with more tafte and richnefs than in any town I had feen; their linen is, as I have obferved of *Rio Grande*, peculiarly fine and white. They live in a moft fociable and pleafant manner, but whenever they meet, cards are introduced as a matter indifpenfable. Some very fumptuous dinners are given, and at every table the greateft variety of fweetmeats are ferved; this is the more eafily done, as there fugar is equally cheap and good,

and

and their fruits not lefs abundant than deli-
cious.

The town ftands on the declivity of a hill fo
fteep that the communication between the upper
and lower part is difficult. The lower part is
bufy, full of warehoufes and fhops; it is reck-
oned very unhealthy, and therefore the elegance
of the place is chiefly to be feen in the upper
part. There is a neat but fmall dock-yard,
where fhips of every fort are excellently well
built; in particular moft of the fhips employed
in the Brazil trade are built here or at *Rio de
Janeiro.* The view of the bay from the town is
beautiful, and at the back upon the height is
an indifferent fort, once taken by the Dutch,
and kept by them for fome fhort time. The
adjacent country is charmingly laid out in cultivation and gardens, among which a great
number of elegant country-feats arife, and give
an air of gaiety and population to the fcene.

Minchin, notwithftanding his *prudence,* one
day fell in my way, and had certainly no great
reafon to boaft of his good fortune; notwithftanding, when the Rear-Admiral refufed to
liften to his requeft of ftaying behind, he made
application to me. I took Dr. *Azeredo* to vifit
him, and though he declared that his cafe was
no way dangerous, I prevailed with the Admiral to grant him permiffion to ftay.

U 3.

The

The *Princeffa da Beira*, a line-of-battle fhip, commanded by Commodore *Diego da Piva*, and belonging to our fquadron, fprung a leak, when we were about to put to fea, this circumftance delayed us a confiderable time, for the leak being near her keel, every thing was obliged to be taken out, an event fortunate for the Court of Portugal and our Commodore. On moving a cheft of gold, of which there were three on board of immenfe value, it was difcovered to have been broke into, and on examining, fome inconfiderable part was miffing. Had it not been for the circumftance of the leak, this cheft, in all probability, would have arrived at Lifbon empty.

Some little time before our departure from *Bahia de Todos os Santos*, while I was confined to my houfe by indifpofition, a Portuguefe fhip from Bengal bound to Lifbon arrived in that harbour, on board of which came a paffenger, Mr. Stewart. The officers of the fleet who went on board that fhip as fhe came into port, mentioned my name to him, and that I was in town; they, as himfelf told me, fpoke fo handfomely of me that he felt a defire to fee me. He landed the fame day, and went to the houfe of an eminent merchant (Mr. Lifboa,) where I was particularly intimate; he enquired after me in that houfe, and every individual of the

family

family said so much in my favour, that his wish to see me encreased. It happened that while they were talking on my subject I sent a messenger there on some business, and Mr. Stewart being informed of it, directed my messenger to tell me, that if I was able to come out he would be glad that I would dine at Mr. Lisboa's; that it would give him pleasure to be of service to me, and he would furnish me with any money I might have occasion for. I sent a servant back to tell him, that I would certainly dine where he was, and that had I been dressed I would then have paid him a visit; upon this he came with my servant to me, and in person repeated the message he had before sent. As I was no more within the reach of the good Admiral Antonio Januario de Valle, and having, on account of my long and unexpected detention here occasion for a few guineas, I accepted from Mr. Stewart the loan of about twenty pounds. This money he lent me; and would have lent me as much more, merely from the reputation which my conduct, during the eight months which I had been in Brazil, had acquired me.

In the mean time a packet arrived from *Rio de Janeiro* on her way to Europe, and by her I wrote a detailed account of the mutiny on board the Lady Shore to his Grace of Portland, promising

mising

mifing to attend his commands at Lifbon. The letter was enclofed to his Excellency the Britifh Envoy at that place, to whom I propofed to furrender, and was by him forwarded to the Duke.

Mr. Stewart had been introduced by me to the Governor-General, from whom I now folicited a paffage for him and myfelf in the packet, which we both much wifhed for, to avoid the delays naturally incident to a convoy. But owing to fome vague reports brought from India by the fhip in which Mr. Stewart came, refpecting a probability of hoftilities between Britain and Portugal, our requeft was refufed. His Excellency having been much irritated by fome vexatious circumftances which had juft occurred, expreffed his difapprobation of my requeft in fomewhat violent terms; thefe I was rafh enough to refent in a manner that might have occafioned an irreparable breach with a lefs amiable character; but that excellent nobleman, whofe refentment never extended beyond the moment of heat, not only forgave me, but that very evening invited me to his box in the theatre.

After Mr. Stewart's apparently generous conduct, I naturally held him in fome eftimation, thinking that I alfo poffeffed his good opinion, but fome one, I know not who, having acquainted

quainted him with my difgrace in England, he fo conducted himfelf, that if we had not imme-diately failed he would have had fome caufe to repent his illiberality.

Such was the return he made for my having embroiled myfelf with my beft friend, the Go-vernor General! This was the man, my com-plaifance for whom tempted me to throw my-felf into a pofition of refiftance againft the re-prefentative, the kinfman of Majefty! and when anger, at the indignities offered me by this oriental mufhroom, extorted from me a letter the dictates of paffion! *this* was the man who could cooly fend it to the Intendant of Police in Portugal, from whom I afterwards received it among other papers.

If it may be allowed a man who has feen al-moft all the world, and been an attentive ob-ferver of what he has feen, to judge, Brazil is the richeft country in the world; for though fome may more abound in particular commo-dities, none produces in fuch plenty every thing neceffary for life. Of the articles ufually ex-ported I have already fpoken; but in my excur-fions into the country (and the Portuguefe al-low that no European ever faw fo much of it,) I found it vaftly richer than I expected. The beft and moft various kinds of timber abound here, and of thefe I carefully collected and pre-

ferved

ferved famples. Thofe ufed for furniture and ship-building are very hard and durable; and the opinion of the beft informed Portuguefe is, that without arrogating any fuperiority of valour and feamanfhip to their failors, no Britifh fhip could cope with one of theirs of equal force, owing to the fuperior ftrength of the timber; in this opinion I, however, do not coincide with them.

On or about the 1ft of June we failed from Brazil with a convoy of one hundred and fifteen fail, moft of them very large fhips; and after a tedious paffage, during which nothing material occurred, we reached the river Tagus on the 9th September, 1798. On entering the harbour, and before I difembarked, an opportunity offering, I difpatched a fecond letter to the Duke of Portland, recapitulating what I had before written, concerning the mutiny, and mentioning my intention of awaiting his Grace's commands at Lifbon.

CHAP. XXIV.

The author arrives at Lifbon, writes to the Minifters, and offers to furrender himfelf.—Is arrefted.—Applies to the Conful-General for Madeira, who can obtain no fatisfactory anfwer from the Intendant of Police

Police.—He learns at length that his confinement is owing to the quarrels in Brazil—Is suddenly removed at midnight to a house at Belem.—Is sent on board a ship.—Some account of the city of Lisbon, and of the manners of the Portuguese.—The Portuguese army miserably bad.—The author sails for Gibraltar.— Unable to reach that port, they make Tangier.— With a Lieutenant and some of the people of the Dorothea, the author gains Gibraltar.—The narrow escape of Captain Grey and his lady.

THE moment I arrived in the *Tagus*, I wrote to the British Minister at Lisbon, apprising him of my arrival, and that I was come with the intention of surrendering myself to him, begging him, at the same time, to appoint an hour when I might have the honour of waiting upon him. He returned me a polite answer, and pursuant to my request fixed an hour for my visit. He received me with much civility, and on my repeating my offer to surrender, declined taking charge of me; he told me, that he had received my dispatch, which he had forwarded, but had not yet been informed of any determination of his Court on my subject, and that this was an affair too delicate for him to interfere in without positive instructions.

I now

I now felt the ill effects of the broils I had imprudently engaged in before I left Brazil; though I could hardly have imagined that *gentlemen* would have taken vengeance in such a manner. When I parted from the British Envoy I went and presented my letters of recommendation to such of the Portuguese Ministers as they were addressed; I then went to a hotel, to which I had been recommended, intending to take up my residence there till the determination of the British Court should be known. I had been in Lisbon only a few days when I was desired to go to the dock-yard, where I was told that the Commissioner (a Rear-Admiral) wanted me. I attended as I was directed, and to my great surprise was told, that at the instance of the Minister of Marine and the British Envoy I was to be sent to the *Castello de St. Jorge*, where, however, I was to be treated in every respect as a gentleman.

This intelligence could not but excite my surprise; I had not long left Mr. Walpole, who seemed very differently disposed, and I was not less conscious of having done nothing that could merit such treatment from the Government of Portugal; I nevertheless obeyed the order, though I could not reconcile the idea that Mr. Walpole, after what he had said to me, should have demanded my arrestation. In this state

of

of uneafinefs and fufpenfe I addreffed myfelf to Charles Murray, Efq. Conful-General from his Britannic Majefty at the Madeiras, a man whofe reputation for benevolence, and whofe confequence in the world pointed him out to me as the moft likely perfon to obtain an account of the true caufe of my imprifonment.

In the mean time my fervant and little Richards learnt my fituation, when the former fled for fear; but the latter, though in a ftrange country, and under fifteen years of age, delivered himfelf up, and defired to fhare my confinement. He was accordingly fent to the *Caftello de St. Jorge,* but with a pofitive injunction to be kept apart from me, and orders were at the fame time given, that I fhould not be informed of his imprifonment. I, however, immediately became acquainted with it, and fent for the Governor, who, at my earneft requeft, allowed him the range of the caftle, on my promife to hold no communication with him.

A fufficiently plentiful table was found for me, and my lodgings were extremely good, but for above a week I could not obtain my baggage. At length my trunks were fent to me, and, to my great furprife, without having paffed any examination though they contained many papers, yet a few immaterial ones
which

which laid loofe in a bureau belonging to the hotel where I lodged were eagerly feized and tranfmitted to *Manique*, the Intendant-General of the Police. I applied to every one I could think of to learn what was the caufe of my imprifonment, and was told by all that it was at the requeft of Mr. Walpole and the *Minifter of the Marine* of Portugal; in a few days, however, I received from the humane Mr. Murray a letter in anfwer to that I have already mentioned to have fent him, of which the following is an extract:

LISBON, SEPTEMBER 18th, 1798.

"———— As it appeared to me that
" at prefent, you are hardly, nay unjuftly dealt
" by, being imprifoned here, without having
" committed any crime againft the laws of this
" country, and without even being told the
" reafon of your commitment, I refolved to
" comply with your requeft, I endeavoured to
" find out the caufe of that extraordinary pro-
" ceeding, for your information.
" To this purpofe I called firft on Mr. Wal-
" pole, his Majefty's Envoy at this court, and
" had I found that it was at his defire, I fhould
" have afked no further queftions; but his
" Secretary affured me, (for Mr. Walpole
" was

" was in the country,) that it was not; that
" you had been with Mr. Walpole foon after
" your arrival from Brazil, offering to deliver
" yourfelf up to him to be fent home to Eng-
" land, but that he, having no orders from
" home concerning you, had declined taking
" charge of you; all which the Envoy himfelf
" has fince confirmed to me.

" I next went to the Conful-General's office,
" and fpoke to the Secretary there; Mr. God-
" dard the Conful, being at prefent in England,
" who alfo affured me that nothing had ema-
" nated from that office tending to induce your
" imprifonment; judging therefore that it muft
" have proceeded from the Government of
" this country, and having fome bufinefs with
" his Excellency, *Don Rodrigo de Souza Coutinbo*,
" Secretary of State for the marine, and fo-
" reign dominions, in whofe department cog-
" nizance is taken of all tranfactions from the
" Brazils, I called upon him the next mor-
" ning, and took occafion to mention your fi-
" tuation to him. He affured me that her
" Majefty had given no order whatever con-
" cerning you; that no complaint had come
" from the Brazils to this government againft
" you, fo that he fuppofed your confinement
" muft proceed from fome infinuation of the
" Britifh Minifter; I affured him that was not
the

" the cafe; then, faid he, it muft be merely an
" official affair of the Intendant of the Police,
" in which the Government takes no part.
" Being acquainted with Mr. Manique, the
" Intendant, I fpoke to him on the fubject, but
" could get no fatisfactory anfwer as to the
" immediate caufe of your imprifonment. "

This letter at once opened my eyes, and as I
had been fent to the *Caftello* by the Commif-
fioner of the dock-yard, I entertained very
little doubt but that the whole had been a manœuvre of the *gallant* Rear-Admiral *Francifco
de Paula Leite*, to prevent me from calling him
to account for his conduct at *Bahia de Todos ôs
Santos*, which he perfectly well knew to be my
intention. Among others, I applied to Major
General *Gomez Frere d'Andrade*, a very diftinguifhed foldier, who had ferved in Ruffia with
much reputation, and is of one of the moft
noble families in Portugal; he reprefented my
cafe to the Intendant, and folicited my difcharge.

His Majefty's Envoy, Mr. Murray, Mr.
Crifpin, the Pro-Conful, alfo ufed their utmoft
exertions to afcertain the caufe of my arreft,
but they were not able to learn any thing pofitive: however, after much folicitation, the Intendant, afhamed I fuppofe of his conduct, confented that little Richards fhould be lodged in
the

the fame apartments which were allotted to me. About the fame time he likewife gave me up my papers, and among them, by miftake, as I imagine, the individual letter I had wrote to Mr. Stewart in *Bahia de Todos os Santos*.

At length, after much folicitation, he avowed that the caufe of my confinement was the violence of my behaviour in Brazil, and recapitulated, with great accuracy, the actions I have already related; he further declared, that it was to *prevent my doing mifchief* that he could not confent to my being at liberty; but that I fhould have no reafon to complain of my treatment, and whenever Mr. Walpole chofe to fend me away, that I fhould have immediate permiffion to depart.

During my imprifonment I had reprefented my cafe to the Duke of Portland, and defired of him that I might be claimed: I likewife fhould imagine that Mr. Walpole did the fame; but before an anfwer could be received, *Manique*, the Intendant of Police, prevented my receiving any benefit from the Court of London. Perceiving, as he might eafily do, that the number of my friends increafed, and that it was probable my cafe might be properly reprefented to his Royal Highnefs the Prince of Brazil, with the fupport of a very powerful intereft, he thought proper, without a moment's

X

notice,

notice, to remove me from the *Castello de St. Jorge.*

On the 5th of November, about twelve at night, as I was undressing, I was waited upon by two persons belonging to *Manique*'s office; they told me they were going to conduct me, at Mr. Walpole's request, on board a ship which was already down the river, and would sail with the morning's tide for a British port. I received this intimation with the greatest pleasure; I hurried on my cloths, and in a moment was ready to attend them. Two of the chaises of the country were at the door, my baggage was fixed; *Manique*'s secretary got into the carriage with me, one of his domestics into the chaise with Richards, and we set out. We were conducted to the lower end of *Belem*, about two leagues distant from the Castle, and arrived there about three in the morning; I was carried to the house of M.ʳ *Joaquim Jozé de Abreu,* Surveyor of the Customs, who received me with great civility. He told me at first, that in the course of an hour or two the fleet with which I was to sail would drop down the river; but after I had waited with him till day-light, he altered his tone, and told me that the fleet would not probably sail for a day or two; but rather than I should return, he would accommodate me for that time with apartments in his

house,

houfe, provided I would promife to take no advantage of his confidence, but remain quietly
in the rooms he fhould affign me. In reply I
affured him, that he had nothing to apprehend
from me, as no event could give me fo much
pleafure as leaving a country where a wretch
like *Manique* was an abfolute fovereign, and
fuffered to exercife his tyranny on any one who
had not the good fortune to pleafe him in all his
caprices; it was not, therefore, into fuch a
country, but out of it, that I might be expected
to fly.

I was immediately fhewn into a fuite of
apartments, fmall, but very handfome; thefe
were, for the prefent, to be my prifon, and I
was ferved in a ftyle of elegance which aftonifhed me. I defired leave to write his Britannic
Majefty's Envoy, in whofe poffeffion I had left
fome papers abfolutely neceffary; for the fame
reafon I defired likewife to write to Mr. Murray, his Majefty's Conful-General for Madeira,
of whofe kindnefs to me I have before made
mention. Paper, pens, and ink, being brought
to me, I wrote the letters, and committed them
to the care of my entertainer; he told me he
muft fend them to *Manique*, who, he made no
doubt, would forward them according to my
defire.

I had

'I had paffed about eight days under this gentleman's hofpitable roof, receiving every day
marks of politenefs and attention; which rendered my abode very pleafant, but without
hearing from Mr. Walpole or Mr. Murray:
That they had been fent to Manique; the perpetual good offices I was daily experiencing
left me no room to doubt; but the Intendant
I knew to be capable of any act of cruelty or
meannefs; I therefore concluded that he had
fuppreffed them, and that Mr. Walpole was as
unacquainted with my removal as he had been
with my arreft, to which they had proftituted
his name; nor was I without fufpicions that
they had now recurred to the fame impudent
project.

While thefe reflections occupied my mind I
was fuddenly informed that the fleet was drop-
ping down, and that I muft prepare to embark;
I needed very little preparation, and in a few
minutes was ready. My kind landlord gave
me a lift of the ftores he had laid in for me,
which were more than fufficient for a much
longer voyage than that I was about to take;
then putting a paffport into my hand, he informed me, that as there was no fhips going to
England for fome time, *Manique* had directed
him to put me on board one of the convoy going to Gibraltar. He affured me, as was the

fact,

fact, that the accommodation provided for me was extremely good ; that the paſſage was paid, and that the maſter of the ſhip was directed to put me on board any veſſel we might meet at ſea bound for the Britiſh Channel. This excellent man added, "As you have neither heard "from Mr. Walpole nor Mr. Murray during "the time you were at my houſe, it is poſſible "you may be unprovided with money ſufficient "for your preſent uſe, I will therefore advance "you any ſum I can afford." I took a few pounds, and gave him a line to Mr. Murray, who, with his uſual goodneſs, immediately repaid M. *De Abreu.*

I now went on board. The convoy was under ſail, and I never in my life felt more happineſs than at quitting a country where men may be deprived of liberty without being told why, without having committed any crime, and without being permitted to vindicate themſelves. My diſputes in Brazil came not within the cognizance of an Intendant of Police of Liſbon ; the government of that country adminiſters the juſtice of it, and to the Governor belonged the power of puniſhing me if I had merited puniſhment ; but that he had made no complaint is evident from the declaration of the Miniſter of the Marine and Tranſmarine Department to Mr. Murray, an extract of whoſe

X 3

letter

letter to me has been already given. As *Ma-nique* knew nothing of me, it should seem that some *weighty* arguments had been made use of to him by some of those *gentlemen* I had offended in Brazil, and who there made an attempt to assassinate me. Whether he who had the politeness to declare to my face that "the English "troops were good for nothing!" and had learnt that I did not suffer such insolence to pass with impunity, joined his mite of influence to injure me, he must determine.

The air and climate of Portugal are well known for their salubrity and pleasantness, the weather being seldom inconveniently hot in summer, nor is the winter ever so cold as to require the use of fires, so that hardly such a thing as a fire-place is seen. The inhabitants are so intolerably lazy, that it is no unusual matter to see a parcel of lusty fellows sitting on the ground picking the vermin off each other; and their superstition surpasses all imagination. The churches here are numerous and fine; in that of St. Antonio they shew a stone in which the holy man, as they believe, made the figure of the cross with his finger: the marks of the chizzel are not, however, so totally obliterated but that the imposture strikes the most superficial observer.

Portugal

Portugal formerly was famous for its enterprifing navigators, but of late their fpirit feems
nearly extinct. Literature never was at a high
pitch in this country; a few poets were formerly found here, among whom *Camoens* bears
the greateft reputation; but for works of wit
and humour we may in vain look among the literary archives of Portugal. This feems to be
principally owing to the bufy interference of
the church, which eternally is endeavouring to
fmell out herefy or impiety; and as few priefts
can take a jeft, a writer who dared to make the
world laugh, would ftand in an awkward predi-
cament. The fame confcioufnefs of importance
tempts them to intrude fpies into every private
family, a practice that has not a little contributed
to the referve and gloom that feems to pervade
every houfe. Their habitual lazinefs is alfo
another caufe of their jealoufy, for many of the
ancient nobility being extremely poor, were
out-done in point of appearance by the merchants, whofe origin nobody knew; they affected referve, and pretended to defpife thofe
whom they had not the energy to imitate. The
peafantry, too, are fuch fervile dependants on
the will of the lords, that their daughters, if
handfome, were almoft fure to fall victims to
the luft of the young nobility; and I fhould
fuppofe that thefe youthful debauchees, not

X 4

ftopping

ſtopping at theſe low intrigues, would ſoon in-
vade the females of ſuperior rank, which would
be a ſufficient caution to fathers and huſbands,
whoſe youth had been ſpent in ſimilar exploits,
to truſt more to locks and bolts than to male
continence and female chaſtity.

There are ſeveral theatres in Liſbon, one of
which is very fine, but no women are allowed
to perform on the ſtage; to ſupply their want
they employ the moſt delicate boys and young
men, who, at the diſtance of the boxes, are not
to be diſtinguiſhed from women. This cuſtom
may poſſibly have given riſe to an abominable
vice, which is ſhockingly frequent here.

There is a dock-yard which is ſaid to be very
good, but I never ſaw it, except when I was
weak enough to go there through the contri-
vance of *Manique*; but certainly the ſhips built
there are extremely handſome *while new*. When
they have been at ſea a few years they, however,
loſe their ſhape, and become what the ſailors
call *hogged*, that is, inſtead of forming a beautiful curve, loweſt in the middle and higher at
the ſtem and ſtern; the ends fall and the middle riſes, ſo as to reſemble, in ſome degree,
the back of a hog. This defect I have heard
attributed, with what juſtice I know not, to the
enormous weight of their guns; for though
their iron is ſo much better than ours, that,

from

from the hammer marks I have feen upon new guns, I have reafon to believe that they are hammered after they are caft, and they far furpafs in weight Britifh pieces of equal calibre; I think I do not exceed the truth when I eftimate the difference of weight at one fourth.

The Portuguefe failors are by all nations allowed to be expert in their occupation; thofe that I faw in the whole fquadron, and particularly aboard her moft Faithful Majefty's fhip the Ulyffes, were fine ftout young men, remarkably quiet and orderly. Their pay is good, and they are perfectly happy in their fituation, to which the greateft attention is paid by their officers, feveral of whom are every way qualified for fupporting their rank with mildnefs, firmnefs, judgment, and dignity. Far different is the condition of their land forces. The only regiments I faw that were at all fit for fervice were two of infantry; one was that which ftill bears the name of La Lippe, the celebrated Field-Marfhal and Captain-General of Portugal; the other was that of *Gomez Frere d'Andrade*, which is ftill better, and of its commander I may with propriety fay, that no fervice can boaft of a more able officer. The other regiments of infantry that I faw were miferable in every refpect, and only exceeded in point of wretchednefs by the cavalry, whofe appearance,

in

in fact, would rather require Hogarth's pencil than my pen to convey an adequate idea of them. The enormous long fwords of this grotefque cavalry add not a little to the general oddity of their look; fuch is the length of thefe monftrous weapons, that they cannot be drawn at one motion by men of fmall or even moderate ftature. The ftrait fword is certainly far preferable to the crooked one on every account. The crooked fword being only fit for cutting, deprives the wearer of his beft mode of affault, and is, to fay no worfe of it, a very ineffectual weapon. The ftrait blade, in order to give it all the advantage of which it is capable, ought to be fharp at the point as well as the edge, of fufficient ftrength, and *long*; ftill it muft be proportioned to the ftature of the man who is to wield it, and not like thofe of Portugal, fo long that the *Cavalier* can neither draw nor return it with eafe.

As we paffed the bar of Lifbon I perceived that we were under the convoy of his Majefty's fhip *Dorothea*, and I feized the opportunity which offered of addreffing a few lines to her Commander to acquaint him in what manner I had been placed in one of the fhips under his command. In fact, my arreft at Lifbon had become a common fubject of converfation there; and many very refpectable characters had be-

come

come friends, becaufe I had forced pride to re-
ftrain itfelf within the bounds of good manners ;
my letter to the Captain of the *Dorothea* was
therefore a kind of a marine gazette extraordinary. Our paffage was tedious, and the weather
unpleafant; our fhip fprung the head of her
main-maft, which difabled her from carrying
fail, and this occafioned us to fall far aftern of
the reft of the fleet. When we made the mouth
of the Gut of Gibraltar, we were unable to follow the convoy through, and confequently
fteered for Tangier Bay, which we reached in
the middle of the night. Soon after day-break,
I was aftonifhed to fee the *Dorothea*'s boat with
the Lieutenant and the Purfer come along-fide;
they informed us that when the frigate firft made
that land, they had gone on fhore to buy ftock ;
but the wind becoming more favourable, the
frigate and convoy proceeded up the Gut and
left them behind. They were in hopes that we
were in a condition to venture the paffage without convoy, as the wind was fair, and the weather too boifterous to fuffer either gun-boats or
the fmall privateers, which fwarm there, to attack us: but feeing our difabled ftate, and that
the Mafter durft not venture to fail without an
efcort, they returned to the town of Tangier,
and I accompanied them. I there found that
amiable and hofpitable character, Mr. Matra,

his

his Majesty's Conful-General for Morocco, and with him we fpent that day.

Lieutenant Down, being very apprehenfive that the Dorothea might fail from Gibraltar up the Mediterranean, determined, (for what will not Britifh feamen do?) to leave the ftock he had purchafed, and proceed next morning at day-break in his yawl for Gibraltar. I folicited his leave to accompany him, which he granted; but as we were preparing to depart, we perceived his Majefty's fhip *El Corfo*, with a French privateer, her prize, which had arrived duri g the night. I immediatly fuggefted to Lieutenant Down, that it might accommodate the Commander of *El Corfo*, and perfectly anfwer our purpofe, fhould we offer to take charge of the prize and carry her to Gibraltar. The Lieutenant approved my plan, and inftantly propofed it to the Commander of *El Corfo*, who was much pleafed to have the means of fending his prize into port without weakening his fhip, and readily complied with our requeft. She was therefore delivered over to Lieutenant Down, with only four men belonging to *El Corfo*. Thefe, with the Purfer, the nephew of the Vice-Conful, the boat's crew, and myfelf, made up the whole of his ftrength; we failed with a brifk wefterly breeze, and in a very few hours we reached the Rock, juft as

the

the Dorothea and her convoy got in. All the Spanish gun-boats had come out to attack them; the Dorothea had been vigouroufly affailed, and Captain Grey, who, with his Lady, came paffengers in that fhip from Lifbon, had nearly loft their lives.

The Dorothea came to an anchor within Europa Point, while the gun-boats kept a heavy and well-directed fire upon her. Captain and Mrs. Grey went into one of the barges to land, and juft as they pufhed off from the fhip, one of the top-mafts was fhot away and fell fo near the boat that it almoft funk her; they however reached the fhore in fafety, though compleatly drenched.

CHAP. XXV.

The author arrives fafe at Gibraltar.—Is arrefted on account of the difcovery of a confpiracy there.— Difcharged from confinement.—Extraordinary exertions of Earl St. Vincent.—The author arrives at Tangier, where he is moft kindly treated by the Conful-General.—Refolves to wait there for the Duke of Portland's orders.—Defcription of Tangier.—Manner of building houfes there.—The

gaiety

*gaiety occasioned by the presence of the Consuls.—
Mosques.—Gates of the town.—Abject state of the
Jews.—Character of the Moors.—Their funerals.
—Moorish troops.—Their arms.—Their horses.—
Their cavalry.—Remark on horses' bits.—Their
evolutions.—Surprised that any one could perform
their manœuvres on a plain saddle.—The Moorish
mode of shoeing horses.—The author procures a
horse to be shoed in the European fashion.—Barbarous manner of fastening horses in the stable.—
Manner of travelling in Barbary.*

WE brought *El Corso*'s prize safe into Gibraltar; and as Lieutenant Down went ashore
before we came to anchor, I sent a letter by
him to General O'Hara, Governor of that garrison. In this letter, which I had prepared at
Tangier, when I did not expect so soon to reach
Gibraltar, I had explained my situation to that
General; I had in fact given him a brief recital
of the most material events in which I had been
involved since I left England; and this I intended to have sent by the earliest opportunity.

I reached the Rock however in a very unlucky
moment; for just before our arrival a plot had
been discovered, which was said to have for its
object the burning of the arsenal: this occasioned a general alarm; and an order to apprehend all strangers and foreigners; the latter of
whom

whom were fent out of the garrifon, and fuch
as were able, were compelled to ferve on board
the fleet.   By this judicious manœuvre, the
gallant Earl St. Vincent converted the very
fcum of the earth into ufeful fubjects; proving
clearly, that, with a good commander, the
worft of materials will make excellent foldiers
or failors, provided difcipline and fubordination be duly kept up.   It is by no means my
intention to derogate from the bravery of our
Britifh feamen, whofe excellent conduct has at
all times been a pattern to the world; yet
thefe ruffians, fnatched from fhops, from ftalls,
and from futtling-houfes, were made their companions in glory; and proved themfelves worthy the honour of fighting by their fides.
What they might have done under an officer
of a lefs decided character than Earl St. Vincent is hard to fay; but they knew him to be
brave, and that to difobey was to die; to his
firmnefs alone, therefore, his country owes
thofe acts of valour performed by this motley
affemblage of outcafts.

I fhared the fate of other fufferers, and was
arrefted along with the nephew of the Britifh
Vice-Conful, and feveral others, who like us
were about to land.   As I had already fent my
letter to General O'Hara, I intended to have
waited patiently his anfwer, as in fact the ordinary

nary ceremony of obtaining permiffion to proceed to land, takes up, even in peaceable
times, fome hours; but the officers of the navy
whom I faw there, informed me that as I was
on board one of his Majefty's fhips, I was at
the difpofal of Earl St. Vincent, who muft do
with me as he fhould think fit. By them I was
told that it was believed that I belonged to the
privateer, as I fhould naturally fuppofe, from
the circumftance of my having been feen upon
her deck in an uniform which they did not
know; in fhort, I underftand my perfon was
recognized by fome one who knew me, but who
never dreamt of my being there as one of the
perfons employed in bringing the prize into
port, imagining, on the contrary, that I had
joined the enemies of my country.

This news, I was told, had been carried to
Earl St. Vincent, who, taking it to be true,
was very juftly enraged at my fuppofed treafon,
and ordered me immediately to be fent in arreft
on board his Majefty's fhip the Aurora. I was
carried thither with the nephew of the Vice-
Conful, who, as I before obferved, had been
arrefted in the general confufion; this circumftance afforded me fome confolation, for if a
man *known*, provided with every neceffary paffport, and bearing even letters of recommendation to the Governor, could be arrefted, it was

no

no way aftonifhing that I fhould be detained; I therefore maintained my tranquillity pretty well, and was, I muft own, not a little diverted at the difmay and confternation of my fellow-prifoner, who, being unpractifed in alarms, feemed fufficiently uneafy under this temporary reftraint.

. When I learnt that it was fuppofed by all, even by Lord St. Vincent, that I belonged to the privateer, I immediately took the proper fteps to clear myfelf from fuch a fufpicion. Early next morning, Captains Lord William Stewart and Newhoufe, of the royal navy, called upon me by the Admiral's command, to en-quire how I came there, and what my purpofe was; a very fhort explanation alone was necef-fary, and all reftraint was immediately taken off. Nothing then remained for me but to fo-licit to be fent to Tangier; this adventure, however, I hold to be fortunate, as it afforded me an opportunity of explaining myfelf to men fo juftly the object of public admiration as the Governor and Admiral.

The day following, Earl St. Vincent directed Captain Selby, of his Majefty's fhip Mondovi, to land me at Tangier. This direction was in-timated to me in the morning, at which time the fhip was laying with her main-maft out, and all her rigging down; I was ordered to em-

Y

bark

bark at eleven; and such was the difpatch ufed to prepare her for fea, that by one o'clock, not more than five hours from the iffuing of the orders, we were under way. This was, however, but a trifle, compared with the active exertions of Earl St. Vincent; for more than once, when a crippled prize has been brought in *one tide*, *the very next tide* fhe has been fent out completely refitted, armed, and manned, a cruizer in the Britifh fervice.

The attention paid by this great Admiral, and the fatigues he muft have neceffarily undergone, are aftonifhing; at the earlieft dawn of morning he was feen attending to the bufinefs of the dock-yard, where the fmalleft minutia did not efcape his eye; and in the evening, till the utmoft glimpfe of twilight was obfcured, he never quitted the work carrying on there, unlefs other parts of the fervice required his prefence. He did away the ceremonious formality of going on board and on fhore practifed by commanders of fhips of war; the fplendid barge, with its fmart crew, were no more feen; a boat of any fort that could be procured, with perhaps a couple of boys to work it, ferved not only the Captains but the Admiral himfelf; who found fufficient employ for every hand, without fuffering them to throw away their time in empty parade.

The

The manner of his watering and refitting the
fhips that for fo long a time blocked up Cadiz,
deferves notice. The fleet was at firft totally
fupplied with water brought by tranfports from
Lifbon; this was a tedious and expenfive bufinefs, but he found the way to diminifh it, by
fending the fhips of war to Gibraltar for a fupply. One fhip only at a time ufed to leave the
fleet, and proceed for the garrifon, where fhe
took in not her own complement of water alone,
but as much more as fhe could; the firft
fair wind was her fignal for failing, nor would
the Admiral admit any excufe for even a moment's delay. On her return, the inftant fhe
hove in fight of the fleet, the next in rotation
failed, and the fuperfluous water was forthwith
diftributed among thofe that moft wanted a fupply. The fame ftrictnefs and regularity was
obferved refpecting fhips that wanted repairs,
nor was every trifling deficiency allowed to be
an excufe for coming into port; when there,
no delay was admitted, the repairs were conducted with furprifing rapidity, and the fhips
quickly refumed their ftation.

This unufual alertnefs was extremely harraf-
ing to the officers, yet they all admired their
indefatigable chieftain, who, like the Great
Frederick of Pruffia, had the fingular fortune
to be beloved in proportion to the feverity of

Y 2

the

the duty he impofed. Neverthelefs, a thoufand attempts were made to evade fervices which they thought troublefome, and to elude the vigilance of the Admiral, and a thoufand droll adventures were the refult; but though they were fometimes fuccefsful, he was generally an over-match for them.

On my arrival at Tangier, Mr. Matra, the Conful-General, received me with his ufual benevolent kindnefs, and did every thing in his power to make me forget my diftreffing circumftances. My earneft wifh was to have reached Germany, but the journey was difficult, and my finances required that I fhould do fomething to avoid the preffure of want. *Morocco* did not promife any thing very advantageous, and was, befides, a country where a man, accuftomed to the elegance of fociety, could hardly think of an eftablifhment; but excepting *that*, no other country unlefs Spain, was within my reach; and to ferve in a country at war with my own, was to me infupportable. Neceffity, therefore, determined my choice; and notwithftanding the ample and honourable provifion which Spain would have afforded me, I preferred, without much hefitation, the forlorn hope which Barbary held out. I therefore candidly laid my whole hiftory before the Conful-General, and explained to him the neceffity under

which

which I lay of looking out for employment
somewhere. He, I may venture to say, in
common with every one who really knows my
case, thought me hardly dealt by, and with a
franknefs which I very gratefully remember,
humanely offered me his good offices.

I determined to write again to his Grace of
Portland, before I refolved to fix myfelf in any
fituation whatever, making another offer to
come forward, not only to clear up the honour
and propriety of my own conduct, but to fub-
ftantiate thofe charges of fcandalous negligence
and imbecile want of fortitude in others, which
occafioned the unfortunate lofs of the Lady
Shore. This I conceived to be no more than
my duty, fince his Majefty's Minifters had already heard from me in the fame ftyle, and it
was therefore my endeavour to place the mutiny,
and the caufe of its fuccefs, in the cleareft point
of view, in order that they might not only bring
the guilty to condign punifhment, but by pointing out where the error had been, enable others
to procced with more fafety in future.

In this letter I affured his Grace that I would
endeavour to exift where I was, without con-
tracting any obligation ; that, in hopes of receiving his commands, I would wait a reafonable time ; but if I heard nothing from his Majefty's Minifters, I muft, from dire neceffity,

                    accept

accept the firſt employment that offered, and could no more engage myſelf to anſwer their call.

The town of *Tangier* lays in a bay at the mouth of the Gut of *Gibraltar*, in lat 35° 43' N. long. 5° 18' W. about fourteen leagues W. S. W. from that garriſon. It is ſheltered on the north behind that ridge of hills called Cape *Spartel*, which forms the ſouthern ſide of the entrance into the Gut. The entrance of the bay is commanded by very high land on both ſides, and might, with no great labour, be made extremely ſtrong ; at preſent there are no works near it, except a few ſmall batteries, and thoſe only the ſide next the town. The bay is expoſed to different winds, which, beſides the badneſs of the anchorage, render it an unſafe harbour at all times.

The town does not lay at the bottom of the bay, but on the weſtern ſide of it ; it is not very conſiderable, and is ſurrounded by a high wall hardly muſket-proof. The ſtreets are all, except one, ſo narrow, that two people can hardly paſs each other; and ſo dirty, that no place I have ever ſeen, except Liſbon, can bear the leaſt compariſon with them ; the town is no where regularly paved ; but in ſome places a few ſtones are laid, as if dropped there by chance. The houſes are, for the moſt part, only one ſtory high,

high, with no windows towards the ſtreet, and
very few any where elſe; they are all flat roofed,
and, from the badneſs of the workmanſhip, the
roof is ſure to ſink in the middle, thereby forming a ſort of reſervoir for the rain-water, which
drops plentifully through, and renders the
apartments very damp and diſagreeable. Every
houſe, great or ſmall, encloſes a quadrangle,
where the gloomy maſter can ſit, ſtupified with
opium, ſmoaking his pipe, afraid leſt any ſtran-
ger, ſhould get a peep at his women, who, though
perhaps objects of jealouſy to their huſbands,
are certainly not objects of temptation to any
one who has ever beheld the blaze of Britiſh
beauty. The entrance into their houſes is by a
winding paſſage, which leads into the quadrangle, from whence are the entrances into all the
apartments, and I no where ſaw the door of one
room lead into another; theſe doors are large,
with two folding flaps, like thoſe of a coach
gateway, and in them is a little wicket, ſcarce
big enough for a man to paſs in a ſtooping poſ-
ture. The apartments are ſmall, and very narrow in proportion to their lengths, being like
partitioned ſpaces taken out of a gallery, and
have ſeldom any light but what they receive from
the wicket.

This town is, however, rendered very pleaſant, as it is the reſidence of all the Conſuls-

Y 4

General,

General, whofe gay mode of living forms a very ftriking contraft with that of their gloomy neighbours. Their houfes are built and furnifhed in the European tafte, and Mr. Matra's in particular, fo very neat and elegant, that I feemed to be in England whenever I entered it. The Confuls live in great fplendour, and inftead of practifing that œconomy which in that place they might readily do, they feem to vie with each other in fumptuous elegance at their dinners, balls, and concerts; this fociety is further improved by the addition of fome French families, who, on account of the war, have removed from Gibraltar to fettle here.

Some of the Confuls have country-feats and gardens in the vicinity of the town; the Britifh and the American Conful, Mr. Simpfon, have each of them a retreat of this kind, beautifully fituated, on the face of the mountain, which forms the entrance of the Gut. The gardens of both, but particularly Mr. Simpfon's, who principally refides there, are very well laid out, but the way to them is infamoufly bad. None but the horfes of that country would be able to afcend the mountains; the road requires almoft climbing, and the path (efpecially that which leads to Mr. Simpfon's,) is nothing but a channel, worn through the foil of the mountain down to the rock by the winter rains; it is fo

rough,

rough, fteep, and ftoney, that it is not lefs dangerous to defcend to the bottom than difficult
to afcend to the top.

In Tangier are feveral mofques, but of their
interior I can give no defcrip ion, it being forbidden to Chriftians to enter them ; and if any
one fhould accidentally ftray within their gates,
which are always open, he muft either inftantly
fubmit to circumcifion, and become a Mahometan, or his life muft pay the forfeit. Some
mofques have fmall courts before them, paved
with tiles of different colours, and in the middle is a fountain for the ablutions practifed according to the Mahometan ritual. In the interior parts of the country all Chriftians who
pafs muft take off their hats and fhoes, but this
being the feat of the Confuls, they are excufed
the filly ceremony ; the Jews are, however,
obliged to fubmit to it in the fulleft extent.

The gates of Tangier, and indeed of every
other town in Barbary, are fhut at fun-fet and
opened at fun-rife ; no intereft, no perfuafion,
can prevail upon them to keep thofe towards
the fea open after the time allotted, or to unbar
them a moment earlier.

The Jews are very numerous here, as
well as in every other part of Barbary ; by
them, and through their means, all the trade
of the country is carried on ; neverthelefs they

are

are treated in the moſt barbarous manner. They are the moſt abjeƈt of ſlaves; any Moor, even a child, will abuſe and ſtrike them whenever he thinks proper; complaint at beſt would avail nothing, but probably would draw down upon them new and aggravated inſults. Their houſes muſt at all times be open, and the Moors go in when they pleaſe. It could not be ſuppoſed that theſe viſits were of the moſt polite kind; but Britiſh urbanity can with difficulty form an idea of the brutalities praƈtiſed by thoſe ſavage intruders.

The induſtry of theſe oppreſſed Iſraelites is aſtoniſhing; patient, perſevering, and dexterous, they accumulate fortunes; and, amidſt all their ſufferings, they never ceaſe to have in view their ſole objeƈt, intereſt; yet they are for the moſt part fair traders, and contented with moderate profits. Such is their humiliating ſtate, that even the richeſt of them are glad to be ranked among the ſervants of any Chriſtian, whoſe official ſituation can afford them protection againſt the oppreſſions under which they groan.

They are allowed to have their ſynagogue; but whenever the Emperor wants money, he lays them under contribution, ſometimes by ſeizing their place of worſhip, under pretence that the ground it ſtands upon is wanted for his

ſervice,

fervice. The late Emperor, who hated the Jews, found another, and a very ingenious way of extorting money from them. The Jewifh women, from fome motives, probably of religion, wear no colour in their petticoats except green : and, as the fureft way of diftreffing them, this *enlightened Prince* iffued a prohibition againft that article of drefs. His edicts waited no formality ; the poor Jeweffes muft either ftrip, and the dealers lofe the fale of all the ftock they had, or make the beft terms they could. A fum of money was propofed and accepted ; the edict was repealed, and the petticoat again difplayed its verdant hue.

The Moors, from their education, and their want of intercourfe with ftrangers, are rude and uncouth in their manners ; of fociety they have no idea ; what little converfation they hold with each other is in the open air ; and I cannot think that their difcourfe will abound with wit or erudition. Brutally ignorant, they look upon the Jews and Chriftians with ineffable contempt ; fo far indeed do they carry their arrogance, that a Moor, rather than tell either to go out of his way, will ride, or drive his cattle over him. They have, however, fome idea of police, for guards are placed in the ftreets, and every perfon who walks out after fun-fet muft have a lantern carried before him. Whenever, likewife,

likewife, a Chriftian goes into the country to any diftance from the gates of the town, the Governor will not be anfwerable for any confequences, unlefs he takes a Moor with him, one of whom he will order to attend the traveller on application being made. I, however, difpenfed with this ceremony, and when the Governor fent to tell me that I fhould take a Moor foldier with me when I went any diftance, to prevent infult or ill treatment, I anfwered, that Britifh dragoons were accuftomed to guard others, and not to be guarded themfelves, and that I wore a fword, to which I could perfectly truft my own fafety.

The funerals of the Moors are conducted in a way fufficiently ftriking to a ftranger; they are followed by a numerous croud, finging in the country fafhion; the body is depofited in a fort of bier, and covered over, if a male, with a woollen cloth, called there *al baik*; and the whole machine completely rolled up in it, if a female.

The troops of this country, in their prefent ftate, are by no means fit to be oppofed to European forces of any defcription; they have no idea of difcipline, and their arms and drefs are extremely ill calculated for the purpofes of war. Their cavalry is the moft numerous and beft part of their forces; their horfes are excellent

and

and abundant every where, though for the road and for carriage of merchandize, the mule and the camel are moft ufed. The Moors are excellent horfemen, and their cavalry, with very little trouble, might be made the fineft in the world. The men in general are handfome, of a good fize, ftout, active, and can endure fatigue and hunger furprifingly well; their horfes too, have every quality defirable, fo that nothing is wanting but proper arms, harnaffing, and training. At prefent, they wear a fort of loofe pantaloon, no ftockings, a loofe robe, flippers, and fpurs with one prodigious long iron fpike, which ferves at once for neck and for rowel; fuch indeed is the drefs of the whole country. Their arms confift of a very long mufket, and a very bad fhort fword; their fad‑dle has a rifing behind, which reaches a confiderable height up the back, and another before, but the thigh is no way confined. The ftirrup is in the Tartar fafhion, as long and as broad as the foot, and the form of the faddle neceffarily obliges them to ride with very fhort ftirrups; for if they could not raife themfelves much above the feat of the faddle, it would be impof‑fible for them to feat themfelves in it.

The bridle is the fame as that ufed by the Tartars in general, and which I have already marked to have excited my aftonifhment, at

finding

finding among the inhabitants of Brazil. It is worthy of remark, that the horfes in Barbary, as well as Brazil, are remarkably tender mouthed, contrary to what my Englifh readers would expect; but thefe powerful bridles keep a horfe in awe, and the fmalleft touch makes him obey, fo that there needs not that conftant pulling which my countrymen are fo fond of. I am aware of the force of prejudice, and that I fhall be laughed at by many, when I affert, that a fnaffle bit and a tight rein are good for nothing but to fpoil a horfe; let, however, any one for a moment confider whether any animal can move fo brifkly when reftrained as when all its limbs have their free motion, and then let them fay, what will be the effect of the perpetual pulling and fawing of a fnaffle bit. Befides, the horfe by degrees gets accuftomed to this teafing but infignificant bit; a ftrong pull becomes neceffary to check him, and the rider, as is too often the cafe with Englifhmen, confiders his bridle as a kind of fupport to himfelf. In a word, wherever a powerful bit is ufed, I have obferved the horfes to be tender mouthed, and the reverfe in thofe where the fnaffle is employed. The only evolution they practife is to form in line of battle, then in fubdivifions to advance, with aftonifhing rapidity, fome diftance in front of the line; when they have made their career, in full

fpeed,

speed, they in an inftant throw their horfes on their haunches, and ftop as if nailed to the ground; they then fire, and return to the pofition they left, and this manœuvre they practife fo often, that their horfes are very foon ruined. They feemed to have no idea that an European could ride with dexterity, unlefs taught by them, and were much aftonifhed at feeing me, on a fmooth faddle, behind them in no feat of horfemanfhip. They fire with great exactnefs, but the fire of cavalry never can be made redoubable; to give, therefore, to a horfeman, more than one piftol, is, as I have elfewhere obferved, only to encumber him, and to take from his activity.

Their manner of fhoeing horfes is awkward in the extreme; inftead of forming the fhoe in the European manner, they make the two heels crofs each other, leaving an opening fomething like a loop before, They cut away the fore part of the hoof as much as they well can, but allow it to fpread on the fides, by which means the foot not only becomes unfhapely, but it occafions the horfe to cut. The fhoe is only fixed on with three or four nails on each fide of the loops, and the croffes behind are bent up and hammered into the heel.

On my arrival at Tangier, Mr. Matra had given me the privilege of ufing his horfes when
I pleafed;

I pleafed; I therefore took upon me to put at leaft one into decent trim. The fhoe was the firft point that I proceeded to reform; for which purpofe having myfelf made a proper model, I took it to a Moorifh blackfmith for his imitation. It is but juftice to thofe artifts to fay, that they are ingenious; for the man after a few trials, compleated a fet of very decent fhoes, which I then nailed on to fhew him the method of doing it. He feemed furprifed at my mode of trimming the hoof; however, he foon acquirer a competent knowledge, though I had much difficulty in prevailing upon him to fix the fhoes fufficiently forward. I fitted up an old faddle of Mr. Matra's, in the huzar ftyle, but the ftirrups were loft, nor could I get a pair in all Tangier; I had, therefore, recourfe to my ingenious fmith, who, by the help of a model, made a pair that would not have difgraced a Birmingham artift. My thus being my own blackfmith, fadler, and farrier, gave the Moors a ftrange idea of me, as they had hitherto imagined themfelves to be the only perfons in the world that were capable of managing a horfe.

Their ftables are likewife a fcene of abfurdity and cruelty; they do not faften their horfes by the head, but by the fore-legs, with ftraps, to a chain, which is ftretched the whole length of the manger, fo that the poor animals cannot

lay

lay down; if the horfe be unruly, he is alfo faftened by the hinder legs, and I have actually feen a mettlefome ftallion (for fuch are all the horfes here) not only faftened by the fore-legs in the ufual way, but with one hind-leg faften- ed, fo as to be capable only of moving forward, and the other capable only of moving backward. I have juft faid that the horfes are fo faftened that they cannot lay down, but this the Moors confider as no hardfhip; for they *endeavour* to prevent them from it, under the notion that *a horfe that lays down is fick.* Of their horfes, however, they are very fond, and none are per- mitted to be exported, except fuch as are pre- fents from the Emperor.

Travelling is very inconvenient in Barbary; every perfon muft have a pafs, and to make the road any way comfortable, an efcort is neceffary both for protection and to procure provifions; befides, there are only two fhort feafons, one in fpring, and one in autumn, when travelling is decently practicable; for in winter, the whole country is deluged with rain, and in fummer, the ground cracks in fuch a manner, that a horfe is in danger of breaking his legs by ftep- ping into the chinks.

CHAP. XXVI.

*Treatment of Christian slaves in Barbary.—The au-
thor receives notice of the demand of the British
Court for his surrender.—Complies with it, and
sails for Gibraltar.—His letter to the Governor,
and the answer.—Sails for Lisbon.—Politely received by the British officers there.—Writes to
the British Envoy and Mr. Murray, with their
answers.—Sails for Portsmouth.—His letter to
the Duke of Portland.—Sent for to town.*

I REMAINED some time at Tangier, enjoying
every amusement that place could afford; I vi-
sited the several Consuls, who, notwithstanding
any war, always live upon friendly terms, much
to the benefit of their several sovereigns, whose
affairs would be materially injured by any dis-
agreement, as the Moors would not fail to turn
it to their disadvantage. I likewise amused myself with excursions into the country, but these
the rain often rendered unpleasant; however, as
I wished to see all I could, I disregarded petty
inconveniences. One of my principal amusements was the improving of my friend and benefactor, Mr. Matra's horses; and to this I so
far devoted myself, that when (as will hereafter
be related,) Earl St. Vincent dispatched an

officer

officer for me, I was found in the act of shoeing one of them.

I had one day an opportunity of knowing the treatment of the European slaves from their own mouths. Walking on the beach with an officer of the navy, we saw some of these captives, one of whom addressed himself to me in German; he informed me that they were *Lubckers* and *Hamburghese*, and had been some time in slavery. Their treatment does not, however, seem at all bad; their allowance is about six-pence a day, at least equal to one shilling and six-pence here; they are not compelled to work, and some of them who had acknowledged themselves to be boat-builders, having been employed at their trade, received additional wages in consequence of the representation of the Consuls, who insisted that they should not work without being paid.

In the month of December a letter came from General O'Hara to Mr. Matra, acquainting him that I was ordered home in custody; and at the same time Captain Newhouse, of his Majesty's ship Peterell, was directed to receive me, *if I chose to go.* I readily consented to obey the order, but wrote to General O'Hara, that it would be impossible for me to comply with it so soon as twenty-four hours, which was all the time Captain Newhouse could allow me; if, how-

ever,

ever, any other ship came in a few days, or if the Petterell would look in on her return from the expedition on which she was going, I would not require her to come to anchor, as upon hoisting red at the main I would instantly repair on board.

On the 8th of January, 1799, fourteen days after, the Petterell hove in sight, and having made the signal previously agreed upon, I repaired on board ; a few hours conveyed us to Gibraltar, where I no sooner arrived than I sent the following letter to General O'Hara :

" SIR,

        " IN obedience to your Excellency's
" commands, and the directions of the benevo-
" lent Mr. Matra, whose singular bounties to me
" have given him the privilege of disposing of
" me as *he* pleases, I yesterday embarked on
" board his Majesty's ship Petterell, and now
" surrender myself to your Excellencies dispo-
" sition. From you, Sir, I am assured of liberal
" treatment, therefore I have only to solicit the
" honour of an early audience. Confident in
" the rectitude of my own conduct, and the
" justice of my country, I can entertain no ap-
" prehension; but did there even exist a possi-
" bility of converting any act of mine into a
                                    " crime;

" crime, long accuſtomed to adverſity, I have
" learnt to meet with firmneſs all man can do.
" I am,
" Moſt perfectly and reſpectfully,
" Sir,
" Your Excellency's
" Very devoted ſervant.
" J. G. S. LISLE."

" *Gibraltar Bay,*
" *On board his M. S. Petterell,*
" *8th Jan.* 1799."

The General, probably feeling himſelf a lit-
awkward at the proſpect of being drawn into
converſation upon an affair of ſome delicacy,
thought proper to decline complying with my
requeſt, and returned me the following anſwer:

" GIBRALTAR, the 9th JAN. 1799.
" SIR,
" IN conſequence of orders from Go-
"' vernment, through his Majeſty's Principal
" Secretary of State, you are to be ſent to
" England in cuſtody, and having no will of
" my own upon this occaſion, I cannot but de-
" cline an interview, which, without ſerving
" you, could only give pain to
" SIR,
" Your obedient ſervant,
" CHA. O'HARA."

" *To Major Liſle.*"

Notwith-

Notwithstanding this refusal I, however, received marks of polite and kind attention from that excellent General.

It was the province of Earl St. Vincent to dispose of me as he pleased; and as his Majesty's ship *Mondovi* hove in sight the day after my arrival, I intreated his Lordship, that as she would, in all probability, soon return to Lisbon, I might be permitted to go in her; I particularly asked this, as I had some knowledge of Captain Selby, who commanded her, and who had before taken me to Tangier. I was honoured by his Lordship's consent, and he gave immediate orders to the *Mondovi* to prepare for her return as soon as she had delivered her dispatches and received those from the Garrison.

Next morning Captain Grey, whom I have before mentioned, came to me, and acquainted me, that the *Mondovi* was on the point of sailing; I therefore immediately repaired on board; and after a short voyage, during which I was treated with the utmost kindness and attention, arrived at Lisbon.

At Lisbon I was sent on board the Brilliant, commanded by that excellent officer and accomplished gentleman, Captain Blackwood. Here I enjoyed every pleasure the place would admit; and it is but justice to the several British

tish

tifh Commanders then in the Tagus, to declare, that I never, in the moft aufpicious fituation of my life, was treated with more kindnefs and politenefs. As foon as I arrived at Lifbon, I wrote to the Britifh Envoy, Mr. Walpole, to whofe humanity I had been fo much indebted at my former vifit to this place. To this he returned the following anfwer:

LISBON, 18th JANUARY, 1799.

" SIR,

" I HAVE been favoured with your
" letter of yefterday's date, and I take this op-
" portunity of confirming to you the orders
" which I have received from his Majefty to
" fend you home in cuftody; and I have, in
" obedience to his Majefty's commands, de-
" fired Captain Selby to convey you on board
" his Majefty's fhip Brilliant, commanded by
" Captain Blackwood, and I am perfuaded that
" you will receive every attention poffible from
" Captain Blackwood.

" Under thefe circumftances you will per-
" ceive the impoffibility of my acquiefcing in
" your wifhes to come on fhore.
" I am, SIR,
" Your moft obedient,
" humble Servant,
" ROB. WALPOLE."

" *Major J. G. Semple Lifle.*"

Z 4

I like-

I likewife wrote to Mr. Murray, the Conful-General, who had fo kindly interfered for my liberation; and his anfwer, as explaining not only fome parts of Mr. Walpole's, but feveral other circumftances, much better than I am able, I fubjoin:

" SIR,

" I RECEIVED yefterday evening a let-
" letter from you without a date, and this
" morning, at 11 o'clock, one dated this
" morning. Before I fay any thing on your
" prefent fituation, let me acquaint you that
" I received a letter from you, from on board
" the veffel in which you left this river,
" after fhe was under weigh, fo could not
" anfwer it to you then. I afterwards re-
" ceived that you left with the Portuguefe gen-
" tleman at Belem, and paid him the two
" pieces you requefted of me; the other two
" which you mention to have been put into the
" hands of the Intendant of Police I have never
" feen, nor ever will; it is in vain to expect it.
" All your papers left in my hands, with the
" certificate you defired from me, I fent Mr.
" J. Fox, at Falmouth, to lie till called for,
" as you defired, and I know they have got to
" hand.

" I obferve what has paffed with you fince
" you left this. I went laft night to the rooms
" ex-

" expecting to meet Mr. Walpole; he did not
" come there; and I am fo much and fo in-
" difpenfibly employed at prefent, writing to
" Madeira and England, by veffels ready to fail,
" that it is impoffible for me to go to his houfe,
" which is at a diftance from mine; befides, it
" appears to me, that it could be of no fervice
" to you, not only becaufe his conference with
" Captain Selby muft have been over this morn-
" ing before I got your letter; but ftill more,
" becaufe, as he now acts under orders from
" home, he cannot give fcope to his own incli-
" nations towards indulgencies to you, if con-
" trary to thofe orders; and for that reafon I
" dare fay he will decline giving you a meet-
" ing. But there is ftill a further and more
" powerful reafon; after you went away, fome
" difagreeable circumftances took place be-
" tween him and the Intendant; on that ac-
" count an application to Court became necef-
" fary, which the Intendant refented fo much,
" and laid before her Majefty the contents of
" your, what he ftyled, petulent and infulting
" letter to him, after your return from on board
" the packet, that I am certain he would clap
" you again into confinement the moment you
" put your foot on fhore here; and from the
" nature of his office, he can do fo, in fpite of
" all Mr. Walpole's endeavour to prevent it.
" Nothing but the Queen turning the Intend-

" ant

" ant out of office could prevent it, and that
" you may believe is totally out of the queſtion.
" All that Mr. Walpole could do, would be to
" inſiſt on your being delivered up whenever
" he pointed out the veſſel in which he wanted
" to ſend you to England ; and even then the
" Intendant would have it in his power to ſend
" you on board a priſoner, and with what diſ-
" agreeable marks he might chuſe to call ne-
" ceſſary, on the ſcore of ſecurity for your not
" being one inſtant at liberty in this city : all
" this he can do, and I dare ſay, would not
" bate one diſagreeable item. As for me, I
" cannot ſpeak to the Intendant, having been
" implicated in the buſineſs between him and
" the Envoy, in ſo much, that we have had no
" communication ſince.

" From all this you will gather that it is my
" opinion that you have nothing for it but pa-
" tience, and to make the beſt of it you can ;
" and when you arrive in England, I doubt not
" your readineſs to ſurrender yourſelf to your
" country will have full weight, and be of that
" ſervice to you there, which it cannot poſſibly
" be here. I return you Governor O'Hara's
" letter.

" I am, Sir,

" Your obedient Servant,

(Signed)   " CHAS. MURRAY."

" *Liſbon, Jan.* 18, 1799."

Not-

Notwithstanding these friendly cautions, as there were no apprehensions entertained of my deserting, I frequently went on shore in the most perfect contempt of *Manique* and his authority.

About the 10th of February we sailed for England, and after a pleasant passage, arrived at Portsmouth on the 22d of the same month. Immediately on my arrival I announced myself to his Grace of Portland in the following letter:

"*On board his M. Ship* BRILLIANT, *22d Feb.* 1799.

" MY LORD,

" I had the honour to inform your
" Grace from Tangiers, that in consequence of
" the extraordinary events with which you are
" acquainted, I had found myself reduced to
" the necessity of looking for hospitality on the
" shores of Barbary, where I engaged myself to
" remain inactive, a time more than sufficient
" for your Grace to convey to me your com-
" mands, which I bound myself to obey. About
" six weeks after my arrival in that country it
" was intimated by General O'Hara to Mr.
" Matra, his Majesty's Consul-General, (whose
" bounties to me had given him a right to dif-
" pose of me as he pleased,) that the British
Envoy

" Envoy at the Court of Lisbon had received
" an order to send me home in custody, and
" that such an order had been communicated
" to his Excellency. Having furnished your
" Grace with every information, having surren-
" dered myself to the British Envoy at Portu-
" gal, according to the promise I made your
" Grace in my letter from Brazil, having so
" repeatedly solicited you to permit that I
" should come to London ; in short, after hav-
" ing done every thing honourable, and every
" thing that it is possible for a man, well dif-
" posed to do, I felt myself mortified to learn,
" that it had been found necessary to order,
" that I should be sent home in *custody*; ne-
" verthelefs, though, when such intelligence
" reached me, I was no longer in the power of
" the British Government, though I was in a
" position from whence neither force or inge-
" nuity could have taken me, I instantly pre-
" pared to obey the summons of the Crown.
" I wrote General O'Hara, assuring him that I
" would surrender myself in his garrison in the
" course of a fortnight ; and farther told his
" Excellency, that the better to enable me to
" accomplish that purpose, I had already soli-
" cited the Commander of his Majesty's ship
" Petterell, who was then leaving Tangiers,
" bound on an expedition of a few days to the
" South-

" Southward, to call for me on his return.
" Such a delay was the more neceſſary for me,
" that when I eſtabliſhed myſelf at Tangiers,
" ſuppoſing I ſhould find myſelf obliged to re-
" main there at leaſt for ſome months, I had
" contracted ſome ſmall obligations in fitting
" up a houſe, which I was not able immedi-
" ately to diſcharge. His Excellency removed
" theſe obſtacles ; his Majeſty's ſhip Petterell
" ſoon afterwards appeared in the bay, made
" the ſignal agreed on between her Commander
" and myſelf, and I embarked for Gibraltar,
" where I had the ſatisfaction to find that my
" conduct met the approbation of the Governor
" and Admiral. To the humanity and libe-
" rality of Earl St. Vincent, and thoſe invin-
" cible heroes by whom he is ſurrounded, I
" am indebted for an inexhauſtible fund of con-
" ſolation.

" Committed to the charge of Captain Black-
" wood, by his Majeſty's Envoy at Liſbon, I
" have at length reached this port ; and after
" having well weighed every act of mine ſince
" I left theſe ſhores ; after calling to my recol-
" lection that it muſt be known to your Grace
" that my conduct has been approved of by
" every reſpectable character in the ſervice
" of the Britiſh crown, in whoſe way dame
" Fortune has toſſed me. After its being eſta-
" bliſhed

" blifhed beyond all poffibility of doubt, that
" I have furrendered myfelf a volunteer to the
" order of Government, and fince that period
" I have in nothing felt myfelf in cuftody, I
" venture to pray, that I may be permitted to
" *prefent myfelf* wherever his Majefty may be
" pleafed to command; but fhould there, in
" your Grace's opinion, exift reafons to confti-
" tute me, for a time, a prifoner, confident in
" the rectitude of my own conduct, and the
" juftice of my country, I moft cheerfully fub-
" mit to fuch a decifion; but humbly intreat,
" that the place of my confinement may be
" where it was when I was lefs intitled to in-
" dulgence—the ftate fide of Newgate—This re-
" queft will, I hope, appear the more reafon-
" able to your Grace, that the accufer as I am
" of the mutineers, and others more guilty
" than they are, I fhould, were I to mingle with
" the crowd, be treated by them as it is ufual
" to treat a King's evidence, a character which,
" if to fhare in the guilt be a neceffary qualifi-
" cation, I cannot be fuppofed to exhibit.

" I have the honour to be,

" With the higheft refpect,

" My LORD DUKE, &c. &c. &c.

" J. G. S. LISLE."

I wrote

I wrote likewife to Earl Spencer, fending him the famples of wood I had collected at Brazil, of which, though I had loft fome few during my arreft at Lifbon, I had preferved the moft valuable.

During my ftay at Portfmouth, Enfign Prater, whofe officioufnefs I have before had occafion to mention, thought proper to publifh a detail of the mutiny on board the Lady Shore. In this curious production (which appeared in the *Star* of the 2d of April, 1799,) he fays, " On our " firft arrival at Port Saint Pedroes, Adjutant " Minchin, *of his own accord*, allowed James " George Semple Lifle, who was a convict on " board, to make out a Report to the Governor, " that he the faid Semple was a Major in the " Dutch Cavalry; and Adjutant Minchin fanc- " tioned it." To this I fhall only reply, that I made *no report* as has been already feen, and that it was not Minchin alone that figned it, but, as his Majefty's Minifters know, *every offi- cer* of the fhip and troops. He goes on, " the " officer in whofe houfe I was quartered, afked " me why the faid Major had not his uniform, " belt, breaft-plate, fafh, &c. as Adjutant M. " and myfelf? I not wifhing to deceive the " officer, informed him, that *he never had any*." If by the good-natured and perfpicuous reply Mr. Prater ftates himfelf to have given to

the

the officer he meant, that *I never had any* uniform, he was furely miftaken; and in fact I
never wore any other drefs during my ftay in
Brazil; if he alluded to the breaft-plate, (meaning, I fuppofe,) the *gorget*, he is perfectly correct, for, as an officer of dragoons, it was not a
part of my uniform; in fact, he wifhed to injure
me, and threw himfelf into the fituation of
Pope's dunce, who,

" *Means not, but blunders round about a meaning.*"

As to fwords, we were all alike, for
thanks to him and his Commander Minchin,
who prudently declined drawing upon the mutineers, they had been all taken away, as being
.what *fome* of us had no occafion for. He likewife infinuates, that Minchin and myfelf had
confpired againft him; whether I confpired or
bore him any malice, nay, whether I had not
been his friend and benefactor, let the following
elegant letter fhew: --

" BAHAI, MAY 2d, 1797.
" To
" Major J. G. S. Lifle
" SIR,
        " I return your Trowfers with many
" thanks. Should have returned before but
" the Taylor difappointed me in getting mine
" done until this day
                        " I defired

" I defired Welfh to get a Bundle contain-
" ing four Muflinet waifcoats & a Reg^{tle}. Coat.
" in your Poffeffion but he told me you had
" detaind them till I paid you what you paid
" the Surgeon at Rio de Janeiro; the fmall
" pittance I received. the other day was Bearly
" fufficient to pay for what Clothes &c. I was
" in want of; you Certainly cannot be igno-
" rant of my diftrefs in Refpect of thofe necef-
" fary article, & the dearnefs of this Country.
" now I have nothing to get a fmall fea ftock.
" for the reft of the Voyage; but you fhall be
" pay'd at Lifbon on our arrival at that port,
" & you will oblige me in giving the Articles
" to Welfh not that they worth your keeping
", as the waiftcoats too fmall for you and the
" Coat not worth your ufe;
" I am Sir

" Yours obediently

" W_M. PRATER

" Enfign N. S. Wales Corp's

" of Foot."

I only remark, that I knew nothing about
his cloaths, which it feems he had left in the
care of my fervant, and which I ordered to be
given him as foon as I knew of his demand;
he forgot to pay me the money he mentions,
either at Lifbon or any where elfe. The pan-
A a   taloons

taloons and fhirt I never meant to receive, as they were not lent but given; for feeing him come along the front of a regiment drawn up to receive the Governor of *Minas* as he landed at *Bahia*, with fafh, gorget, and uniform, in a dirty fhirt, and a pair of white pantaloons mended acrofs the fore-part with brown thread, I told him to difappear from where he then was, and to go to my fervant, who would fupply him with pantaloons and a fhirt.

As foon as his account of the mutiny appeared, I replied to his fcurrility in the fame paper of the 8th April. My anfwer I here fubjoin; and have only to add, that he had treated the great and dignified characters I mention, with an indecency not fit for a gentlemen even to repeat.

Extract of a Letter from the STAR.

April 8, 1799.

" It was my wifh to have avoided every pub-
" lic difcuffion on the fubject of the mutiny on
" board the Lady Shore, until a court of juftice
" had given their opinion. The trial is not
" delayed by any fault of mine. I left a ftate
" of happinefs in Barbary. I came forward the
" moment I was called upon by my country,
" and have been in perfect readinefs to meet in-
" veftigation

" veſtigation theſe ſix weeks ; nor have I ceaſed
" ſubmiſſively, to ſolicit that it may be brought
" on. But ſince Enſign Prater has publiſhed,
" through the channel of your paper, a ſtate-
" ment prejudicial to me, and ſince you cannot
" publiſh the relation of facts, to which I fur-
" niſh vouchers*, do me the favour to aſk that
" gentleman (who ſeems ſo well acquainted
" with the particulars of the mutiny,) who it
" was that, abſent from his cabin in the mo-
" ment of the mutiny, and miſſing for ſeveral
" hours after the affray was over, was found
" concealed in the fore-part of the ſhip, where
" the women convicts were confined? and, who
" ſought for ſhelter underneath the bed of the
" ſurgeon ?

" Mr. Prater, on the ſcore of Commodore
" Hancorne, is ſo far correct, that that truly
" reſpectable and amiable character did render
" me many ſervices in Brazil, and did refuſe to
" receive his viſits : it is true the Commodore

---

* " The *relation of facts* here referred to was refuſed inſer-
" tion, not from any doubt of its correctneſs; for in ſupport
" of it we were referred to gentlemen whoſe reputations are
" unſullied, viz. Mr. Black, the Purſer, Mr. Fyfe, the Sur-
" geon, Mr. Murchiſon, the Second Mate, and Mr. Lewes,
" the Steward ; but becauſe in the preſent ſtate of the buſi-
" neſs we thought ſome parts of it unſeaſonable, and there-
" fore likely to be deemed libellous.

" EDIT."

A a 2 had

" had once the honour of being a Lieutenant in
" the moft glorious navy under heaven; he is
" proud to fay fo, nor did he, at once, jump
" into the diftinguifhed fituation he now occu-
" pies with fo much reputation, he obtained it
" by length of fervice and by dint of merit!
" But Mr. Prater fhould have accufed the Com-
" manding Admiral of the fleet, Antonio Ja-
" nuario de Valle, and not Commodore Han-
" corne, of having fupplied my wants, and his
" Excellency the Vice-Roy, of having given
" me a handfome houfe, while he lodged Pra-
" ter, Drummond, the foldiers, women, &c.
" without diftinction, in an hofpital; thefe
" great men knew every thing unfavourable to
" me, but they had alfo the means of learning
" how I behaved in the moment of the mutiny:
" and how fome others. My difpute with Mr.
" Prater differs in fomething from his account
" of it: Reafons, more than fufficient, induced
" me (while at Rio Grande) to put my fword
" in my hand againft him, but he was refcued
" from the danger into which he had drawn
" himfelf, by the interference of Mr. Murchi-
" fon; who himfelf received what was meant
" for Prater.
                    " I am, SIR,
           " Your moft obedient Servant,
                         " J. G. S. LISLE."

" Portfmouth, April 5, 1759."

                                        During

During my stay at Portsmouth I received the same attention and politeness I had met with at Lisbon. As no doubts were entertained concerning my safety, I was permitted to amuse myself as I pleased; but as a life of indolence never suited my disposition, I again and again made application to his Majesty's Ministers to send for me to town. I could not indeed suppose that they would order me to be brought to England without some reason, and I naturally concluded, that they had for their object the investigation of the mutiny on board the Lady Shore; two months and upwards, however, elapsed before I was sent for.

At length, either in consequence of my applications, or from some other motive, Mr. Townshend was sent for me. He found me early in the morning on board the Brilliant; and after acquainting me with his mission, he left me, and returned to his inn, where I engaged to join him before eleven o'clock; this engagement I fulfilled, and we immediately set off to town. From him I received the most polite treatment; I was laid under no restraint whatever, and so far from being disarmed, I not only travelled with my side-arms, but Mr. Townshend, who knew my disposition, furnished me with a brace of pistols for our mutual

A a 3　　　　defence

defence on the road; in short, his humanity and politeness made me forget that I was a prisoner.

CHAP. XXVII.

The author arrives in town, is sent to Tothil-Fields Bridewell.—Character of that prison.—The author's exploits with bailiffs.—Conclusion.

At my arrival in town I was deposited in Tot-hil-Fields Bridewell, where I have ever since remained, to use the phraseology of the place, like a parcel left at an inn till called for. Here I have received the utmost politeness, and the most humane attention, from Mr. Fenwick, the Governor, and his family, who seem, in short, to be formed by nature for softening the rigours of captivity; such, too, is the force of example, that the same humanity pervades all his servants, and guilt, though nothing human can divest it of its horrors and remorse, feels them as its worst evils, without the aggravation of tortures, equally cruel, unnecessary, and impolitic.

Thus far has been, what we may call, the more serious part of my history; and many of

my

my readers will, perhaps, be much furprifed at
not finding it a counter-part to that of Jona-
than Wild; but, in truth, my life has rather
confifted of ferious, than of comic fcenes, and
my adventures, befide thofe already enume-
rated, are not, I hope, of a very criminal dye.
I have, it is true, had a thoufand hair-breadth
efcapes from bailiffs, and among the reft, one
or two laughable ones, which I fhall relate; but
as to the trafh fold by Kearfley as my hiftory, I
know nothing of it, farther, than that it is, with
the exception of a very few inftances, totally
falfe, and where true, fhamefully diftorted. For
inftance, I was by him accufed of having defrauded Lord Eardley, Lord Salifbury, and
Meffrs. Grimwood, Hudfon, and Barret, all of
whom lived in the fame ftreet; I fent to them
to know if they had any charge againft me, and
received from each a certificate, acknowledging, that I never had cheated them, and that
they had nothing to lay to my charge. I mean,
not, however, to deny that I have neglected
punctuality in my payments, and that when I
wanted money, I have, without thinking how
it would be paid, accepted the loan of a few
guineas from any friend; taylors have, likewife,
found me not fo ready to pay as to order; and
thus I became acquainted with bailiffs.

A a 4

One

One of my best manœuvres to avoid them was, before my person was known to them, to pretend business in all the different spunging-houses: I thus knew their faces, and by the help of a good look-out, for a long time avoided them. One day, however, near Charing-cross, I was met in a hackney-coach by two bailiffs, who had a writ against me; as soon as I perceived them, I ordered the coachman to drive as fast as he possibly could into the Horse Guards, promising to take all consequences upon myself, and to give him a guinea for his trouble. The descendant of Jehu exerted his utmost skill, but without being able to prevent one from attempting to seize the horses, while the other attempted to storm the door; a dexterous application of the whip, however, made the post the former had taken very uneasy, and I repelled, as well as I could, the attacks of the other invader. Both clung, however, to the sides of the coach, till we drove altogether into the Horse Guards; there I leaped out, and having explained the matter to the officer then on duty, made a bow to the bailiffs, and walked through the Park, while they returned by the gate they had entered, amidst the laughter of all who beheld the scene.

Another time, sitting at breakfast, I was attacked by three of them, and got off by the following
lowing

lowing ftratagem: I then lived in Oxendon-ftreet; and almoft oppofite to me lodged Lord (then the honourable Mr.) Semple, who bore a commiffion in the Guards; the fimilarity of names, as both were called Captain Semple, had occafioned many miftakes; but though our names were alike, our circumftances differed widely; for he owed nobody a farthing, and I owed every body who would give me credit. As foon as thefe vultures of the law entered the room, they, with the ufual etiquette, made me acquainted with the purport of their vifit, and concluded, by giving me a very preffing invi-tation to a houfe kept by one of them. As I wifhed to decline this honour, I affected much furprize, and told them they muft needs be miftaken, as I was in debt to nobody; they afked me if I was not Captain Semple? "Then, "gentlemen," faid I, "the whole is cleared "up, there is another Captain Semple lives in "this ftreet, I fee him now," pointing at his lodgings, "looking through the window; and "this is not the firft, nor hardly the twentieth "time, that I have been arrefted for him; in. "fhort, his attornies, his duns, and his bailiffs, "will force me to quit this ftreet." I then profeffed myfelf perfectly ready to go with them, if they infifted upon it; but that I was quite wearied with fuch inceffant vifits of that nature;

and

and muſt, for my own ſake, bring any illegal
act before a Court of Juſtice, that I might be
rid of ſuch plagues for the future. This puz-
zled the bailiffs, who, with ſome reluctance,
went down ſtairs, and, at the door, enquired of
the ſervant of the houſe, if there was *any other
Captain Semple* in that ſtreet; ſhe told him there
was, and opening the door, pointed out to them
the ſame houſe that I had done. This ſatisfied
them, and I profited by the diverſion thus made
in my favour to eſcape, leaving my honourable
nameſake to ſettle the affair with them as he
could. In a word, he was taken to a ſpunging-
houſe, in ſpite of all his remonſtrances, till the
agent of the regiment releaſed him; I have been
told, he afterwards attempted a proſecution
againſt the bailiff, but it appearing that no
wanton uſe had been made of the writ, and that
the miſtake was almoſt unavoidable, he obtained
no ſatisfaction.

Another time Colonel ———— had the miſ-
fortune to be arreſted, and two *good ſureties* being demanded, I undertook to procure them for
my old friend and companion. Two were accordingly found ; but, alas! notwithſtanding
they ſwore poſitively, they were not credited,
and we were forced to come again into court
next day; then, however, we ſucceeded, for
having procured *a new face*, I dreſſed one of the

former

former (a Jew, who fold flippers about the ftreets) in fuch a manner, that he was no longer recognized by the Court, and we came off triumphant.

This dexterity in avoiding the common courfe of law, however, eventually coft me dear; I was fo well known for out-witting bailiffs, that there was hardly one who would undertake to arreft me; and this it was, as I am well convinced, that induced Mr. Lycett to proceed againft me criminally. In confequence of this ambiguity thruft into the law, nobody knows how, men are intrapped; and, if carried to its extent, there may foon be no impoffibility in taking an infolvent merchant from the Royal Exchange, and fending him to New South Wales.

I now return to the fubject of my more ferious bufinefs; and here I muft beg my readers' patience till I lay before them a concife view of my viciffitudes. Born of an antient and noble race, but not poffeffed of riches equal to their rank, I naturally imbibed ideas of a too lofty kind; flattered in my youth by my rich and powerful friends, I formed to myfelf plans of future grandeur; plans, which my impetuofity of difpofition prevented me from realizing. With abundance of fire, and not a fingle atom of prudence, I launched into the world; my

friends

friends fupplied me with money even to profu‑
fion; and as I got it without trouble, I fpent it
without reluctance. Liberal as they were, my
extravagance outftripped their bounty, and I
was repeatedly involved in debt; ftill their
purfes were not fhut; they fatisfied my credi‑
tors, and, with fhame I relate, their generofity
only impelled me to new expences!

Accuftomed, from my earlieft infancy, to the
moft elevated fociety, my ideas imperceptibly
affimilated themfelves to theirs. I entertained
views of grandeur while yet a child; I felt my‑
felf born a foldier, and implicitly trufted to my
fword for opening to me the way to the Temple
of Glory. When little beyond the age of a
fchool-boy, I was diftinguifhed by the moft re‑
nowned generals; I had feen the immenfe ar‑
mies of Ruffia cloathed in an uniform of my own
contriving, and the celebrated Prince Potemkin
had, as is well known, honoured me with par‑
ticular marks of his approbation. Flattering,
as are the diftinctions I received, I will not re‑
late them all; but my reception by the *Prince
de Ligne* was in a ftyle of compliment too fingular
to be omitted.

Coming to Brabant, on my return from the
Black Sea, I had the honour of becoming ac‑
quainted with that great and moft amiable
Prince. To the utmoft politenefs, he fuper‑
added

added an invitation, in confequence of which I went to Antwerp, where his Highnefs then lay with a corps of army, as the Emperor, Jofeph II. then threatend to attack Holland. Such was the opinion of my military talents, which this veteran foldier entertained, that in compliment, he ordered his regiment, which was certainly one of the fineft in the world, to parade before the hotel where I lodged : not fatisfied with this, though he was an old Imperial General, and I was a very young Major, he placed me at his right-hand, and went with me along the front. The very inftant too that I was receiving this moft honourable and pleafing compliment, as if every thing meant to confpire to inflate my vanity, Earl Cholmondely, with another gentleman and a lady, arrived at the *Grande Laboureur*, the hotel where I was.

A conftant repetition of thofe praifes might have intoxicated a much cooler head than mine; my pride had now its full fcope ; I was already in idea a General in Chief; my brain teemed with improvements in tactics and evolutions, till my expences fo far out-grew my income, that I was involved in debt and difficulties.

Even when I was difgraced at home, I was admitted to the favour and familiarity of the firft generals upon the Continent : what their

opinion

opinion of me was, the following anecdote will shew. Just after I had joined the allied army in the Low Countries, a British General who knew me and my whole history, one day asked the Duke F. of Brunswick, how he, knowing my disgrace, and that I had just come from France, could put such confidence in me? " Were I a taylor, or a boot-maker," replied the Duke, " I certainly should be somewhat " cautious in giving him *credit*, but as a soldier, " I know that I might safely trust him with the " whole Prussian army."

Of my sufferings since I left the allies I need not say another word; my readers are fully acquainted with them, and I cannot submit to the whining tone of complaint. I have, I trust, amidst them all, acted in such a manner as to give my friends no reason to blush for me; my actions were such as I thought my duty required, though I cannot help thinking myself somewhat hardly treated, at being left for near six months in a prison, without even the smallest allowance for subsistence.

I have now performed what I promised, by giving my own history, such as it has really been; and the reader has, I hope, seen, amidst all my errors, something that may be commended, much that may be pardoned, and still more

that

that must be pitied.   That I meant to vindicate every part of my conduct could not be suppofed; but, alas! man is the creature of circumftances, and let him not prefume to expect, that no preffure is heavy enough to drive him to a wrong action.   Violent paffions, the almoft infeparable companions of a vigorous conftitution, call upon youth, with an importunity nearly unceafing; experience, the fureft guide, is inevitably wanting;   example invites, fplendour difplays its allurements, fafhion leads the way, and ruin too often follows.   Gay, honeft, unfufpecting, and generous, the young man rufhes on to pleafure, and confidering intereft as trafh, is apt to weigh the property of others as lightly as he does his own; amufements incur expence, and expence degenerates into prodigality.   To fupply thofe pleafures now become almoft neceffary to his exiftence; he contracts debts, which he cannot pay;   he fhifts from his creditors; his gay companions forfake him, as an incumbrance on their joyous moments; poverty ftares him in the face, and actions, at which his foul recoils, become the only poffible means of fubfifting.   If an accidental fupply falls in his way, his relifh for pleafure returns; he embraces it with an appetite fharpened by abftinence; he is again involved, and difgrace fucceeds to ruin.

Once.

Once difgraced, thofe *prudent* friends, whom the law alone reftrains from open plunder, abandon him; they do worfe, they fhut the door of fociety againft him by their calumnies; his faults are the theme of their converfation, and they fhelter their own want of honefty behind his lofs of fame; they hunt him down with unceafing clamour, till it needs more than common difcernment and common firmnefs even to dare to befriend him; his timid well-wifhers will not venture to give their countenance to him; and he is left to perifh!

Did it always happen that men of warm paffions, hurried away by pleafures, were villains; or did it always happen that the cold, the folemn, the plegmatic, were honeft; fome excufe might be found for fuch perfecutions. But as it happens on the contrary, that the man who is without vices is alfo, for the moft part, without virtues; and that prudence is very often nothing better than low felfifhnefs in difguife, little can be faid for fuch gratuitous feverity; befides, if one good action is not fufficient to conftitute the man of worth, why fhould one bad one be allowed to conftitute the villain? A ferious turn, the effect of experience, may reclaim the libertine, his unruly paffions may fubfide, and he may, if the gate of fociety be left open to him, fome time or other, re-enter it; but, if

hunted

hunted into villainy, by the clamours of hypocrify, the die is caft, and his perdition is inevitable.

Too often do talents and accomplifhments prove the ruin of the owner; he is befet by the envy of little minds, they endeavour to reduce him to their own level, by drawing him into debauches; they flatter him while in his prefence, but no fooner is he gone than they revile him: if his intimacy with them can give probability to their tales, they fabricate calumnies which pafs for truths; if he makes one falfe ftep, he falls unpitied, and they are the firft to trample upon him.

It is a trite obfervation, that men of talent are generally poor, and feldom rife to any high preferment; it is true! for if they depend folely on their merit, no fooner does that begin to difplay itfelf, than it is invefted on all fides by an army of blockheads, who, having no merit of their own, cannot bear it in others. But where a youth fets out with high fpirits, confpicuous talents, indulgent friends, and a fmall fortune, his ruin is next to inevitable; life is to him a perpetual ambufcade, with a thoufand mafked batteries ready to play upon him at every turn; his vanity is flattered, his fenfes amufed, his companions prefs him to become

B b

the

the partaker of their pleafures, his enemies endeavour to entice him to deftruction; he yields
himfelf up to gaiety and expence, till at length
he falls, and dunces rife on his ruin.

APPENDIX.

APPENDIX.

IT was not my intention to have added another word to the preceding sheets; but, on looking over Mr. Prater's account of the mutiny, I thought it a pity that such a *beau morceau* should be entrusted to the perishable archives of a newspaper. It is in fact an *unique*, and will, no doubt, recommend him to promotion, as it is plain that no such petty impediments as fogs or mists can obstruct the lyncean eye of one that (according to his own account) can see through an oak plank; besides, as he can describe affairs which he never saw, with all the precision of an eye-witness, his talents, at making official reports, must be truly wonderful. In order to do him justice, I cannot forbear giving his own words; and I doubt not that my readers will, with me, pronounce him

Tam Marti quam Mercurio.

Extract

Extract from the STAR, *of Ensign* PRATER'S
Narrative of the Mutiny on board the LADY
SHORE.

" On the 1ſt day of Auguſt, 1797, about
" four o'clock A. M. the French emigrants,
" and a number of deſerters (ſent on board the
" Lady Shore) bound to New Holland, aſ-
" ſiſted by the ſeamen,* revolted, and took poſ-
" ſeſſion of the ſhip, guns, ſmall arms, and the
" arm-cheſt. Mr. Lambert, Chief Mate, whoſe
" watch it was upon deck, having obſerved
" them for ſome time loading their muſkets at
" the main hatchway, without alarming the
" Captain or Officers commanding the troops,
" imprudently went into the cabin, loaded his
" piſtols, and diſcharging one of them, ſhot a
" Frenchman, named de la Hay; the muti-
" neers immediately ſhot Mr. Lambert dead
" on the ſpot. As Captain Wilcox, hearing
" a noiſe, was coming out of his cabin, he was
" ſtabbed in the right ſide of his neck, and in
" his left breaſt, which occaſioned him to fall
" down the companion ladder into the great ca-
" bin, which was our apartment. By this time the

* The ſeamen evidently lent no aſſiſtance in the time of the
mutiny, they afterwards were compelled to aſſiſt in working
the ſhip. (P. 206.)

                                    " revolters

" revolters had entire poſſeſſion of the ſhip, ſta-
" tioning ſentries at every hatchway, with their
" arms loaded, pointing two guns down the
" main hatchway, loaded with grape-ſhot and
" broken bottles; alſo two guns on the fore-
" caſtle, pointed aft, loaded in the like man-
" ner; laying on the gratings at every hatch-
" way, to ſtop any one from coming upon
" deck.

" About eight o'clock A. M.* the chiefs and
" ſeveral others came down below into the
" great cabin, and demanded our arms, which
" were given them; at the ſame time Adjutant
" Minchin gave orders to the ſerjeants to deli-
" ver up what arms and what ammunition they
" had amongſt them, and deſired them not to
" make any reſiſtance. Adjutant M. gave his
" word and honour that no reſiſtance ſhould be
" made on his part, or any of his people, againſt
" them. Serjeant Hughes informed Adjutant
" M. he had about twenty-eight ſtand of arms,
" and about thirty or forty rounds of ball car-
" tridges, which Adjutant M. ordered him to
" deliver up.

* Mr. Prater muſt either poſſeſs the faculty of ſeeing
through three bulk-heads of ſtout oak plank, or elſe he muſt
relate this from hearſay, as he was, at the time he mentions,
concealed among the women convicts. (P. 199.)

B b 3

" They

" They informed us, that in a few days they
" intended to give us the long-boat, and fend
" us away, which they performed on the 15th
" day, at eight o'clock P. M. diftance about
" 100 leagues off land, at the entrance of the
" river de la Plata, in the latitude of Cape St.
" Mary; fending in the long-boat twenty-nine
" perfons, men, women, and children, the
" youngeft child not five weeks old.   After
" meeting with very tempeftuous weather and
" heavy feas, in forty-eight hours we arrived at
" a Portuguefe fettlement, called Port Saint
" Pedroes, Rio Grande, where we were received
" by the Governor and inhabitants in a very
" humane manner.   On our firft arrival at Port
" Saint Pedroes, Adjutant Minchin, of his own
" accord,* allowed James George Semple Lifle,
" who was a convict on board, to make out a
" Report to the Governor, that he the faid
" Semple was a Major in the Dutch cavalry,
" and Adjutant M. fanctioned him in it.
" Some few days after, the officer, at whofe
" houfe I was quartered, afked me the reafon
" why the faid Major had not his uniform, belt,
" breaft-plate, fafh, &c. as well as Adjutant

* I have elfewhere remarked the grofs faifehood of this relation, for further fatisfaction, the reader may, however, refer to P. 215—217.

" M. and

" M. and felf? I, not wifhing to deceive the
" officer, informed him he never had any; and
" that he was nothing but a convict, and was
" fent out for feven years tranfportation.   The
" Governor was informed what I had re-
" ported, and acquainted Semple with it, who
" went to Minchin's quarters, and afked his
" advice what he fhould do in the bufinefs?
" Minchin advifed him to feek and run me
" through, and there would be nothing more
" faid about his character.   Minchin being
" very intimate with Semple, went next morn-
" ing, in company with him, to the Governor's,
" carrying a parcel of papers belonging to him,
" one of them faid to be a Dutch Commiffion
" in the cavalry *: and Minchin told the Go-
" vernor the faid Semple was a gentleman of
" rank and fortune, a paffenger on board the
" Lady Shore; and that he knew him to be an

---

* I am more afhamed, if poffible, of Prater's folly and
bafenefs, than of the trouble I give my readers in remarking
it.   There was, it feems, a paper which he could not read,
and this I called, what it really was, a Dutch Commiffion;
but furely his own ignorance was no fufficient reafon for his
affertion.   By the fame rule he might deny any other paper
to be authentic; he wifhed to vilify me in the eyes of all
mankind, and therefore finding his ftory difregarded by the
diftinguifhed perfonages of *Rio Grande*, he attempted to circulate it in England, where, to his difgrace, the falfehood of
his affertion is univerfally known.

B b 4" officer

" officer in Dutch cavalry, and what I had
" reported was an infamous lie; and he the said
" Minchin hoped the Governor would chaftife
" me. Minchin took Semple's advice in every
" thing,* and always kept him company.

" On the 23d September, 1797, we were
" embarked on board fmall craft for Rio de Ja-
" neiro. Semple, Mr. Black, and Michael
" Richards, a boy, made intereft to go by land
" to St. Catharine's. We arrived at Rio de
" Janeiro on the 23d of October, fome time
" after the above-mentioned people had reached
" that fettlement from St. Catharine's, on board
" the Portuguefe men of war. Semple was on
" board the Admiral's fhip, Signior Antoine
" Janeiro's; Mr. Black on board a 64 gun fhip,
" commanded by one Thompfon,† an Englifh-
" man. On board the Admiral's fhip was an-
" other Englifhman (named Philip Anvorn, a

* Neither Minchin nor Prater were MY *companions*, and had *either of them taken my advice* during the mutiny, I have little doubt of having faved the fhip; and had they taken it when they were in Brazil, they would have met with more refpect than they received.

† Since the time of *one Arnold*, I have not heard of even an enemy being treated with fuch indecency. But to the truth of the next obfervation I readily and heartily fubfcribe; Mr. Prater was *fincerely* forry that I was treated with refpect by the moft diftinguifhed officers in the Portuguefe fervice.

" Lieutenant

"Lieutenant in our fervice, but rank of Major
" General in the Portuguefe fervice) who, I
" am forry to fay, paid every attention to
" Semple, fupplying him with cafh, and in-
" troducing him to the firft company in Rio
" de Janeiro. Although I had applied to him
" in perfon for affiftance, and to ufe his intereft
" for us to be better treated than what we were,
" he, knowing our fituation, many days with-
" out fubfiftence, actually in a ftate of ftarva-
" tion, the allowance from the Viceroy being
" only twelve venteens, fterling about $13\frac{1}{2}$d.
" per day, for fifty days; and that was actually
" ftopped from all of us for four or five days,
" except Drummond, without our having a
" morfel of bread to eat.

" On the 23d of January, 1798, we were em-
" barked on board the different Brazil mer-
" chantmen, for St. Salvadore's and Lifbon,
" and arrived at St. Salvadore's the 5th of
" April; being very ill treated on board the
" merchantmen, having nothing to eat but
" ftinking falt beef, cafade root, and horfe
" beans. We reprefented our ill treatment to
" Francifco Paulo de Lait, Admiral, and com-
" manding our convoy, who took no notice of
" it. We ftaid at St. Salvadore's two months,
" receiving no fubfiftence either from the Go-
" vernor or Commodore. On board the fhip
" with

" with myfelf was Lieutenant Drummond. On
" our coming out of the Bay of All-Saints, we
" unfortunately carried away our rudder, and
" were obliged to return to refit, when, on ap-
" plying to the Governor for a paffage in the
" fecond convoy, he kindly ordered us on board
" the frigate Carlotta, the Commodore of the con-
" voy where we cannot fay, with truth, we were
" treated like gentlemen.   On our going into
" the Tagus, we got aground on the Bar of
" Lifbon, but in twenty-four hours we happily
" got off, by the affiftance of the Almighty,
" and not by the good management of the Por-
" tuguefe.*   Witnefs my hand this 1ft Septem-
" ber, 1798.

" W_M. PRATER, Enfign,
" N. S. W. Corps of Foot."

* Mr. Prater grows wondrous pious towards his conclufion;
and indeed if his piety there arofe from repentance for the
falfehoods that he had uttered, it might be, perhaps, a confolation to the godly part of his friends. Without, however,
the leaft intention of under-rating the mercies of God, or over-
rating the feamanfhip of the Portuguefe failors, had they not
been on board, the fhip had, I doubt, remained on the Bar
of Lifbon till this day.

" *Copy*

" *Copy of Lieutenant* GERARD DRUMMOND'S
Certificate.

" Enfign Prater having defired me to look
" into the above Report of the feizure, &c. of
" the fhip Lady Shore, on the 1ft day of Au-
" guft, 1797; I do hereby declare the above re-
" port to be true, as I was on board the fhip at
" the time, and have been with Mr. Prater
" fince leaving the fhip, in the long boat, to
" our arrival at this place.

(Signed) " GERARD DRUMMOND,
" Lieutenant Bombay Marines Hon.
" Eaft-India Company's Service."*

---

* This was a moft convenient certificate; it was, without
a date, tacked, like an epaulet on a military coat, to any thing
that required it, and fhifted as occafion offered. Mr. Drummond is in the Eaft Indies, or I might anfwer his certificate by
afking, who it was that hid himfelf under the furgeon's bed?

(COPIE.)

A Monfieur,

　　Monfieur le Baron D'OMPTEDA,

　　　　*Envoyé d'*HANOVRE,

　　　　　　a RATISBONNÉ.

" SOUFFREZ, Monfieur, que je vous
" demande raifon de votre conduite a mon
" egard.

" En 1º. A quel titre, et de quel droit avez
" vous en la témérité, de me faire arrêtter?
" Etoit-ce comme Miniftre de fa Majefté Bri-
" tannique? Mais, Monfieur, etiez vous revêtu
" de ce caractere? Vous qui n'etes recu a la
" Diette de Ratifbonne que comme le Miniftre
" de l'Electeur de Brunfwic Lunebourg, et en
" qui le Senat d'Augfburg n'a reconnu que ce
" titre, dans fon decret ci joint, du 11 Mars,
" 1794.

" Vous avez donc eu tort de vous qualifier de
" Miniftre de fa M. Britannique comme vous
" l'avez fait a Augfburg le 11 Decembre, 1793;
" et dont je vous envoye un fidele extrait. Ce
" n'eft donc point a ce titre que vous avez pu
" avoir authorité fur moi

" Mais encore, etoit-ce en qualité d'autho-
" rifé de fa M. B.? Mais comment auriez vous
　　　　　　　　　l'impudence

" l'impudence de le dire ? Vous qui fcavez que
" le veritable Miniftre de la Cour Britannique
" a Ratifbonne, a declaré qu' elle n'avoit pas
" demandé mon arreftation, et que le Roi n'a-
" voit aucun fujet de plainte contre moi.

" Vous n'aviez donc, Monfieur, aucune au-
" thorité fur moi, ni comme Miniftre, ni comme
" authorifé de fa Majefté Britannique, vous
" avez donc outre paffé les pouvoirs qui vous
" ont été confiés par votre Souverain, et par
" confequent compromis le caractere dont il
" vous avoit revêtu,

" Mais 2°. Quand vous auriez été revêtu de
" tous les titres que vous avez eu la prefomp-
" tion d'emprunter, ma conduite méritoit-elle
" de fi mauvais traitements de votre part? les
" temoignages flatteurs et les grades honnora-
" bles que m'ont accordé les Princes fous les
" drapeaux defquels j'ai fervir ne la juftifient-
" ils pas fuffifamment ?

" Je ne parlerai point ici de mes campagnes
" au fervice de la Ruffie, ni de celles que j'ai
" fait en Amerique dans les armées de S. M. B.
" mon Souverain, mais je parle de la maniere
" dont je me fuis montré en 1793 en combat-
" tant fous les ordres de S. A. S. Monfeigneur
" le Duc de Brunfwic Oels, et en fuite fons
" ceux de S. A. S. Monfeigneur le Prince d'
" Orange, le grade honorable que cet augufte
" Prince

" Prince m'a accordé dans l'armée de L. L. HH.
" PP. prouve la confiance qu'il avoit en moi,
" et si j'ai manqué à mon devoir, c'est à lui
" et nullement à vous, Monsieur, à s'en plain-
" dre.

" D'après m'avoir fait éprouver les plus ...
" ... vexations, m'avoir condamné ... ...
" ...reur, d'une prison de trois mois ... ...
" ... ainsi que mes domestiques, et après ...
" ... une autre ... ... ville pour ...
" ... le temps de ... la grâce, qu'...
" ... avez ... ...
" ... pu en ... un ... , il ... ...
" plus ... nant, Monsieur, que de me rendre
" raison de si iniques procédés. J'... une
" réparation, vous l'avez de quel genre. Vous
" ... voulu me ... ... à la face de ... ...
" ... ... à la face de l'Europe qui ... ...
" ... la satisfaction qui m'est due.

" Je suis ... ... votre ... ...
" que je dois l'être.

                    " Monsieur,

            " Votre très humble ... ...

                        J. G. E. LISLE.

" ... 1764.   " ... "

                    DE ...
            ————————